The Eternal Husband

AND OTHER STORIES

THE ETERNAL HUSBAND

AND OTHER STORIES

by

FYODOR DOSTOEVSKY

Translated and Annotated

by

RICHARD PEVEAR

and

LARISSA VOLOKHONSKY

Bantam Books

New York   Toronto   London   Sydney   Auckland

THE ETERNAL HUSBAND AND OTHER STORIES
A Bantam Book / October 1997

Translation copyright © 1997 by Richard Pevear and Larissa Volokhonsky
Preface copyright © 1997 by Richard Pevear

BOOK DESIGN BY JAMES SINCLAIR

Library of Congress Cataloging-in-Publication Data
Dostoyevsky, Fyodor, 1821–1881.
[Short stories. English. Selections]
The eternal husband and other stories / by Fyodor Dostoevsky ; translated
and annotated by Richard Pevear and Larissa Volokhonsky.
p.   cm.
Contents: A nasty anecdote—The eternal husband—Bobok—The meek
one—The dream of a ridiculous man.
ISBN 0-553-37912-7 (pbk.)
1. Dostoyevsky, Fyodor, 1821–1881—Translations into English.
2. Russia—Social life and customs—Fiction.   I. Pevear, Richard,
1943–   .   II. Volokhonsky, Larissa.   III. Title.
PG3326.A2   1997
891.73'3—dc21   97-2938
                                                                 CIP

Published simultaneously in the United States and Canada

Bantam Books are published by Bantam Books, a division of Bantam
Doubleday Dell Publishing Group, Inc. Its trademark, consisting of the
words "Bantam Books" and the portrayal of a rooster, is Registered in U.S.
Patent and Trademark Office and in other countries. Marca Registrada.
Bantam Books, 1540 Broadway, New York, New York 10036.

PRINTED IN THE UNITED STATES OF AMERICA

FFG   10 9 8 7 6 5 4 3 2 1

Contents

PREFACE

It is the road of every Christian man, who starts
from the senses, who is endowed with reason as
a dialectical principle which, in the drama of his
earthly life, must make a decision between ever
increasing participation and eternal defection.

—Erich Auerbach,
Dante, Poet of the Secular World

Dostoevsky's work represents a life-long meditation on the
same few themes, motifs, and figures. The love triangle, for
instance, with all its ambiguities of pride and humiliation,
outward magnanimity, and inner rivalry, entered his work
with his very first book, *Poor Folk,* finished in 1845, when he
was twenty-four. Some ten years later, after passing through
many of his early stories (*The Landlady, A Faint Heart, White
Nights*), the motif entered the writer's own life in the form of
his friendship with the Isaev family in Semipalatinsk and his
later courtship of the widowed Marya Dmitrievna Isaev.
Marya Dmitrievna eventually became his first wife, but before
accepting his proposal she hesitated for a long time between
Dostoevsky and a young schoolteacher by the name of Vergu-
nov. Dostoevsky thus got to play two roles—the family friend
who falls in love with the mistress of the house, and then the
older rival of a handsome young suitor. The various moves of
this elaborate game are detailed in the letters he wrote at the
time, which read like pages from one of his own epistolary
tales. So he found himself in situations he had already portrayed and would portray again and again in his later novels,

culminating in the three (or four) interlocking love triangles of *The Brothers Karamazov.* This close exchange between life and literature, with literature sometimes strangely anticipating life, is a Dostoevskian feature.

The figure of the "dreamer" also entered Dostoevsky's work with *Poor Folk,* took a central part in much of his early writing, both fiction and journalism, re-emerged quite changed in *Notes from Underground* (1864), and continued to appear in virtually all his later work. Mikhail Bakhtin notes in *Problems of Dostoevsky's Poetics:* "Dostoevsky made very wide use of the artistic possibilities of the dream in almost all its variations and nuances. Indeed, in all of European literature there is no writer for whom dreams play such a large and crucial role as Dostoevsky." We must distinguish, however, between the dreamer and the dream, because dreaming takes two main forms in Dostoevsky. The first is the form of a reverie produced by the dreamer, who longs to transform the squalid reality around him into something nobler, loftier, more beautiful. The dreamer is a fervent idealist, a great reader of German romantic poetry, but his consciousness is isolated and he usually ends badly. Reality triumphs. Yet the dreamer's aspirations receive a backhanded vindication: aesthetically he is right; art and sensibility are exalted in his person above the meanness of the world. The bubble of this sort of romantic dreaming, which Dostoevsky himself indulged in as a young liberal of the 1840s, was definitively pricked in *Notes from Underground.* There the dreamer becomes a far more complex and contradictory figure; his tone changes from sentimental idealism to bitter sarcasm, much of the sarcasm directed against himself and his own former dreams: ". . . to tell long stories of how I defaulted on my life through moral corruption in a corner, through an insufficiency of milieu, through unaccustom to what is alive, and through vainglorious spite in the underground—is not interesting, by God; a novel needs a hero, and here there are *purposely* collected all the features for an antihero . . ." Isolated consciousness has recognized its isolation. This recognition marked all of Dostoevsky's work after *Notes.*

The second form dreaming takes in Dostoevsky is that of an unexpected and intense vision, which comes to the dreamer in sleep as a gift or a final revelation, a "living image" that awakens him to a truth he had not suspected or had not understood before. Such are Alyosha's dream of the messianic banquet and Mitya's dream of "the wee one" in *The Brothers Karamazov*. These are confirming, saving dreams. They have a negative counterpart, ultimately serving the same purpose, in the nightmares of Raskolnikov and Svidrigailov in *Crime and Punishment*, of Stavrogin in *Demons*, and finally in Ivan Karamazov's "hallucination" of the devil.

With his second book, *The Double* (1846), another key motif of Dostoevsky's work appears. The story tells about the emergence of a "Mr. Golyadkin Jr." in the government office where the petty clerk Golyadkin serves, a parody and rival of himself who eventually drives him mad. Mr. Golyadkin Sr. is a proud man and keeps aloof from his fellow clerks; his double is the reverse. Golyadkin Sr. says of him: "He has such a playful, nasty character . . . He's such a scoundrel, such a fidget, a licker, a lickspittle," but then adds, *"such a Golyadkin."* Here Dostoevsky first came upon the surprising truth that pride, far from unifying and fortifying the person, as we might think, is the source of all inner divisions. In *The Double* it literally splits Mr. Golyadkin in two. Dostoevsky did not repeat this bold artistic experiment, which in fact never satisfied him, but the motif of the double occurs in subtler forms throughout his work. It raises by implication the question of human unity, the oneness of the person and of mankind, which Dostoevsky explored all his life—politically in his involvement with revolutionary groups in the 1840s, spiritually in his subsequent religious meditations.

The phenomenon of the double in Dostoevsky's work is not subject to purely psychological explanation. There is always a social nexus, an outer and collective world that is reflected in or impinges upon the inner, personal world. In *The Double* this nexus is the administrative bureaucracy introduced by the emperor Nicholas I, in which, as the critic Konstantin

Mochulsky wrote, "the schema of human values was replaced by the table of ranks." Administrative unity is external and imposed; behind it there is a growing disintegration of human life. To dramatize this disunity, Dostoevsky often resorts to the device of the "scandalous feast" or "inappropriate gathering" (as one book of *The Brothers Karamazov* is entitled). So he does with the farewell party in *Notes from Underground,* the funeral dinner for Marmeladov in *Crime and Punishment,* and, more scandalous still, the gathering of all the main characters of *Demons* in Varvara Petrovna's drawing room. "Here," says Bakhtin, "everything is unexpected, out of place, incompatible and impermissible if judged by life's ordinary 'normal' course." Things usually hidden are brought to light, unspeakable words are spoken, people are exposed, denounced, humiliated; in tone and effect these scenes are somewhere between wild farce and hysteria. They are marked by a particular shamelessness.

Scandal scenes are loud and chaotic, but the true scandal, the "scandalous victim," is silent or inarticulate in Dostoevsky. Separation from "what is living" leads to violence against what is living, to a violation of the living, to violated innocence. Most often the victim is a child; in both *Crime and Punishment* and *Demons* it is a sexually abused little girl. Among all the thinkers, talkers, and writers who populate Dostoevsky's works, the child stands mute, unable to comprehend or protest. Certain women play a similar role—Sonya Marmeladov, for instance, and the half-mad Marya Lebyadkin. Through them the theme deepens until it touches, in Mochulsky's words, on "the eternal feminine principle of the world, the mystical soul of the earth."

Dostoevsky composed with these motifs and figures like a musician, playing variations on them, combining them in new ways, working them out in different keys and with different harmonies and tempos. In his novels they are formed into extremely complex structures. In his shorter works they appear in an uncombined state. That may be why some of the most penetrating commentaries on Dostoevsky—I am thinking particularly of Bakhtin's *Problems of Dostoevsky's Poetics* and two books by René Girard: *Deceit, Desire, and the Novel* and *Dostoïevski, du double à l'unité*—give so much attention to the stories we have collected here.

Along with the consistency of its themes, Dostoevsky's work exhibits a constant formal inventiveness. This, too, can be seen in a pure state in his shorter pieces. Hailed by earlier critics (Vyacheslav Ivanov in his 1916 study *Freedom and the Tragic Life,* and Konstantin Mochulsky in his critical biography, among others) as the creator of the "novel-tragedy"—a concept fitting the high seriousness and dramatic form of his art—Dostoevsky has been called by Bakhtin the innovator of "a completely new type of artistic thinking, which we have provisionally called *polyphonic* . . . It could even be said that Dostoevsky created something like a new artistic model of the world, one in which many basic aspects of old artistic form were subjected to a radical restructuring." The stories in this collection bear out and support Bakhtin's findings in his discussion of the "characteristics of genre" in Dostoevsky—the presence in his work of elements of Menippean satire (the most well-known ancient examples are *The Golden Ass* of Apuleius and Petronius's *Satyricon*), of the allegorical mystery plays of the Middle Ages, of the Voltairean philosophical tale—all genres with a marked popular and comic spirit. This is not to say that Dostoevsky imitated old forms or combined them in some peculiar hybrid; his work is artistically of a piece and unmistakably his own; but the formal demands imposed on him by his vision forced him to expand the limits of nineteenth-century realism. (Commenting on the scandalous drawing-room scene in *Demons,* Bakhtin notes: "It is absolutely impossible to imagine such a scene in, say, a novel by Leo Tolstoy or Turgenev. This is no grand drawing room, it is the public square with all the specific logic of carnivalized public-square life.") Dostoevsky's formal inventiveness came in part, then, from a listening to tradition. It was this that gave his work its historical depth and resonance. Behind these tales of the most ordinary, obscure lives, there are the broader features of the menippea—the free use of the fantastic, the polemicizing with conflicting ideas, and, above all, the testing of truths in extreme situations. Yet we also hear, suddenly, the tones of high tragedy. *The Meek One* reaches, in the end, the harrowing grief of Lear's last scene with the dead Cordelia (the story has, in fact, not a little in common with *King Lear*). At the same time, precisely in this story we also have one of Dostoevsky's boldest experiments in fictional form, what may be the first appearance in literature of the "stream of consciousness"—a point the writer himself comments on in his opening note. Most of Dostoevsky's writings contain direct or hidden comments on their own "poetics." There are no outpourings of psychic magma here, but the explorations of a highly conscious artist. Like each of his novels, each of these stories is formally unique, each is a fresh response to the expressive challenge posed by the thematic materials of his art.

The development of Dostoevsky's work was by no means the smooth, orderly unfolding of a successful writer's career. Here the biographical factor, to which I have already alluded, comes to the fore again. The turbulence of Dostoevsky's life is well known: his involvement in revolutionary politics during the late 1840s, his arrest together with other members of the Petrashevsky circle in 1849, his mock execution, stayed at the last minute on orders from the emperor, his four years at hard labor in the prison of Omsk, followed by six years of service "in the ranks" in Semipalatinsk, his return to Petersburg and literary activity in 1859, the painful difficulties that ensued (deaths in the family, the failures of two magazines he edited with his brother, the accumulation of debts, the beginning of his addiction to gambling), his flight abroad in 1866 to escape his creditors, the precarious and nomadic existence he led there with his second wife, gambling away everything including her wedding ring and writing all the while (*The Idiot, The Eternal Husband,* the first drafts of *Demons*), his return to Russia in 1871, to find relative peace and eventual fame, which was at its height when he died in 1881 at the age of sixty. Yet the decisive break in this much-disrupted life is not to be found in any of these external events, not even the break in his career caused by ten years of prison and exile. Dostoevsky went on writing in more or less the same way after those ten years as before. The decisive break occurred in his "spiritual biography" some five years after his return, with the seemingly sudden discovery of what he called the "underground."

The emergence of the underground is the turning point in Dostoevsky's work. What he wrote before *Notes from Underground* was talented, certainly. What he wrote after was far more than talented. The shift in tone that signals the emergence of the underground indicates a deeper shift, an inner displacement, a peripeteia. As René Girard explains it, the love triangles and dreamers of Dostoevsky's early work *reflect* a certain state of affairs (not peculiar to Dostoevsky); with the underground, the reality behind that state of affairs is *revealed* for the first time. Error gives form to the truth that corrects it. The underground appears doubly in *Notes,* through the nameless hero as he tells his story, and through the author as he portrays this "man from underground." Despite the markedly personal tone of the writing, the two are not the same. The narrator is *in* the underground, Dostoevsky is some way out of it.

The underground brings out the rivalry hidden behind romantic sentiments and ideals, the exchanges of pride and humiliation that govern the relations between people and even within the singular person, who turns out to be multiple. Spiritual pride, the separation from one's fellow creatures, the will to autonomy, *produces* the rival, and thus brings about its own humiliation. The scale of this imitative rivalry is a richly chromatic one, running through all degrees of envy, jealousy, and duplicity, conscious and unconscious. But the question, finally, is of the place of imitation in human life. Here matters of art and education come together with the highest spiritual endeavor because the ideal offered to the Christian is also a way of imitation—the *imitatio Christi,* the "imitation of Christ." The sheer original does not exist; we cannot escape imitation. René Girard observes: "In the universe structured by the Gospel revelation, individual existence remains essentially imitative, even, and perhaps above all, when it rejects with horror any thought of imitation. The Fathers of the Church held as evident a truth that later became obscured and that the novelist wins back step by step through the terrible consequences of that obscuring" (*Dostoïevski, du double à l'unité*). The way of imitation revealed by the Gospels may be denied, rejected, but the structure remains, only turned another way. The original model is exchanged for another. Girard's term for this exchange is "deviated transcendence." The most extreme example in Dostoevsky is furnished by Kirillov in *Demons,* whose suicide for the salvation of mankind is a parody rather than an imitation of Christ, betraying the demonic wrenching of the deviation. Dostoevsky did not expound this as a whole and ready-made truth in his work; he came to it precisely step by step on his way through the underground.

The present collection represents, in miniature, the inner development of Dostoevsky's later work. The stories here, with one exception, were written after *Notes from Underground.* And even that one exception, *A Nasty Anecdote,* written in 1862, may be described as verging on the underground. It is one of the broadest satires in Dostoevsky, and the most farcical of his scandalous feasts. The target of the satire is the spirit of reform that spread through Russia in the early years of the reign of the "tsar-liberator" Alexander II, who came to the throne in 1855. More specifically, the target is the "festival of reconciliation" that Dostoevsky himself had looked forward to even quite recently in his journalism. Here, when the wealthy liberal official Pralinsky, whose name in English as in Russian suggests the sweetness of praline, appears uninvited at the wedding party of his subordinate Pseldonymov, the "festival" actually takes place, with disastrous consequences. What erupts into Pralinsky-Dostoevsky's dream of all people "embracing morally" is a world that Pralinsky has never known but that Dostoevsky knew quite well—the world of wretchedly poor clerks and young nihilists, the underside of the bureaucracy of which

Pralinsky and his fellow generals are the top, and along with that the world of carnival humor. Pralinsky wants to "embrace morally" while keeping his distance ("I'll delicately give a reminder that they and I are—different, sirs. Earth and sky"). He finds himself, however, in a very physical predicament: his first act is to step into a cooling galantine, and he ends with his face in the blancmange. No distances are respected; all distinctions break down. This is not the sort of union Pralinsky dreamed of. He gets drunk, and his great word, meant to bring all people together, the word "humaneness," comes out as "hu-humaneness." Instead of proving himself a statesman, he makes himself the subject of a "nasty anecdote." The structure of the story is particularly effective: by postponing his account of Pseldonymov's life until the end, Dostoevsky leaves us with two monumental portraits, absolutely irreconcilable, standing side by side.

These portraits are still single, anecdotal figures. Their opposition is mainly social and external. In the underground, the divisions become internal and rivalry acquires a metaphysical dimension. This is shown clearly in *The Eternal Husband*, written in 1870. Dostoevsky said at the time, in a letter to his friend and editor N. Strakhov: "I thought of writing this story four years ago, the year of my brother's death, in response to the words of Apollon Grigoriev, who praised my *Notes from Underground* and said to me then: 'That is how you should write.' But this is not *Notes from Underground*, it is quite different in form, though the essence is the same, my usual essence, if only you, Nikolai Nikolaevich, will acknowledge that, as a writer, I have some particular essence of my own." The more spectacular ideological elements of Dostoevsky's work, such as the polemical monologue of the man from underground or the "poem" of the Grand Inquisitor, which have drawn so much commentary from critics and philosophers, are entirely absent from *The Eternal Husband*. They are not of the essence, then. What is of the essence, of his "usual essence," is the mechanism of metaphysical rivalry and deviated transcendence, which is portrayed here in its purest form, as a kind of duel, almost a prizefight, its rounds signaled by the ringing of bells.

There is a certain way in which the double makes his appearance in Dostoevsky's work. Raskolnikov, in acute anguish at the end of the third part of *Crime and Punishment,* dreams that he is murdering the old woman again, but this time she does not die but instead laughs wildly at him. Terrified, he attempts to cry out and wakes up:

> He drew a deep breath—yet, strangely, it was as if the dream were still going on: his door was wide open, and a man completely unknown to him was standing on the threshold, studying him intently.
>
> Raskolnikov had not yet managed to open his eyes fully, and he instantly closed them again. He lay on his back without stirring. "Is this the dream still going on, or not?" he thought, and again imperceptibly parted his eyelashes a little: the stranger was standing in the same place and was still peering at him! . . . Finally it became unbearable: Raskolnikov raised himself all at once and sat up on the sofa.
>
> "Speak, then. What do you want?"
>
> "Ah, I just knew you were not asleep, but only pretending," the unknown man answered strangely, with a quiet laugh. "Allow me to introduce myself: Arkady Ivanovich Svidrigailov. . . ."

Similarly, Ivan Karamazov finds himself in an inexplicable state of anguish as he approaches his father's house:

> Above all this anguish was vexing and annoyed him by the fact that it had some sort of accidental, completely external appearance; this he felt. Somewhere some being or object was standing and sticking up, just as when something sometimes sticks up in front of one's eyes and one doesn't notice it for a long time, being busy or in heated conversation, and meanwhile one is clearly annoyed, almost suffer-

ing, and at last it dawns on one to remove the offending object, often quite trifling and ridiculous, something left in the wrong place, a handkerchief dropped on the floor, a book not put back in the bookcase, or whatever. At last, in a very bad and irritated state of mind, Ivan Fyodorovich reached his father's house, and suddenly, glancing at the gate from about fifty paces away, he at once realized what was tormenting and worrying him so.

On the bench by the gate, idly enjoying the cool of the evening, sat the lackey Smerdyakov, and Ivan Fyodorovich realized at the first sight of him that the lackey Smerdyakov was also sitting in his soul, and that it was precisely this man that his soul could not bear.

Or there is the moment a little later in the same novel when Alyosha, in great grief and temptation over the death and "disgrace" of the elder Zosima, meets the dubious novice Rakitin:

. . . some vague but tormenting and evil impression from the recollection of the previous day's conversation with his brother Ivan now suddenly stirred again in his soul, demanding more and more to come to the surface. It was already quite dark when Rakitin, passing through the pine grove from the hermitage to the monastery, suddenly noticed Alyosha lying face down on the ground under a tree, motionless and as if asleep.

Rakitin seems suddenly to materialize from the evil impression in Alyosha's soul, evoked by the abrupt shift in point of view. So Smerdyakov "sticks up" in Ivan's soul, and so Svidrigailov emerges from Raskolnikov's dream and steps across his threshold. There is the same premonitory anguish, the same mingling of inner and outer reality, when Pavel Pavlovich, the "eternal husband," appears in the way and only then in the memory of the "eternal lover" Velchaninov. But here the confrontation is more elaborately and mysteriously delayed, being more exclusively the subject of the story.

Formally, *The Eternal Husband* is the most classically pro-
portioned and perfectly constructed of Dostoevsky's works.
There are no digressions, no subplots, no secondary characters,
no personified narrator, no accompanying commentary or
analysis. With an extreme economy of means, Dostoevsky is
able to portray people acting in ways they themselves do not
understand, so that we see both their acts and their own incomprehension, and glimpse through their partial explanations
the puzzle of their true motives. The question of who knows
what and how much remains open almost to the end of the
story. But behind that *obvious* question is a vanishing sequence
of others. Narrative omniscience is limited to Velchaninov, a
sort of underground Pralinsky (he twice uses the term "underground" himself, once referring to Pavel Pavlovich, the second
time referring to himself as well). The "eternal husband" of
the title remains more shadowy, impenetrable—buffoon, victim, avenger, rival, admirer, and even lover of the handsome
younger man. Yet the final mystery lies in Velchaninov, who is
unable to free himself from the mechanism of his own behavior, who is as automatic in his gallantry as Pavel Pavlovich is in
his cuckoldry. He knows that some power contradicts him at
the very center of his personality, and the knowledge humili-
ates him, but only at moments. Then he glides on his way.
The death of "their daughter Liza" in the middle of the story
is a loss the meaning of which is beyond the grasp of both
protagonists. They seem to forget her almost at once, Pavel
Pavlovich in his new courtship, Velchaninov in his own self-
admiration. Sentimental complacency has seldom been so
chillingly portrayed as in the scene of Velchaninov's visit to the
cemetery:

> It was a clear evening, the sun was setting; round about,
> near the graves, lush green grass was growing; not far away
> amid the eglantines, a bee buzzed; the flowers and wreaths
> left on Liza's little grave by the children and Klavdia Pe-
> trovna after the burial still lay there, half their leaves blown
> off. Even some sort of hope, for the first time in a long

while, refreshed his heart. "What lightness!" he thought, feeling the silence of the cemetery and gazing at the clear, serene sky. A flood of some pure, untroubled faith in something filled his soul. "Liza sent it to me, it's she talking to me," came the thought.

This passage epitomizes the expressive concision of style in *The Eternal Husband*.

Tragedy is singular, comedy repetitive. The tragedy of Liza's death is the hidden heart of the story, hidden precisely by the ongoing "duel" of her two "fathers." In the epilogue, comedy asserts itself, almost to the point of scandal, in the absurd repetition of the same relations and the same automatic behavior we have just witnessed. Everything is about to begin over again. At that moment the final bell rings.

Two of the last three stories here Dostoevsky specifically labeled "fantastic," but in fact all three are fantastic stories. Their narrators are all underground men, though at different depths of the underground. All are nameless, like the hero of *Notes from Underground*. Like him, they have fallen out of normal human society, they despise and are despised by everyone, they nurse their own separate plans and intentions. We will have more to say about these special cases in a moment.

Bobok and *The Dream of a Ridiculous Man* are examples of Dostoevsky's use of Menippean satire, a genre that includes fantastic voyages, dream visions, and dialogues of the dead. Bakhtin finds these stories "menippea almost in the strict sense of the term, so precisely and fully manifest in them are the classical characteristic features of the genre." We shall not try to summarize his detailed discussion here. "We would hardly be mistaken," he concludes, "in saying that *Bobok*, in all its depth and boldness, is one of the greatest menippea in all world literature." If *A Nasty Anecdote* is the most farcical, *Bobok* is the most shameless and outrageous of Dostoevsky's scandal scenes, a dialogue not of the illustrious dead in the realm beyond the grave, but of rotting "contemporary dead men." Through the half-mad narrator, an unsuccessful writer,

Dostoevsky connects the satire with his own polemics and thus with the society of the living, so sharply mirrored in the society of the dead. The little story is an acute formulation of the theme of social decay among people who have lost their faith in God (only the simple tradesman here is still a believer). Such punning literalism is part of the story's humor.

The Meek One grew out of Dostoevsky's meditations on the suicide of a young woman, mentioned briefly in the October 1876 installment of his *Diary of a Writer,* the issue before the one in which the story itself was published. "About a month ago," he wrote, "there appeared in all the Petersburg newspapers a few short lines in small type about a certain Petersburg suicide: a poor young girl, a seamstress, threw herself out of a fourth-story window—'because she simply could not find work to feed herself.' It was added that she threw herself out and fell to the ground *holding an icon in her hands.* This holding of an icon is a strange and unheard-of feature in suicides! So then this was some sort of *meek,* humble suicide." In shaping a story around this incident, Dostoevsky went back to the "love story" in the second part of *Notes from Underground,* where the hero, in indirect revenge for an earlier humiliation, first "rescues" and then rejects a young prostitute. He is such an underground reasoner that he never imagines the girl may have her own mind and will. "For me to love meant to tyrannize and to preponderize morally," he explains. "All my life I've been incapable even of picturing any other love, and I've reached the point now of sometimes thinking that love consists precisely in the right, voluntarily granted by the beloved object, to be tyrannized over." The girl leaves, the man rushes after her a moment later, but then stops: "Why am I running after her? Why? To fall down before her, to weep in repentance, to kiss her feet, to beg forgiveness! . . . But—why? . . . Won't I hate her, maybe tomorrow even, precisely for kissing her feet today? . . . Won't I torment her to death?" In *The Meek One,* the hero marries the girl, and proceeds to do just that. But there are significant differences.

These appear clearly in the form of the two works. *The*

Meek One has none of the discursive and polemical character of *Notes*. It is the most intimate of Dostoevsky's stories; reading it seems almost like a profanation. The man from underground is a writer, though a careless and defiant one; the narrator here is a desperately speaking voice. But despite his rambling efforts to "collect his thoughts to a point," the story is highly unified, concentrated into the few hours following the catastrophe, during which he tries to understand what has happened. As in *The Eternal Husband,* Dostoevsky shows himself a master at revealing events through the incomprehension of the person who experiences them. But here the double story of the marriage and the "attempt to understand" unfolds simultaneously. There is a difference, too, in the consciousness of the hero, who is in the process of exchanging defiance for grief. All this gives his voice a piercing urgency.

Like *Bobok,* the brief *Dream of a Ridiculous Man* is a compendium of themes central to Dostoevsky's work. One of these is the theme of "ridiculousness." The fear of being or looking ridiculous marks most of Dostoevsky's underground heroes, including the suave Velchaninov and even the proud Nikolai Stavrogin. Ridiculousness is the shameful other face of pride. The narrator of *The Meek One* refuses to challenge a fellow officer, not from fear of a duel but from fear of looking ridiculous in the theater buffet, and for that he pays the most terrible price. In this last story, the label of "ridiculous" is fastened on the narrator from the start. The second paragraph is a succinct description of the doubled personality of all of Dostoevsky's ridiculous men. The metaphysical malady it leads to is the same that afflicts Kirillov in *Demons:* "The conviction was overtaking me," says the ridiculous man, "that everywhere in the world it *made no difference.*" It is an ethical solipsism the implications of which the narrator ponders for a long time while sitting in his Voltaire armchair. And he resolves on the Kirillovian solution of suicide, though without the messianic ambition that pushes Kirillov into demonic parody. At this extremity he is granted two things which are really one—first, a moment of "irrational" pity, which he repulses, and then a saving dream. In the end, which is the beginning, he not only loses his shame at being ridiculous, but even embraces his ridiculousness. He has gone through the underground and come out on the other side.

These ridiculous narrators are all extreme cases. Dostoevsky was obviously drawn to such cases, perhaps for the reason suggested by the man from underground at the end of his story: "As far as I myself am concerned, I have merely carried to an extreme in my life what you have not dared to carry even halfway, and, what's more, you've taken your cowardice for good sense, and found comfort in thus deceiving yourselves. So that I, perhaps, come out even more 'living' than you. Take a closer look!" The extreme and eccentric have a heroic and representative quality, despite their social isolation. Bakhtin goes so far as to say that "Dostoevsky's mode of artistic thinking could not imagine anything in the slightest way humanly significant that did not have certain elements of *eccentricity* (in all its diverse manifestations)." *The Dream of a Ridiculous Man* was Dostoevsky's last artistic work before *The Brothers Karamazov* and points to that novel's hero, Alyosha Karamazov, who is beyond the fear of being ridiculous, that is, beyond the doubled consciousness of the underground. The author says of Alyosha in his opening note: ". . . not only is an odd man 'not always' a particular and isolated case, but, on the contrary, it sometimes happens that it is precisely he, perhaps, who bears within himself the heart of the whole, while the other people of his epoch have all for some reason been torn away from it for a time by some kind of flooding wind."

The dream that saves the ridiculous man is a vision of the earthly paradise—a "second earth" that has not known the Fall into sin and evil. Similar dreams come to Stavrogin in *Demons* and to Versilov in *The Adolescent,* but the theme is treated most fully here. Stavrogin discovers the "tiny red spider" of his own terrible sin in the center of his vision, and it is suddenly dispelled. The Fall is not absent from the ridiculous man's dream either: he brings it about himself. What comes then is a condensed and somewhat polemicized history of humanity, which so fills the dreamer's heart with guilt, pity, grief, and love that he wakes up—and for him it is a true awakening, to life, "life—and preaching!" In the terms of the epigraph I have placed at the head of this preface, he moves from "eternal defection" to "ever increasing participation." He will preach because he has seen the "living image" of the truth, beyond conceptual understanding. It has shown him "that people can be beautiful and happy without losing the ability to live on earth." And he goes and finds the little girl he offended. *The Dream of a Ridiculous Man* thus resolves a whole series of interlocking motifs in Dostoevsky's work.

This book begins and ends with attempts to speak the saving word that will unite mankind. But Pralinsky's absurd "hu-humaneness" had to pass through the underground of duplicity and silence—the failure of Velchaninov to tear "the very last word" either from Pavel Pavlovich or from himself in *The Eternal Husband;* the putrefaction of souls leading to the senselessly repeated "bobok, bobok" that haunts the writer of *Bobok;* and finally the hell of "silent speaking" in *The Meek One*—before it could emerge in the ridiculous man's preaching, the same yet quite transformed.

—Richard Pevear

THE ETERNAL HUSBAND

AND OTHER STORIES

A Nasty Anecdote

A STORY

This nasty anecdote occurred precisely at the time when, with such irrepressible force and such touchingly naive enthusiasm, the regeneration of our dear fatherland began, and its valiant sons were all striving toward new destinies and hopes. Then, one winter, on a clear and frosty evening, though it was already past eleven, three extremely respectable gentlemen were sitting in a comfortably and even luxuriously furnished room, in a fine two-storied house on the Petersburg side,[1] and were taken up with a solid and excellent conversation on a quite curious subject. These three gentlemen were all three of general's rank.[2] They were sitting around a small table, each in a fine, soft armchair, and as they conversed they were quietly and comfortably sipping champagne. The bottle was right there on the table in a silver bucket with ice. The thing was that the host, privy councillor Stepan Nikiforovich Nikiforov, an old bachelor of about sixty-five, was celebrating the housewarming of his newly purchased house, and, incidentally, his birthday, which happened to come along and which he had never celebrated before. However, the celebration was none too grand; as we have already seen, there were only two guests, both former colleagues of Mr. Nikiforov and his former subordinates, namely: actual state councillor Semyon Ivanovich Shipulenko and the other, also an actual state councillor, Ivan Ilyich Pralinsky. They came at around nine o'clock, had tea, then switched to wine, and knew that at exactly eleven-thirty they should go home. The host had liked regularity all his life. A couple of words about him: he began his career as a fortuneless petty clerk, quietly endured the drag for forty-five years on end, knew very well how far he would be promoted, could not bear having stars in his eyes, though he was already wearing two of them,[3] and particularly disliked expressing his own personal opinion on any subject whatsoever. He was also honest, that is, he had never happened to do anything particularly dishonest; he was a bachelor because he was an egoist; he was far from stupid, but could not bear to display his intelligence; he particularly disliked sloppiness and rapturousness, which he considered moral sloppiness, and toward the end of his life sank entirely into some sweet, lazy comfort and systematic solitude. Though he himself sometimes visited people of the better sort, from his youth he could never bear to receive guests, and of late, when not playing patience, he was content with the company of his dining-room clock, imperturbably listening, as he dozed in his armchair, to its ticking under the glass dome on the mantelpiece. He was of extremely decent and clean-shaven appearance, looked younger than his years, was well preserved, promising to live a long time, and adhered to the strictest gentlemanliness. His post was rather comfortable: he sat somewhere and signed something. In short, he was considered a most excellent man. He had only one passion, or, better, one ardent desire: this was to own his own house, and precisely a grand house, not simply a solid one. His desire was finally realized: he picked out and purchased a house on the Petersburg side, far away, true, but the house had a garden, and was elegant besides. The new owner reasoned that far away was even better: he did not like receiving at home, and as for going to visit someone or to work—for that he had a fine two-place carriage of chocolate color, the coachman Mikhei, and two small but sturdy and handsome horses. All this had been duly acquired by forty years of painstaking economy, and so his heart rejoiced over it all. This was why, having acquired the house and moved into it, Stepan Nikiforovich felt such contentment in his peaceful heart that he even invited guests for his birthday, which before he used carefully to conceal from his closest acquaintances. He even had special designs on one of the invited. He himself occupied the upper story of the house, and he needed a tenant for the lower one, which was built and laid out in the same way. So Stepan Nikiforovich was counting on Semyon Ivanovich Shipulenko, and during the evening even twice turned the conversation to that subject. But Semyon Ivanovich kept silent in that regard. This was a man who had also had a long and difficult time cutting a path for himself, with black hair and side-whiskers and a permanently bilious tinge to his physiognomy. He was a married man, a gloomy homebody, kept his household in fear, served self-confidently, also knew very well what he would achieve and still better what he would never achieve, sat in a good post and sat very solidly. At the new ways that were beginning he looked, if not without bile, still with no special alarm: he was very confident of himself and listened not without mocking spite to Ivan Ilyich Pralinsky's expatiating on the new themes. However, they were all somewhat tipsy, so that even Stepan Nikiforovich himself condescended to Mr. Pralinsky and entered into a light dispute with him about the new ways. But a few words about His Excellency Mr. Pralinsky, the more so as he is the main hero of the forthcoming story.

Actual state councillor Ivan Ilyich Pralinsky had been called "Your Excellency" for only four months—in short, he was a young general. He was young in years, too, about forty-three, certainly not more, and in looks he appeared and liked to appear still younger. He was a tall, handsome man, who made

a show of his dress and of the refined solidity of his dress, wore
an important decoration on his neck[4] with great skill, from
childhood had managed to adopt a few high-society ways,
and, being a bachelor, dreamed of a rich and even high-society
bride. He dreamed of many other things as well, though he
was far from stupid. At times he was a great talker and even
liked to assume parliamentary poses. He came from a good
family, was a general's son and a sybarite, in his tender childhood wore velvet and cambric, was educated in an aristocratic
institution, and, though he did not come out of it with much
learning, was successful in the service and even got himself as
far as a generalship. His superiors considered him a capable
man and even placed hopes in him. Stepan Nikiforovich, under whom he began and continued his service almost up to
the generalship, never considered him a very practical man and
did not place any hopes in him. But he liked that he was from
a good family, had a fortune, that is, a big rental property with
a manager, was related to some not-insignificant people, and,
on top of that, carried himself well. Stepan Nikiforovich inwardly denounced him for surplus imagination and light-
mindedness. Ivan Ilyich himself sometimes felt that he was too
vain and even ticklish. Strangely, at times he was overcome by
fits of some morbid conscientiousness and even a slight repentance for something. With bitterness and a secret sting in his
soul, he sometimes admitted that he had not flown at all as
high as he thought. In those moments he would even fall into
some sort of despondency, especially when his hemorrhoids
were acting up, called his life *une existence manquée*,[5] ceased
believing (privately, of course) even in his parliamentary abilities, calling himself a *parleur*, a *phraseur*,[6] and though all this
was, of course, very much to his credit, it in no way prevented
him from raising his head again half an hour later, and with
still greater obstinacy and presumption taking heart and assuring himself that he would still manage to show himself and
would become not only a dignitary, but even a statesman
whom Russia would long remember. At times he even imagined monuments. From this one can see that Ivan Ilyich aimed

high, though he kept his vague hopes and dreams hidden deep in himself, even with a certain fear. In short, he was a kind man, and even a poet in his soul. In recent years, painful moments of disappointment had begun to visit him more often. He became somehow especially irritable, insecure, and was ready to consider any objection an offense. But the reviving Russia suddenly gave him great hopes. The generalship crowned them. He perked up; he raised his head. He suddenly started talking much and eloquently, talking on the newest topics, which he adopted extremely quickly and unexpectedly, to the point of fierceness. He sought occasions for talking, drove around town, and in many places managed to become known as a desperate liberal, which flattered him greatly. That evening, having drunk some four glasses, he got particularly carried away. He wanted to make Stepan Nikiforovich, whom he had not seen for a long time prior to that and till then had always respected and even obeyed, change his mind about everything. For some reason he considered him a retrograde and attacked him with extraordinary heat. Stepan Nikiforovich made almost no objections and only listened slyly, though the topic interested him. Ivan Ilyich was getting excited and in the heat of the imagined dispute sampled from his glass more often than he should have. Then Stepan Nikiforovich would take the bottle and top up his glass at once, which, for no apparent reason, suddenly began to offend Ivan Ilyich, the more so in that Semyon Ivanych Shipulenko, whom he particularly despised and, moreover, even feared on account of his cynicism and malice, was most perfidiously silent just beside him, and smiled more often than he should have. "They seem to take me for a mere boy," flashed in Ivan Ilyich's head.

"No, sir, it's time, it's long since time," he went on with passion. "We're too late, sir, and, in my view, humaneness is the first thing, humaneness with subordinates, remembering that they, too, are people. Humaneness will save everything and keep it afloat . . ."

"Hee, hee, hee, hee!" came from Semyon Ivanovich's direction.

"But, anyhow, why are you scolding us so?" Stepan Nikiforovich finally objected, smiling amiably. "I confess, Ivan Ilyich, so far I'm unable to get the sense of what you're so kindly explaining. You put forward humaneness. That means the love of mankind, doesn't it?"

"Yes, if you wish, the love of mankind. I . . ."

"Excuse me, sir. As far as I'm able to judge, the point is not just in that. Love of mankind is always proper. But the reform is not limited to that. Questions have come up about the peasants, the courts, management, tax-farming,[7] morality, and . . . and . . . and there's no end to them, these questions, and all together, all at once, they may produce great, so to speak, upheavals. That's what we're worried about, not just humaneness . . ."

"Yes, sir, the thing goes a bit deeper," Semyon Ivanovich observed.

"I understand very well, sir, and allow me to observe, Semyon Ivanovich, that I shall by no means agree to lag behind you in the depth of my understanding of things," Ivan Ilyich observed caustically and much too sharply. "However, even so I shall make so bold as to observe that you, Stepan Nikiforovich, also have not quite understood me . . ."

"No, I haven't."

"And yet I precisely hold to and maintain everywhere the idea that humaneness, and precisely humaneness with subordinates, from clerk to scrivener, from scrivener to household servant, from servant to peasant—humaneness, I say, may serve, so to speak, as the cornerstone of the forthcoming reform and generally toward the renewal of things. Why? Because. Take the syllogism: I am humane, consequently they love me. They love me, therefore they feel trust. They feel trust, therefore they believe; they believe, therefore they love . . . that is, no, I mean to say, if they believe, they will also believe in the reform, understand, so to speak, the very essence of the matter, will, so to speak, embrace each other morally and resolve the whole matter amicably, substantially. Why are you laughing, Semyon Ivanovich? Is it not clear?"

Stepan Nikiforovich silently raised his eyebrows; he was surprised.

"I think I've had a bit too much to drink," Semyon Ivanych observed venomously, "that's why I'm hard of understanding. A certain darkening of the mind, sir." ·

Ivan Ilyich winced.

"We won't hold out," Stepan Nikiforovich said suddenly, after slight reflection.

"That is, how is it we won't hold out?" asked Ivan Ilyich, surprised at Stepan Nikiforovich's sudden and fragmentary observation.

"Just so, we won't hold out." Stepan Nikiforovich obviously did not wish to expand further.

"You don't mean about new wine in new bottles?"[8] Ivan Ilyich objected, not without irony. "Ah, no, sir; I can answer for myself."

At that moment the clock struck half past eleven.

"They sit and sit, then up and go," said Semyon Ivanych, preparing to get up from his place. But Ivan Ilyich forestalled him, rising from the table at once and taking his sable hat from the mantelpiece. He looked as if offended.

"Well, then, Semyon Ivanych, you'll think?" said Stepan Nikiforovich, seeing his guests off.

"About the apartment, you mean? I'll think, I'll think, sir."

"And let me know quickly once you decide."

"Still business?" Mr. Pralinsky observed amiably, fawning somewhat and playing with his hat. It seemed to him that he was being forgotten.

Stepan Nikiforovich raised his eyebrows and said nothing, as a sign that he was not keeping his guests. Semyon Ivanych hastily took his leave.

"Ah . . . well . . . as you wish, then . . . since you don't understand simple amiability," Mr. Pralinsky decided to himself, and somehow with particular independence offered his hand to Stepan Nikiforovich.

In the front hall Ivan Ilyich wrapped himself in his light, expensive fur coat, trying for some reason to ignore Semyon

Ivanych's shabby raccoon, and they both started down the stairs.

"Our old man seemed offended," Ivan Ilyich said to the silent Semyon Ivanych.

"No, why?" the other replied calmly and coldly.

"The flunky!" Ivan Ilyich thought to himself.

They came out on the porch, and Semyon Ivanych's sleigh with its homely gray stallion drove up.

"What the devil! Where has Trifon gone with my carriage!" Ivan Ilyich cried, not seeing his equipage.

They looked this way and that—no carriage. Stepan Nikiforovich's man had no idea about it. They turned to Varlaam, Semyon Ivanych's coachman, and received the answer that he had been standing there all the while, and the carriage had been there, too, but now they were no more.

"A nasty anecdote!" said Mr. Shipulenko. "Want me to give you a lift?"

"Scoundrelly folk!" Mr. Pralinsky cried in rage. "The rascal asked me to let him go to some wedding here on the Petersburg side, some female crony was getting married, devil take her. I strictly forbade him to leave. And now I'll bet he's gone there!"

"Actually," Varlaam observed, "he did go there, sir, and he promised to manage it in just one minute, that is, to be here right on time."

"So there! I just knew it! He'll catch it from me!"

"You'd better give him a couple of good whippings at the police station, then he'll follow your orders," Semyon Ivanych said, covering himself with a rug.

"Kindly don't trouble yourself, Semyon Ivanych!"

"So you don't want a lift?"

"Safe journey, *merci*."

Semyon Ivanych drove off, and Ivan Ilyich went by foot along the wooden planks, feeling a rather strong irritation.

"No, you'll catch it from me now, you rogue! I'll go by foot on purpose so that you'll feel it, so that you'll get scared! He'll

come back and find out that the master went by foot . . .
blackguard!"

Ivan Ilyich had never cursed like that before, but he was
very furious, and besides there was a clamor in his head. He
was not used to drinking and therefore some five or six glasses
worked quickly. But the night was delightful. It was frosty,
but unusually calm and windless. The sky was clear, starry.
The full moon flooded the earth with a matted silver gleam. It
was so good that Ivan Ilyich, having gone some fifty steps,
almost forgot his troubles. He was beginning to feel somehow
especially pleasant. Besides, tipsy people change impressions
quickly. He was even starting to like the plain wooden houses
on the deserted street.

"It's really nice that I went by foot," he thought to himself,
"both a lesson to Trifon and a pleasure for me. Indeed, I must
go by foot more often. So what? On Bolshoi Prospect I'll find
a cab at once. A nice night! What wretched little houses here.
Must all be petty folk, clerks . . . merchants, maybe . . .
that Stepan Nikiforovich! and what retrogrades they all are,
the old nightcaps! Precisely nightcaps, *c'est le mot!*[9] He's an
intelligent man, though; he has this *bon sens,*[10] a sober, practical understanding of things. No, but these old men, old men!
They lack . . . what do you call it? Well, they lack something . . . We won't hold out! What did he mean by that?
He even fell to thinking when he said it. By the way, he didn't
understand me at all. But how could he not? It's harder not to
understand than to understand. Above all, I'm convinced,
convinced in my soul. Humaneness . . . love of mankind.
Restore man to himself . . . revive his personal dignity, and
then . . . with this ready material get down to business.
Seems clear! Yes, sir! I beg your pardon, Your Excellency, take
the syllogism: we meet a clerk, for instance, a poor, downtrod-
den clerk. 'Well . . . what are you?' Answer: 'A clerk.' All
right, so he's a clerk; then: 'What kind of a clerk?' Answer:
such-and-such kind. 'You're in the civil service?' 'I am!' 'Want
to be happy?' 'I do.' 'What does one need for happiness?' This
and that. 'Why?' Because . . . And so the man understands
me after a couple of words: the man is mine, the man is

caught, so to speak, in the net, and I can do whatever I like with him—for his own good, that is. A nasty man, this Semyon Ivanych! And such a nasty mug . . . A whipping at the police station—he said it on purpose. No, lies, you do the whipping, I won't; I'll get Trifon with words, I'll get him with reproaches, and he'll feel it. About birch rods,[11] hm . . . an unsolved problem, hm . . . But shouldn't I stop at Emerance's? Pah, the devil, you cursed planks!" he cried, suddenly tripping. "And this is the capital! Enlightenment! You could break a leg. Hm. I hate this Semyon Ivanych; a most disgusting mug. He sniggered at me tonight when I said they'd embrace each other morally. So they will, and what do you care? You I won't embrace; sooner a peasant . . . I'll meet a peasant, and talk with a peasant. Anyhow, I was drunk, and maybe didn't express myself properly. Maybe I'm not expressing myself properly now either . . . Hm. I'm never going to drink. You babble in the evening, then the next day you repent. So what, I'm not staggering as I walk . . . And anyhow, they're all rogues!"

So Ivan Ilyich reasoned, desultorily and incoherently, as he went on down the sidewalk. The fresh air affected him and, so to speak, got him going. Another five minutes and he would have calmed down and wanted to sleep. But suddenly, about two steps from Bolshoi Prospect, he heard music. He looked around. On the other side of the street, in a very decrepit, one-story, but long wooden house, a great feast was going on, fiddles hummed, a string bass droned, and a flute spouted shrilly to a very merry quadrille tune. The public was standing under the windows, mostly women in quilted coats with kerchiefs on their heads; they strained all their efforts to make something out through the chinks in the blinds. Obviously there was merriment. The sound of the dancers' stomping reached the other side of the street. Ivan Ilyich noticed a policeman not far away and went up to him.

"Whose house is that, brother?" he said, throwing his expensive fur coat open slightly, just enough so that the policeman could notice the important decoration on his neck.

"The clerk Pseldonymov's, a legistrar,"[12] the policeman, who instantly managed to make out the decoration, replied, straightening up.

"Pseldonymov? Hah! Pseldonymov! . . . What's he doing, getting married?"

"Getting married, Your Honor, to a titular councillor's daughter. Mlekopitaev,[13] a titular councillor . . . served on the board. That house comes with the bride, sir."

"So it's already Pseldonymov's house, not Mlekopitaev's?"

"Pseldonymov's, Your Honor. Used to be Mlekopitaev's, and now it's Pseldonymov's."

"Hm. I'm asking, brother, because I'm his superior. I'm general over the place where Pseldonymov works."

"Right, Your Excellency." The policeman drew himself all the way up, but Ivan Ilyich seemed to have lapsed into thought. He was standing and reflecting . . .

Yes, Pseldonymov actually was from his department, from his own office; he recalled that. He was a petty clerk, with a salary of about ten roubles a month. Since Mr. Pralinsky had taken over his office still very recently, he might not have remembered all his subordinates in too much detail, but Pseldonymov he did remember, precisely apropos of his last name. It had leaped out at him from the very first, so that he had been curious right then to have a closer look at the owner of such a name. He now recalled a man still very young, with a long, hooked nose, with blond and wispy hair, skinny and malnourished, in an impossible uniform, and unmentionables impossible even to the point of indecency. He remembered how the thought had flashed in him right then: should he not award the wretch some ten roubles to fix himself up for the holiday? But since the wretch's face was all too lenten, and had an extremely unpleasant look, even causing disgust, the good thought somehow evaporated of itself, and so Pseldonymov remained without a bonus. The greater was his amazement when this same Pseldonymov, not more than a week ago, put in a request to get married.[14] Ivan Ilyich remembered that he had somehow had no time to occupy himself with the matter more thoroughly, so that the matter of the wedding had been decided lightly, hastily. But all the same he remembered with precision that Pseldonymov was taking his bride together with a wooden house and four hundred roubles in cash; this circumstance had surprised him then; he remembered even cracking a light joke about the encounter of the names Pseldonymov and Mlekopitaev. He clearly recalled it all.

As he went on recollecting, he fell to thinking more and more. It is known that whole trains of thought sometimes pass instantly through our heads, in the form of certain feelings, without translation into human language, still less literary language. But we shall attempt to translate all these feelings of our hero's and present the reader if only with the essence of these feelings, with what, so to speak, was most necessary and plausible in them. Because many of our feelings, when translated into ordinary language, will seem perfectly implausible. That is why they never come into the world, and yet everybody has them. Naturally, Ivan Ilyich's feelings and thoughts were a bit incoherent. But you know the reason why.

"What then!" flashed in his head. "So we all talk and talk, but once it gets to business, only a fig comes out. Here's an example, this very same Pseldonymov: he's just come from the church, all excited, all hopeful, expecting to taste . . . This is one of the most blissful days of his life . . . Now he's busy with the guests, giving a feast—modest, poor, but merry, joyful, sincere . . . What, then, if he knew that at this very moment I, I, his superior, his chief superior, am standing right here by his house and listening to his music! But how, in fact, would it be with him? No, how would it be with him if I should suddenly up and walk in now? hm . . . Naturally, he'd be frightened at first, numb with bewilderment. I'd be interfering with him, I'd probably upset everything . . . Yes, that's how it would be if any other general walked in, but not I . . . Here's the thing, that any other, only not I . . .

"Yes, Stepan Nikiforovich! You didn't understand me just now, but here's a ready example for you.

"Yes, sir. We all shout about humaneness, but heroism, a great deed, that we're not capable of.

"What kind of heroism? This kind. Just consider: given the present-day relations between all members of society, for me, for me to come after midnight to the wedding of my subordinate, a registrar, who makes ten roubles—after all, this is bewilderment, this is a turnabout of ideas, the last day of Pompeii,[15] bedlam! No one will understand it. Stepan Nikiforovich would die before he understood it. Didn't he say: we won't hold out. Yes, but that's you old people, people of paralysis and stagnation, but I will hold out! I'll turn the last day of Pompeii into the sweetest day for my subordinate, and a wild act into a normal, patriarchal, lofty and e-thi-cal one. How? Like this. Be so good as to listen . . .

"Well . . . here I am, suppose, going in: they're amazed, interrupt their dancing, stare wildly, back away. Right, sir, but here I show myself: I go straight to the frightened Pseldonymov and, with the tenderest smile, in the simplest words possible, say: 'Thus and so,' I say, 'I was visiting His Excellency Stepan Nikiforovich. I suppose you know, it's here in the neighborhood . . .' Here I tell, lightly, in some amusing way, the adventure with Trifon. From Trifon I pass on to how I went by foot . . . 'Well—I hear music, I ask a policeman, and find out that you, brother, are getting married. Why don't I stop at my subordinate's, I think, to see how my clerks make merry and . . . get married. Now, you're not going to drive me out, I suppose!' Drive out! What a phrase for a subordinate. The devil he'll drive me out! I think he'll lose his mind, he'll rush headlong to sit me in an armchair, he'll tremble with delight, he won't even know what to make of it at first! . . .

"Well, what could be simpler, more gracious, than such an act! Why did I come? That's another question! That's, so to speak, the moral side of the matter. There's where the juice is!

"Hm . . . What was I thinking about? Ah, yes!

"So then, of course, they'll seat me next to the most important guest, some titular councillor, or a relative, a retired staff captain with a red nose . . . Gogol described these originals nicely. So, naturally, I make the acquaintance of the bride, praise her, encourage the guests. I beg them not to be embarrassed, to make merry, to go on dancing, I joke, I laugh, in

short—I'm amiable and charming. I'm always amiable and
charming when I'm pleased with myself. Hm . . . the thing
is that I still seem to be a bit . . . that is, not drunk, but
just . . .

". . . Naturally, being a gentleman, I'm on an equal footing with them and by no means demand any special tokens
. . . But morally, morally it's another matter: they'll understand and appreciate . . . My act will resurrect in them all
the nobility of . . . And so I sit there for half an hour . . .
Even an hour. I'll leave, naturally, just before supper, otherwise they'll start bustling about, baking, frying, they'll bow
low before me, but I'll just drink a glass, congratulate them,
and decline supper. I'll say: business. And as soon as I pronounce 'business,' their faces will all become respectfully stern
at once. By this I'll delicately give a reminder that they and I
are—different, sirs. Earth and sky. Not that I'd want to im-
pose it, but it's needed . . . even in the moral sense it's necessary, whatever you say. However, I'll smile at once, even
laugh, perhaps, and everyone will instantly cheer up . . . I'll
joke once more with the bride; hm . . . and even this: I'll
hint that I'll come again in exactly nine months as a godfather,
heh, heh! And she'll certainly give birth by then. Because they
multiply like rabbits. So everyone bursts out laughing, the
bride blushes; I kiss her on the forehead with feeling, even
bless her, and . . . tomorrow my deed is already known in
the office. Tomorrow I'm stern again, tomorrow I'm demanding again, even implacable, but by now they all know who I
am. They know my soul, they know my essence: 'He's stern as
a superior, but as a man he's an angel!' And so I'm victorious;
I've caught them with some one small act that wouldn't even
occur to you; they're mine now; I'm the father, they're the
children . . . Go on, Stepan Nikiforovich, Your Excellency,
try doing something like that . . .

". . . But do you know, do you understand, that Pseldonymov will recall for his children how the general himself
feasted and even drank at his wedding! And those children will
tell their children, and they will tell their grandchildren, like a

sacred anecdote, that a dignitary, a statesman (and I'll be all that by then) deigned . . . etc., etc. But I'll raise the humiliated one morally, I'll restore him to himself . . . He gets a salary of ten roubles a month! But if I were to repeat this or some such thing five or ten times, I'd win popularity everywhere . . . I'd be impressed on everybody's heart, and the devil alone knows what might come of it later, this popularity! . . ."

Thus or almost thus reasoned Ivan Ilyich (gentlemen, a man sometimes says all sorts of things to himself, and in a somewhat peculiar state besides). All this reasoning flashed through his head in about half a minute, and, of course, he might have limited himself to these little dreams and, having mentally shamed Stepan Nikiforovich, gone quite calmly home and to bed. And it would have been well if he had! But the whole trouble was that the moment was a peculiar one.

As if on purpose, suddenly, at that very instant, his susceptible imagination pictured the complacent faces of Stepan Nikiforovich and Semyon Ivanovich.

"We won't hold out!" Stepan Nikiforovich repeated, smiling superciliously.

"Hee, hee, hee!" echoed Semyon Ivanovich with his nastiest smile.

"And now let's see how we won't hold out!" Ivan Ilyich said resolutely, and his face even flushed hotly. He stepped off the planks and with firm tread went straight across the street to the house of his subordinate, the registrar Pseldonymov.

His star drew him on. He walked briskly through the open gate and in disdain shoved aside with his foot the hoarse, shaggy little cur that, more for decency's sake than meaning any business, rushed at his legs with a rasping bark. By a wooden boardwalk he reached a covered porch, jutting like a booth into the yard, and by three decrepit wooden steps he went up to a tiny entryway. Though a tallow candle-end or something like a lamp was burning somewhere in a corner, that did not prevent Ivan Ilyich, just as he was, in galoshes, from stepping with his left foot into a galantine set out to cool. Ivan Ilyich bent down and, looking with curiosity, saw standing there two more dishes of some sort of aspic, as well as two molds, obviously of blancmange. The squashed galantine embarrassed him a bit, and for one tiny instant the thought flitted through him: shouldn't I slip away right now? But he considered it too low. Reasoning that no one had seen and that no one was going to suspect him, he quickly wiped off the galosh, so as to conceal all traces, groped for the felt-upholstered door, opened it, and found himself in the tiniest of anterooms. One half of it was literally heaped with over-coats, caftans, cloaks, bonnets, scarves, and galoshes. In the other half the musicians had settled: two fiddles, a flute, and a string bass, four men in all, brought in, naturally, from the street. They were sitting by an unpainted wooden table, with one tallow candle, and sawing away for all they were worth at the last figure of a quadrille. Through the open door to the main room people could be seen dancing, in dust, smoke, and haze. It was somehow furiously merry. Guffaws, shouts, and ladies' shrieks were heard. The cavaliers were stomping like a squadron of horses. Above this whole pandemonium sounded the commands of the master of ceremonies, probably an ex-tremely unconstrained and even unbuttoned man: "Cavaliers, step out, *chaîne de dames, balancez!*"[16] and so on and so forth. Ivan Ilyich, in some slight agitation, threw off his fur coat and galoshes and, holding his hat, entered the room. Anyhow, he was no longer reasoning . . .

For the first moment no one noticed him: they were all finishing the end of the dance. Ivan Ilyich stood as if stunned and could make out nothing of this porridge in detail. Ladies' dresses, cavaliers with cigarettes in their teeth flashed by . . . some lady's light blue scarf flashed by and brushed his nose. After her, in furious ecstasy, a medical student swept, his tou-sled hair all in a whirl, and shoved him hard on his way. Before him also flashed, long as a milepost, an officer of some regiment. Someone shouted in an unnaturally shrill voice as he flew by, stomping, with everyone else: "E-e-eh, Pseldony-mushka!" There was something sticky under Ivan Ilyich's feet: the floor must have been waxed. In the room, not a small one incidentally, there were upward of thirty guests.

But a minute later the quadrille was over, and almost at once the very thing took place which Ivan Ilyich had imagined as he was dreaming on the plank sidewalk. Some sort of hum, some sort of extraordinary whisper passed through the guests and dancers, who had not yet had time to catch their breath and wipe the sweat from their faces. All eyes, all faces quickly began to turn to the newly entered guest. Then at once every-one started slowly retreating and backing away. Those who had not noticed were pulled by the clothes and brought to reason. They would look around and at once start backing away along with the others. Ivan Ilyich went on standing by the door, not taking one step forward, and the open space between him and the guests, the floor strewn with countless candy wrappers, tickets, and cigarette butts, was growing wider and wider. Suddenly a young man in a uniform, with wispy blond hair and a hooked nose, timidly stepped into this space. He moved forward, bending, and looked at the unexpected guest in exactly the same way as a dog looks at its master who has called it in order to give it a kick.

"Hello, Pseldonymov, recognize me? . . ." said Ivan Ilyich, and in that same instant felt that he had said it terribly awk-wardly; he also felt that at that moment he was, perhaps, com-mitting the most frightful foolishness.

"Y-Y-Your Ex-cellency! . . ." mumbled Pseldonymov.

"Well, so there. I stopped entirely by chance, brother, as you can probably imagine . . ."

But Pseldonymov obviously could not imagine anything. He stood, goggle-eyed, in terrible bewilderment.

"You won't drive me out, I suppose . . . Glad or not, wel-come the guest! . . ." Ivan Ilyich went on, feeling that he was abashed to the point of indecent weakness, that he wished to smile but no longer could; that the humorous story about

Stepan Nikiforovich and Trifon was becoming more and more impossible. But Pseldonymov, as if on purpose, would not come out of his stupor and went on staring at him with an utterly foolish look. Ivan Ilyich cringed, he felt that another minute like this and an incredible bedlam would break out.

"Maybe I've interfered with something . . . I'll go!" he barely uttered, and some nerve twitched at the right corner of his mouth . . .

But Pseldonymov recovered himself . . .

"Your Excellency, good heavens, sir . . . The honor . . ." he was mumbling, bowing hurriedly, "deign to sit down, sir . . ." And, still more recovered, he showed him with both hands to the sofa, from which the table had been moved aside for the dancing . . .

Ivan Ilyich felt relieved and lowered himself onto the sofa; someone rushed at once to move the table back. He glanced around cursorily and noticed that he alone was sitting down, while all the others were standing, even the ladies. A bad sign. But it was not yet time to remind and encourage. The guests still kept backing away, and before him, bent double, there still stood Pseldonymov alone, who still understood nothing and was far from smiling. It was nasty; in short: during this moment our hero endured such anguish that his Harun-al-Rashidian[17] invasion of his subordinate, for the sake of principle, could actually have been considered a great deed. But suddenly some little figure turned up beside Pseldonymov and started bowing. To his inexpressible pleasure and even happiness, Ivan Ilyich at once recognized him as a chief clerk from his office, Akim Petrovich Zubikov, with whom he was not, of course, acquainted, but whom he knew to be an efficient and uncomplaining official. He immediately rose and proffered Akim Petrovich his hand, the whole hand, not just two fingers. The man received it in both of his palms with the deepest reverence. The general was triumphant; all was saved.

And actually Pseldonymov was now, so to speak, not the second, but the third person. He could turn directly to the chief clerk with his story, necessarily taking him as an acquaintance and even a close one, and Pseldonymov meanwhile could simply keep silent and tremble with awe. Consequently, decency was observed. And the story was necessary; Ivan Ilyich felt it; he saw that all the guests were expecting something, that even all the domestics were crowding both doorways, almost climbing on one another in order to see and hear him. The nasty thing was that the chief clerk, in his stupidity, still would not sit down.

"Come, come!" said Ivan Ilyich, awkwardly indicating the place beside him on the sofa.

"Good heavens, sir . . . here's fine, sir . . ." and Akim Petrovich quickly sat down on a chair, offered him almost in flight by Pseldonymov, who stubbornly remained on his feet.

"Can you imagine what's happened," Ivan Ilyich began, addressing Akim Petrovich exclusively, in a somewhat trembling but now casual voice. He even drew out and separated the words, emphasized their syllables, began to pronounce the letter *a* somehow like *ah*—in short, he himself felt and was aware that he was being affected, but was no longer able to control himself; some external force was at work. He was painfully aware of terribly much at that moment.

"Can you imagine, I'm only just coming from Stepan Nikiforovich Nikiforov's—you've heard of him, perhaps, a privy councillor. Well . . . on that commission . . ."

Akim Petrovich leaned his whole body forward deferentially, as if to say: "How could I have not heard, sir."

"He's your neighbor now," Ivan Ilyich went on, momentarily addressing Pseldonymov, for the sake of propriety and naturalness, but quickly turning away, seeing at once from Pseldonymov's eyes that it made decidedly no difference to him.

"The old man, as you know, was raving all his life about buying himself a house . . . So now he's bought it. The prettiest little house. Yes . . . And today also happened to be his birthday, though he never celebrated it before, even concealed it from us, making excuses out of stinginess, heh, heh! and now he's so glad of his new house that he invited me and Semyon Ivanovich. You know—Shipulenko."

Akim Petrovich leaned forward again. Zealously leaned forward! Ivan Ilyich was somewhat comforted. For it had already occurred to him that the chief clerk might perhaps surmise that, at that moment, he was a necessary point of support for His Excellency. That would have been nastiest of all.

"Well, we three sat there, he stood us to some champagne, talked about business . . . Well, about this and that . . . about pro-blems . . . Even had a little dis-pute . . . Heh, heh!"

Akim Petrovich deferentially raised his eyebrows.

"Only that's not the thing. I finally say good night to him, he's a punctual old man, goes to bed early—old age, you know. I go out . . . my Trifon isn't there! I worry, I ask: 'What did Trifon do with the carriage?' It turns out that, in hopes I'd stay long, he went to the wedding of some female crony of his or else his sister . . . God knows with him. Somewhere here on the Petersburg side. And incidentally took the carriage." Again, for propriety's sake, the general glanced at Pseldonymov. The man bent double instantly, but not at all in the way the general would have liked. "No sympathy, no heart," flashed in his head.

"You don't say!" said the deeply struck Akim Petrovich. A little hum of astonishment went through the whole crowd.

"Can you imagine my position . . ." (Ivan Ilyich glanced at them all.) "No help for it, I set out by foot. I thought I'd toddle along to Bolshoi Prospect, and there find some cabbie . . . heh, heh!"

"Hee, hee, hee!" Akim Petrovich echoed deferentially. Again a hum, now on a merry note, passed through the crowd. At that moment the glass of a wall lamp cracked with a loud noise. Someone zealously rushed to put it right. Pseldonymov roused himself and gave the lamp a stern look, but the general did not even pay attention, and everything quieted down.

"I'm walking . . . and the night is so beautiful, still. Suddenly I hear music, stomping, dancing. I ask a policeman: Pseldonymov's getting married. So, brother, you're throwing a ball for the whole Petersburg side? ha, ha," he suddenly addressed Pseldonymov again.

"Hee, hee, hee! yes, sir . . ." echoed Akim Petrovich; the guests stirred again, but the stupidest thing of all was that Pseldonymov, though he did bow again, even now did not smile, just as if he were made of wood. "Is he a fool, or what?" thought Ivan Ilyich. "The ass ought to have smiled now, then everything would go swimmingly." Impatience raged in his heart. "I thought, why not visit my subordinate. He won't drive me out . . . glad or not, welcome the guest. Excuse me, please, brother. If I'm interfering, I'll go . . . I only stopped to have a look . . ."

But little by little a general movement was beginning. Akim Petrovich gazed with a sweetened air, as if to say: "Could Your Excellency possibly interfere?" All the guests were stirring and beginning to show the first tokens of casualness. The ladies almost all sat down. A good and positive sign. Those who were braver fanned themselves with handkerchiefs. One of them, in a shabby velvet dress, said something deliberately loudly. The officer she had addressed also wanted to reply loudly, but since the two of them were the only loud ones, he passed. The men, most of them clerks, plus two or three students, exchanged glances, as if urging each other to loosen up, coughed, and even began making a couple of steps in different directions. Anyhow, none of them was particularly timid, only they were all uncouth and almost all of them looked with animosity at the person who had barged in on them to disrupt their merry-making. The officer, ashamed of his pusillanimity, gradually began to approach the table.

"But listen, brother, allow me to ask your name and patronymic?" Ivan Ilyich asked Pseldonymov.

"Porfiry Petrovich, Your Excellency," the man replied, goggle-eyed, as if on review.

"Now then, Porfiry Petrovich, introduce me to your young wife . . . Take me to . . . I . . ."

And he made a show of getting up. But Pseldonymov rushed headlong to the drawing room. The young bride, however, had been standing right at the door, but on hearing that the talk was about her, she hid at once. A minute later Pseldonymov led her out by the hand. Everyone made way, letting them pass. Ivan Ilyich rose solemnly and addressed her with a most amiable smile.

"Very, very glad to make your acquaintance," he said with a most high-society half bow, "and what's more on such a day . . ."

He gave a most insidious smile. The ladies got pleasantly excited.

"Sharmay," the lady in the velvet dress said almost aloud.

The bride was worthy of Pseldonymov. This was a thin little damsel, still only some seventeen years old, pale, with a very small face and a sharp little nose. Her small eyes, quick and furtive, were not at all abashed, but, on the contrary, looked at him intently and even with a certain tinge of spite. Obviously, Pseldonymov had not taken her for her beauty. She was wearing a white muslin dress with pink doubling. Her neck was skinny, her body like a chicken's, all protruding bones. To the general's greeting she was able to say precisely nothing.

"Yes, you got yourself a pretty little thing," he went on in a low voice, as if addressing Pseldonymov alone, but purposely so that the bride heard it, too. But Pseldonymov said precisely nothing here as well, and this time did not even sway. It even seemed to Ivan Ilyich that there was in his eyes something cold, secretive, even something kept to himself, peculiar, malignant. And yet he had at all costs to get at some feeling. It was for that he came.

"A fine pair, though," he thought. "However . . ."

And he again addressed himself to the bride, who was placed beside him on the sofa, but all he received to his two or three questions was again only a "yes" or a "no," and in fact he did not quite receive even that.

"If only she'd get a little embarrassed," he went on to himself. "Then I could start joking. Otherwise there's no way out." And Akim Petrovich, as if on purpose, was also silent, though only out of stupidity, but still it was inexcusable.

"Gentlemen! am I not perhaps interfering with your pleasures?" he tried to address everyone in general. He felt that his palms were even sweating.

"No, sir . . . Don't worry, Your Excellency, we'll get started right away, and for now . . . we're cooling our heels, sir," the officer replied. The bride glanced at him with pleasure: the officer was still young and wore the uniform of some command or other. Pseldonymov stood right there, thrusting himself forward, and seemed to stick his hooked nose out still more than before. He listened and watched, like a lackey who stands holding a fur coat and waiting for the parting words of his masters to come to an end. Ivan Ilyich made this comparison himself; he was at a loss, felt that he was ill at ease, terribly ill at ease, that the ground was slipping from under his feet, that he had gotten somewhere and could not get out, as if in the dark.

Suddenly everyone stepped aside, and a heavyset and not very tall woman appeared, elderly, simply dressed though with some festiveness, a big shawl around her shoulders, pinned at the throat, and wearing a bonnet to which she was obviously not accustomed. In her hands was a small, round tray on which stood a not yet started, but already uncorked, bottle of champagne and two glasses, no more nor less. The bottle was evidently meant for only two guests.

The elderly woman went straight up to the general.

"Don't find fault, Your Excellency," she said, bowing, "but since you haven't disdained us, doing us the honor of coming to my son's wedding, be so kind as to congratulate the young folk with wine. Don't disdain it, do us the honor."

Ivan Ilyich seized upon her as his salvation. She was not such an old woman, about forty-five or -six, no more. But she had such a kind, red-cheeked, such an open, round Russian face, she smiled so good-naturedly, bowed so simply, that Ivan Ilyich was almost reassured and began to have hopes.

"So yo-o-ou are the ma-ter-nal pa-a-arent of your so-o-on?" he said, rising from the sofa.

"The maternal parent, Your Excellency," Pseldonymov maundered, stretching his long neck and again sticking his nose out.

"Ah! Very glad, ve-ry glad to make your acquaintance."

"Don't scorn us, then, Your Excellency."

"Even with the greatest pleasure."

The tray was set down, Pseldonymov leaped over and poured the wine. Ivan Ilyich, still standing, took the glass.

"I am especially, especially glad of this occasion, since I can . . ." he began, "since I can . . . herewith pay my . . . In a word, as a superior . . . I wish you, madam" (he turned to the bride), "and you, my friend Porfiry—I wish you full, prosperous, and enduring happiness."

And, even with emotion, he drank off the glass, his seventh that evening. Pseldonymov looked serious and even sullen. The general was beginning to hate him painfully.

"And this hulk" (he glanced at the officer) "is stuck here, too. Why doesn't he shout 'hurrah!' Then it would take off, take right off . . ."

"And you, too, Akim Petrovich, drink and congratulate them," added the old woman, addressing the chief clerk. "You're a superior, he's your subordinate. Look after my boy, I ask you as a mother. And don't forget us in the future, dear Akim Petrovich, kind man that you are."

"How nice these Russian old women are!" thought Ivan Ilyich. "She's revived them all. I've always liked our folkways . . ."

At that moment another tray was brought to the table. It was carried by a wench in a rustling, not yet laundered calico dress with a crinoline. She could barely get her arms around the tray, it was so big. On it was a numberless multitude of little plates with apples, bonbons, gumdrops, candied fruit, walnuts, and so on and so forth. Till then the tray had been in the drawing room, for the pleasure of all the guests, mainly the ladies. But now it was brought over to the general alone.

"Don't scorn our victuals, Your Excellency. What we've got, we're glad to give," the old woman repeated, bowing.

"Heavens . . ." said Ivan Ilyich, and even with pleasure he took and crushed between his fingers a single walnut. He was resolved to be popular to the end.

Meanwhile the bride suddenly began to giggle.

"What, ma'am?" Ivan Ilyich asked with a smile, glad of some signs of life.

"It's Ivan Kostenkinych there, making me laugh, sir," she replied, looking down.

The general actually made out a blond youth, not bad-looking at all, hiding on the other side of the sofa in a chair, who kept whispering something to Madame Pseldonymov. The youth got up. He was apparently very timid and very young.

"I was telling her about the 'dream book,'[18] Your Excellency," he murmured, as if making an excuse.

"About what dream book?" Ivan Ilyich asked indulgently.

"The new one, sir, the literary one. I was telling her, sir, that if you see Mr. Panaev[19] in your dreams, it means you'll spill coffee on your shirtfront, sir."

"What innocence," thought Ivan Ilyich, even angrily. The youth, though he became very red as he was saying it, was still incredibly glad that he had told about Mr. Panaev.

"Well, yes, yes, I've heard . . ." responded His Excellency.

"No, there's an even better one," another voice said, right beside Ivan Ilyich, "there's a new lexicon being published, they say Mr. Kraevsky himself will write articles, Alferaki . . . and *es*posé literature . . ."[20]

This was said by a young man, not a bashful one this time, but a rather casual one. He was wearing gloves, a white waistcoat, and held his hat in his hand. He did not dance, had a supercilious look, because he was a collaborator on the satirical magazine *The Firebrand,* set the tone, and showed up at this wedding by chance, invited as a guest of honor by Pseldonymov, with whom he was on intimate terms and with whom, still last year, he had shared a life of poverty "in corners"[21] rented from some German woman. He did drink vodka, however, and for that purpose had already absented himself more than once to a cozy little back room, the way to which was known to all. The general took a terrible dislike to him.

"And that's funny, sir, because," the blond youth suddenly

interrupted joyfully, the one who had told about the shirtfront and to whom the collaborator in the white waistcoat had given a hateful look for it, "funny because, Your Excellency, the writer assumes that Mr. Kraevsky doesn't know how to spell and thinks that 'exposé literature' should be written 'esposé literature' . . ."

But the poor youth barely finished. He could see by his eyes that the general had known that long ago, because the general also became as if abashed himself, obviously because he did know it. The young man was incredibly ashamed. He managed hurriedly to efface himself somewhere, and for the rest of the time afterward was very sad. Instead, the casual collaborator on *The Firebrand* came closer still and, it seemed, was intending to sit down somewhere nearby. To Ivan Ilyich such casualness seemed a bit ticklish.

"Yes! tell me, please, Porfiry," he began, in order to talk about something, "why—I've been wanting to ask you personally about it—why are you called Pseldonymov, and not Pseudonymov? Surely you're Pseudonymov?"

"I'm unable to give a precise report, Your Excellency," Pseldonymov replied.

"It must have been mixed up already on his father's papers, sir, when he entered the service, sir, so now he's stayed Pseldonymov," Akim Petrovich responded. "It happens, sir."

"Ab-so-lutely," the general picked up heatedly, "ab-so-lutely, because, consider for yourself: Pseudonymov—that comes from the literary word 'pseudonym.' Well, and Pseldonymov doesn't mean anything."

"Out of stupidity, sir," Akim Petrovich added.

"That is, what, in fact, is out of stupidity?"

"The Russian people, sir; out of stupidity they sometimes change letters, sir, and pronounce things sometimes in their own way, sir. For instance, they say ninvalid, when they ought to say invalid, sir."

"Well, yes . . . ninvalid, heh, heh, heh . . ."

"They also say liberry, Your Excellency," the tall officer blurted out, having long had an itch to distinguish himself somehow.

"That is, liberry meaning what?"

"Liberry instead of library, Your Excellency."

"Ah, yes, liberry . . . instead of library . . . Well, yes, yes . . . heh, heh, heh! . . ." Ivan Ilyich was obliged to chuckle for the officer as well.

The officer straightened his tie.

"And they also say perfick," the collaborator on *The Firebrand* attempted to mix in. But His Excellency tried this time not to hear. He was not going to chuckle for everyone.

"*Perfick* instead of *perfect*," the "collaborator" went on pestering with visible irritation.

Ivan Ilyich gave him a stern look.

"Stop pestering him!" Pseldonymov whispered to the collaborator.

"What do you mean, I'm just talking. What, can't I talk?" the other objected in a whisper, but nevertheless fell silent and with concealed rage left the room.

He made his way straight to the alluring little back room where, ever since the evening began, a small table had been placed for the dancing gentlemen, covered with a Yaroslavl tablecloth, on which stood vodka of two kinds, pickled herring, cheap caviar, and a bottle of the strongest sherry from the national cellar.[22] With spite in his heart, he was just pouring himself some vodka, when suddenly in ran the medical student with the tousled hair, the foremost dancer and cancanner at Pseldonymov's ball. With hasty greed he rushed for the decanter.

"They're starting now!" he said, hurriedly serving himself. "Come and watch: I'll do a solo upside down, and after supper I'll risk the *fish*.[23] It's even suitable for a wedding. A friendly hint, so to speak, to Pseldonymov . . . She's nice, this Kleopatra Semyonovna, you can risk whatever you like with her."

"He's a retrograde," the collaborator said gloomily, drinking his glass.

"Who's a retrograde?"

"That one, that personage, sitting in front of the gumdrops. A retrograde, I tell you!"

"Ah, you!" the student muttered, and dashed out of the room, hearing the ritornello of the quadrille.

The collaborator, left alone, poured himself some more for the sake of greater bravado and independence, drank up, ate a bite, and never before had the actual state councillor Ivan Ilyich acquired for himself a fiercer enemy or a more implacable avenger than this slighted-by-him collaborator on *The Firebrand,* especially after two glasses of vodka. Alas! Ivan Ilyich suspected nothing of the sort. Nor did he yet suspect another capital circumstance, which had an influence on all further mutual relations of the guests with His Excellency. The thing was that, though for his part he had given a decent and even detailed explanation of his presence at his subordinate's wedding, this explanation had not in fact satisfied anyone, and the guests went on being embarrassed. But suddenly everything changed, as if by magic; they all calmed down and were ready to make merry, guffaw, squeal, and dance just as if the unexpected guest were not in the room at all. The reason for it was the rumor, the whisper, the news which suddenly spread, no one knew how, that the guest seemed to be . . . under the influence. And though the matter had, at first glance, the look of the most terrible slander, it gradually began to justify itself, as it were, so that everything suddenly became clear. What's more, they suddenly became extraordinarily free. And it was at this same moment that the quadrille began, the last one before supper, to which the medical student had hastened so.

And just as Ivan Ilyich was addressing himself to the bride again, trying this time to get at her with some quip, the tall officer suddenly jumped over to her and swung himself down on one knee. She jumped up from the sofa at once and fluttered off with him to line up for the quadrille. The officer did not even apologize, nor did she even glance at the general as she left, as if she were even glad of her deliverance.

"However, essentially she's in her rights," thought Ivan Ilyich, "and besides, they don't know propriety."

"Hm . . . you mustn't stand on ceremony, brother Porfiry," he turned to Pseldonymov. "Perhaps you have something there . . . to tend to . . . or whatever . . . please, don't be embarrassed.—Is he keeping watch on me, or what?" he added to himself.

He was beginning to find Pseldonymov unbearable, with his long neck and eyes fixed intently on him. In short, all this was not it, not it at all, but Ivan Ilyich was still far from wanting to admit it.

The quadrille began.

"Shall I, Your Excellency?" Akim Petrovich asked, deferentially holding the bottle in his hands and preparing to fill His Excellency's glass.

"I . . . I don't really know if . . ."

But Akim Petrovich, with a reverently beaming face, was already pouring the champagne. Having filled his glass, he also, as if on the sly, as if thievishly, shrinking and cringing, filled his own, with the difference that he filled it one whole finger less, which was somehow more deferential. He was like a woman in childbirth sitting next to his immediate superior. What indeed was he to talk about? Yet he had to entertain His Excellency even out of duty, since he had the honor of keeping him company. The champagne served as a way out, and it was even pleasing to His Excellency to have his glass filled— not for the sake of the champagne, which was warm and the most natural swill, but just so, morally pleasing.

"The old boy wants a drink himself," thought Ivan Ilyich, "and he doesn't dare without me. I mustn't hinder . . . And it's ridiculous if the bottle just stands between us."

He took a sip, which in any case seemed better than just sitting there.

"I'm here," he began, with pauses and emphases, "I'm here, so to speak, by chance, and, of course, it may be that the others find . . . that it's . . . so to speak, in-ap-propriate for me to be at such a . . . gathering."

Akim Petrovich was silent and listened with timid curiosity.

"But I hope you understand why I'm here . . . It's not really that I came to drink wine. Heh, heh!"

Akim Petrovich was about to chuckle along with His Excellency, but somehow stopped short and again did not respond with anything reassuring.

"I'm here . . . in order, so to speak, to encourage . . . to show, so to speak, a moral, so to speak, goal," Ivan Ilyich went on, vexed at Akim Petrovich's obtuseness, but suddenly fell silent himself. He saw that poor Akim Petrovich had even lowered his eyes, as if he were guilty of something. The general, in some perplexity, hastened to take another sip from his glass, while Akim Petrovich, as if his whole salvation lay in it, seized the bottle and poured more.

"It's not that you have so many resources," thought Ivan Ilyich, looking sternly at poor Akim Petrovich. The latter, sensing this stern general's glance on him, resolved now to be definitively silent and not raise his eyes. So they sat facing each other for two minutes or so, a painful two minutes for Akim Petrovich.

A couple of words about this Akim Petrovich. He was a placid man, like a hen, of the oldest cast, nurtured on obsequiousness, and yet a kind man and even a noble one. He came from Petersburg Russians—that is, both his father and his father's father were born, grew up, and served in Petersburg and never once left Petersburg. These are a totally special type of Russian people. They have scarcely the faintest notion of Russia, and that does not trouble them at all. Their whole interest is confined to Petersburg and, above all, to the place where they serve. All their cares are concentrated around penny preference, grocery shop, and monthly salary. They do not know even a single Russian custom, nor a single Russian song, except "Luchinushka,"[24] and that only because barrel organs play it. However, there are two essential and unshakable tokens by which you may instantly distinguish a true Russian from a Petersburg Russian. The first is that all Petersburg Russians, all, without exception, always say *Academic Bulletin* and never *Petersburg Bulletin*.[25] The second, equally essential token is that a Petersburg Russian never uses the word "breakfast," but always says "Frühstück,"[26] putting special emphasis on the *Früh*. By these basic and distinctive tokens you can always distinguish them: in short, this is a humble type and was formed definitively over the last thirty-five years. However, Akim Petrovich was by no means a fool. Had the general asked him something appropriate for him, he would have replied and kept up the conversation, whereas it was quite unfitting for a subordinate to answer such questions, though Akim Petrovich was dying of curiosity to learn something more specific about His Excellency's real intentions . . .

And meanwhile Ivan Ilyich was falling more and more into reverie and into a certain round of ideas; distracted, he imperceptibly but ceaselessly sipped from his glass. Akim Petrovich at once and most diligently poured more. Both were silent. Ivan Ilyich was beginning to watch the dancing, and soon it attracted his attention somewhat. Suddenly one circumstance even surprised him . . .

The dancing was indeed merry. Here people danced precisely in simplicity of heart, to make merry and even get wild. Among the dancers very few were adroit; but the non-adroit stomped so hard that they might have been taken for adroit. The officer distinguished himself above all: he especially liked the figures where he remained alone, as in a solo. Then he would bend himself amazingly—namely, standing straight as a milepost, he would suddenly lean to one side so that you would think he was about to fall over, but at the next step he would suddenly lean to the opposite side, at the same sharp angle to the floor. He maintained a most serious expression and danced with the full conviction that everyone was amazed at him. Another gentleman, after getting potted beforehand, prior to the quadrille, fell asleep beside his partner at the second figure, so that his lady had to dance alone. A young registrar, who was dancing away with the lady in the blue scarf, in all the figures and all five quadrilles that had been danced that evening, kept pulling one and the same stunt—namely, he would lag behind his partner a little, pick up the end of her scarf, and, in air, at the changing of partners, would manage to plant about twenty kisses on it. The lady would go sailing on ahead of him as if she noticed nothing. The medical student indeed performed a solo upside down and provoked furious rapture, stomping, and squeals of pleasure. In short, there was unconstraint in the extreme. Ivan Ilyich, in whom the wine was also having its effect, was beginning to smile, but gradually some bitter doubt began to creep into his soul: of course, he very much liked casualness and unconstraint; he had desired, his soul had even called for this casualness, as they were all backing away, but now this casualness was beginning to go beyond limits. One lady, for instance, wearing a shabby blue velvet dress, bought at fourth hand, pinned her skirt up for the sixth figure in such a way that it was as if she were wearing trousers. This was that same Kleopatra Semyonovna with whom one could risk anything, as her partner, the medical student, had put it. Of the medical student there was nothing else to say: simply Fokine.[27] How could it be? First they backed away, and then suddenly they got so quickly emancipated! It seemed like nothing, yet this transition was somehow strange: it foreboded something. As if they had totally forgotten there was any Ivan Ilyich in the world. Naturally, he was the first to laugh and he even risked applauding. Akim Petrovich deferentially chuckled in unison with him, though, by the way, with obvious pleasure and not suspecting that His Excellency was already beginning to nurse a new worm in his heart.

"You dance nicely, young man," Ivan Ilyich felt forced to say to the student as he was passing by: the quadrille had just ended.

The student turned sharply to him, pulled some sort of grimace, and, bringing his face indecently close to His Excellency's, gave a loud cock-crow. This was too much. Ivan Ilyich got up from the table. In spite of that, there followed a burst of irrepressible laughter, because the cock-crow was astonishingly natural, and the whole grimace was completely unexpected. Ivan Ilyich was still standing in perplexity when Pseldonymov himself suddenly came and, bowing, began inviting him to supper. After him came his mother.

"Your Excellency," she said, bowing, "do us the honor, dearie, don't scorn our poverty . . ."

"I . . . I really don't know . . ." Ivan Ilyich began, "it was not for this that I . . . I . . . was just about to leave . . ."

He was indeed holding his hat in his hand. Not only that: just then, at that very instant, he had given himself his word of honor that he would leave without fail, at once, whatever the cost, and not stay for anything, and . . . and he stayed. A minute later he was leading the procession to the table. Pseldonymov and his mother went ahead, clearing the way for him. He was seated in the place of honor, and again a full bottle of champagne appeared before him. There were appetizers: herring and vodka. He reached out, poured himself a huge glass of vodka, and drank it. He had never drunk vodka before. He felt as if he were tumbling down a mountain, falling, falling, falling, that he must hold on, get a grip on something, but there was no opportunity for that.

His position was indeed becoming more and more peculiar. Not only that: it was some sort of mockery of fate. God knows what had happened to him in one little hour. When he came in, he was, so to speak, opening his embrace to all mankind and all his subordinates; and here, before one little hour had passed, he felt and knew with all his aching heart that he hated Pseldonymov, cursed him, and his wife, and his wedding. Not only that: from his face, from his eyes alone, he could see that Pseldonymov also hated him, that his eyes were all but saying: "Go to blazes, curse you! Fastened yourself on my neck! . . ." All this he had long since read in his look.

Of course, even now, as he was sitting down at the table, Ivan Ilyich would sooner have let his hand be cut off than admit sincerely, not only aloud, but even to himself, that all this was indeed exactly so. The moment had not yet fully come, and for now there was still a certain moral balance. But his heart, his heart . . . it was sick! it begged for freedom, air, rest. Ivan Ilyich was all too kindly a man.

He knew, he knew very well, that he should have left long

ago, and not only so as to leave, but so as to save himself. That all this had suddenly become something else—well, had turned out totally unlike his dream on the planks that evening.

"Why did I come? Did I really come to eat and drink here?" he asked himself, munching on pickled herring. He even got into negation. There were moments when irony at his great deed stirred in his soul. He was even beginning not to understand himself why, in fact, he had come.

But how could he leave? To leave like that, without going through with it, was impossible. "What will people say? They'll say I go dragging myself around to indecent places. In fact, it will even come out that way if I don't go through with it. What, for instance, will be said tomorrow (because it will spread everywhere), by Stepan Nikiforovich, by Semyon Ivanych, in the offices, at the Shembels', at the Shubins'? No, I must leave in such a way that they all understand why I came, I must reveal the moral purpose . . ." And meanwhile this touching moment refused to be caught. "They don't even respect me," he went on. "What are they laughing at? They're so casual, as if unfeeling . . . Yes, I've long suspected the whole younger generation of being unfeeling! I must stay, whatever the cost! . . . They've just been dancing, but once they've gathered around the table . . . I'll start talking about problems, about reforms, about Russia's greatness . . . I'll still get them carried away! Yes! Maybe absolutely nothing is lost yet . . . Maybe this is how it always is in reality. Only how shall I begin with them so as to attract them? What sort of method must I come up with? I'm at a loss, simply at a loss . . . And what do they want, what do they demand? . . . I see they're laughing at something over there . . . Can it be at me, oh, Lord God! But what is it that I want . . . why am I here, why don't I leave, what am I after? . . ." He thought this, and some sort of shame, some deep, unbearable shame wrung his heart more and more.

But it all went on that way, one thing after another.

Exactly two minutes after he sat down at the table, a dreadful thought took possession of his whole being. He suddenly felt that he was terribly drunk, that is, not as before, but definitively drunk. The cause of it was the glass of vodka, which, drunk on top of the champagne, produced an immediate effect. He felt, he sensed with his whole being, that he was definitively weakening. Of course, this greatly increased his bravado, yet consciousness did not abandon him, but cried out: "Not nice, not nice at all, and even quite indecent!" Of course, his unsteady, drunken thoughts could not settle on any one point: suddenly, even tangibly for himself, something like two sides appeared in him. On one was bravado, a yearning for victory, the overthrowing of obstacles, and a desperate conviction that he would still reach his goal. The other side made itself known to him by a tormenting ache in his soul and some gnawing at his heart. "What will people say? where will it end? what will tomorrow bring, tomorrow, tomorrow! . . ."

Earlier he had somehow vaguely sensed that he already had enemies among the guests. "That's because I was drunk then, too," he thought with tormenting doubt. What was his horror now, when he indeed became convinced, by indubitable signs, that he indeed had enemies at the table, and it was no longer possible to doubt it.

"And for what? for what?" he thought.

At this table all thirty guests were placed, some of whom were definitively done in. The others behaved with a certain nonchalant, malignant independence; they all shouted, talked loudly, offered premature toasts, fired bread balls with the ladies. One, a sort of uncomely person in a greasy frock coat, fell off his chair as soon as he sat at the table, and remained that way until the end of the supper. Another absolutely insisted on climbing onto the table and delivering a toast, and only the officer, who grabbed him by the coattails, restrained his premature enthusiasm. The supper was a perfect omnium-gatherum, though a cook had been hired to prepare it, some general's serf: there was a galantine, there was tongue with potatoes, there were meat cakes with green peas, there was, finally, a goose, and, to crown it all, blancmange. For drinks there were beer, vodka, and sherry. A bottle of champagne stood in front of the general alone, which forced him to pour for Akim Petrovich as well, since the man no longer dared use his own initiative at supper. For toasts the rest of the guests were meant to drink Georgian wine or whatever there happened to be. The table itself consisted of many tables put together, among them even a card table. It was covered with many tablecloths, including a colored Yaroslavl one. Gentlemen and ladies were seated alternately. Pseldonymov's maternal parent did not want to sit at the table; she bustled about and gave orders. Instead there appeared a malignant female figure who had not made an appearance earlier, in a sort of reddish silk dress, with a bound cheek, and in the tallest of bonnets. As it turned out, this was the bride's mother, who had finally agreed to come from the back room for supper. She had not come out till then on account of her implacable enmity for Pseldonymov's mother; but of that we shall speak later. This lady looked spitefully, even mockingly, at the general, and apparently did not wish to be introduced to him. To Ivan Ilyich this figure seemed highly suspect. But, besides her, certain other persons were also suspect and inspired an involuntary apprehension and alarm. It even seemed that they were in some conspiracy among themselves, and precisely against Ivan Ilyich. At least it seemed so to him, and in the course of the supper he became more and more convinced of it. Namely: there was malignancy in one gentleman with a little beard, a free artist of some sort; he even glanced several times at Ivan Ilyich and then, turning to his neighbor, whispered something in his ear. Another, a student, was in truth already thoroughly drunk, but all the same was suspect by certain tokens. The medical student also boded ill. Even the officer himself was not altogether trustworthy. But an especial and obvious hatred shone from the collaborator on *The Firebrand:* he sprawled so in his chair, had such a proud and presumptuous air, snorted so independently! And though the rest of the guests did not pay any special attention to the collaborator, who had written only four little ditties for *The Firebrand,* thus becoming a liberal, and evidently even disliked him, still, when a bread ball suddenly fell next to Ivan Ilyich, obviously sent in his direction, he was ready to stake his head that the perpetrator of this bread ball was none other than the collaborator on *The Firebrand*.

All this, of course, affected him in a lamentable fashion.

Particularly disagreeable was yet another observation: Ivan Ilyich was fully convinced that he was beginning to articulate words somehow unclearly and with difficulty, that he wanted to say a great deal, but his tongue would not move. Then, that he had suddenly begun as if to forget himself and, above all, out of the blue, would suddenly snort and laugh when there was nothing at all to laugh at. This disposition quickly passed after a glass of champagne, which Ivan Ilyich, though he had poured it for himself, had no wish to drink, but suddenly drank somehow quite accidentally. After this glass, he suddenly almost wanted to weep. He felt he was lapsing into the most peculiar sentimentality; he was beginning to love again, to love everybody, even Pseldonymov, even the collaborator on *The Firebrand*. He suddenly wanted to embrace them all, to forget everything and make peace. Not only that: to tell them everything frankly, everything, everything, that is, what a kind and nice man he was, with what excellent abilities. How he was going to be useful to the fatherland, how he was able to make the fair sex laugh, and, above all, what a progressist he was, how humanely he was prepared to condescend to everyone, to the most lowly, and, finally, in conclusion, to tell frankly the whole motive that had induced him to come, uninvited, to Pseldonymov's, drink two bottles of champagne, and overjoy them with his presence.

"The truth, the sacred truth first of all, and frankness! I'll get them with frankness. They'll believe me, I see it clearly; they even look hostile, but when I reveal everything to them, I'll subject them irresistibly. They'll fill their glasses and, with a shout, drink my health. The officer, I'm sure of it, will break his glass on his spur. There may even be a shout of 'hurrah!' Even if they should decide to toss me hussar fashion, I wouldn't resist, it would even be rather nice. I'll kiss the bride on the forehead; she's a sweetie. Akim Petrovich is also a very good man. Pseldonymov, of course, will improve in time. He lacks, so to speak, this worldly polish . . . And though, of course, this whole new generation lacks this delicacy of heart, but . . . but I'll tell them about the modern destiny of Russia among the other European powers. I'll mention the peasant question, too, yes, and . . . and they'll all love me, and I'll come out with glory! . . ."

These dreams were, of course, very pleasant, but the unpleasant thing was that amid all these rosy hopes Ivan Ilyich suddenly discovered in himself yet another unexpected ability: namely, spitting. At least the saliva suddenly began leaping from his mouth quite regardless of his will. He noticed it because Akim Petrovich, whose cheek he had sprayed, was sitting there not daring, out of deference, to wipe it off right away. Ivan Ilyich took a napkin and suddenly wiped it off himself. But this at once appeared so preposterous to him, so beyond anything reasonable, that he fell silent and began to be surprised. Akim Petrovich, though he had been drinking, sat all the same as if he were in shock. Ivan Ilyich now realized that, for almost a quarter of an hour already, he had been telling him about some most interesting topic, but that Akim Petrovich, while listening to him, was as if not only embarrassed, but even afraid of something. Pseldonymov, who was sitting two chairs away, also kept stretching his neck toward him, his head inclined to one side, listening with a most disagreeable air. He actually was as if keeping watch on him. Glancing around at the guests, he saw that many were looking straight at him and guffawing. But the strangest thing of all was that this did not embarrass him in the least; on the contrary, he sipped once more from his glass and suddenly started speaking for all to hear.

"I was saying!" he began as loudly as he could, "gentlemen, I was just saying to Akim Petrovich that Russia . . . yes, precisely Russia . . . in short, you understand what I mean to sa-sa-say . . . Russia, in my deepest conviction, experiences hu-humaneness . . ."

"Hu-humaneness!" came from the other end of the table.

"Hu-hu!"

"Coo-coo!"

Ivan Ilyich paused. Pseldonymov rose from his chair and started peering: who had shouted? Akim Petrovich was covertly shaking his head, as if admonishing the guests. Ivan Ilyich noticed it very well, but painfully held his tongue.

"Humaneness!" he went on stubbornly. "And this evening . . . and precisely this evening I was saying to Stepan Niki-ki-forovich . . . yes . . . that . . . that the renewal, so to speak, of things . . ."

"Your Excellency!" came loudly from the other end of the table.

"What can I do for you?" the interrupted Ivan Ilyich replied, trying to make out who had shouted.

"Precisely nothing, Your Excellency, I got carried away, please continue, con-tin-ue!" the voice came again.

Ivan Ilyich winced.

"The renewal, so to speak, of these very things . . ."

"Your Excellency!" the voice shouted again.

"What is it you want?"

"Hello there!"

This time Ivan Ilyich could not restrain himself. He interrupted his speech and turned to the offender and violator of order. This was a still very young student, totally crocked and arousing enormous suspicion. He had been hollering for a long time and even broke a glass and two plates, insisting that that was what was done at weddings. At the same moment that Ivan Ilyich turned to him, the officer began to reprimand the shouter sternly.

"What's with you, why are you hollering? You ought to be taken out, that's what!"

"It's not about you, Your Excellency, it's not about you! Do continue!" shouted the merrymaking schoolboy, sprawling on his chair. "Do continue, I'm listening and I'm very, ve-ry, ve-ry pleased with you! Pra-aiseworthy, pra-aiseworthy!"

"A drunken brat!" Pseldonymov prompted in a whisper.

"I can see he's drunk, but . . ."

"It's that I just told an amusing anecdote, Your Excellency!" the officer began. "About a certain lieutenant of our command, who had exactly that way of talking to superiors; so now he's imitating him. To every word of his superior, he would add: pra-aiseworthy, pra-aiseworthy! He was expelled from the service for it ten years ago."

"Wha-what lieutenant is that?"

"From our command, Your Excellency, he went mad over this praiseworthy. First they admonished him with milder measures, then they put him under arrest . . . His superior officer admonished him like a father; and all he said was: pra-aiseworthy, pra-aiseworthy! And it's strange: he was a courageous officer, six foot six. They wanted to court-martial him, but noticed that he was crazy."

"Meaning . . . a prankster. For prankishness they shouldn't be so severe . . . I, for my part, am ready to forgive . . ."

"There was medical evidence, Your Excellency."

"What! an autopsy?"

"Good heavens, he was perfectly alive, sir."

A loud and almost general burst of laughter came from the guests, who in the beginning had behaved themselves decorously. Ivan Ilyich became furious.

"Gentlemen, gentlemen!" he cried, at first almost without stammering, "I am quite well able to distinguish that autopsies are not performed on the living. I thought that in his madness he was no longer living . . . that is, already dead . . . that is, I mean to say . . . that you don't love me . . . And yet I love you all . . . yes, and I love Por . . . Porfiry . . . I humiliate myself by saying so . . ."

At that moment an enormous spit flew out of Ivan Ilyich's mouth and spattered on the tablecloth in a most conspicuous place. Pseldonymov rushed to wipe it up with his napkin. This last disaster finally crushed him.

"Gentlemen, this is too much!" he cried out in despair.

"A drunk man, Your Excellency," Pseldonymov prompted again.

"Porfiry! I see that you . . . all . . . yes! I say that I hope
. . . yes, I challenge you all to say: how have I humiliated
myself?"

Ivan Ilyich was on the verge of tears.

"Your Excellency, good heavens, sir!"

"Porfiry, I turn to you . . . Say, if I came . . . yes . . .
yes, to the wedding, I had a goal. I wanted to morally uplift
. . . I wanted them to feel. I address you all: am I very humiliated in your eyes, or not?"

Deathly silence. That was just the thing, that there was
deathly silence, and to such a categorical question. "Why, why
don't they cry out at least at such a moment!" flashed in His
Excellency's head. But the guests only exchanged looks. Akim
Petrovich was sitting there more dead than alive, and Pseldonymov, numb with fear, repeated to himself a terrible question,
which had already presented itself to him long before:

"What am I going to get for all this tomorrow?"

Suddenly the already very drunk collaborator on *The Firebrand*, who had been sitting in glum silence, addressed Ivan
Ilyich directly and, his eyes flashing, began to reply on behalf
of the whole company.

"Yes, sir!" he cried in a thundering voice, "yes, sir, you've
humiliated yourself, yes, sir, you're a retrograde . . . Re-tro-
grade!"

"Young man, come to your senses! To whom, as it were, are
you speaking!" Ivan Ilyich cried furiously, again jumping up
from his seat.

"To you, and, secondly, I'm not a young man . . . You
came to show off and seek popularity."

"Pseldonymov, what is it!" cried Ivan Ilyich.

But Pseldonymov jumped up in such horror that he stood
like a post and absolutely did not know what to start doing.
The guests, too, froze in their places. The artist and the student were applauding and shouting, "bravo, bravo!"

The collaborator went on shouting with irrepressible rage:

"Yes, you came to flaunt your humaneness! You interfered
with everybody's merrymaking. You drank champagne without realizing that it was too expensive for a clerk who makes

ten roubles a month, and I suspect that you're one of those superiors who relish their subordinates' young wives! Not only that, I'm convinced that you're in favor of tax-farming . . . Yes, yes, yes!"

"Pseldonymov, Pseldonymov!" Ivan Ilyich cried, holding his arms out to him. He felt that each of the collaborator's words was like a new dagger in his heart.

"Wait, Your Excellency, kindly do not worry!" Pseldonymov cried out energetically, jumped over to the collaborator, grabbed him by the scruff of the neck, and pulled him away from the table. It was even impossible to expect such physical strength from the scrawny Pseldonymov. But the collaborator was very drunk, and Pseldonymov perfectly sober. Then he gave him several whacks on the back and chucked him out the door.

"You're all scoundrels!" the collaborator cried. "By tomorrow I'll make caricatures of you all in *The Firebrand*! . . ."

They all jumped up from their seats.

"Your Excellency, Your Excellency!" cried Pseldonymov, his mother, and some of the guests, crowding around the general. "Calm yourself, Your Excellency!"

"No, no!" cried the general, "I'm destroyed . . . I came . . . I wanted, so to speak, to baptize. And look here, for all that, for all that!"

He sank onto the chair as if unconscious, put both hands on the table, and lowered his head to them, right into a dish of blancmange. No need to describe the universal horror. A minute later he rose, as if wishing to leave, staggered, tripped against the leg of a chair, fell flat on the floor, and started snoring . . .

This happens to non-drinkers when they accidentally get drunk. To the last stroke, to the last instant they remain conscious, and then suddenly fall as if cut down. Ivan Ilyich lay on the floor, having lost all consciousness. Pseldonymov seized himself by the hair and froze in that position. The guests hastily began to depart, each discussing in his own way what had happened. It was about three o'clock in the morning.

The main thing was that Pseldonymov's situation was much worse than could have been imagined, quite apart from the whole unattractiveness of the present circumstances. And while Ivan Ilyich is lying on the floor, with Pseldonymov standing over him, desperately tugging himself by the hair, let us interrupt the chosen current of our story and give a few words of explanation about Porfiry Petrovich Pseldonymov himself.

Still as recently as a month before his marriage, he was perishing quite irretrievably. He came from the provinces, where his father had once served as something and where he had died while under prosecution. When, some five months before the wedding, after perishing for a whole year in Petersburg, Pseldonymov got his ten-rouble post, he was resurrected in body and spirit, but circumstances soon laid him low again. In the whole world there remained only two Pseldonymovs, he and his mother, who had left the provinces after her husband's death. Mother and son were perishing together in the cold and feeding on doubtful substances. There were days when Pseldonymov took a mug and went to the Fontanka himself to fetch water, which he also drank there. Having obtained his post, he and his mother somehow settled themselves in corners somewhere. She began taking in laundry, and he knocked together some savings over four months, so as somehow to provide himself with boots and a bit of an overcoat. And how much grief he endured in his office: his superiors would approach him asking if it was long since he had taken a bath. There was a rumor that he had nests of bedbugs thriving under the collar of his uniform. But Pseldonymov was a man of firm character. In appearance, he was quiet and placid; he had very little education, and hardly ever was any conversation heard from him. I do not know positively whether he thought, made plans and systems, or dreamed of anything. But instead he was developing some instinctive, deep-seated, unconscious resolve to make his way out of his nasty situation. There was an antlike persistence in him: destroy an anthill and they will immediately start rebuilding it, destroy it again—again they will rebuild it, and so on without tiring. This was a nest-building and domestic being. One could see written on his brow that he would find his way, make his nest, and perhaps even put something aside. His mother alone in the whole world loved him and loved him to distraction. She was a firm, tireless, hardworking woman, and kind besides. They would just have gone on living in their corners for another five or six years, until circumstances changed, had they not run into the retired titular councillor Mlekopitaev, who had been a treasurer serving somewhere in the provinces, but had recently moved to Petersburg and settled there with his family. He knew Pseldonymov and had once owed something to his father. He had a bit of money, not much, of course, but he did have it; how much there was in reality—of this no one knew anything, neither his wife, nor his elder daughter, nor his relations. He had two daughters, and since he was a terrible despot, a drunkard, a domestic tyrant, and ailing besides, he suddenly took a notion to marry one daughter to Pseldonymov: "I know him," he said, "the father was a good man, and the son will be a good man." Whatever Mlekopitaev wanted, he did; no sooner said than done. He was a very strange despot. He spent most of his time sitting in his armchair, some illness having deprived him of the use of his legs, though that did not prevent him from drinking vodka. He drank and swore the whole day long. He was a wicked man; he absolutely had to torment someone constantly. For that he kept several distant female relations around him: his own sister, ailing and shrewish; his wife's two sisters, also wicked and multiloquent; and then his old aunt, who had broken a rib on some occasion. He kept yet another sponger, a Russified German woman, for her talent in telling him tales from *The Thousand and One Nights*. All his pleasure consisted in picking on these unfortunate hangers-on, cursing them constantly and seven ways to Sunday, though none of them, including his wife, who had been born with a toothache, dared to make a peep before him. He got them to quarrel among themselves, invented and fomented gossip and strife among them, and afterward guffawed and rejoiced seeing how they all nearly came to blows among themselves. He was overjoyed when his elder daughter, who for about ten years had lived in poverty with some officer, her husband, was finally widowed and moved in with him, bringing three small, ailing children. Her children he could not stand, but since their appearance increased the material on which his daily experiments could be conducted, the old man was very pleased. This whole heap of wicked women and ailing children, together with their tormentor, crowded into a wooden house on the Petersburg side, not eating enough, because the old man was miserly and handed out money by kopecks, though he did not stint on his vodka; not sleeping enough, because the old man suffered from insomnia and demanded to be entertained. In short, the whole thing lived in poverty and cursed its fate. It was at this time that Mlekopitaev sought out Pseldonymov. He was struck by his long nose and humble look. His puny and homely younger daughter had then turned seventeen. Though she had once attended some German *Schule,* she had not learned much more in it than the rudiments. After that, she grew up, scrofulous and sapless, under the crutch of her lame and drunken parent, amid a bedlam of household gossip, spying, and calumny. She never had any girlfriends, or any intelligence. She had long been wishing to get married. With other people she was silent, but at home, by her mummy and the spongers, she was wicked and piercing as a little drill. She particularly liked pinching and dealing out swats to her sister's children, peaching on them for stolen sugar or bread, which caused an endless and unquenchable quarrel between her and her elder sister. The old man himself offered her to Pseldonymov. But he, wretched though he was, nevertheless asked for some time to reflect. He and his mother pondered long together. But the house was to be registered in the bride's name, and though it was wooden, though it was one-storied and disgusting, it was still worth something. On top of that came four hundred roubles—when would he ever save up so much! "Why am I taking a man into my house?" the drunken tyrant shouted. "First, since you're all females, and I'm sick of just females. I want Pseldonymov to dance to my music, too, because I'm his benefactor. Second, I'm taking him, because you all don't want it and you're angry. So I'll do it just to spite you. What I've said I'll do, I'll do! And you, Porfirka, beat her when she's your wife; she's had seven demons sitting in her since the day she was born. Drive them all out, I'll even get the stick ready . . ."

Pseldonymov kept silent, but he had already decided. He and his mother were received into the house still prior to the wedding, washed, clothed, shod, given money for the wedding. The old man patronized them, perhaps precisely because the whole family spited them. He even liked the old Pseldonymov woman, so he restrained himself and did not pick on her. However, Pseldonymov himself he made dance the Little Cossack[28] for him a week before the wedding. "Well, enough, I just wanted to make sure you don't forget yourself with me," he said when the dance was finished. He gave just enough money for the wedding and invited all his relations and acquaintances. On Pseldonymov's side there were only the collaborator on *The Firebrand* and Akim Petrovich, the guest of honor. Pseldonymov knew very well that the bride loathed him and that she would much rather be marrying an officer and not him. But he endured it all, for such was his arrangement with his mother. The whole day of the wedding and the whole evening the old man spent drinking and cursing in nasty language. The whole family, on account of the wedding, huddled in the back rooms, which were crowded to the point of stinking. The front rooms were reserved for the ball and the supper. Finally, when the old man fell asleep, completely drunk, at around eleven o'clock in the evening, the bride's mother, who had been especially angry with Pseldonymov's mother that day, decided to exchange her wrath for mercy and come out for the ball and the supper. Ivan Ilyich's appearance upset everything. Mrs. Mlekopitaev became embarrassed, offended, and began accusing them of not warning her that a general had been invited. They assured her that he had come on his own, uninvited—she was so stupid that she refused to believe it. Champagne was necessary. Pseldonymov's mother had only one rouble, Pseldonymov himself—not a kopeck. They had to bow and scrape before the wicked old Mlekopitaev woman, begging money for one bottle, then for another. They pictured future official relations for her, the career, trying to bring her to reason. She finally gave her own money, but she made Pseldonymov drink such a cup of gall and vinegar[29] that he ran more than once into the little room where the nuptial bed had been prepared, seized himself silently by the hair, and threw himself headfirst onto the bed destined for paradisal delights, all atremble with impotent rage. No! Ivan Ilyich did not know the cost of the two bottles of Jackson he had drunk that night. What was Pseldonymov's horror, anguish, and even despair, when the business with Ivan Ilyich ended in so unexpected a way! Again there was going to be a fuss, and maybe a whole night of shrieking and tears from the capricious bride, and reproaches from her muddleheaded relations. He already had a headache without that, already without that the fumes and darkness clouded his eyes. And now Ivan Ilyich needed help, they had to look for a doctor or a carriage at three o'clock in the morning, to take him home, and it must be a carriage, not a hired hack, because it was impossible for such a person, and in such a state, to be sent home in a cab. And where find money at least for the carriage? The Mlekopitaev woman, infuriated that the general had not said even two words to her, nor so much as glanced at her during supper, announced that she did not have a kopeck. And perhaps she really did not have a kopeck. Where to find the money? What to do? Yes, he did have cause for pulling his hair.

Meanwhile, Ivan Ilyich was moved temporarily to a small leather sofa that stood right there in the dining room. While they were clearing and separating the tables, Pseldonymov rushed to all corners to borrow money, even tried borrowing from the servants, but no one turned out to have anything. He even risked troubling Akim Petrovich, who stayed longer than the others. But he, though he was a good man, became so bewildered and even frightened at the mention of money, that he came out with the most unexpected rubbish.

"At some other time, it would be my pleasure," he mumbled, "but now . . . really, you must excuse me . . ."

And, taking his hat, he quickly fled the house. Only the kindhearted youth who had told about the book of dreams proved good for anything, and inopportunely at that. He, too, stayed longer than the rest, taking a heartfelt interest in Pseldonymov's calamities. Finally, Pseldonymov, his mother, and the youth decided in general council not to send for a doctor, but rather to send for a carriage to take the sick man home, and meanwhile, before the carriage, to try some household remedies on him, such as wetting his temples and head with cold water, putting ice on the top of his head, and the like. This was undertaken by Pseldonymov's mother. The youth flew off to look for the carriage. Since at that hour there were not even any hacks on the Petersburg side, he set off for a carriage stand somewhere far away, where he woke up the coachmen. They started bargaining, saying that at such an hour even five roubles would not be enough to charge for a carriage. They settled, however, for three. But when, at almost four o'clock, the youth arrived at Pseldonymov's in the hired carriage, their decision had long since been changed. It turned out that Ivan Ilyich, who was still unconscious, had become so ill, was groaning and tossing so much, that to move him and take him home in such condition became completely impossible and even risky. "What will come of it?" said the completely discouraged Pseldonymov. What was to be done? A new question arose. If the sick man was to be kept at home, where was he to be moved to and where was he to be put? In the whole house there were only two beds: one huge double bed on which old man Mlekopitaev slept with his spouse, and another, newly purchased, with walnut veneer, also a double bed, intended for the newlyweds. All the other inhabitants, or, better to say, female inhabitants, of the house slept on the floor beside each other, mostly on featherbeds, but rather worn-out and malodorous ones, that is, altogether indecent, and of these there was barely enough; or not even that. Where, then, to put the sick man? They might, perhaps, produce a featherbed—they could pull one out from under somebody as a last resort, but where, and upon what, to put it? It turned out that it would have to be put in the big room, because it was farthest removed from the depth of the family and had its own separate exit. But what to put it on? surely not on chairs? It is known that beds are made up on chairs only for boarding-school students when they come home on Saturday to stay overnight, but for such a person as Ivan Ilyich it would be very disrespectful. What would he say the next morning, seeing himself on some chairs? Pseldonymov would not hear of it. One thing remained: to move him to the nuptial bed. This nuptial bed, as we have already mentioned, was set up in a small room just next to the dining room. On the bed was an as yet unused, newly purchased double mattress, clean linen, four pillows covered in pink calico, and, over that, muslin pillowcases trimmed with ruche. The coverlet was of satin, pink, with a quilted pattern. From a golden ring above, muslin curtains hung down. In short, everything was as it ought to be, and the guests, almost all of whom had visited the bedroom, had praised the furnishings. The bride, though she could not stand Pseldonymov, had nevertheless run over several times during the evening, especially, on the sly, to have a peek. What was her indignation, her anger, when she learned that they wanted to put on her nuptial bed a man sick with something like cholerine! The bride's mama tried to intercede for her, cursing, vowing to complain to her husband the next day; but Pseldonymov showed his mettle and insisted: Ivan Ilyich was moved, and the bed for the newlyweds was made up in the drawing room on chairs. The young woman sniveled, was ready to start pinching, but dared not disobey: her papa

had a stick she was very well acquainted with, and she knew
that the next day her papa was sure to demand a detailed
account of a certain something. To comfort her, the pink coverlet and the pillows in pink cases were moved to the drawing
room. At that moment the youth arrived with the carriage; on
learning that the carriage was no longer needed, he became
terribly frightened. He had to pay for it himself, and he had
never yet had even ten kopecks. Pseldonymov declared his total bankruptcy. They tried to reason with the driver. But he
started making noise and even rapped on the shutters. How it
ended, I do not know in detail. It seems the youth went in the
carriage as a hostage to Peski,[30] to the Fourth Rozhdestvensky
Street, where he hoped to awaken some student who was
spending the night with his acquaintances and see if he might
not have some money. It was already past four in the morning
when the young couple was left alone and the door of the
room was closed. Pseldonymov's mother stayed at the suf-
ferer's bedside all night. She huddled on the floor, on a little
rug, and covered herself with a fur jacket, but was unable to
sleep, because she was forced to get up every moment: Ivan
Ilyich had a terribly upset stomach. Mrs. Pseldonymov, a courageous and magnanimous woman, undressed him herself,
took off all his clothes, looked after him as after her own son,
and spent the whole night carrying the necessary vessels from
the bedroom to the corridor and back again. And yet the disasters of this night were far from over.

Ten minutes had not passed since the young couple was shut
in the drawing room, when a rending cry was suddenly heard,
a cry not of joy, but of a most malignant quality. The cries
were followed by a noise, a crash, as of the falling of chairs,
and instantly, into the still dark room, there unexpectedly
burst a whole crowd of gasping and frightened women in all
possible dishabille. These women were: the bride's mother, her
elder sister, who for the time had abandoned her ailing children, her three aunts, even the one with the broken rib came

padding in. Even the cook was there, even the sponging German woman who told fairy tales, from under whom her own featherbed had been pulled by force for the newlyweds, which was the best one in the house and constituted her entire property, came padding in along with the rest. All these respectable and perspicacious women had already stolen on tiptoe from the kitchen to the corridor some quarter of an hour earlier, and were eavesdropping in the anteroom, consumed by the most inexplicable curiosity. Meanwhile someone quickly lighted a candle, and they all beheld an unexpected sight. The chairs, unable to bear the double weight and supporting the heavy featherbed only on the edges, had slid apart, and the featherbed had fallen on the floor between them. The young woman was sniveling with anger; this time she was offended to the heart. The morally crushed Pseldonymov stood like a criminal caught in his evildoing. He did not even try to justify himself. Gasps and shrieks came from all sides. Pseldonymov's mother also came running at the noise, but this time the bride's mummy was fully on top of things. First she showered Pseldonymov with strange and for the most part unjust reproaches on the theme of "What kind of husband are you after that, my dear? What are you good for, my dear, after such shame?" and so on, and finally, taking her daughter by the hand, she drew her from her husband to her own room, taking upon herself personally the next day's responsibility before the terrible father when he called for an account. Everyone cleared out after her, saying "ah" and wagging their heads. Only his mother stayed with Pseldonymov and tried to comfort him. But he immediately drove her away from him.

He could not be bothered with comforting. He made his way to the sofa and sat down in the gloomiest pondering, barefoot as he was and in only the most necessary underwear. Thoughts crossed and tangled in his head. At times, as if mechanically, he glanced around this room where so recently there had been wild dancing and where cigarette smoke still hung in the air. Cigarette butts and candy wrappers were still lying on the spilt-upon and dirtied floor. The wreckage of the nuptial bed and the overturned chairs testified to the frailty of the best and surest of earthly hopes and dreams. He went on sitting like that for nearly an hour. Heavy thoughts kept coming into his head, as for example: what now awaited him at work? He was painfully aware that he had to change his place of work at all costs, and that it was impossible to remain at his former place, precisely owing to all that had happened that evening. He also thought about Mlekopitaev, who, perhaps the very next day, would make him dance the Little Cossack again, in order to test his meekness. He also realized that, though Mlekopitaev had given him fifty roubles for the wedding day, which had been spent to the last kopeck, he had not yet dreamed of giving him the four hundred roubles of the dowry, there had not been any mention of it. And the house itself had not yet been formally transferred. He also thought about his wife, who had abandoned him at the most critical moment of his life, about the tall officer who had gone on one knee before her—he had managed to notice that. He thought about the seven demons who were sitting in his wife, by her father's own testimony, and about the stick ready to drive them out . . . Of course, he felt strong enough to endure a lot, but fate kept slipping in such surprises as could make one finally doubt one's strength.

Thus Pseldonymov grieved. Meanwhile the candle-end was going out. Its glimmering light, falling directly on Pseldonymov's profile, reproduced him in colossal form on the wall, with outstretched neck, hooked nose, and two wisps of hair sticking up from his crown and forehead. Finally, when morning's freshness was already wafting, he got up, chilled and benumbed of soul, made his way to the featherbed lying between the chairs, and, not straightening anything, not blowing out the candle-end, not even putting a pillow under his head, crawled onto it on all fours and fell into that dead, leaden sleep that must be the sleep of those sentenced to civil execution the next day.

On the other hand, what could compare with the painful night Ivan Ilyich Pralinsky spent on the nuptial bed of the unfortunate Pseldonymov! For some time the headache, vomiting, and other most unpleasant attacks would not leave him for a minute. These were the torments of hell. Consciousness, though barely flickering in his head, lit up such abysses of horror, such dismal and loathsome pictures, that it would have been better not to regain consciousness. However, everything was still mixed up in his head. He recognized Pseldonymov's mother, for instance—heard her gentle admonishments, such as: "Be patient, dovey, be patient, my dear, nothing ventured, nothing gained"—recognized her and yet was unable to give himself any logical account of her presence at his side. Loathsome phantoms pictured themselves to him: most often it was Semyon Ivanych, but, on closer inspection, he noticed that this was not Semyon Ivanych at all, it was Pseldonymov's nose. Before him also flitted the free artist, and the officer, and the old woman with the bound cheek. Most of all he was preoccupied with the golden ring that hung over his head, from which the curtains came. He made it out clearly by the dim light of a candle-end, and kept seeking mentally: what is the purpose of this ring, why is it there, what does it signify? He asked the old woman about it several times, but obviously did not say what he meant to say, and she evidently did not understand him, no matter how he sought to explain. Finally, toward morning, his attacks ceased, and he fell asleep, fast asleep, without dreams. He slept for about an hour, and when he woke up, he was already almost fully conscious, feeling an unbearable ache in his head, and in his mouth, on his tongue, which had turned into some piece of flannel, the foulest taste. He sat up in bed, looked around, and fell to thinking. The pale light of the dawning day, stealing in narrow strips through the cracks in the blinds, trembled on the wall. It was about seven o'clock in the morning. But when Ivan Ilyich suddenly realized and recalled all that had happened to him since evening; when he recalled all the adventures at supper, his miscarried great deed, his speech at the table; when he imagined all at once, with horrifying clarity, all that might come of it now, all that would now be said and thought about him; when he looked around and saw, finally, to what a sad and hideous state he had brought the peaceful nuptial bed of his subordinate—oh, then such mortal shame, such torment descended suddenly into his heart, that he cried out, covered his face with his hands, and in despair threw himself down on the pillow. A moment later he jumped out of bed, saw his clothes right there on a chair, properly folded and already cleaned, grabbed them, and quickly, hurrying, looking over his shoulder and terribly afraid of something, began pulling them on. Right there on the other chair lay his fur coat, and his hat, and in the hat his yellow gloves. He was about to slip away quietly. But the door suddenly opened and old Mrs. Pseldonymov came in with an earthenware bowl and a washstand. On her shoulder hung a towel. She set the washstand down and, without further talk, announced that it was absolutely necessary to wash.

"Come now, dearie, wash yourself, you can't go without washing . . ."

And at that moment Ivan Ilyich realized that if there was at least one being in the whole world of whom he now could neither be ashamed nor afraid, it was precisely this old woman. He washed himself. And for a long time afterward, in difficult moments of his life, he recalled, amid other pangs of conscience, all the circumstances of this awakening, this earthenware bowl with the faience washstand, filled with cold water in which pieces of ice still floated, and the soap in its pink wrapper, of an oval shape, with some letters stamped on it, fifteen kopecks' worth, obviously bought for the newlyweds, but of which Ivan Ilyich was to be the first user; and the old woman with the damask towel on her left shoulder. The cold water refreshed him, he dried himself off, and, without saying a word, not even thanking his sister of mercy, seized his hat, took on his shoulders the fur coat held for him by Mrs. Pseldonymov, and through the corridor, through the kitchen, where the cat was already miaowing and the cook, raising herself on her pallet, gazed after him with greedy curiosity, ran out to the courtyard, to the street, and rushed for a passing cab. The morning was frosty, a chilled yellowish fog still enveloped the houses and all objects. Ivan Ilyich turned up his collar. He thought that everyone was watching him, that everyone knew him, that everyone recognized him . . .

For eight days he did not leave his house or go to work. He was ill, painfully ill, but more morally than physically. In those eight days he lived through an entire hell, and they must have been counted to his credit in the other world. There were moments when he would start thinking about becoming a monk. There really were. His imagination would even run particularly free on those occasions. He pictured quiet underground singing, an open coffin,[31] life in a secluded cell, forests and caves; but, coming to his senses, he would realize almost at once that all this was the most terrible nonsense and exaggeration, and he was ashamed of this nonsense. Then moral fits began, concerned with his *existence manquée*. Then shame again flared up in his soul, taking possession of it all at once, burning and exacerbating everything. He shuddered, imagining various pictures to himself. What would they say about him, what would they think, how would he enter the office, what whispering would pursue him for a whole year, for ten years, all his life? His anecdote would be handed down to posterity. Sometimes he even lapsed into such faintheartedness that he was ready to go at once to Semyon Ivanych and beg for his forgiveness and friendship. Himself he did not even try to justify, he blamed himself definitively: he found no justifications for himself and was ashamed of them.

He also thought of taking his retirement immediately and thus, simply, in solitude, devoting himself to the happiness of mankind. In any case, he certainly had to change all his acquaintances and in such fashion as to eradicate any memory of himself. Then the thought came to him that this was all nonsense and that through increased strictness with his subordinates the whole thing could still be mended. Then he would begin to have hope and take courage. Finally, after a whole eight days of doubt and torment had passed, he felt he could endure the uncertainty no longer, and *un beau matin*[32] he decided to go to the office.

Before, when he was still sitting at home, in anguish, he had imagined a thousand times how he would enter his office. He was convinced, to his horror, that he was sure to hear ambiguous whispers behind his back, to see ambiguous faces, to reap the most malignant smiles. What was his amazement when none of it in fact happened. He was met deferentially; he was bowed to; everyone was serious; everyone was busy. Joy filled his heart as he made his way to his inner office.

He at once and most seriously got down to business, listened to some reports and explanations, made decisions. He felt he had never yet reasoned and decided so intelligently, so efficiently, as that morning. He saw that people were pleased with him, honored him, treated him with respect. The most ticklish insecurity would have been unable to notice anything. Business went splendidly.

Finally Akim Petrovich also appeared with some papers. At his appearance something as if stung Ivan Ilyich in his very heart, but only for an instant. He got busy with Akim Petrovich, talked gravely, showed him what needed to be done, and gave explanations. He noticed only that he as if avoided looking at Akim Petrovich for too long, or, better to say, that Akim Petrovich was afraid to look at him. But then Akim Petrovich was finished and began to gather up the papers.

"And here is another petition," he began as dryly as he could, "from the clerk Pseldonymov, about his transfer to the ———— department. His Excellency Semyon Ivanovich Shipulenko has promised him a post. He asks your gracious assistance, Your Excellency."

"Ah, so he's transferring," Ivan Ilyich said, and felt an enormous weight lift from his heart. He looked at Akim Petrovich, and at that moment their eyes met.

"Why, then I, for my part . . . I will employ," Ivan Ilyich replied, "I am prepared."

Akim Petrovich obviously wanted to slip away quickly. But Ivan Ilyich suddenly, on an impulse of nobility, decided to speak himself out definitively. Apparently inspiration had come over him again.

"Tell him," he began, directing a clear and profoundly meaningful look at Akim Petrovich, "tell Pseldonymov that I wish him no evil; no, I do not! . . . That, on the contrary, I am even ready to forget all the past, to forget all, all . . ."

But suddenly Ivan Ilyich stopped short, staring in amazement at the strange behavior of Akim Petrovich, who from a sensible man suddenly turned out, for some reason, to be a most terrible fool. Instead of listening and hearing him out, he suddenly blushed to the point of ultimate stupidity, began bowing somehow hastily and even indecently with some sort of little bows and at the same time backing toward the door. His whole look expressed a wish to fall through the floor, or, better to say, to get quickly back to his desk. Ivan Ilyich, left alone, rose from his chair in perplexity. He was looking into the mirror without noticing his own face.

"No, strictness, strictness, strictness alone!" he was whispering to himself almost unconsciously, and suddenly bright color poured all down his face. He suddenly felt so ashamed, so distressed, as he had not felt in the most unbearable moments of his eight-day illness. "I didn't hold out!" he said to himself, and sank weakly into his chair.

THE ETERNAL HUSBAND

A STORY

I

Velchaninov

Summer came—and Velchaninov, beyond all expectation, stayed in Petersburg. His trip to the south of Russia fell through, and there was no end to his case in sight. This case— a lawsuit over an estate—was taking a most nasty turn. Three months earlier it had looked quite uncomplicated, all but indisputable; but everything had changed somehow suddenly. "And generally everything has begun to change for the worse!"—Velchaninov began repeating this phrase to himself gloatingly and frequently. He hired a clever, expensive, famous lawyer, and did not mind the cost; but in impatience and from insecurity he got to busying himself with the case as well: read and wrote documents which the lawyer uniformly rejected, kept running around to various offices, made inquiries, and most likely hindered everything considerably; at least the lawyer complained and urged him to go to the country. But he could not even make up his mind to go to the country. The dust, the stuffiness, the white nights of Petersburg, which chafed his nerves—this was what he enjoyed in Petersburg. His apartment, recently rented, was somewhere near the Bolshoi Theater, and this, too, had not worked out; "nothing works out!" His hypochondria was increasing day by day; but he had long been inclined to hypochondria.

This was a man who had lived much and broadly, now far from young, about thirty-eight or even thirty-nine, and all this "old age"—as he himself put it—had come upon him "almost quite unexpectedly"; but he understood himself that he had aged not in the quantity, but rather, so to speak, in the quality of his years, and that if his infirmities had indeed begun, it was rather from within than from without. By the look of him, he still seemed a fine man. He was a tall and sturdy fellow, with thick, light brown hair and not a trace of gray on his head, and with a long brown beard almost halfway down his chest; as if somewhat clumsy and gone to seed at first sight, but, on closer inspection, you would at once discern in him a gentleman of excellent seasoning and who had once received a most high-society upbringing. Now, too, Velchaninov's manners were free, bold, and even graceful, despite all his well-acquired peevishness and bagginess. And even to this day he was filled with the most unshakable, most impudent high-society self-confidence, the extent of which he perhaps did not suspect in himself, despite his being not only an intelligent, but sometimes even a sensible man, almost educated and unquestionably gifted. The color of his face, open and ruddy, had been distinguished in the old days by a feminine tenderness and had attracted the attention of women; now, too, someone would look at him and say: "There's a hale fellow! Hale and hearty!" And yet this "hale fellow" was cruelly afflicted with hypochondria. His eyes, large and pale blue, also used to have much winsomeness in them ten years ago; they were such light, such merry and carefree eyes, that they inadvertently attracted everyone he came across. Now, nearing the age of forty, the brightness and kindness had almost died out in these eyes, already surrounded with light wrinkles; there appeared in them, on the contrary, the cynicism of a weary and not entirely moral man, cunning, mockery most often, and another new shade that had not been there before: a shade of sorrow and pain—a sort of distracted sorrow, as if without object, but intense. This sorrow was especially manifest when he was left alone. And, strangely, this man, so boisterous, merry, and carefree just two years ago, who was so good at telling such amusing stories—now liked nothing better than to be left entirely alone. He deliberately abandoned his numerous acquaintances, whom even now he might not have abandoned, despite the definitive disorder of his financial situation. True, vanity also helped here: with his insecurity and vanity it was impossible to endure former acquaintances. But his vanity, too, began gradually to change in isolation. It did not diminish—even quite the contrary; but it began to degenerate into some peculiar sort of vanity, which had not been there before; he began to suffer sometimes from entirely different causes than usual before—from unexpected causes, entirely unthinkable before, from "more higher" causes than previously—"if it can be put that way, if there actually are higher and lower causes . . ." That he added himself.

Yes, he did come to that as well; he was now struggling with some *higher* causes, of which he had not even stopped to think before. In his mind and according to his conscience, he called "higher" all those "causes" which (to his surprise) he was in no way able to laugh at in himself—something which had not happened till then—in himself, naturally; oh, in society it was a different matter! He knew perfectly well that the circumstances needed only to arise—and the next day he would quite calmly renounce, aloud, despite all the mysterious and reverential decisions of his conscience, all these "higher causes" and himself be the first to make fun of them, naturally without admitting anything. And this was indeed so, despite the certain, even quite considerable, share of independence of thought he had won lately from the "lower causes" that had hitherto possessed him. And how many times, getting out of bed in the morning, had he begun to be ashamed of the thoughts and feelings he had lived through during the night's insomnia! (And of late he had been suffering constantly from insomnia.) He had long since noticed that he was becoming extremely insecure in all things, both important and trifling, and therefore he resolved to trust himself as little as possible. However, certain facts stood out which could in no way be acknowledged as actually existing. Of late, at night sometimes, his thoughts and sensations changed almost completely as compared with his usual ones and for the most part did not at all resemble those that fell to the first half of his day. He was struck by this—and even consulted a famous doctor, though, true, the man was his acquaintance; naturally, he brought it up jokingly. He received the response that the fact of a change and even a splitting of thoughts and sensations at night during insomnia, and at night generally—is a universal fact among people of "strong thoughts and strong feelings"—that the convictions of a whole lifetime would sometimes change all at once under the melancholy influence of night and insomnia; suddenly, out of the blue, the most fateful decisions would be taken; but that, of course, there is measure in all things—and if, finally, the subject feels this split too much, so that it reaches the point of suffering, that is unquestionably a sign that illness has set in; and therefore something ought to be undertaken without delay. Best of all would be to change one's way of life radically, to change one's diet or even undertake a journey. A laxative would, of course, be helpful.

Velchaninov listened no further, but for him the illness was fully proven.

"And so all this is just an illness, all this 'higher' is just an illness and nothing more!" he sometimes exclaimed caustically to himself. He wanted very much not to agree.

Soon, however, the same thing that used to happen in exclusively nighttime hours began to repeat itself in the mornings, but with greater bile than at night, with anger instead of repentance, with mockery instead of tenderheartedness. Essentially, it was certain events from his past and long-past life that returned more and more often to his memory, "suddenly and God knows why," but that returned in some special way.

Velchaninov had long been complaining, for instance, of a loss of memory: he would forget the faces of his acquaintances, who would get offended with him when they met; a book read six months earlier would sometimes be completely forgotten in that length of time. And what then?—despite this obvious daily loss of memory (which worried him very much)—all that had seemed long past, all that had even been completely forgotten for ten, for fifteen years—all this now suddenly came back to his memory, but with such an amazing precision of impressions and details that it was as if he were living it over again. Some of the facts he remembered had been so well forgotten that it seemed miracle enough to him that they could be remembered. But that was not yet all; for who among people who have lived broadly does not have memories of a certain sort? But the thing was that all these remembrances now came back as if with some completely new, unexpected, and previously quite unthinkable point of view on the fact, as if prepared by someone. Why did certain memories now seem altogether criminal to him? And these mental judgments were not the only thing; his dark, solitary, and sick mind he might not have believed; but it went as far as curses and all but tears, inwardly if not outwardly. Two years ago he would not have believed it if he had been told he would one day weep! At first, however, what he remembered was more of a caustic than of a sentimental sort: he remembered certain social mishaps, humiliations; he recalled, for instance, how he had been "slandered by some intriguer," with the result that he stopped being received in a certain house—how, for instance, and even not so long ago, he had been positively and publicly offended and had not challenged the offender to a duel—how he had once been brought up short by a most witty epigram, in a circle of the prettiest women, and had been at a loss for a reply. He even remembered two or three unpaid debts, trifling ones, true, but debts of honor, and to such people as he no longer kept company with and of whom he had even begun to speak ill. He also suffered (but only in the most evil moments) from the remembrance of two most foolishly squandered fortunes, each of them considerable. But soon he also began to have remembrances of "higher" things.

Suddenly, for instance, "out of the blue" he remembered the forgotten—and forgotten by him in the highest degree— figure of one kindly little official, gray-haired and ridiculous, whom he had insulted once long, long ago, publicly and with impunity and solely from braggadocio: only so as not to lose a funny and fortunate quip, which brought him fame and was repeated afterward. He had forgotten the fact so well that he could not even remember the old man's last name, though all the circumstances of the adventure presented themselves with inconceivable clarity. He vividly remembered that the old man was then defending his daughter, who lived with him and had gone too long unmarried, and of whom some sort of rumors had begun to spread in town. The old man tried to respond and got angry, but suddenly burst into sobs before the whole company, which even produced a certain impression. They ended by getting him drunk on champagne for the fun of it, and had themselves a good laugh. And now, when Velchaninov remembered "out of the blue" how the old fellow had wept, covering his face with his hands like a child, it suddenly seemed to him that he had never forgotten it. And, strangely, all this had seemed very funny to him at the time; but now— quite the contrary, and precisely in the details, precisely in the covering of his face with his hands. Then he remembered how, solely for the sake of a joke, he had slandered the very pretty wife of a schoolteacher, and the slander had reached the husband. Velchaninov had soon left that little town and did not know how the consequences of his slander had ended, but now he suddenly began to imagine the end of those conse- quences—and God knows where his imagination might have taken him, if a much closer memory had not suddenly pre- sented itself, of a certain girl, from simple tradespeople, whom he did not even like and of whom, he had to confess, he was ashamed, but whom, not knowing why himself, he got preg- nant, and then just abandoned along with the child, without even saying good-bye (true, he had no time), when he left

Petersburg. Afterward he looked for the girl for a whole year, but was simply unable to find her. However, there turned out to be perhaps hundreds of such memories—and it even seemed that each memory dragged dozens of others after it. Gradually his vanity also began to suffer.

We have already said that his vanity degenerated into something peculiar. That was true. There were moments (rare, however) when he sometimes reached such self-abandon that he was not even ashamed of not having his own carriage, of dragging about on foot to official places, of having become somewhat negligent in his dress—and if perchance one of his old acquaintances looked him over mockingly in the street, or simply decided not to recognize him, he truly had enough arrogance not even to wince. Seriously not to wince, in reality, not only in appearance. Naturally, this happened rarely, these were only moments of self-abandon and irritation, but even so his vanity began gradually to withdraw from former pretexts and to concentrate itself around one question that constantly came to his mind.

"So then," he would sometimes begin thinking satirically (and he almost always began with the satirical when thinking about himself), "so then, someone there is concerned with correcting my morals and is sending me these cursed memories and 'tears of repentance.' Let them, it's nothing! it's all shooting with blanks! Don't I know for sure, for surer than sure, that despite all these tearful repentances and self-condemnations, there isn't a drop of independence in me, despite my most stupid forty years! If some such temptation should happen along tomorrow, well, for instance, if the circumstances were again such that it would profit me to spread the rumor that the teacher's wife was receiving presents from me—I'd be sure to spread it, I wouldn't flinch—and the thing would turn out even worse, more vile, than the first time, because this would already be the second time and not the first. Well, if I were to be insulted again, now, by that princeling, his mother's only son, whose leg I shot off eleven years ago—I'd challenge him at once and set him on a peg leg again. Well, aren't these blank shots, then, and what's the sense in them! and why these reminders, if I can't settle things for myself with any degree of decency!"

And though the fact with the teacher's wife was not repeated, though he did not set anyone on a peg leg, the mere thought that this would certainly have to be repeated, if the circumstances were such, nearly killed him . . . at times. One could not, in fact, suffer from memories constantly; one could rest and enjoy oneself—in the intermissions.

And so Velchaninov did: he was ready to enjoy himself in the intermissions; but, all the same, the longer it went on, the more disagreeable his life in Petersburg became. July was approaching. A resolve sometimes flashed in him to drop everything, including the lawsuit itself, and go off somewhere without looking back, somehow suddenly, inadvertently, down to the Crimea, for instance. But an hour later, usually, he was already despising his thought and laughing at it: "These nasty thoughts won't cease in any South, if they've already started and if I'm at least a somewhat decent man, and that means there's no point in running away from them, and no reason to.

"And why run away?" he went on philosophizing from grief. "It's so dusty here, so stuffy, everything's so dirty in this house; in these offices I hang about in, among all these practical people—there's so much of the most mousy bustle, so much of the most jostling worry; in all these people who stay on in the city, in all these faces flitting by from morning to evening—all their selfishness, all their simple-hearted insolence, all the cowardice of their little souls, all the chickenness of their little hearts is so naively and frankly told—that it's really a paradise for a hypochondriac, speaking most seriously! Everything's frank, everything's clear, everything even finds it unnecessary to cover itself up, the way our ladies do somewhere in the country or taking the waters abroad—and therefore everything's much more worthy of the fullest respect, if only for this frankness and simplicity alone . . . I won't go anywhere! I may crack here, but I won't go anywhere! . . ."

II

The Gentleman with Crape on His Hat

It was the third of July. The stuffiness and heat were unbearable. For Velchaninov the day turned out to be a most bustling one: all morning he had to walk and drive around, and the future held for him the absolute need to visit that evening a certain necessary gentleman, a businessman and state councillor, at his country house somewhere on the Black River,[1] and catch him unexpectedly at home. Sometime after five, Velchaninov finally entered a certain restaurant (rather dubious, but French) on Nevsky Prospect, near the Police Bridge, sat down in his usual corner at his table, and asked for his daily dinner.

He ate a one-rouble dinner daily and paid separately for the wine, considering this a sacrifice sensibly offered up to his disordered circumstances. Surprised that it was possible to eat such trash, he nevertheless finished everything to the last crumb—and each time with such appetite as if he had not eaten for three days. "There's something morbid about it," he occasionally muttered to himself, noting his appetite. But this time he sat down at his table in the nastiest state of mind, vexedly flung his hat away somewhere, leaned on his elbow, and fell to thinking. Let his neighbor, having dinner at the next table, make some noise, or a serving boy not understand him from the first word—and he, who knew so well how to be polite and, when necessary, so haughtily imperturbable, would surely raise a row like a cadet, and perhaps make a scandal.

The soup was served, he took the spoon, but suddenly, before dipping it, he dropped the spoon on the table and all but jumped up from his chair. An unexpected thought suddenly dawned on him: at that moment—and God knows by what process—he suddenly understood fully the cause of his anguish, his special, particular anguish, which had already tormented him for several days in a row, the whole time lately, which had fastened on to him God knows how and, God knows why, refused to get unfastened; and now he all at once saw and understood everything like the palm of his hand.

"It's all that hat!" he murmured as if inspired. "Just simply and solely that cursed round hat with the loathsome funeral crape on it, that's the cause of it *all*!"

He began to think—and the further he thought into it, the gloomier he became and the more astonishing "the whole event" became in his eyes.

"But . . . but what sort of event is it, anyhow?" he tried to protest, not trusting himself. "Is there anything in it that remotely resembles an event?"

The whole thing consisted in this: almost two weeks ago (he really did not remember, but it seemed like two weeks), he had met for the first time, in the street, somewhere at the corner of Podiachesky and Meshchansky Streets, a gentleman with crape on his hat. The gentleman was like everybody else, there was nothing special about him, he had passed by quickly, but he had glanced at Velchaninov somehow much too intently and for some reason had at once greatly attracted his attention. At least his physiognomy had seemed familiar to Velchaninov. He had apparently met it sometime somewhere. "Ah, anyhow, haven't I met thousands of physiognomies in my life? One can't remember them all!" Having gone on some twenty paces, he seemed to have forgotten the encounter already, despite his first impression. But the impression nevertheless lingered for the whole day—and a rather original one: in the form of some pointless, peculiar anger. Now, two weeks later, he recalled it all clearly; he also recalled failing completely to understand the source of his anger—to the point of not even once connecting and juxtaposing his nasty state of mind all that evening with the morning's encounter. But the gentleman hastened to give a reminder of himself, and the next day again ran into Velchaninov on Nevsky Prospect and again looked at him somehow strangely. Velchaninov spat, but, having spat, was at once surprised at his spitting. True, there are physiognomies that instantly provoke a pointless and aimless revulsion. "Yes, I actually met him somewhere," he muttered pensively, half an hour after the encounter. Then again for the whole evening he was in the nastiest state of mind; he even had some bad dream during the night, and still it did not occur to him that the whole cause of this new and peculiar spleen of his—was just merely the earlier encounter with the mourning gentleman, though that evening he had remembered him more than once. He even had a fleeting fit of anger, that "such trash" dared to get remembered for so long; and he would certainly have considered it humiliating to ascribe all his anxiety to the man, if such a thought had occurred to him. Two days later they met again, in a crowd, getting off some Neva steamer. This third time Velchaninov was ready to swear that the gentleman in the mourning hat recognized him and strained toward him, drawn back and pushed by the crowd; it seemed he even "dared" to reach out his hand to him; perhaps he even cried out and called him by name. This last, however, Velchaninov did not hear clearly, but . . . "who, however, is this rascal and why doesn't he approach me, if in fact he recognizes me and would like so much to approach?" he thought spitefully, getting into a cab and going off toward the Smolny monastery. Half an hour later he was arguing loudly with his lawyer, but that evening and night he was again in the vilest and most fantastic anguish. "Is my bile not rising?" he asked himself suspiciously, looking in the mirror.

This was the third encounter. Then for five days in a row he encountered decidedly "no one," and of the "rascal" there was not a sound. And yet every now and then the gentleman with crape on his hat would be remembered. Velchaninov caught himself at it with some surprise. "Am I pining for him, or what?—Hm! . . . And it must be that he also has a lot to do in Petersburg—and for whom is this crape of his? He evidently recognized me, but I don't recognize him. And why do these people wear crape? It somehow doesn't become them . . . I suppose if I look at him more closely, I'll recognize him . . ."

And something was as if beginning to stir in his memories,

like some familiar but for some reason suddenly forgotten word, which you try as hard as you can to remember; you know it perfectly—and you know that you know it; you know precisely what it means, you circle around it; but the word simply refuses to be remembered, no matter how you struggle over it!

"It was . . . It was long ago . . . and it was somewhere . . . There was . . . there was . . . —well, devil take it all, whatever there was or wasn't! . . ." he suddenly cried out spitefully. "And is it worth befouling and humiliating myself over this rascal! . . ."

He got terribly angry; but in the evening, when he suddenly recalled that he had gotten angry that day, and "terribly" so— it felt extremely unpleasant to him; as if someone had caught him at something. He was embarrassed and surprised:

"It means, then, that there are reasons for my getting so angry . . . out of the blue . . . just from remember- ing . . ." He did not finish his thought.

And the next day he got still angrier, but this time it seemed to him that there was a cause and that he was perfectly right; it was "an unheard-of impertinence": the thing was that a fourth encounter had taken place. The gentleman with the crape had appeared again, as if from under the ground. Velchaninov had only just caught in the street that very state councillor and necessary gentleman whom he was now trying to catch by coming upon him by chance at his country house, because this official, barely acquainted with Velchaninov, but needed for his case, refused to be caught, then as now, and was hiding as well as he could, not wishing for his part to meet with Velchaninov; rejoicing that he had finally run into him, Velchaninov walked beside him, hurrying, peeking into his eyes, and trying as well as he could to guide the gray-haired old fox toward a certain theme, toward a certain conversation in which he might divulge and let drop one much-sought and long-awaited little phrase; but the gray-haired old fox also kept his own counsel, laughed it off, and said nothing—and then, precisely at this extremely tricky moment, Velchaninov's eye suddenly picked out, across the street, the gentleman with crape on his hat. He was standing there and gazing intently at them both; he was watching them—that was obvious—and even seemed to be chuckling.

"Devil take it!" Velchaninov flew into a rage, having already parted from the official and ascribing all his failure with him to the sudden appearance of this "impudent fellow." "Devil take it, is he spying on me, or what! He's obviously keeping watch on me! Has somebody hired him, or what, and . . . and . . . and, by God, he was chuckling! I'll beat him up, by God . . . Too bad I don't carry a stick! I'll buy a stick! I won't leave it like this! Who is he? I absolutely must know who he is!"

Finally—exactly three days after this (fourth) encounter— we find Velchaninov in his restaurant, as we have already described him, now completely and seriously alarmed, and even somewhat at a loss. He even could not help admitting it himself, despite all his pride. He was forced, finally, to realize, having juxtaposed all the circumstances, that all his spleen, all this *peculiar* anguish and all his two-week-long alarm—had been caused by none other than this same mourning gentleman, "despite all his nonentity."

"Granted I'm a hypochondriac," thought Velchaninov, "and am therefore ready to make an elephant out of a gnat, but, all the same, is it any easier for me if all this *might be* merely a fantasy? If every such rogue is able to turn a man completely upside down, then it's . . . it's . . ."

Indeed, in this (fifth) encounter today, which so alarmed Velchaninov, the elephant seemed almost altogether a gnat: the gentleman, as before, whisked past, but this time no longer examining Velchaninov and not making a show, as before, of recognizing him—but, on the contrary, lowering his eyes and seeming to wish very much not to be noticed himself. Velchaninov turned and shouted to him at the top of his voice:

"Hey, you! crape-hat! So now you're hiding! Wait—who are you?"

The question (and the whole shout) was quite witless. But Velchaninov realized it only after he shouted. At this shout—the gentleman turned, paused for a moment, became flustered, smiled, was about to say something, to do something—for a moment, obviously, was in terrible indecision, and suddenly—turned and ran away without looking back. Velchaninov gazed after him in astonishment.

"And what?" he thought, "what if it's not in fact he who is bothering me, but, on the contrary, I him, and that's the whole thing?"

After dinner, he hastened off to the official in his country house. He did not find the official; he was told that "the master has not come back since morning, and is unlikely to come back tonight before three or four o'clock, because he is staying in town for a name-day party." This was such a "bother" that, in his first fit of rage, Velchaninov decided to go to the name-day party himself and in fact even set off; but, realizing on the way that this was going too far, he dismissed the coachman halfway there and dragged himself on foot to his place near the Bolshoi Theater. He felt a need for movement. To calm his agitated nerves, he needed to have a good night's sleep at all costs, despite his insomnia; and to fall asleep, he had at least to be tired. Thus he reached his place only at half past ten, for it was no small distance—and he indeed got very tired.

The apartment he had rented in March, which he so gleefully denounced and criticized, making excuses to himself that it was "all on the march," and that he "got stuck" in Petersburg accidentally, because of this "cursed lawsuit"—this apartment of his was not at all as bad and indecent as he said it was. The entrance was indeed a bit dark and "grimy," under the gateway; but the apartment itself, on the second floor, consisted of two big, bright, high-ceilinged rooms, separated from each other by a dark hall, and thus looking one onto the street, the other onto the courtyard. The one with windows on the courtyard had an adjacent little study meant to serve as a bedroom; but Velchaninov had books and papers there, lying

about in disorder; he slept in one of the big rooms, the one
with windows on the street. His bed was made up for him on
the sofa. He had quite good, though secondhand, furniture,
and there were, besides, even some expensive objects—frag-
ments of former well-being: porcelain and bronze knick-
knacks, large and genuine Bukhara rugs; even two rather good
paintings survived; but everything had been in obvious disorder, not in place and even covered with dust, since his servant
girl Pelageya went to visit her family in Novgorod and left him
alone. This strange fact of a bachelor and man of society, who
still wished to preserve his gentlemanliness, keeping a single
girl as a servant, almost made Velchaninov blush, though he
was very pleased with this Pelageya. The girl had entered his
employment at the moment of his moving into this apartment
in the spring, from the household of acquaintances of his who
had gone abroad, and she had brought order to the place. But
at her departure he had not ventured to hire another female
servant; nor was it worthwhile hiring a lackey for a short term,
and besides he did not like lackeys. So it was arranged that the
tidying up would be done each morning by Mavra, the sister
of the caretaker's wife, with whom he left the key on his way
out, and who did precisely nothing, took the money, and, it
seems, was pilfering. But he had already waved his hand at it
all and was even pleased to be left at home quite alone. Yet
there is measure in all things—and his nerves decidedly refused at times, in certain bilious moments, to endure all this
"muck," and, returning home, he entered his rooms almost
every time with disgust.

But this time he barely took the trouble to undress, threw
himself on his bed, and irritably decided not to think about
anything, but to fall asleep at all costs "this very minute."
And, strangely, he suddenly fell asleep as soon as his head
touched the pillow; this had not happened to him for almost a
month.

He slept for about three hours, but it was a troubled sleep;
he dreamed some strange dreams, such as one dreams in fever.
They had to do with some crime he had supposedly commit-

ted and kept secret, and of which he was unanimously accused by people who were constantly coming into his place from somewhere. A terrible crowd gathered, yet people still kept coming in, so that the door could no longer be closed, but stood wide open. But all interest finally concentrated on one strange man, someone very closely acquainted with him at some time, who had since died, and now for some reason also suddenly came into his room. The most tormenting thing was that Velchaninov did not know who the man was, had forgotten his name and simply could not remember it; he knew only that he had once loved him very much. It was as if all the rest of the people who had come also expected the most important word from this man: either an accusation or a vindication of Velchaninov—and they were all impatient. But he sat motionless at the table, kept silent, and refused to speak. The noise would not subside, his vexation grew stronger, and suddenly Velchaninov, in a rage, struck the man, because he refused to speak, and felt a strange pleasure in it. His heart sank with horror and suffering at his action, yet it was in this sinking that the pleasure consisted. Completely frenzied, he struck a second and a third time, and in some sort of intoxication from fury and fear, which reached the point of madness, but also contained in itself an infinite pleasure, he no longer counted the blows, but struck without stopping. He wanted to destroy all, all of *it*. Suddenly something happened; everyone shouted terribly and turned expectantly to the door, and at that moment there came three resounding strokes of the bell, with such force as if someone wanted to tear it off the door. Velchaninov woke up, instantly came to his senses, flew out of bed, and rushed to the door; he was absolutely sure that the ringing of the bell had not been a dream and that someone had actually rung for him that minute. "It would be far too unnatural if such a clear, such an actual, tangible ringing were just my dream!"

But, to his surprise, the ringing of the bell also turned out to be a dream. He opened the door and went out to the hall, even peeked onto the stairs—there was decidedly no one. The

bell hung motionless. Marveling, but also rejoicing, he went
back to the room. As he was lighting the candle, he remembered that the door had only been shut, but not locked with
key or hook. Before, too, when he came home, he had often
forgotten to lock the door for the night, considering it a matter of no importance. Pelageya had reprimanded him several
times for it. He went back to the hall to lock the door, opened
it once more and looked out, then closed it just with the
hook, but was still too lazy to turn the key. The clock struck
two-thirty; it meant he had slept for three hours.

His dream had agitated him so much that he did not want
to go back to bed right away and decided to pace the room for
some half an hour—"time enough to smoke a cigar." Having
dressed hastily, he went up to the window, raised the thick
damask curtain and the white blind behind it. Outside it was
already quite light. The bright summer Petersburg nights always produced a nervous irritation in him and lately had only
contributed to his insomnia, so that about two weeks ago he
had purposely provided his windows with these thick damask
curtains, which did not let in any light when completely
closed. Having let in the light and forgetting the burning candle on the table, he began pacing back and forth still with
some heavy and sick feeling. The impression of the dream still
worked. The serious suffering at having raised his hand against
this man and beaten him went on.

"And this man doesn't even exist and never did, it's all a
dream, so what am I whining about?"

With bitterness and as if all his cares converged in this, he
began to think that he was decidedly becoming sick, a "sick
person."

It had always been hard for him to admit that he was getting old or feeble, and out of spite, in his bad moments, he
exaggerated both the one and the other, on purpose, to taunt
himself.

"Old age! I'm getting quite old," he muttered, pacing, "I'm
losing my memory, seeing phantoms, dreams, bells ringing
. . . Devil take it! I know from experience that such dreams

have always been a sign of fever in me . . . I'm sure this whole 'story' with this crape is also perhaps a dream. I decidedly thought right yesterday: it's I, I who keep bothering him, and not he me! I made up a poem out of him, and hid under the table from fear myself. And why do I call him a rascal? He may be quite a decent man. True, his face is disagreeable, though nothing especially unattractive; he's dressed like everybody else. Only his look is somehow . . . I'm at it again! about him again!! and what the devil do I care about his look? What, can't I live without this . . . gallowsbird?"

Among other thoughts that popped into his head, one also wounded him painfully: he suddenly became as if convinced that this gentleman with the crape had once been acquainted with him in a friendly way and now, meeting him, was making fun of him, because he knew some big former secret of his, and saw him now in such humiliating circumstances. Mechanically, he went up to the window to open it and breathe the night air, and—and all at once gave a great start: it seemed to him that something unheard-of and extraordinary suddenly occurred before him.

He had not yet had time to open the window, but hastened to slip behind the corner of the window niche and hide himself: on the deserted sidewalk opposite he had suddenly seen, right in front of the house, the gentleman with crape on his hat. The gentleman was standing on the sidewalk facing his windows, but evidently without noticing him, and was examining the house with curiosity, as if trying to figure something out. It seemed he was pondering something and as if making up his mind to do it; he raised his hand and as if put a finger to his forehead. Finally, he made up his mind: he looked furtively around and, on tiptoe, stealthily, began hurriedly to cross the street. That was it: he went to their gate, through the door (which in summer sometimes stayed unbolted till three in the morning). "He's coming to me," quickly flashed in Velchaninov, and suddenly, headlong and also on tiptoe, he rushed to the door and—stopped in front of it, stock-still in expectation, lightly resting his twitching right hand on the door hook he had fastened earlier and listening as hard as he could for the rustle of the expected footsteps on the stairs.

His heart was pounding so that he was afraid he might not hear the stranger tiptoeing up the stairs. He did not understand the fact, but he felt everything with some tenfold fullness. As if his earlier dream had merged with reality. Velchaninov was brave by nature. He liked sometimes to carry his fearlessness in the face of danger to the point of a certain swagger—even if no one was watching him, just so as to admire himself. But now there was something else there as well. The recent hypochondriac and insecure whiner was completely transformed; this was now a totally different man. Nervous, inaudible laughter was bursting from his breast. From behind the closed door he could guess the stranger's every move.

"Ah! there he is coming up, he's here, he's looking around; listening down the stairs; barely breathing, sneaking . . . ah! he's taken hold of the handle, he's pulling, trying! he was counting on finding my place unlocked! That means he knows I sometimes forget to lock it! He's pulling the handle again; what, does he think the hook will pop out? He's sorry to go away! Sorry to leave with nothing?"

And, indeed, everything must certainly have been happening as he pictured it: someone was indeed standing outside the door and kept gently, inaudibly trying the lock and pulling at the handle and—"so, naturally, had some purpose." But Velchaninov already had the solution of the problem ready, and, with a sort of ecstasy, was waiting for the right moment, calculating and taking aim; he had an invincible desire to suddenly lift the hook, suddenly fling the door open and find himself face-to-face with the "bogey." To say, "And what are you doing here, my dear sir?"

And so it happened; seizing the moment, he suddenly lifted the hook, pushed the door, and—nearly bumped into the gentleman with crape on his hat.

III

Pavel Pavlovich Trusotsky

The man as if froze on the spot. The two stood opposite each other on the threshold, and looked fixedly into each other's eyes. Several moments passed in this way, and suddenly—Velchaninov recognized his visitor!

At the same time, the visitor evidently also guessed that Velchaninov recognized him perfectly: it flashed in his eyes. In one instant his whole face as if melted into the sweetest smile.

"I surely have the pleasure of speaking with Alexei Ivanovich?" he nearly sang out in the tenderest voice, comically unsuited to the circumstances.

"But can it be that you are Pavel Pavlovich Trusotsky?" Velchaninov, too, finally managed to say with a puzzled look.

"You and I were acquainted some nine years ago in T——, and—if you will permit me to recall—were friendly acquaintances."

"Yes, sir . . . maybe so, sir . . . but it's now three o'clock, and you spent a whole ten minutes trying to see if my door was locked or not . . ."

"Three o'clock!" the visitor cried, taking out his watch and even being ruefully surprised. "Exactly right: three! Excuse me, Alexei Ivanovich, I ought to have realized it when I came in; I'm even ashamed. I'll stop by and have a talk with you one of these days, but now . . ."

"Ah, no! if we're to have a talk, let's have it right now, please!" Velchaninov recollected himself. "Kindly come this way, across the threshold; to my rooms, sir. You yourself, of course, were intending to come in, and not just to pass by at night to check the locks . . ."

He was agitated and at the same time as if taken aback, and felt unable to collect himself. He was even ashamed: no mystery, no danger—nothing remained of the whole phantasmagoria; there turned up only the stupid figure of some Pavel Pavlovich. But, nevertheless, he by no means believed it was as simple as that; he had a vague and fearful presentiment of something. Seating the visitor in an armchair, he impatiently sat down on his bed, a step away from the armchair, leaned forward, his palms resting on his knees, and waited irritably for the man to speak. He greedily examined and recalled him. But, strangely, the man was silent and seemed not to understand at all that he was "obliged" to speak immediately; on the contrary, he himself looked at his host with eyes that were as if expecting something. It might have been that he was simply timid, feeling some initial awkwardness, like a mouse in a mousetrap; but Velchaninov got angry.

"What's with you!" he cried. "I don't suppose you're a fantasy or a dream! Have you shown up here to play the dead man? Explain yourself, my dear!"

The visitor stirred, smiled, and began warily: "As far as I can see, you find it, first of all, even striking that I came at such an hour and—under such particular circumstances, sir . . . So that, remembering all past things and how we parted, sir—I find it strange even now, sir . . . However, I did not even have any intention of calling on you, and if it has turned out this way, it was—accidentally, sir . . ."

"How, accidentally! I saw you from the window, running across the street on tiptoe!"

"Ah, you saw!—well, then perhaps you now know more about it all than I do, sir! But I'm only vexing you . . . Here's the thing, sir: I came here three weeks ago, on my own business . . . I am Pavel Pavlovich Trusotsky, you recognized me yourself, sir. My business is that I'm soliciting to be transferred to another province and to another job, sir, to a post with a considerable promotion . . . But, anyhow, all that is also not it, sir! . . . The main thing, if you wish, is that it's the third week I've been hanging around here, and it seems I've been putting my business off on purpose—that is, about the transfer, sir—and, really, even if it does come off, for all I know I may forget that it came off, sir, and not move out of your Petersburg in the mood I'm in. I'm hanging around as if I'd lost my purpose, and as if I were even glad I'd lost it—in the mood I'm in, sir . . ."

"What mood is that?" Velchaninov was frowning.

The visitor raised his eyes to him, raised his hat, and now with firm dignity pointed to the crape.

"Yes—here's what mood, sir!"

Velchaninov gazed dumbly now at the crape, now into his visitor's face. Suddenly a blush poured instantly over his cheeks, and he became terribly agitated.

"Not Natalia Vassilievna!"

"Herself, sir. Natalia Vassilievna! This past March . . . Consumption, and almost suddenly, sir, in some two or three months! And I've been left—as you see!"

Having said this, the visitor, with strong emotion, spread his arms to both sides, holding his hat with the crape in his left hand and bowing his bald head very deeply for at least ten seconds.

This look and this gesture suddenly as if refreshed Velchaninov; a mocking and even provocative smile flitted over his lips—but as yet only for a moment: the news of the death of this lady (with whom he had been acquainted so long ago and whom he had so long ago managed to forget)—now made an unexpectedly staggering impression on him.

"How can it be!" he muttered the first words that came to his lips. "And why didn't you come straight to tell me?"

"I thank you for your sympathy, I see and appreciate it, despite . . ."

"Despite?"

"Despite so many years of separation, you have now treated my grief and even myself with such perfect sympathy that I naturally feel grateful. That is the only thing I wished to say, sir. And it is not that I doubted my friends, even now I can find the most sincere friends here, sir (take just Stepan Mikhailovich Bagautov alone), but my acquaintance with you, Alexei Ivanovich (friendship, perhaps—for I recall it with gratitude)—was nine years ago, sir, you never came back to us; there were no letters on either side . . ."

The visitor was reciting as if by rote, but all the while he spoke, he looked at the ground, though, of course, he could

see everything above as well. But the host, too, had managed
to collect himself a little.

With a certain quite strange impression, which was growing
more and more, he listened to and observed Pavel Pavlovich,
and suddenly, when the man paused—the most motley and
unexpected thoughts unexpectedly flooded his head.

"But why did I keep not recognizing you till now?" he cried
out, becoming animated. "We ran into each other some five
times in the street!"

"Yes, I also remember that; you kept coming toward me,
sir—twice, maybe even three times . . ."

"That is—it was *you* who *kept* coming toward me, not I
toward you!"

Velchaninov got up and suddenly laughed loudly and quite
unexpectedly. Pavel Pavlovich paused, looked attentively, but
at once began to go on:

"And you didn't recognize me because, first of all, you
might have forgotten, sir, and, finally, I even had smallpox
during this time, which left some traces on my face."

"Smallpox? Why, he did in fact have smallpox! but how on
earth did you . . ."

"Manage that? All sorts of things happen, Alexei Ivanovich;
every now and then one manages!"

"Only it's terribly funny all the same. Well, go on, go on—
my dear friend!"

"And I, though I also kept meeting you, sir . . ."

"Wait! Why did you just say 'manage that'? I was going to
put it much more politely. Well, go on, go on!"

For some reason he was feeling merrier and merrier. The
staggering impression was replaced by something quite different.

He paced up and down the room with quick steps.

"And I, though I also kept meeting you, sir, and as I was
coming here to Petersburg I was even intending to look you
up without fail, but, I repeat, I'm now in such a state of mind
. . . and so mentally broken since that same month of
March . . ."

"Ah, yes! broken since the month of March . . . Wait, you don't smoke?"

"You know, I, while Natalia Vassilievna . . ."

"Ah, yes, yes; but since the month of March?"

"Maybe a little cigarette."

"Here's a cigarette; light up and—go on! go on, I'm terribly . . ."

And, lighting a cigar, Velchaninov quickly sat down on his bed again. Pavel Pavlovich paused.

"But you yourself, however, are somehow quite agitated—are you well, sir?"

"Ah, to the devil with my health!" Velchaninov suddenly got angry. "Go on!"

The visitor, for his part, seeing the host's agitation, was growing more pleased and self-confident.

"What's the point of going on, sir?" he began again. "Imagine to yourself, Alexei Ivanovich, first of all, a man who is crushed—that is, not simply but, so to speak, radically crushed; a man who, after twenty years of marriage, changes his life and hangs about in dusty streets without any suitable purpose, as if in the steppes, all but forgetting himself, and even reveling somewhat in this self-forgetting. After that it's natural if sometimes, meeting an acquaintance or even a true friend, I may avoid him on purpose, so as not to approach him at such a moment—of self-forgetting, that is. And at another moment, one remembers everything so well and thirsts so much to see at least some witness and partaker of that recent but irretrievable past, and one's heart starts pounding so, that not only in the daytime but even at night one risks throwing oneself into a friend's arms, even if one has to wake him up especially for that purpose past three in the morning, sir. I only got the hour wrong, but not the friendship; for at the present moment I'm only too well rewarded, sir. And concerning the hour, really, I thought it wasn't twelve yet, being in that mood. One drinks one's own sorrow and is as if intoxicated by it. And not even sorrow, but precisely this novicondition is what keeps hitting me . . ."

"What a way to put it, though!" Velchaninov, having suddenly become terribly serious again, observed somehow gloomily.

"Yes, sir, I put it strangely . . ."

"And you're . . . not joking?"

"Joking!" exclaimed Pavel Pavlovich in mournful perplexity, "at the very moment when I announce . . ."

"Ah, keep quiet about that, I beg you!"

Velchaninov got up and again began pacing the room.

And in this way about five minutes went by. The visitor, too, made as if to get up, but Velchaninov cried out: "Sit, sit!"—and the man at once obediently lowered himself into the armchair.

"How changed you are, though!" Velchaninov began talking again, suddenly stopping in front of him—just as if suddenly struck by the thought. "Terribly changed! Extremely! Quite a different man!"

"No wonder, sir: it's nine years."

"No, no, no, it's not a matter of years! You haven't changed in appearance, God knows: you've changed in something else!"

"Also, maybe, these nine years, sir."

"Or since the month of March!"

"Heh, heh," Pavel Pavlovich chuckled slyly, "you've got some playful thought . . . But, if I dare ask—what essentially is this change?"

"What indeed! Before there was such a solid and decent Pavel Pavlovich, such a smarty of a Pavel Pavlovich, and now—a perfect *vaurien*[2] of a Pavel Pavlovich."

He was in that degree of vexation in which the most restrained people sometimes start saying unnecessary things.

"*Vaurien!* You think so? And no longer a 'smarty'? Not a smarty?" Pavel Pavlovich tittered delightedly.

"The devil you're a 'smarty'! Now, maybe, you're thoroughly *smart.*

"I'm impudent," Velchaninov went on thinking, "but this rascal is more impudent still. And . . . and what's his purpose?"

"Ah, my dearest, ah, my most priceless Alexei Ivanovich!" The visitor suddenly became extremely agitated and started fidgeting in his armchair. "But what's that to us? We're not in society now, not in brilliant, high-society company! We're—two most sincere and ancient former friends, and, so to speak, have come together in the fullest sincerity to mutually recall that precious connection, in which the deceased woman constituted so precious a link in our friendship!"

And he was as if so carried away by the rapture of his feelings that he again bowed his head, as earlier, but now he covered his face with his hat. Velchaninov studied him with loathing and uneasiness.

"And what if he's simply a buffoon?" flashed in his head. "But n-no, n-no! it seems he's not drunk—however, maybe he is; his face is red. Though even if he is drunk—it comes out the same. What has he got up his sleeve? What does the rascal want?"

"Remember, remember," Pavel Pavlovich cried out, uncovering his face little by little and as if getting more and more carried away by his memories, "remember our excursions outside of town, our evenings and evening parties with dances and innocent games at His Excellency the most hospitable Semyon Semyonovich's? And our evening readings, just the three of us? And our first acquaintance with you, when you came to me one morning to get information about your lawsuit, and even started shouting, sir, and suddenly Natalia Vassilievna came out and ten minutes later you were already a true friend of our house, for precisely one whole year, sir—just as in *The Provincial Lady*, Mr. Turgenev's play . . ."[3]

Velchaninov was pacing slowly, looking at the ground, listening with impatience and loathing, but—listening hard.

"*The Provincial Lady* never entered my head," he interrupted, somewhat at a loss, "and you never spoke in such a squeaky voice before, or in this . . . not your own style. Why are you doing it?"

"Indeed, I was mostly silent before, sir—that is, I was more silent," Pavel Pavlovich picked up hastily. "You know, before I preferred to listen when my late wife spoke. You remember how she spoke, with what wit, sir . . . And concerning *The Provincial Lady* and in particular concerning *Stupendiev*—you're right there, too, because it was later that we ourselves, I and my priceless late wife, remembering you, sir, in some quiet moments, after you'd already left, compared our first meeting to this theater piece . . . because there was in fact a resemblance, sir. And particularly concerning *Stupendiev* . . ."

"What's this *Stupendiev*, devil take it!" Velchaninov shouted and even stamped his foot, being completely put out at the word *Stupendiev*, owing to a certain uneasy remembrance that flashed in him at this word.

"*Stupendiev* is a role, sir, a theatrical role, the role of 'the husband' in the play *The Provincial Lady*," Pavel Pavlovich squeaked in the sweetest little voice, "but that belongs to another category of our dear and beautiful memories, already after your departure, when Stepan Mikhailovich Bagautov graced us with his friendship, just as you did, sir, and for a whole five years."

"Bagautov? What's that? Which Bagautov?" Velchaninov suddenly stopped dead in his tracks.

"Bagautov, Stepan Mikhailovich, who graced us with his friendship precisely a year after you and . . . like you, sir."

"Ah, my God, but that I know!" Velchaninov cried, finally figuring it out. "Bagautov! but he served with you . . ."

"He did, he did! at the governor's! From Petersburg, a most elegant young man of the highest society!" Pavel Pavlovich cried out, decidedly enraptured.

"Yes, yes, yes! How could I! And so he, too . . ."

"And he, too! And he, too!" Pavel Pavlovich, having picked up his host's imprudent phrase, echoed with the same rapture. "And he, too! It was then that we produced *The Provincial Lady* in His Excellency the most hospitable Semyon Semyonovich's home theater—Stepan Mikhailovich was 'the count,' I was 'the husband,' and my late wife was 'the provincial lady'—only the role of 'the husband' was taken from me at the insistence of my late wife, so I didn't play 'the husband,' being supposedly unable to, sir . . ."

"No, the devil you're Stupendiev! You're Pavel Pavlovich Trusotsky first of all, and not Stupendiev!" Velchaninov said rudely, unceremoniously, and all but trembling with vexation. "Only, excuse me, this Bagautov is here in Petersburg; I saw him myself, in the spring! Why don't you go to him, too?"

"I've called on him every blessed day for three weeks now, sir. He won't receive me! He's ill, he can't receive me! And, imagine, I found out from the foremost sources that he really is extremely dangerously ill! Such a friend for six years! Ah, Alexei Ivanovich, I'm telling you and I repeat that in this mood one sometimes wishes simply to fall through the earth, even in reality, sir; and at other moments it seems I could just up and embrace precisely some one of these former, so to speak, witnesses and partakers, and with the sole purpose of weeping—that is, absolutely for no other purpose than weeping! . . ."

"Well, anyhow, you've had enough for today, right?" Velchaninov said sharply.

"More, more than enough!" Pavel Pavlovich rose at once from his place. "It's four o'clock and, above all, I've disturbed you so egoistically . . ."

"Listen, now: I'll call on you myself, without fail, and then I do hope . . . Tell me directly, frankly tell me: you're not drunk today?"

"Drunk? Not a whit . . ."

"You didn't drink before coming, or earlier?"

"You know, Alexei Ivanovich, you're completely feverish, sir."

"I'll call on you by tomorrow, in the morning, before one . . ."

"And I've long been noticing that you're as if delirious, sir." Pavel Pavlovich interfered delightedly, pressing the point. "I really am so ashamed that I, in my awkwardness . . . but I'm leaving, I'm leaving! And you go to bed and sleep!"

"And why didn't you tell me where you live?" Velchaninov, recollecting himself, shouted after him.

"Didn't I, sir? In the Pokrovsky Hotel . . ."

"What Pokrovsky Hotel?"

"Why, right next to the Pokrov church, there in the lane, sir—only I forget which lane, and the number as well, but it's right next to the Pokrov church . . ."

"I'll find it!"

"You'll be a most welcome guest."

He was already going out to the stairs.

"Wait!" Velchaninov cried again, "you're not going to give me the slip?"

"How do you mean, 'give you the slip'?" Pavel Pavlovich goggled his eyes at him, turning and smiling from the third step.

Instead of an answer, Velchaninov noisily slammed the door, locked it carefully, and put the hook into the eye. Going back to his room, he spat as if he had been befouled by something.

After standing motionlessly for five minutes in the middle of the room, he threw himself down on the bed, without undressing at all, and instantly fell asleep. The forgotten candle burned all the way down on the table.

IV

Wife, Husband, and Lover

He slept very soundly and woke up at exactly half past nine; rose instantly, sat on his bed, and at once began thinking about the death of "that woman."

Yesterday's staggering impression from the unexpected news of this death had left him in some bewilderment and even pain. This bewilderment and pain had only been stifled in him for a time yesterday, in Pavel Pavlovich's presence, by one strange idea. But now, on awakening, all that had happened nine years earlier suddenly stood before him with extreme vividness.

He had loved and been the lover of this woman, the late

Natalia Vassilievna, wife of "this Trusotsky," when, on his own business (and also on occasion of a lawsuit about an inheritance), he had spent a whole year in T———, though the business itself had not called for such long-term presence; the real reason had been this liaison. This liaison and love had possessed him so strongly that he had been as if the slave of Natalia Vassilievna and, indeed, would have ventured at once upon anything even of the most monstrous and senseless sort if it had been demanded only by the merest caprice of this woman. Never, either before or afterward, had anything similar happened to him. At the end of the year, when parting was already imminent, Velchaninov had been in such despair as the fatal hour drew near—in despair, despite the fact that the parting was supposed to be for the shortest time—that he suggested to Natalia Vassilievna that he carry her off, take her away from her husband, drop everything, and go abroad with him forever. Only the mockery and firm persistence of this lady (who at first fully approved of the project, but probably only out of boredom or else to make fun of it) could have stopped him and forced him to leave alone. And what then? Two months had not passed since their parting, and he, in Petersburg, was already asking himself that question which remained forever unresolved for him: did he really love this woman, or had it all been only a certain "bedevilment"? And it was not at all out of light-mindedness or under the influence of a new passion starting in him that the question was born in him: for those first two months in Petersburg he was in some sort of frenzy and was unlikely to notice any woman, though he at once took up with his former society and had occasion to see hundreds of women. Nevertheless, he knew very well that if he found himself at once back in T———, he would immediately fall again under all the oppressive charm of this woman, despite all the questions that had been born in him. Even five years later he was still of the same conviction. But five years later he had already admitted it to himself with indignation and even remembered "that woman" herself with hatred. He was ashamed of his T——— year; he could not understand how such a "stupid" passion had even been possible for him, Velchaninov! All memories of this passion turned to disgrace for him; he blushed to the point of tears and suffered remorse. True, after another few years, he managed to calm himself down somewhat; he tried to forget it all—and nearly succeeded. And now all at once, nine years later, it all suddenly and strangely rose up again before him after yesterday's news about Natalia Vassilievna's death.

Now, sitting on his bed, with vague thoughts crowding disorderedly in his head, he felt and realized clearly only one thing—that despite all yesterday's "staggering impression" from this news, he was all the same very calm regarding the fact of her death. "Am I not even going to feel sorry about her?" he asked himself. True, he no longer felt hatred for her now and could judge more impartially, more justly about her. In his opinion, which, by the way, had been formed early on in this nine-year period of separation, Natalia Vassilievna belonged to the number of the most ordinary provincial ladies of "good" provincial society, and—"who knows, maybe that's how it was, and only I alone made up such a fantasy out of her?" He had always suspected, however, that this opinion might contain an error; he felt it now, too. Besides, the facts contradicted it; this Bagautov had also had a liaison with her for several years, and, it seems, was also "under all her charms." Bagautov was indeed a young man of the best Petersburg society and, being "a most empty man" (as Velchaninov said of him), could therefore make his career only in Petersburg. Now he had, nevertheless, neglected Petersburg—that is, his chiefest profit—and lost five years in T——— solely on account of this woman! And he had finally returned to Petersburg, perhaps, only because he, too, had been discarded like "a worn-out old shoe." So there was something extraordinary in this woman—a gift of attraction, enslavement, domination!

And yet it would seem that she had no means of attracting and enslaving: "she wasn't even so beautiful, and perhaps simply wasn't beautiful at all." Velchaninov had met her when she was already twenty-eight years old. Her not very handsome face was able sometimes to be pleasantly animated; but her eyes were not nice: there was some unnecessary hardness in her look. She was very thin. Her intellectual education was weak; her intelligence was unquestionable and penetrating, but nearly always one-sided. The manners of a provincial society lady, but, true, one with considerable tact; elegant taste, but mainly just in knowing how to dress herself. A resolute and domineering character; there could be no halfway compromise with her in anything: "either all, or nothing." A surprising firmness and steadfastness in difficult matters. A gift of magnanimity and nearly always right beside it—a boundless unfairness. It was impossible to argue with this lady: two times two never meant anything to her. She never considered herself unfair or guilty in anything. Her constant and countless betrayals of her husband did not weigh on her conscience in the least. In Velchaninov's own comparison, she was like "a flagellant's Mother of God,"[4] who believes in the highest degree that she is indeed the Mother of God—so did Natalia Vassilievna believe in the highest degree in each of her actions. She was faithful to her lovers—though only until she got tired of them. She liked to torment a lover, but also liked to reward him. She was of a passionate, cruel, and sensual type. She hated depravity, condemned it with unbelievable violence, and—was depraved herself. No facts could ever have brought her to an awareness of her own depravity. "Doubtless she *sincerely* doesn't know it," Velchaninov had thought to himself still in T———. (While participating in her depravity himself, be it noted in passing.) "She's one of those women," he thought, "who are as if born to be unfaithful wives. These women never fall before marriage: the law of their nature is that they must be married first. The husband is the first lover, but not otherwise than after the altar. No one marries with more ease and adroitness. For the first lover, the husband is always to blame. And everything happens with the highest degree of sincerity; to the end they feel themselves justified in the highest degree and, of course, perfectly innocent."

Velchaninov was convinced that there indeed existed such a

type of such women; but then, too, he was convinced that there existed a corresponding type of husband, whose sole purpose consisted of nothing but corresponding to this type of woman. In his opinion, the essence of such husbands lay in their being, so to speak, "eternal husbands," or, better to say, in being *only* husbands in life and nothing else. "Such a man is born and develops solely in order to get married, and having married, to turn immediately into an appendage of his wife, even if it so happens that he happens to have his own indisputable character. The main feature of such a husband is—a well-known adornment. It is as impossible for him not to wear horns as it is for the sun not to shine; but he not only never knows it, but even can never find it out by the very laws of nature." Velchaninov deeply believed that these two types existed and that Pavel Pavlovich Trusotsky of T——— was a perfect representative of one of them. Yesterday's Pavel Pavlovich, naturally, was not the Pavel Pavlovich he had known in T———. He found the man incredibly changed, but Velchaninov also knew that he could not but have changed and that all this was perfectly natural; Mr. Trusotsky could be all he had been before only with his wife alive, but now this was only part of the whole, suddenly set free—that is, something astonishing and unlike anything else.

As for the Pavel Pavlovich of T———, this is what Velchaninov remembered and recalled about him now:

"Of course, in T——— Pavel Pavlovich was only a husband" and nothing more. If, for instance, he was, on top of that, also an official, it was solely because for him the service, too, had turned, so to speak, into one of the duties of his married life; he served for the sake of his wife and her social position in T———, though he was in himself quite a zealous official. He was thirty-five years old then and possessed a certain fortune, even a not altogether small one. He did not show any particular ability in the service, nor inability either. He kept company with all that was highest in the province and was reputed to be on an excellent footing. Natalia Vassilievna was perfectly respected in T———; she, however, did not value that very much, accepting it as her due, but at home she always knew how to receive superbly, having trained Pavel Pavlovich so well that his manners were ennobled enough even for receiving the highest provincial authorities. Maybe (so it seemed to Velchaninov) he was also intelligent: but since Natalia Vassilievna rather disliked it when her spouse did much talking, his intelligence went largely unnoticed. Maybe he had many good innate qualities, as well as bad ones. But the good qualities were as if under wraps, and the bad impulses were stifled almost definitively. Velchaninov remembered, for instance, that there occasionally arose in Mr. Trusotsky an impulse to mock his neighbor; but this was strictly forbidden him. He also liked occasionally to tell some story; but this, too, was supervised: he was allowed to tell only something of the more insignificant and short variety. He had an inclination for friendly circles away from home and even—for having a drink with a friend; but this last was even exterminated at the root. And with this feature: that, looking from outside, no one could tell that he was a husband under the heel; Natalia Vassilievna seemed to be a perfectly obedient wife and was per-haps even convinced of it herself. It might have been that Pavel Pavlovich loved Natalia Vassilievna to distraction; but no one was able to notice it, and it was even impossible—also probably following the domestic orders of Natalia Vassilievna herself. Several times during his T———— life, Velchaninov asked himself: does this husband have at least some suspicion that he is having a liaison with his wife? Several times he seriously asked Natalia Vassilievna about it and always received the response, uttered with some vexation, that her husband knew nothing and could never learn anything, and that "whatever there is—is none of his business." Another feature on her part: she never laughed at Pavel Pavlovich, and found him neither ridiculous nor very bad in anything, and would even intercede for him very much if anyone dared to show him any sort of discourtesy. Having no children, she naturally had to become predominantly a society woman; but her own home was necessary for her as well. Society pleasures never fully ruled her, and at home she liked very much to occupy herself with the household and handwork. Pavel Pavlovich had recalled yesterday their family readings in T——— of an evening; this did happen: Velchaninov read, Pavel Pavlovich also read; to Velchaninov's surprise, he was very good at reading aloud. Natalia Vassilievna meanwhile would do embroidery and always listened to the reading quietly and equably. They read novels by Dickens, something from Russian magazines, and sometimes also something "serious." Natalia Vassilievna highly esteemed Velchaninov's cultivation, but silently, as something finished and decided, which there was no more point in talking about; generally her attitude to everything bookish and learned was indifferent, as to something completely alien, though perhaps useful; but Pavel Pavlovich's sometimes showed a certain ardor.

The T——— liaison broke off suddenly, having reached on Velchaninov's part the fullest brim and even almost madness. He was simply and suddenly chased away, though everything was arranged in such fashion that he left perfectly ignorant of the fact that he had already been discarded "like a useless old shoe." About a month and a half before his departure, there appeared in T——— a certain little artillery officer, a very young man, just graduated from cadet school, who took to visiting the Trusotskys; instead of three, there came to be four. Natalia Vassilievna received the boy benevolently, but treated him as a boy. Velchaninov had decidedly no inkling of anything, nor could he have thought anything then, because he had suddenly been informed of the necessity of parting. One of the hundred reasons put forth by Natalia Vassilievna for his unfailing and most speedy departure was that she thought she was pregnant; and so it was natural that he had unfailingly and at once to disappear for at least three or four months, so that nine months later it would be more difficult for the husband to suspect anything, if any calumny should come up afterward. The argument was rather farfetched. After Velchaninov's stormy proposal of running away to Paris or America, he left alone for Petersburg, "no doubt just for a brief moment"—that is, for no more than three months, otherwise he would not have left for anything, despite any reasons or arguments. Exactly two months later, in Petersburg, he received a letter from Natalia Vassilievna with a request that he not come back, because she already loved another; about her pregnancy she informed him that she had been mistaken. The information about the mistake was superfluous, everything was clear to him: he remembered the little officer. With that the matter ended forever. He heard something afterward, already several years later, about Bagautov turning up there and staying for a whole five years. Such an endless duration of the liaison he explained to himself, among other things, by the fact that Natalia Vassilievna must have aged a lot, and therefore would herself become more attached.

He stayed sitting on his bed for almost an hour; finally, he came to his senses, rang for Mavra with coffee, drank it hastily, got dressed, and at precisely eleven o'clock went to the Pokrov church to look for the Pokrovsky Hotel. Concerning the Pokrovsky Hotel proper he had now formed a special morning impression. Incidentally, he was even somewhat ashamed of his treatment of Pavel Pavlovich yesterday, and this now had to be resolved.

The whole phantasmagoria yesterday with the door latch he explained by an accident, by the drunken state of Pavel Pavlovich, and perhaps by something else as well, but essentially he had no precise idea why he was going now to start some new relationship with the former husband, when everything between them had ended so naturally and of itself. He was drawn by something; there was some special impression here, and as a result of this impression he was drawn . . .

V

Liza

Pavel Pavlovich had no thought of "giving him the slip," and God knows why Velchaninov had asked him that question yesterday; veritably, he himself had had a darkening. At his first inquiry in the grocery shop near the Pokrov church, he was directed to the Pokrovsky Hotel, two steps away in a lane. At the hotel it was explained to him that Mr. Trusotsky was now "putting up" there in the yard, in the wing, in Marya Sysoevna's furnished rooms. Going up the narrow, slopped, and very filthy stone stairway of the wing to the second floor, where those rooms were, he suddenly heard weeping. It was as if a child of seven or eight were weeping; it was heavy weeping, stifled sobs could be heard bursting through, accompanied by a stamping of feet and also as if stifled but violent shouts in some hoarse falsetto, but now of a grown man. This grown man seemed to be quieting the child and wishing very much for the weeping not to be heard, but was making more noise himself. The shouts were merciless, and the child was as if begging forgiveness. Entering a small corridor with two doors on each side of it, Velchaninov met a very fat and tall woman, disheveled in a homey way, and asked her about Pavel Pavlovich. She jabbed her finger toward the door behind which the weeping could be heard. The fat and purple face of the forty-year-old woman expressed some indignation.

"See what fun he has!" she bassed in a half voice and went past him to the stairs. Velchaninov was about to knock, but changed his mind and simply opened Pavel Pavlovich's door. In the middle of a small room, crudely but abundantly furnished with simple painted furniture, Pavel Pavlovich stood, dressed only by half, without frock coat or waistcoat, his face flushed with vexation, trying to quiet with shouts, gestures, and perhaps (as it seemed to Velchaninov) also kicks, a little girl of about eight, dressed poorly, though like a young lady, in a short black woolen dress. She, it seemed, was in genuine hysterics, hysterically sobbing and reaching out her arms to Pavel Pavlovich, as if wishing to put them around him, to embrace him, to plead and entreat something from him. In an instant everything changed: seeing the visitor, the girl gave a cry and shot into the tiny adjoining room, while Pavel Pavlovich, momentarily taken aback, melted all at once into a smile, exactly as yesterday, when Velchaninov had suddenly opened the door to the stairs.

"Alexei Ivanovich!" he exclaimed in decided surprise. "In no way could I have expected . . . but come, come! Here, on this sofa, or this armchair, while I . . ." And he rushed to get into his frock coat, forgetting to put his waistcoat on.

"Don't be ceremonious, stay as you are." Velchaninov sat down on a chair.

"No, allow me to be ceremonious, sir; there, now I'm a bit more decent. But why are you sitting in the corner? Here, in the armchair, by the table . . . Well, I never, never expected!"

He, too, sat down on the edge of a wicker chair, though not next to the "unexpected" visitor, but turning his chair at an angle so as to face Velchaninov more fully.

"And why didn't you expect me? Didn't I precisely arrange yesterday that I'd come to you at this time?"

"I thought you wouldn't come, sir; and once I realized the whole thing yesterday, on waking up, I decidedly despaired of seeing you, even forever, sir."

Velchaninov meanwhile was looking around. The room was in disorder, the bed was not made, clothes were strewn about, on the table were glasses with drunk coffee, bread crumbs, and a bottle of champagne, half-finished, uncorked, with a glass beside it. He looked out of the corner of his eye into the adjoining room, but all was quiet there; the girl kept silent and did not stir.

"You don't mean you're drinking this now?" Velchaninov pointed to the champagne.

"Leftovers, sir . . ." Pavel Pavlovich was embarrassed.

"Well, you really have changed!"

"Bad habits, and suddenly, sir. Really, since that time; I'm not lying, sir! I can't restrain myself. Don't worry now, Alexei Ivanovich, I'm not drunk now and won't pour out drivel, like yesterday at your place, sir, but I'm telling you the truth, it's all since that time, sir! And if someone had told me half a year ago that I'd get so loose as I am now, sir, had showed me myself in a mirror—I wouldn't have believed it!"

"So you were drunk yesterday?"

"I was, sir," Pavel Pavlovich admitted in a half whisper, lowering his eyes abashedly, "and you see, not so much drunk as somewhat past it, sir. I wish to explain this, because past it is worse for me, sir: there's not much drunkenness, but some sort of cruelty and recklessness remain, and I feel grief more strongly. Maybe I drink for the sake of grief, sir. And then I may pull some pranks, even quite stupidly, sir, and get at people with insults. I must have presented myself to you very strangely yesterday?"

"You don't remember?"

"How not remember, I remember everything, sir . . ."

"You see, Pavel Pavlovich, I thought it over and explained it to myself in exactly the same way," Velchaninov said conciliatorily, "and besides, I was somewhat irritable myself yesterday and . . . overly impatient with you, which I freely admit. Sometimes I don't feel myself quite well, and your unexpected arrival in the night . . ."

"Yes, in the night, in the night!" Pavel Pavlovich shook his head as if surprised and disapproving. "And what on earth prompted me! I wouldn't have come in for anything if you yourself hadn't opened the door, sir; I'd have gone away. I came to you about a week ago, Alexei Ivanovich, and didn't find you at home, but afterward I might never have come another time, sir. All the same, I also have a touch of pride, Alexei Ivanovich, though I'm aware that I'm in . . . such a state. We met in the street, too, but I kept thinking: well, and what if he doesn't recognize me, what if he turns away, nine years are no joke—so I didn't dare approach. And yesterday I came trudging from the Petersburg side, and forgot the time, sir. All on account of this" (he pointed to the bottle) "and from emotion, sir. Stupid! very, sir! and if it was a man not like you—because you did come to me even after yesterday, remembering old times—I'd even have lost hope of renewing the acquaintance."

Velchaninov listened attentively. The man seemed to be speaking sincerely and even with a certain dignity; and yet he had not believed a thing from the very moment he set foot in the place.

"Tell me, Pavel Pavlovich, you're not alone here, then? Whose girl is it that I just found with you?"

Pavel Pavlovich was even surprised and raised his eyebrows, but the look he gave Velchaninov was bright and pleasant.

"Whose girl, you ask? But that's Liza!" he said with an affable smile.

"What Liza?" Velchaninov murmured, and something as if shook in him. The impression was too unexpected. Earlier, when he came in and saw Liza, he was surprised, but felt decidedly no presentiment, no special thought in himself.

"Why, our Liza, our daughter Liza!" Pavel Pavlovich went on smiling.

"How, daughter? You mean you and Natalia . . . and the late Natalia Vassilievna had children?" Velchaninov asked mistrustfully and timidly, somehow in a very soft voice.

"But, how's that, sir? Ah, my God, but who indeed could you have learned it from? What's the matter with me! It was after you that God granted us!"

Pavel Pavlovich even jumped up from his chair in some excitement, also as if pleasant, however.

"I never heard a thing," Velchaninov said and—paled.

"Indeed, indeed, who could you have learned it from, sir!" Pavel Pavlovich repeated in a tenderly slack voice. "We had lost all hope, my late wife and I, you remember it yourself, and suddenly God blessed us, and what came over me then— he alone knows that! exactly a year after you, it seems, or not, not a year after, much less, wait, sir: you left us then, unless memory deceives me, in October or even November?"

"I left T———— at the beginning of September, on the twelfth of September; I remember it well . . ."

"In September was it? hm . . . what's the matter with me?" Pavel Pavlovich was very surprised. "Well, if so, then permit me: you left on the twelfth of September, and Liza was born on the eighth of May, so that makes it September, October, November, December, January, February, March, April— after eight months and something, there, sir! and if only you knew how my late wife . . ."

"But show me . . . call her . . ." Velchaninov babbled in some sort of breaking voice.

"Certainly, sir!" Pavel Pavlovich bustled, interrupting at once what he had intended to say, as altogether unnecessary. "Right away, I'll introduce her to you right away, sir!" and he hurriedly went to Liza's room.

Perhaps a whole three or four minutes went by; there was quick and rapid whispering in the little room, and the sounds of Liza's voice were faintly heard. "She's begging not to be brought out," Velchaninov thought. They finally came out.

"Here, sir, she's all embarrassed," Pavel Pavlovich said, "she's so bashful, so proud, sir . . . just like her late mother!"

Liza came out without tears now, her eyes lowered, her father leading her by the hand. She was a tall, slim, and very pretty little girl. She quickly raised her large blue eyes to the guest, looked at him with curiosity, but sullenly, and at once lowered her eyes again. There was in her gaze that child's seriousness, as when children, left alone with a stranger, go into a corner and from there keep glancing, seriously and mistrustfully, at the new, first-time visitor; but perhaps there was also another thought, as if no longer a child's—so it seemed to Velchaninov. Her father brought her over to him.

"This nice man used to know Mama, he was our friend, don't be shy, give him your hand."

The girl bowed slightly and timidly offered her hand.

"Natalia Vassilievna wanted not to teach her to curtsy in greeting, but simply to bow slightly in the English manner and offer her hand to a guest," he added in explanation to Velchaninov, studying him intently.

Velchaninov knew he was studying him, but he no longer cared at all about concealing his excitement; he was sitting motionlessly on the chair, holding Liza's hand in his, and gazing intently at the child. But Liza was very preoccupied with something and, forgetting her hand in the visitor's hand, would not take her eyes off her father. She listened timorously to everything he said. Velchaninov recognized those large blue eyes at once, but most of all he was struck by the astonishing, remarkably tender whiteness of her face and the color of her hair; these signs were all too significant for him. The shape of the face and the curve of the lips, on the other hand, distinctly resembled Natalia Vassilievna. Pavel Pavlovich meanwhile had long since begun telling something, with extraordinary ardor and feeling, it seemed, but Velchaninov did not hear him at all. He caught only one last phrase:

". . . so that you cannot even imagine, Alexei Ivanovich, our joy in this gift of the Lord, sir! For me her appearance constituted everything, so that even if by the will of God my quiet happiness should disappear—then, I thought, Liza would be left to me; that at least I knew firmly, sir!"

"And Natalia Vassilievna?" asked Velchaninov.

"Natalia Vassilievna?" Pavel Pavlovich's face twisted. "You know her, remember, sir, she didn't like to say much, but when she was bidding farewell to her on her deathbed . . . it all got said there, sir! And I just said to you 'on her deathbed'; and yet suddenly, the day before she died, she got excited, angry—said they wanted to finish her off with medications, that she just had a simple fever, and that both our doctors knew nothing, and that as soon as Koch (remember, our staff physician, a little old man) came back, she'd be out of bed in two weeks! Not only that, just five hours before passing away, she remembered that we had to be sure and visit her aunt in three weeks, for her name day, on her estate, Liza's godmother, sir . . ."

Velchaninov suddenly got up from his chair, still without

letting go of Liza's hand. It seemed to him, incidentally, that in the burning glance the girl directed at her father there was something reproachful.

"She's not sick?" he asked somehow strangely, hurriedly.

"Seems not, sir, but . . . our circumstances here came together this way," Pavel Pavlovich said with rueful concern. "She's a strange child to begin with, a nervous one, after her mother's death she was sick for two weeks, with hysterics, sir. Just now we've had such weeping, as you came in, sir—do you hear, Liza, do you?—and over what? The whole thing is that I go away and leave her, so it means I no longer love her anymore as I loved her when Mama was alive—that's what she accuses me of. Why should such a fantasy enter the head of a child, sir, who ought to be playing with toys? But there's no one here for her to play with."

"And how is it you're . . . it's really just the two of you here?"

"Quite alone, sir; only a maid comes once a day to straighten up."

"And when you go out, she stays alone like that?"

"And what else, sir? And yesterday as I went out I even locked her in that little room, it's because of that that we're having tears today. But what was there to do, judge for yourself: two days ago she went downstairs without me, and a boy threw a stone at her head. Or else she'll burst into tears and rush around to everyone in the yard asking where I went, and that's not good, sir. And I'm a fine one, too: I leave her for an hour, and come back the next morning—that's how it turned out yesterday. It's a good thing the landlady let her out while I was gone, she called a locksmith to open the lock—it's even a disgrace, sir—I feel myself a veritable monster, sir. It's all from darkening . . ."

"Papa!" the girl said timidly and anxiously.

"What, again! you're at it again! what did I just tell you?"

"I won't, I won't," Liza repeated in fear, hurriedly clasping her hands before him.

"It can't go on with you like this, in such circumstances,"

Velchaninov suddenly spoke impatiently, with the voice of one in authority. "You . . . you are a man of means; how can you live like that—first of all, in this wing, and in such circumstances?"

"In this wing, sir? But we may leave in a week, and we've spent a lot of money as it is, means or no means, sir . . ."

"Well, enough, enough," Velchaninov interrupted him with ever-increasing impatience, as if clearly saying: "No point in talking, I know everything you're going to say, and I know with what intention you're saying it!" "Listen, I'll make you an offer: you just said you'd stay for perhaps a week, maybe two. I have a house here—that is, a certain family—where I'm as if in my own home, for twenty years now. The family of one Pogoreltsev. Pogoreltsev, Alexei Pavlovich, a privy councillor; he might even be helpful to you in your case. They are at their country house now. They have their own quite splendid country house. Klavdia Petrovna Pogoreltsev is like a sister to me, like a mother. They have eight children. Let me take Liza there right now . . . so as not to lose any time. They'll receive her gladly, for the whole time, they'll be good to her, like their own daughter, their own daughter!"

He was terribly impatient and did not conceal it.

"That's somehow impossible, sir," Pavel Pavlovich said with a little grimace and, as it seemed to Velchaninov, peeking slyly into his eyes.

"Why? Why impossible?"

"But how, sir, let the child go like that, and suddenly, sir—even supposing it's with such a sincere well-wisher as yourself, I don't mean that, sir, but all the same to a strange house, and of such high society, sir, where I still don't know how she'll be received."

"But I told you I'm like one of them," Velchaninov cried out almost in wrath. "Klavdia Petrovna will consider it a happiness just at one word from me. Like my daughter . . . but, devil take it, you know yourself you're just babbling . . . what's there to talk about!"

He even stamped his foot.

"I mean, won't it be very strange, sir? After all, I, too, would have to go and see her once or twice, she can't be entirely without a father, sir? heh, heh . . . and in such an important house, sir."

"But it's the simplest house, not at all an 'important' one!" Velchaninov shouted. "I'm telling you, there are lots of children there. She'll resurrect there, that's the whole purpose . . . And I'll introduce you there tomorrow if you like. And you certainly will have to go and thank them; we'll go every day if you wish . . ."

"Still, sir, it's somehow . . ."

"Nonsense! Above all, you know it yourself! Listen, why don't you come to me this evening and spend the night, perhaps, and early in the morning we'll go, so as to be there by noon."

"My benefactor! Even to spend the night with you . . ." Pavel Pavlovich suddenly consented with tender emotion, "a veritable benefactor . . . and where is their country house?"

"Their country house is in Lesnoye."

"Only what about her clothes, sir! Because to go to such a noble house, and in the country besides, you know . . . A father's heart, sir!"

"What's wrong with her clothes? She's in mourning. How can she have any other clothes? This is the most appropriate thing imaginable! Only maybe her linen could be cleaner, and the kerchief . . ." (The kerchief and what could be seen of her linen were indeed very dirty.)

"Right away, she absolutely must change," Pavel Pavlovich started bustling, "and the rest of the necessary linen we'll also collect right away; Marya Sysoevna took it for laundering, sir."

"Send for a carriage, then, " Velchaninov interrupted, "and quickly, if possible."

But an obstacle arose: Liza was decidedly against it, she had been listening all the while in fear, and if, as he talked with Pavel Pavlovich, Velchaninov had managed to observe her well, he would have seen total despair on her little face.

"I won't go," she said firmly and softly.

"There, you see, just like her mama!"

"I'm not like Mama, I'm not like Mama!" Liza cried, wringing her little hands in despair, and as if justifying herself before her father's terrible reproach of being like her mama. "Papa, Papa, if you abandon me . . ."

She suddenly fell upon the frightened Velchaninov.

"If you take me, I'll . . ."

But she had no time to say anything more; Pavel Pavlovich grabbed her by the arm, almost by the scruff of the neck, and now with unconcealed animosity dragged her to the little room. There again followed several minutes of whispering; stifled weeping could be heard. Velchaninov was about to go in himself, when Pavel Pavlovich came out to him and with a twisted smile announced that she would presently come out, sir. Velchaninov tried not to look at him and averted his eyes.

Marya Sysoevna also came, the same woman he had met earlier on entering the corridor, and started packing into Liza's pretty little bag the linen she had brought for her.

"So, dearie, you're going to take the girl?" she addressed Velchaninov. "You've got a family or something? It'll be a good thing to do, dearie: she's a quiet child, you'll deliver her from this Sodom."[5]

"Now, now, Marya Sysoevna," Pavel Pavlovich began to mutter.

"What, Marya Sysoevna! Everybody knows my name. And isn't it a Sodom here? Is it fitting for a child who understands to look at such shame? They've brought a carriage for you, dearie—to Lesnoye, is it?"

"Yes, yes,"

"Well, good luck to you!"

Liza came out with a pale little face, her eyes downcast, and took her bag. Not one glance in Velchaninov's direction; she restrained herself and did not rush, as earlier, to embrace her father, even when saying good-bye; evidently she did not even want to look at him. Her father decorously kissed her on the head and patted it; at that her lips twisted and her chin trembled, but even so she did not raise her eyes to her father. Pavel

Pavlovich looked somewhat pale, and his hands trembled—this Velchaninov noticed clearly, though he tried as hard as he could not to look at him. He wanted one thing: to leave quickly. "And, anyway, what fault is it of mine?" he thought. "It had to be this way." They went downstairs, there Marya Sysoevna kissed Liza, and only when she was already settled in the carriage did Liza raise her eyes to her father—and suddenly clasp her hands and cry out: another moment and she would have rushed to him from the carriage, but the horses had already started off.

VI

The New Fantasy of an Idle Man

"You're not feeling bad?" Velchaninov was frightened. "I'll order them to stop, to fetch water . . ."

She looked up at him with a burning, reproachful glance.

"Where are you taking me?" she said sharply and curtly.

"It's a wonderful family, Liza. They're now living in a wonderful country house; there are many children, they'll love you there, they're kind . . . Don't be angry with me, Liza, I wish you well . . ."

He would have seemed strange at this moment to anyone who knew him, if they could have seen him.

"You're so . . . you're so . . . you're so . . . ohh, how wicked you are!" Liza said, choking with stifled tears, her angry, beautiful eyes flashing at him.

"Liza, I . . ."

"You're wicked, wicked, wicked, wicked!" She was wringing her hands. Velchaninov was completely at a loss.

"Liza, dear, if you knew what despair you drive me to!"

"Is it true that he'll come tomorrow? Is it true?" she asked imperiously.

"It's true, it's true! I'll bring him myself; I'll get him and bring him."

"He'll deceive me," Liza whispered, lowering her eyes.

"Doesn't he love you, Liza?"

"No, he doesn't."

"Has he hurt you? Has he?"

Liza looked at him darkly and was silent. She turned away from him again and sat stubbornly looking down. He started persuading her, spoke heatedly to her, was in a fever himself. Liza listened mistrustfully, hostilely, but she did listen. Her attention gladdened him extremely: he even began to explain to her what a drinking man was. He said that he himself loved her and would look after her father. Liza finally raised her eyes and gazed at him intently. He started telling her how he had once known her mama, and saw that she was getting caught up in his stories. Little by little she began gradually to answer his questions—but cautiously and monosyllabically, with stubbornness. She still did not give any reply to his main questions: she was stubbornly silent about everything concerning her former relations with her father. As he talked with her, Velchaninov took her little hand in his, as earlier, and would not let it go; she did not pull it away. The girl was not totally silent, however; she did let slip in her vague replies that she used to love her father more than her mama, because formerly her father had always loved her more, and her mama formerly had loved her less; but that when her mama was dying, she had kissed her a lot and wept, when everyone left the room and the two of them remained alone . . . and that she now loved her more than anyone, more than anyone, anyone in the world, and every night she loved her more than anyone. But the girl was indeed proud: catching herself letting it slip, she suddenly withdrew into herself again and fell silent; she even looked hatefully at Velchaninov for making her let it slip. Toward the end of their journey, her hysterical state had nearly passed, but she became terribly pensive and looked around like a little savage, sullenly, with a gloomy, predetermined stubbornness. As for the fact that she was now being taken into a strange home, where she had never been before, this seemed for the moment to embarrass her very little. She was tor-

mented by something else, Velchaninov could see that; he
guessed that she was ashamed of *him,* that she was precisely
ashamed that her father had let her go with him so easily, as if
he had thrown her away to him.

"She's ill," he thought, "maybe very; she's been tormented
. . . Oh, mean, drunken creature! I understand him now!"
He kept urging the coachman on; he had hopes in the country
house, the air, the garden, the children, the new, the unfamiliar to her life, and then, later . . . But of what would come
afterward he no longer had any doubts; there were full, clear
hopes. Only one thing he knew absolutely: that he had never
before experienced what he experienced then, and that it
would stay with him for the rest of his life! "Here is the goal,
here is life!" he thought rapturously.

Many thoughts flashed in him now, but he did not dwell
on them and stubbornly avoided details: without the details,
everything was becoming clear, everything was inviolable. His
main plan formed of itself: "We can influence the scoundrel
with our combined forces," he dreamed, "and he will leave
Liza in Petersburg with the Pogoreltsevs, though at first only
temporarily, for a certain period of time, and go away by himself; and Liza will be left for me; and that's all, what more is
there to it? And . . . and, of course, he wishes it himself;
otherwise why would he torment her." They finally arrived.
The Pogoreltsevs' country house was indeed a lovely little
place; they were met first of all by a noisy band of children
who poured onto the porch of the house. Velchaninov had not
visited in far too long, and the children were wild with joy: he
was loved. The older ones shouted to him at once, even before
he got out of the carriage:

"And how's your lawsuit, how's your lawsuit?" This was
picked up by the smallest ones, who laughed and squealed
following the older ones. He was teased there about his lawsuit. But, seeing Liza, they at once surrounded her and began
studying her with silent and intent childish curiosity. Klavdia
Petrovna came out, and her husband after her. She and her
husband also both started from the first word, and laughing,
with a question about the lawsuit.

Klavdia Petrovna was a lady of about thirty-seven, a plump and still beautiful brunette, with a fresh and rosy face. Her husband was about fifty-five, an intelligent and clever man, but a kindly fellow before all. Their house was in the fullest sense "his own home" for Velchaninov, as he himself put it. But a special circumstance also lay hidden here: some twenty years ago this Klavdia Petrovna had almost married Velchaninov, then still almost a boy, still a student. This had been a first love, fervent, ridiculous, and beautiful. It ended, however, with her marrying Pogoreltsev. They met again five years later, and it all ended in serene and quiet friendship. There forever remained a certain warmth, a certain special light shining in this relationship. Here everything in Velchaninov's memories was pure and irreproachable, and all the dearer to him in that it was perhaps so only here. In this family, he was simple, naive, kind, helped with the children, was never affected, admitted everything and confessed everything. More than once he had sworn to the Pogoreltsevs that he would live a little longer in the world and then move in with them completely and start living with them, never to part again. He thought of this intention to himself not at all as a joke.

He gave them quite a detailed account of all that was necessary about Liza; but his request alone, without any special accounts, would have been enough. Klavdia Petrovna kissed the "little orphan" and promised to do everything for her part. The children took Liza up and led her out to play in the garden. After half an hour of lively talk, Velchaninov got up and started saying good-bye. He was so impatient that they all could notice it. They were all surprised: he had not visited in three weeks and was now leaving after half an hour. He laughed and swore to come the next day. It was brought to his notice that he was much too excited; he suddenly took Klavdia Petrovna by the hands and, under the pretext of having forgotten something very important, led her to another room.

"Remember what I told you—you alone, what even your husband doesn't know—about the T——— year of my life?"

"I remember only too well; you spoke of it often."

"I wasn't speaking, I was confessing, and to you alone, you alone! I never told you the woman's last name; she's Trusotsky, the wife of this Trusotsky. It's she who died, and Liza, her daughter—is my daughter!"

"Is it certain? You're not mistaken?" Klavdia Petrovna asked in some agitation.

"Absolutely not, absolutely not!" Velchaninov uttered rapturously.

And, as briefly as possible, hurrying and terribly agitated, he told her—all. Klavdia Petrovna had known it all before, but she had not known the lady's last name. Velchaninov had become so frightened each time at the mere thought that someone he knew might one day meet Mme. Trusotsky and think of *him* having loved this woman *so much,* that he had not dared up to then to reveal "that woman's" name even to Klavdia Petrovna, his only friend.

"And the father knows nothing?" she asked, having heard the whole story.

"N-no, he does . . . That's what torments me, that I haven't made it all out yet!" Velchaninov went on heatedly. "He knows, he knows; I noticed it today and yesterday. But I have to find out how much of it he knows. That's why I'm in a hurry now. He'll come tonight. I'm perplexed, though, where he could have learned it—that is, learned *everything*. About Bagautov he knows everything, no question of it. But about me? You know how wives are able to reassure their husbands on such occasions! If an angel came down from heaven—the husband would believe not him, but her! Don't shake your head, don't condemn me, I condemn myself, and condemned myself for everything long, long ago! . . . You see, earlier, at his place, I was so sure he knew everything that I compromised myself before him. Believe me: I'm quite ashamed and pained that I met him so rudely yesterday. (I'll tell you everything later in more detail!) He came to me yesterday out of an invincible, malicious desire to let me know that he knew his offense and that the offender was known to him! That's the whole reason for this stupid appearance in a drunken state. But it's so natural on his part! He precisely came to reproach me! Generally, I conducted things too hotly this morning and yesterday. Imprudently stupid! I gave myself away! Why did he accost me at such a troubled moment? I tell you, he even tormented Liza, tormented a child, and probably also in reproach, to vent his spite if only on a child! Yes, he's spiteful—nonentity that he is, he's spiteful, even very much so. It goes without saying that he's nothing but a buffoon, though before, by God, he had the look of a decent man, as far as he could, but it's so natural that he's turned dissolute! Here, my friend, one must take a Christian view! And you know, my dear, my good one—I want to change completely toward him: I want to show him kindness. It will even be a 'good deed' on my part. Because, after all, I am guilty before him! Listen, you know, I'll tell you another thing: once in T—— I suddenly needed four thousand roubles, and he gave it to me in a second, without any receipt, sincerely glad that he was able to please me, and I did take it then, I took it from his own hands, took money from him, do you hear, took it as from a friend!"

"Only be more prudent," Klavdia Petrovna observed worriedly to all this. "And how rapturous you are, really, I'm afraid for you! Of course, Liza's now my daughter, too, but there's so much here, so much that's still unresolved! And above all, be more circumspect now; you absolutely must be circumspect when you're in happiness or in such rapture; you're too magnanimous when you're in happiness," she added with a smile.

Everyone came out to see Velchaninov off; the children brought Liza, with whom they had been playing in the garden. They looked at her now, it seemed, with still greater perplexity than before. Liza turned completely shy when Velchaninov, taking his leave, kissed her in front of everyone and warmly repeated his promise to come the next day with her father. She was silent and did not look at him till the last minute, but then she suddenly seized him by the sleeve and pulled him somewhere aside, looking at him with imploring eyes; she wanted to tell him something. He took her to another room at once.

"What is it, Liza?" he asked tenderly and encouragingly, but she, still looking around timorously, pulled him farther into the corner; she wanted to hide completely from everyone.

"What is it, Liza, what is it?"

She was silent and undecided; she looked fixedly into his eyes with her blue eyes, and all the features of her little face expressed nothing but mad fear.

"He'll . . . hang himself!" she whispered as if in delirium.

"Who will hang himself?" Velchaninov asked in fright.

"He will, he will! During the night he wanted to hang himself from a noose!" the girl said, hurrying and breathless. "I saw it myself! Last night he wanted to hang himself from a noose, he told me, he did! He wanted to before, too, he's always wanted to . . . I saw it in the night . . ."

"It can't be!" whispered Velchaninov in perplexity. She suddenly rushed to kiss his hands; she wept, barely catching her breath from sobbing, she begged and pleaded with him, but he could understand nothing of her hysterical prattle. And forever after there remained in his memory, there came to him awake and in his dreams, those tormented eyes of a tormented child, who looked at him in mad fear and with her last hope.

"And can it be, can it be that she loves him so much?" he thought jealously and enviously, going back to town in feverish impatience. "She herself said today that she loved her mother more . . . maybe she hates him and doesn't love him at all . . .

"And what is this: hang himself? What was she saying? A fool like him hang himself? . . . I must find out; I absolutely must find out! I must resolve everything as soon as possible—resolve it definitively!"

VII

Husband and Lover Kiss

He was in a terrible hurry to "find out." "I was stunned earlier; I had no time earlier to reflect on it," he thought, recalling his first encounter with Liza, "but now I must find out." In order to find out the quicker, he gave orders in his impatience to drive straight to Trusotsky's place, but changed his mind at once: "No, better if he comes to me himself, and meanwhile I'll finish this damned business."

He feverishly got down to business; but this time he felt he was very distracted and ought not to be occupying himself with business matters. At five o'clock, on his way to have dinner, suddenly, for the first time, a funny thought came to his head: what if in fact he was, perhaps, only hindering things by interfering in the lawsuit himself, bustling and hanging out in offices and trying to catch his lawyer, who had begun to hide from him. He laughed merrily at his own supposition. "And if this thought had come to my head yesterday, I'd have been terribly upset," he added, still more merrily. Despite the merriment, he was growing ever more distracted and impatient; finally he fell to thinking; and though his uneasy mind kept clinging to many things, on the whole the result was not at all what he needed.

"I need him, this man!" he finally decided. "I've got to figure him out first and then decide. This is—a duel!"

Returning home at seven o'clock, he did not find Pavel Pavlovich there, which first caused him great surprise, then wrath, and then even despondency; finally, he began to be afraid. "God knows, God knows what it will end with!" he repeated, now pacing the room, now stretching out on the sofa, and constantly looking at his watch. Finally, at around nine o'clock, Pavel Pavlovich did appear. "If the man was being cunning, he couldn't have wangled anything better than this—the way I'm upset right now," he thought, suddenly completely cheered up and terribly merry.

To the pert and merry question: why had he taken so long

in coming?—Pavel Pavlovich smiled crookedly, sat down casually, not like the day before, and somehow carelessly flung his
hat with crape onto another chair. Velchaninov noticed the
casualness at once and took it into consideration.

Calmly and without unnecessary words, without his former
agitation, he told, as if making a report, how he had taken
Liza, how nicely she had been received there, how good it was
going to be for her, and little by little, as if completely forgetting Liza, imperceptibly came down to talking only about the
Pogoreltsevs—that is, what nice people they were, how long he
had known them, what a good and even influential man
Pogoreltsev was, and the like. Pavel Pavlovich listened dis-
tractedly and from time to time glanced at the narrator, covertly, with a peevish and sly grin.

"What an ardent man you are," he muttered with some
especially nasty smile.

"You, however, are somehow wicked today," Velchaninov
observed vexedly.

"And why shouldn't I be wicked, sir, like everybody else?"
Pavel Pavlovich suddenly heaved himself up, as if pouncing
from around a corner; even as if he had just been waiting to
pounce.

"That's entirely as you will," Velchaninov grinned. "I
thought something might have happened to you?"

"And so it did happen, sir!" the man exclaimed, as if boasting that it had happened.

"What is it?"

Pavel Pavlovich waited a little before answering:

"Well, you see, sir, it's all our Stepan Mikhailovich at his
whimsies . . . Bagautov, a most elegant Petersburg young
man, of the highest society, sir."

"He didn't receive you again, or what?"

"N-no, this time I precisely was received, I was admitted for
the first time, sir, and looked upon the countenance . . .
only it was already a dead man's! . . ."

"Wha-a-at! Bagautov died?" Velchaninov was terribly surprised, though it would seem there was nothing for him to be
so surprised at.

"Himself, sir! An unfailing friend of six years! He died yesterday around noon, and I didn't know! Maybe it was at the very moment when I came to inquire about his health. The funeral and burial are tomorrow, he's already lying in his little coffin, sir. The coffin's lined with damson velvet, trimmed with gold braid . . . he died of nervous fever, sir. I was admitted, admitted, I looked upon his countenance! I told them at the front door that I was considered a true friend, so I was admitted. What has he been pleased to do to me now, this true friend of six years—I ask you? Maybe I came to Petersburg just for his sake alone!"

"But why are you angry with him," Velchaninov laughed, "he didn't die on purpose!"

"But I'm saying it in pity; such a precious friend; this is what he meant to me, sir."

And Pavel Pavlovich suddenly, quite unexpectedly, put two fingers like horns over his bald forehead and went off into a long and quiet titter. He spent a whole half minute sitting like that, with horns and tittering, looking into Velchaninov's eyes as if reveling in his most sarcastic impudence. The latter was stupefied as if he were seeing some sort of ghost. But his stupefaction lasted no more than a tiny moment; a mocking smile, calm to the point of impudence, slowly came to his lips.

"And what might that signify?" he asked carelessly, drawing out his words.

"That signifies horns, sir," Pavel Pavlovich snapped, finally taking his fingers from his forehead.

"That is . . . your horns?"

"My very own splendid acquisition!" Pavel Pavlovich again made a terribly nasty grimace.

They both fell silent.

"You're a brave man, anyhow!" said Velchaninov.

"Because I showed you the horns? You know what, Alexei Ivanovich, you'd do better to treat me to something! I treated you in T——— for a whole year, sir, every blessed day . . . Send for a little bottle, my throat's dry."

"With pleasure; you should have said so long ago. What'll you have?"

"Why *you*? make it *we*—we'll drink together, won't we?" Pavel Pavlovich peered into his eyes defiantly and at the same time with some strange uneasiness.

"Champagne?"

"What else? It's not vodka's turn yet, sir . . ."

Velchaninov rose unhurriedly, rang for Mavra downstairs, and gave the order.

"For the joy of a happy reunion, sir, after nine years of separation," Pavel Pavlovich tittered along needlessly and inappropriately. "Now you and you alone are left me as a true friend, sir! Stepan Mikhailovich Bagautov is no more! It's as the poet said:

> The great Patroclus is no more,
> Vile Thersites is living still!"[6]

And at the word "Thersites" he jabbed his finger at his own breast.

"You swine, why don't you explain yourself quicker, I don't like hints," Velchaninov thought to himself. Anger seethed in him, for a long time he had barely contained himself.

"Tell me this," he began vexedly, "if you accuse Stepan Mikhailovich so directly" (now he no longer called him simply Bagautov), "then it seems you should rejoice that your offender is dead; so why are you angry?"

"Why rejoice, sir? What's there to rejoice at?"

"I'm judging by your feelings."

"Heh, heh, you're mistaken about my feelings on that account, sir, as in the wise man's saying: 'A dead enemy is good, but a live one is even better,' hee, hee!"

"But you saw him alive every day for five years, I think, didn't you have enough of looking?" Velchaninov observed spitefully and impudently.

"But did I . . . did I know it then, sir?" Pavel Pavlovich suddenly heaved himself up, again as if pouncing from around a corner, even as if with a certain glee at having finally been asked a long-awaited question. "What do you take me for, Alexei Ivanovich?"

And some completely new and unexpected look suddenly flashed in his eyes, which as if completely transformed his spiteful and until then only vilely grimacing face.

"So you really knew nothing!" Velchaninov, perplexed, said with the most sudden amazement.

"So you think I knew, sir? You think I knew! Oh, what a breed—our Jupiters! With you a man is the same as a dog, and you judge everyone by your own paltry nature! There's for you, sir! Swallow that!" And he banged his fist on the table in rage, but at once got scared at his own banging and looked up timorously.

Velchaninov assumed a dignified air.

"Listen, Pavel Pavlovich, it decidedly makes no difference to me, you must agree, whether you knew or not. If you didn't know, it does you honor in any case, though . . . anyhow, I don't even understand why you've chosen me as your confidant . . ."

"I didn't mean you . . . don't be angry, I didn't mean you . . ." Pavel Pavlovich muttered, dropping his eyes.

Mavra came in with the champagne.

"Here it is!" Pavel Pavlovich cried, obviously glad of a way out, "and the glasses, dearie, the glasses—wonderful! Nothing more is required of you, my sweet. Already opened? Honor and glory to you, dear creature! Well, off you go!"

And, cheered up again, he once more looked boldly at Velchaninov.

"And confess," he suddenly tittered, "that you're terribly curious about all this, sir, and it by no means 'decidedly makes no difference,' as you were pleased to declare, so that you'd even be upset if I got up and left this very moment, sir, without explaining anything."

"Actually, I wouldn't be."

"Oh, you liar!" Pavel Pavlovich's smile said.

"Well, sir, let's begin!" and he poured wine in the glasses. "Let's drink a toast," he pronounced, raising his glass, "to the health of our friend, the resting-in-peace Stepan Mikhailovich!"

He raised his glass and drank.

"I won't drink such a toast," Velchaninov put his glass down.

"Why's that? A nice little toast!"

"Listen here: when you came now, you weren't drunk?"

"I'd had a little. What of it, sir?"

"Nothing special, but I had the impression that yesterday, and especially this morning, you sincerely regretted the late Natalia Vassilievna."

"And who told you that I don't sincerely regret her now as well?" Pavel Pavlovich again pounced, as if he had again been jerked by a spring.

"That's not what I mean; but you must agree that you could be mistaken about Stepan Mikhailovich, and it's a serious matter."

Pavel Pavlovich smiled slyly and winked.

"And you'd like so much to find out how I myself found out about Stepan Mikhailovich!"

Velchaninov turned red:

"I repeat to you again that it makes no difference to me." And in rage he thought, "Why don't I throw him out right now, along with his bottle?" and turned redder still.

"Never mind, sir!" Pavel Pavlovich said, as if encouraging him, and poured himself another glass.

"I'll explain to you presently how I found out 'everything,' sir, and thereby satisfy your fiery wishes . . . for you're a fiery man, Alexei Ivanovich, a terribly fiery man, sir! heh, heh! only give me a little cigarette, because since the month of March I . . ."

"Here's your cigarette."

"I've become dissolute since the month of March, Alexei Ivanovich, and this is how it happened, sir, lend me your ear. Consumption, as you know yourself, my dearest friend," he was getting more and more familiar, "is a curious disease, sir. Quite often a consumptive person dies almost without suspecting he might die the next day, sir. I tell you that just five hours before, Natalia Vassilievna was planning to go in two weeks to visit her aunt thirty miles away. Besides, you're probably familiar with the habit, or, better to say, the trait common to many ladies, and perhaps gentlemen as well, sir, of preserving their old trash, such as love correspondence, sir. The surest thing would be the stove, right, sir? No, every scrap of paper is carefully preserved in their little boxes and hold-alls; it's even numbered by years, by dates and categories. Whether it's very comforting or something—I don't know, sir; but it must be for the sake of pleasant memories. Since she was planning, five hours before the end, to go to her aunt's for the celebration, Natalia Vassilievna naturally had no thought of death, even to the very last hour, sir, and kept waiting for Koch. And so it happened, sir, that Natalia Vassilievna died, and a little ebony box inlaid with mother-of-pearl and silver was left in her desk. Such a pretty little box, with a key, sir, an heirloom, handed down from her grandmother. Well, sir—it was in this box that everything was revealed—that is, everything, sir, without any exception, by days and years, over two whole decades. And since Stepan Mikhailovich had a decided inclination for literature, having once even sent a passionate story to a magazine, there turned out to be nearly a hundred numbers of his works in the little chest—true, it was for five years, sir. Some numbers were even marked in Natalia Vassilievna's own hand. A pleasure for a husband, wouldn't you think, sir?"

Velchaninov quickly reflected and remembered that he had never written even one letter, even one note, to Natalia Vassilievna. And though he had written two letters from Petersburg, they had been addressed to both spouses, as had been arranged. And to Natalia Vassilievna's last letter, informing him of his dismissal, he had never replied.

After finishing his story, Pavel Pavlovich was silent for a whole minute, smiling importunately and expectantly.

"Why do you answer nothing to my little question, sir?" he spoke finally with obvious suffering.

"What little question?"

"About the pleasant feelings of a husband, sir, on opening the little chest."

"Eh, what business is that of mine!" Velchaninov waved his hand biliously, got up, and started pacing the room.

"And I bet you're now thinking: 'What a swine you are, to have pointed to your own horns,' heh, heh! A most squeamish man . . . you, sir!"

"I'm thinking nothing of the sort. On the contrary, you are much too annoyed by your offender's death, and you've drunk a lot of wine besides. I see nothing extraordinary in any of it; I understand too well why you needed a live Bagautov, and I'm prepared to respect your vexation, but . . ."

"And what did I need Bagautov for, in your opinion, sir?"

"That's your business."

"I'll bet you had in mind a duel, sir?"

"Devil take it!" Velchaninov restrained himself less and less, "I thought that, like any decent man . . . in such cases—one doesn't stoop to comical babble, to stupid clowning, to ridiculous complaints and vile hints, with which he besmirches himself still more, but acts clearly, directly, openly, like a decent man!"

"Heh, heh, yes, but maybe I'm not a decent man, sir?"

"That, again, is your business . . . and, anyhow, what the devil did you need a live Bagautov for?"

"Why, only so as to have a look at a nice friend, sir. We'd have taken a little bottle and had a drink together."

"He'd never have drunk with you."

"Why? Noblesse oblige? You drink with me, sir; is he any better than you?"

"I didn't drink with you."

"Why such pride all of a sudden, sir?"

Velchaninov suddenly burst into nervous and irritated laughter.

"Pah, the devil! but you're decidedly some sort of 'predatory type'! I thought you were just an 'eternal husband' and nothing more!"

"How's that? an 'eternal husband'? What does it mean?" Pavel Pavlovich suddenly pricked up his ears.

"Just so, one type of husband . . . it's too long a story. You'd better just clear out, your time is up; I'm sick of you!"

"And what's this about predatory? You said predatory?"

"I said you're a 'predatory type'—I said it to mock you."

"What sort of 'predatory type,' sir? Tell me, please, Alexei Ivanovich, for God's sake, or for Christ's sake."

"Well, that's enough, enough!" Velchaninov cried suddenly, again getting terribly angry. "Your time is up, clear out!"

"No, it's not enough, sir!" Pavel Pavlovich, too, jumped up. "Even though you're sick of me, it's still not enough, because first you and I must have a drink and clink glasses! We'll have a drink, and then I'll go, but now it's not enough!"

"Pavel Pavlovich, can you clear the hell out of here today or not?"

"I can clear the hell out of here, sir, but first we'll drink! You said you don't want to drink precisely *with me;* well, but *I want* that you drink precisely with me!"

He was no longer clowning, no longer tittering. Everything in him was again as if transformed suddenly and was now so opposite to the whole figure and tone of the just-now Pavel Pavlovich that Velchaninov was decidedly taken aback.

"Eh, let's drink, Alexei Ivanovich, eh, don't refuse!" Pavel Pavlovich went on, gripping him firmly by the arm and looking strangely into his face. Obviously, this was not just a matter of drinking.

"Yes, perhaps," the man muttered, "and where's . . . this is swill . . ."

"Exactly two glasses left, pure swill, sir, but we'll drink and clink glasses, sir! Here, sir, kindly take your glass."

They clinked and drank.

"Well, and if so, if so . . . ah!" Pavel Pavlovich suddenly seized his forehead with his hand and for a few moments remained in that position. Velchaninov imagined that he was now going to up and speak out the very *last* word. But Pavel Pavlovich did not speak anything out for him; he only looked at him and quietly stretched his mouth again into the same sly and winking smile.

"What do you want from me, you drunk man! You're fooling with me!" Velchaninov cried frenziedly, stamping his feet.

"Don't shout, don't shout, why shout?" Pavel Pavlovich hastily waved his hand. "I'm not fooling with you, I'm not! Do you know what you've—this is what you've become for me now!"

And he suddenly seized his hand and kissed it. Velchaninov had no time to recover himself.

"This is what you are for me now, sir! And now—to all the devils with me!"

"Wait, stop!" the recovered Velchaninov cried, "I forgot to tell you . . ."

Pavel Pavlovich turned around at the door.

"You see," Velchaninov began to mutter extremely quickly, blushing and averting his eyes completely, "you should be at the Pogoreltsevs' tomorrow without fail . . . to get acquainted and to thank them—without fail . . ."

"Without fail, without fail, how could I not understand, sir!" Pavel Pavlovich picked up with extreme readiness, quickly waving his hand as a sign that there was no need to remind him.

"Besides, Liza is also waiting for you very much. I promised . . ."

"Liza," Pavel Pavlovich suddenly came back again, "Liza? Do you know, sir, what Liza was for me, was and is, sir? Was and is!" he suddenly cried almost in frenzy. "But . . . Heh! That's for later, sir; that's all for later . . . and now—it's no longer enough for me that you and I drank together, Alexei Ivanovich, it's another satisfaction that's needed, sir! . . ."

He put his hat on the chair and, as earlier, slightly breathless, gazed at him.

"Kiss me, Alexei Ivanovich," he suddenly offered.

"Are you drunk?" the man cried, and drew back.

"I am, sir, but kiss me anyway, Alexei Ivanovich, eh, kiss me! I did kiss your hand just now!"

Alexei Ivanovich was silent for a few moments, as if hit on the head with a club. But suddenly he bent down to Pavel Pavlovich, who came up to his shoulder, and kissed him on the lips, which smelled very strongly of wine. He was not entirely sure, incidentally, that he had kissed him.

"Well, and now, now . . ." Pavel Pavlovich shouted again in a drunken frenzy, flashing his drunken eyes, "now here's what, sir: I had thought then—'not this one, too? if even this one,' I thought, 'if even this one, too, then who can one believe after that!'"

Pavel Pavlovich suddenly dissolved in tears.

"So do you understand what kind of friend you've remained for me now?!"

And he ran out of the room with his hat. Velchaninov again stood for several minutes in the same spot, as after Pavel Pavlovich's first visit.

"Eh, a drunken buffoon and nothing more!" he waved his hand.

"Decidedly nothing more!" he confirmed energetically when he was already undressed and lying in bed.

VIII

Liza Is Sick

The next morning while waiting for Pavel Pavlovich, who had promised not to be late for going to the Pogoreltsevs', Velchaninov paced the room sipping his coffee, smoking, and being conscious every moment that he was like a man who wakes up in the morning and remembers every instant that he had been slapped the day before. "Hm . . . he understands only too well what the point is, and will take revenge on me with Liza!" he thought in fear.

The dear image of the poor child flashed sadly before him. His heart beat faster at the thought that today, soon, in two hours, he would see *his* Liza again. "Eh, what is there to talk about!" he decided hotly. "My whole life and my whole purpose are now in that! What are all these slaps and remembrances! . . . And what have I even lived for so far? Disorder and sadness . . . but now—everything's different, everything's changed!"

But, despite his rapture, he fell to pondering more and more.

"He'll torment me with Liza—that's clear! And he'll torment Liza. It's over this that he'll finally do me in, for *everything*. Hm . . . no question, I can't allow yesterday's escapades on his part," he suddenly blushed, "and . . . and look, anyhow, he's not here yet, and it's already past eleven!"

He waited a long time, until half past twelve, and his anguish grew more and more. Pavel Pavlovich did not come. At last the long-stirring thought that he would not come on purpose, solely in order to perform yet another escapade like yesterday's, made him thoroughly vexed: "He knows I'm counting on him. And what will happen now with Liza! And how can I come to her without him!"

Finally, he could not stand it and at exactly one in the afternoon he himself went galloping to the Pokrov. In the rooms he was told that Pavel Pavlovich had not slept at home and had come only after eight in the morning, stayed for a brief quarter of an hour, and left again. Velchaninov was standing by the door of Pavel Pavlovich's room, listening to the maid talking to him, and mechanically turning the handle of the locked door, tugging it back and forth. Recollecting himself, he spat, let go of the latch, and asked to be taken to Marya Sysoevna. But she, when she heard him, willingly came out herself.

She was a kind woman, "a woman of noble feelings," as Velchaninov referred to her later when telling Klavdia Petrovna about his conversation with her. After asking briefly how his trip yesterday with the "missy" had gone, Marya Sysoevna at once got to telling about Pavel Pavlovich. In her words, "only except for the little child, she'd have got rid of him long ago. The hotel already got rid of him because he was far too outrageous. Well, isn't it a sin to bring a wench at night when there's a little child there who already understands! He shouts: 'She'll be your mother, if I want her to be!' And, would you believe it, wench as she was, even she spat in his mug. He shouts: 'You're not my daughter—you're a whore's spawn.' "

"What are you saying!" Velchaninov was frightened.

"I heard it myself. Though he's a drunk man, like as if unconscious, still it's no good in front of a little child; youngling as she is, she'll still get it in her mind! The missy cries, I could see she's all tormented. And the other day here in the yard we had a real sin happen: a commissary or whatever, so people said, took a room in the hotel in the evening and by morning he hanged himself. They said he'd squandered money. People come running, Pavel Pavlovich isn't home, and the child goes around unattended, so there I see her in the corridor among the people, peeking from behind, and staring so strangely at the hanging man. I quickly brought her here. And what do you think—she's trembling all over, got all black, and the moment I brought her here she just fell into a fit. She thrashed and thrashed, and wouldn't come out of it. Convulsions or whatever, only from that time on she got sick. He came, found out about it, and pinched her all over, because he doesn't really hit, it's more like pinches, then he got soused with wine, came and started scaring her, saying: 'I'll hang myself, too, on account of you; from this very cord,' he says, 'I'll hang myself from the curtain cord,' and he makes a noose right in front of her. And the girl's beside herself—she cries, puts her little arms around him: 'I won't,' she cries, 'I won't ever.' Such a pity!"

Though Velchaninov had expected something very strange, these stories struck him so much that he did not even believe them. Marya Sysoevna told him much more: there was, for instance, one occasion when, if it had not been for Marya Sysoevna, Liza might have thrown herself out the window. He left the rooms as if drunk himself. "I'll kill him with a stick, like a dog, on the head!" he kept imagining. And for a long time he kept repeating it to himself.

He hired a carriage and set off for the Pogoreltsevs'. Still within the city, the carriage was forced to stop at an intersection, by a bridge across the canal, across which a big funeral procession was making its way. On both sides of the bridge a number of vehicles crowded, waiting; people also stopped. The funeral was a wealthy one and the train of coaches following it was very long, and then in one of these following coaches Pavel Pavlovich's face suddenly flashed before Velchaninov. He would not have believed it, if Pavel Pavlovich had not thrust himself out the window and nodded to him, smiling. Apparently he was terribly glad to have recognized Velchaninov: he even began making signs from the coach with his hand. Velchaninov jumped out of his carriage and, in spite of the crowd and the policemen and the fact that Pavel Pavlovich's coach was already driving onto the bridge, ran right up to the window. Pavel Pavlovich was alone.

"What's the matter with you," Velchaninov cried, "why didn't you come? what are you doing here?"

"My duty, sir—don't shout, don't shout—I'm doing my duty," Pavel Pavlovich tittered, squinting merrily. "I'm accompanying the mortal remains of my true friend Stepan Mikhailovich."

"That's all absurd, you drunken, crazy man!" Velchaninov, puzzled for a moment, cried still louder. "Get out right now and come with me—right now!"

"I can't, sir, it's a duty, sir . . ."

"I'll drag you out," Velchaninov screamed.

"And I'll raise a cry, sir! I'll raise a cry!" Pavel Pavlovich went on with the same merry titter—just as if it were all a game—hiding, however, in the far corner of the coach.

"Watch out, watch out, you'll get run over!" a policeman shouted. Indeed, some extraneous carriage had broken through the train at the descent from the bridge and was causing alarm. Velchaninov was forced to jump down; other vehicles and people pushed him farther back. He spat and made his way to his carriage.

"In any case, I can't take him there the way he is!" he thought with continuing anxious amazement.

When he had related Marya Sysoevna's story and the strange encounter at the funeral to Klavdia Petrovna, she fell to thinking hard: "I'm afraid for you," she said to him, "you must break all relations with him, and the sooner the better."

"He's a drunken buffoon and nothing more!" Velchaninov cried out vehemently. "Why should I be afraid of him! And how can I break relations when Liza's here? Remember about Liza!"

Meanwhile Liza was lying sick in bed; since last evening she had been in a fever, and they were awaiting a well-known doctor from the city, for whom a messenger had been sent at daybreak. All this definitely upset Velchaninov. Klavdia Petrovna took him to the sick girl.

"Yesterday I watched her very closely," she observed, stopping outside Liza's room. "She's a proud and gloomy child; she's ashamed that she's with us and that her father abandoned her like that; that's the whole of her illness, in my opinion."

"How, abandoned her? Why do you think he's abandoned her?"

"From the fact alone that he let her come here to a completely strange house, and with a man . . . also almost a stranger, or in such relations . . ."

"But I took her myself, by force, I don't find . . ."

"Ah, my God, even a child like Liza could find it! In my opinion, he'll simply never come."

Seeing Velchaninov alone, Liza was not surprised, she only smiled sorrowfully and turned her feverish little head to the wall. She did not respond at all to Velchaninov's timid consolations and ardent promises to bring her father to her the next day without fail. Coming out of her room, he suddenly wept.

The doctor came only toward evening. Having examined the sick girl, he frightened everyone from the first word by observing that he ought to have been sent for sooner. When told that the girl had become sick only the evening before, he did not believe it at first. "Everything depends on how this night goes," he finally decided, and, giving his orders, he left, promising to come the next day as early as possible. Velchaninov wanted absolutely to stay overnight, but Klavdia Petrovna herself convinced him to try once more "to bring that monster here."

"Once more?" Velchaninov repeated in frenzy. "Why, I'll tie him up now and bring him here with my own hands!"

The thought of tying Pavel Pavlovich up and bringing him with his own hands suddenly took possession of him to the point of extreme impatience. "Now I don't feel guilty before him for anything, not for anything!" he said to Klavdia Petrovna as he was taking leave of her. "I renounce all the base, tearful words I said here yesterday!" he added indignantly.

Liza was lying with her eyes closed, apparently asleep; she seemed to be better. When Velchaninov bent down carefully to her little head, to kiss at least the edge of her dress in farewell—she suddenly opened her eyes as if she had been waiting for him, and whispered: "Take me away."

It was a quiet, sorrowful request, without any shadow of yesterday's irritation, but at the same time one could hear something in it, as if she herself were completely certain that her request would not be granted for anything. As soon as Velchaninov, quite in despair, began assuring her that it was impossible, she silently closed her eyes and did not say a word more, as if she did not hear or see him.

On reaching the city, he gave orders to drive straight to the Pokrov. It was already ten o'clock; Pavel Pavlovich was not in his rooms. Velchaninov waited for him for a whole half hour, pacing the corridor in morbid impatience. Marya Sysoevna finally convinced him that Pavel Pavlovich would come back perhaps only toward morning, at daybreak. "Well, then I, too, will come at daybreak," Velchaninov resolved, and, beside himself, went home.

But what was his amazement when, even before entering his place, he heard from Mavra that yesterday's visitor had been waiting for him since before ten.

"And he had his tea here, and sent for wine again, and gave me a fiver for the purpose."

IX

A Phantom

Pavel Pavlovich had made himself extremely comfortable. He was sitting in yesterday's chair, smoking cigarettes, and had just poured himself the fourth and last glass from the bottle. A teapot and a glass of unfinished tea stood near him on the table. His flushed face radiated good humor. He had even taken his tailcoat off, summer-fashion, and was sitting in his waistcoat.

"Excuse me, my most faithful friend!" he cried out, seeing Velchaninov and leaping up from his place to put his tailcoat on. "I took it off for the greater enjoyment of the moment . . ."

Velchaninov approached him menacingly.

"You're not completely drunk yet? Can I still talk with you?"

Pavel Pavlovich was somewhat taken aback.

"No, not completely . . . I commemorated the deceased, but—not completely, sir . . ."

"Can you understand me?"

"That's what I came for, to understand you, sir."

"Well, then I'll begin directly with the fact that you are a blackguard!" Velchaninov shouted in a breaking voice.

"If you begin with that, sir, what will you end with?" Pavel Pavlovich, obviously much frightened, made a slight attempt to protest, but Velchaninov was shouting without listening:

"Your daughter is dying, she's sick; have you abandoned her or not?"

"Dying is she, sir?"

"She's sick, sick, extremely dangerously sick!"

"Maybe it's some little fits, sir . . ."

"Don't talk nonsense! She's ex-treme-ly sick! You ought to have gone, if only so as to . . ."

"To express my thanks, sir, my thanks for their hospitality! I understand only too well, sir! Alexei Ivanovich, my dear, my perfect one," he suddenly seized his hand in both of his own, and, with drunken emotion, almost in tears, as if asking forgiveness, proceeded to shout: "Alexei Ivanovich, don't shout, don't shout! If I die, if I fall, drunk, into the Neva now—what of it, sir, considering the true meaning of things? And we can always go to Mr. Pogoreltsev's, sir . . ."

Velchaninov caught himself and held back a little.

"You're drunk, and therefore I don't understand in what sense you're speaking," he remarked severely. "I am always ready to have a talk with you; the sooner the better, even . . . I came so as . . . But before all you must know that I'm taking measures: you must spend the night here! Tomorrow morning I take you and off we go. I won't let you out!" he screamed again. "I'll tie you up and bring you with my own hands! . . . Does this sofa suit you?" Breathless, he pointed to the wide and soft sofa that stood opposite the sofa on which he himself slept, against the other wall.

"Good heavens, sir, but for me, anywhere . . ."

"Not anywhere, but on this sofa! Here's a sheet for you, a blanket, a pillow, take them" (Velchaninov took it all out of a wardrobe and hurriedly threw it to Pavel Pavlovich, who obediently held out his arm). "Make your bed immediately, immed-iate-ly!"

The loaded-down Pavel Pavlovich stood in the middle of the room, as if undecided, with a long, drunken smile on his drunken face; but at Velchaninov's repeated menacing cry, he suddenly started bustling about as fast as he could, moved the table aside, and, puffing, began to spread and smooth out the sheet. Velchaninov came over to help him; he was partly pleased with his guest's obedience and fright.

"Finish your glass and lie down," he commanded again; he felt he could not help but command. "Was it you who ordered wine sent for?"

"Myself, sir, for wine . . . I knew, Alexei Ivanovich, that you wouldn't send for more, sir."

"It's good that you knew that, but you need to learn still more. I tell you once again that I've taken measures now: I'll no longer suffer your clowning, nor yesterday's drunken kisses!"

"I myself understand, Alexei Ivanovich, that it was possible only once, sir," Pavel Pavlovich grinned.

Hearing this answer, Velchaninov, who was pacing the room, suddenly stopped almost solemnly in front of Pavel Pavlovich:

"Pavel Pavlovich, speak directly! You're intelligent, I acknowledge it again, but I assure you that you are on a false path! Speak directly, act directly, and, I give you my word of honor—I will answer to anything you like!"

Pavel Pavlovich again grinned his long smile, which alone was enough to enrage Velchaninov.

"Wait!" he cried again, "don't pretend, I can see through you! I repeat: I give you my word of honor that I am ready to answer to *everything,* and you will receive every possible satisfaction, that is, every, even the impossible! Oh, how I wish you would understand me! . . ."

"If you're so good, sir," Pavel Pavlovich cautiously moved closer to him, "then, sir, I'm very interested in what you mentioned yesterday about the predatory type, sir! . . ."

Velchaninov spat and again began pacing the room, still quicker than before.

"No, Alexei Ivanovich, sir, don't you spit, because I'm very interested and came precisely to verify . . . My tongue doesn't quite obey me, but forgive me, sir. Because about this 'predatory' type and the 'placid' one, sir, I myself read something in a magazine, in the criticism section[7]—I remembered it this morning . . . I'd simply forgotten it, sir, and, to tell the truth, I didn't understand it then, either. I precisely wished to clarify: the late Stepan Mikhailovich Bagautov, sir— was he 'predatory' or 'placid'? How to reckon him, sir?"

Velchaninov still kept silent, without ceasing to pace.

"The predatory type is the one," he suddenly stopped in fury, "is the man who would rather poison Bagautov in a glass, while 'drinking champagne' with him in the name of a pleasant encounter with him, as you drank with me yester-

day—and would not go accompanying his coffin to the cemetery, as you did today, devil knows out of which of your
hidden, underground, nasty strivings and clownings which be-
smirch only you yourself! You yourself!"

"Exactly right, he wouldn't go, sir," Pavel Pavlovich confirmed, "only why is it me, sir, that you're so . . ."

"It's not the man," Velchaninov, excited, was shouting
without listening, "not the man who imagines God knows
what to himself, sums up all justice and law, learns his offense
by rote, whines, clowns, minces, hangs on people's necks,
and—lo and behold—all his time gets spent on it! Is it true
that you wanted to hang yourself? Is it?"

"Maybe I blurted something out when I was drunk—I
don't remember, sir. It's somehow indecent, Alexei Ivanovich,
for us to go pouring poison into glasses. Besides being an
official in good standing—I'm not without capital, and I may
want to get married again, sir."

"And you'd be sent to hard labor."

"Well, yes, there's also that unpleasantness, sir, though in
the courts nowadays they introduce lots of mitigating circumstances. But I wanted to tell you a killingly funny little anecdote, Alexei Ivanovich, I remembered it in the coach earlier,
sir. You just said: 'Hangs on people's necks.' Maybe you remember Semyon Petrovich Livtsov, sir, he visited us in
T——— while you were there; well, he had a younger
brother, also considered a Petersburg young man, served in the
governor's office in V——— and also shone with various
qualities. He once had an argument with Golubenko, a colonel, at a gathering, in the presence of ladies, including the lady
of his heart, and reckoned himself insulted, but he swallowed
his offense and concealed it; and Golubenko meanwhile won
over the lady of his heart and offered her his hand. And what
do you think? This Livtsov—he even sincerely started a friendship with Golubenko, was reconciled with him completely,
and moreover, sir—got himself invited to be best man, held
the crown,[8] and once they came back from church, went up to
congratulate and kiss Golubenko, and in front of the whole

noble company, in front of the governor, in a tailcoat and curled hair himself, sir—he up and stabbed him in the gut with a knife—Golubenko went sprawling! His own best man, it's such a shame, sir! But that's not all! The main thing was that after stabbing him with the knife, he turned around: 'Ah, what have I done! Ah, what is it I've done!'—tears flow, he shakes, throws himself on all their necks, even the ladies', sir: 'Ah, what have I done! Ah, what is it I've done now!' heh, heh, heh! it's killing, sir. Only it was too bad about Golubenko; but he recovered from it, sir."

"I don't see why you've told this to me," Velchaninov frowned severely.

"But it's all on account of that, sir, that he did stab him with a knife, sir," Pavel Pavlovich tittered. "You can even see he's not the type, that he's a sop of a man, if he forgot decency itself out of fear and threw himself on ladies' necks in the presence of the governor—and yet he did stab him, sir, he got his own! It's only for that, sir."

"Get the hell out of here," Velchaninov suddenly screamed in a voice not his own, just as if something had come unhinged in him, "get out of here with your underground trash, you're underground trash yourself—thinks he can scare me—child-tormentor—mean man—scoundrel, scoundrel, scoundrel!" he shouted, forgetting himself and choking on every word.

Pavel Pavlovich cringed all over, the drunkenness even fell from him; his lips trembled.

"Is it me, Alexei Ivanovich, that you're calling a scoundrel—*you* calling *me,* sir?"

But Velchaninov had already recovered himself.

"I'm ready to apologize," he answered, after pausing briefly in gloomy reflection, "but only in the case that you yourself wish to be direct, and that at once."

"And in your place I'd apologize anyway, Alexei Ivanovich."

"Very well, so be it," Velchaninov again paused briefly, "I apologize to you; but you must agree, Pavel Pavlovich, that after all this I no longer reckon myself as owing to you, that is, I'm speaking with regard to the *whole* matter, and not only the present case."

"Never mind, sir, what is there to reckon?" Pavel Pavlovich grinned, looking down, however.

"And if so, all the better, all the better! Finish your wine and lie down, because I'm not letting you go even so . . .'"

"What of the wine, sir . . ." Pavel Pavlovich, as if a bit embarrassed, nevertheless went up to the table and began to finish his already long filled last glass. Perhaps he had drunk a lot before then, so that his hand shook now and he splashed some of the wine on the floor, on his shirt, and on his waistcoat, but he drank it to the bottom even so, just as if he were unable to leave it undrunk, and, having respectfully placed the empty glass on the table, obediently went over to his bed to undress.

"Wouldn't it be better . . . not to spend the night?" he said suddenly, for some reason or other, having taken one boot off already and holding it in his hands.

"No, not better!" Velchaninov replied irately, pacing the room tirelessly, without glancing at him.

The man undressed and lay down. A quarter of an hour later, Velchaninov also lay down and put out the candle.

He had trouble falling asleep. Something new, confusing the *matter* still more, appearing suddenly from somewhere, alarmed him now, and at the same time he felt that, for some reason, he was ashamed of this alarm. He was dozing off, but some sort of rustling suddenly awakened him. He turned at once to look at Pavel Pavlovich's bed. The room was dark (the curtains were fully drawn), but it seemed to him that Pavel Pavlovich was not lying down but had gotten up and was sitting on the bed.

"What's with you?" Velchaninov called.

"A shade, sir," Pavel Pavlovich uttered, barely audibly, after waiting a little.

"What's that? What kind of shade?"

"There, in that room, through the doorway, I saw as if a shade, sir."

"Whose shade?" Velchaninov asked, after a brief pause.

"Natalia Vassilievna's, sir."

Velchaninov stood on the rug and himself peeked through the hall into the other room, the door to which was always left open. There were no curtains on the windows there, only blinds, and so it was much brighter.

"There's nothing in that room, and you are drunk—lie down!" Velchaninov said, lay down, and wrapped himself in the blanket. Pavel Pavlovich did not say a word and lay down as well.

"And have you ever seen a shade before?" Velchaninov suddenly asked, some ten minutes later.

"I think I did once, sir," Pavel Pavlovich responded weakly and also after a while. Then silence fell again.

Velchaninov could not have said for certain whether he slept or not, but about an hour went by—and suddenly he turned over again: was it some kind of rustling that awakened him?—he did not know that either, but it seemed to him that amid the perfect darkness something was standing over him, white, not having reached him yet, but already in the middle of the room. He sat up in bed and stared for a whole minute.

"Is that you, Pavel Pavlovich?" he said in a weakened voice. His own voice, sounding suddenly in the silence and darkness, seemed somehow strange to him.

There came no reply, but there was no longer any doubt that someone was standing there.

"Is that you . . . Pavel Pavlovich?" he repeated more loudly, even so loudly that if Pavel Pavlovich had been peacefully asleep in his bed, he could not have failed to wake up and reply.

But again there came no reply, and instead it seemed to him that this white and barely distinguishable figure moved still closer to him. Then a strange thing happened: something in him suddenly as if came unhinged, just as earlier, and he shouted with all his might in the most absurd, enraged voice, choking on almost every word:

"If you, you drunken buffoon—dare merely to think—that you can—frighten me—I'll turn to the wall, cover my head with the blanket, and not turn around once during the whole night—to prove to you how greatly I value—even if you stand there till morning . . . buffoonishly . . . and I spit on you!"

And, having spat furiously in the direction of the presumed Pavel Pavlovich, he suddenly turned to the wall, wrapped himself, as he had said, in the blanket, and as if froze in that position without moving. A dead silence fell. Whether the shade was moving closer or remained where it was—he could not tell, but his heart was pounding—pounding—pounding . . . At least five full minutes went by; and suddenly, from two steps away, came the weak, quite plaintive voice of Pavel Pavlovich:

"Alexei Ivanovich, I got up to look for . . ." (and he named a most necessary household object). "I didn't find it there where I was . . . I wanted to look quietly by your bed, sir."

"Then why were you silent . . . when I shouted!" Velchaninov asked in a faltering voice, after waiting for about half a minute.

"I was frightened, sir. You shouted so . . . I got frightened, sir."

"It's in the corner to the left, toward the door, in the cupboard, light a candle . . ."

"I'll do without a candle, sir . . ." Pavel Pavlovich said humbly, going to the corner. "Do forgive me, Alexei Ivanovich, for troubling you so . . . I suddenly felt so drunk, sir . . ."

But the man made no reply. He went on lying face to the wall and lay like that for the whole night without turning once. Did he really want so much to keep his word and show his scorn?—He himself did not know what was happening to him; his nervous disorder turned, finally, almost into delirium, and for a long time he could not fall asleep. Waking up the next morning past nine o'clock, he suddenly gave a start and sat up in bed as if he had been pushed—Pavel Pavlovich was no longer in the room! All that was left was an empty, unmade bed, but the man himself had slipped away at daybreak.

"I just knew it!" Velchaninov slapped himself on the forehead.

X

At the Cemetery

The doctor's apprehensions proved justified, and Liza suddenly grew worse—much worse than Velchaninov and Klavdia Petrovna could have imagined the day before. In the morning Velchaninov found the sick girl still conscious, though all burning with fever; he insisted later that she smiled at him and even gave him her hot little hand. Whether this was true or he unwittingly invented it for himself as a consolation—he had no time to check; by nightfall the sick girl was already unconscious, and so it continued throughout her illness. On the tenth day after her move to the country, she died.

This was a sorrowful time for Velchaninov; the Pogoreltsevs even feared for him. The greater part of these difficult days he lived with them. In the very last days of Liza's illness, he spent whole hours sitting alone somewhere in a corner, apparently not thinking of anything; Klavdia Petrovna would come over to distract him, but he responded little, at times clearly finding it burdensome to talk with her. Klavdia Petrovna had not even expected that "all this would produce such an impression" on him. Most of all he was distracted by the children; with them he even laughed at times; but almost every hour he would get up from his chair and go on tiptoe to look at the sick girl. At times it seemed to him that she recognized him. He had no more hope for recovery than anyone else, yet he would not go far from the room in which Liza lay dying, and usually sat in the room next door.

A couple of times, however, during these days as well, he suddenly displayed an extreme activity: he would suddenly get up, rush to Petersburg to see doctors, invite the most famous ones, gather consultations. The second, and last, of these consultations took place on the eve of the sick girl's death. Some three days prior to that, Klavdia Petrovna had talked insistently with Velchaninov about the necessity of finally discovering the whereabouts of Mr. Trusotsky: "In case of a calamity, Liza could not even be buried without him." Velchaninov mumbled that he would write to him. Then old Pogoreltsev announced that he himself would find him through the police. Velchaninov finally wrote a two-line note and took it to the Pokrovsky Hotel. Pavel Pavlovich, as usual, was not at home, and he handed the note to Marya Sysoevna to be passed on.

Finally, Liza died, on a beautiful summer evening, together with the setting sun, and only then did Velchaninov seem to recover himself. When the dead girl was prepared, dressed in a festive white dress from one of Klavdia Petrovna's daughters, and laid out on the table in the drawing room,[9] with flowers in her little folded hands—he went up to Klavdia Petrovna and, flashing his eyes, announced to her that he would at once bring "the murderer" there as well. Ignoring advice that he wait till the next day, he immediately went to town.

He knew where to find Pavel Pavlovich; he had gone to Petersburg not for doctors only. At times during those days it had seemed to him that if he were to bring her father to the dying Liza, she, on hearing his voice, would recover herself; then, like a desperate man, he would start looking for him. Pavel Pavlovich's quarters were still in the rooming house, but there was no point even in asking there. "He doesn't spend the night or even come home for three days in a row," Marya Sysoevna reported, "and when by chance he comes back drunk, he spends less than an hour and then drags himself off again—quite haywire." A floorboy from the Pokrovsky Hotel told Velchaninov, among other things, that Pavel Pavlovich once used to visit some girls on Voznesensky Prospect. Velchaninov immediately found the girls. Showered with gifts and treats, these persons at once remembered their visitor, chiefly by the crape on his hat, and straight away denounced him, of course, for not coming to them anymore. One of them, Katya, undertook "to find Pavel Pavlovich whenever you like, because he never leaves Mashka Prostakova, and there's no bottom to his money, and this Mashka isn't Prostakova, she's Shystakova, and she's been in the hospital, and if she, Katya, wanted to, she could pack her off to Siberia at once, she'd only have to say the word." Katya, however, did not find him that time, but gave a firm promise for the next time. It was in her assistance that Velchaninov now placed his hopes.

Having reached town by ten o'clock, he immediately sent for her, paying where he had to for her absence, and set out with her on his search. He did not yet know himself what, in fact, he was going to do now with Pavel Pavlovich: kill him for something, or simply look for him, so as to inform him of his daughter's death and the need for his assistance in the funeral? First off they had no luck: it turned out that Mashka Shystakova had had a fight with Pavel Pavlovich two days before, and that some cashier had "smashed Pavel Pavlovich's head in with a bench." In short, for a long time he refused to be found and, finally, only at two o'clock in the morning, coming out of some establishment he had been directed to, did Velchaninov himself suddenly and unexpectedly run into him.

Pavel Pavlovich, completely drunk, was being led toward this establishment by two ladies; one of the ladies held him under the arm, and from behind they were accompanied by one stalwart and loose-limbed pretender, who was shouting at the top of his lungs and threatening Pavel Pavlovich terribly with some sort of horrors. He shouted, among other things, that he had "exploited him and poisoned his life." The matter, it seemed, had to do with some money; the ladies were hurrying and very afraid. Seeing Velchaninov, Pavel Pavlovich rushed to him with outstretched arms, shouting bloody murder:

"Brother, dear, protect me!"

At the sight of Velchaninov's athletic figure, the pretender instantly effaced himself; the triumphant Pavel Pavlovich brandished his fist after him and gave a cry of victory; here Velchaninov seized him furiously by the shoulders and, himself not knowing why, started shaking him with both hands, so that his teeth clacked. Pavel Pavlovich stopped shouting at once and stared at his torturer with dim-witted, drunken fright. Probably not knowing what else to do with him, Velchaninov firmly bent him down and sat him on a hitching post.

"Liza died!" he said to him.

Pavel Pavlovich, still not taking his eyes off him, sat on the hitching post, supported by one of the ladies. He understood, finally, and his face suddenly became somehow pinched.

"Died . . ." he whispered somehow strangely. Whether he grinned drunkenly with his long, nasty smile, or something went awry in his face, Velchaninov could not tell, but a moment later Pavel Pavlovich made an attempt to lift his trembling right hand so as to cross himself; the cross, however, did not come off, and the trembling hand sank down. A little later he slowly got up from the hitching post, caught hold of his lady, and, supported by her, went on his way, seemingly oblivious, as if Velchaninov were not there. But he seized him again by the shoulder.

"Do you understand, drunken monster, that without you it won't even be possible to bury her!" he cried, suffocating.

The man turned his head toward him.

"Remember . . . the artillery . . . lieutenant?" he mumbled, moving his tongue thickly.

"Wha-a-at?" Velchaninov screamed, shuddering painfully.

"There's the father for you! Go look for him . . . to bury . . ."

"You're lying!" Velchaninov cried like a lost man. "It's out of spite . . . I just knew you'd have it ready for me!"

Forgetting himself, he raised his terrible fist over Pavel Pavlovich's head. Another moment—and he would perhaps have killed him with one blow; the ladies shrieked and flew off, but Pavel Pavlovich did not bat an eye. Some sort of frenzy of the most beastly spite distorted his whole face.

"And do you know," he spoke much more firmly, almost as if not drunk, "our Russian ———?" (And he uttered a swearword most unfit for print.) "Well, take yourself there!" Then he tore violently from Velchaninov's grip, stumbled, and nearly fell. The ladies picked him up and this time ran, shrieking, and almost dragging Pavel Pavlovich with them. Velchaninov offered no pursuit.

The next day, at one o'clock in the afternoon, a quite decent middle-aged official in uniform came to the Pogoreltsevs' country house and politely handed Klavdia Petrovna a packet addressed to her, on behalf of Pavel Pavlovich Trusotsky. The packet contained a letter with an enclosed three hundred roubles and the necessary certificates concerning Liza. Pavel Pavlovich wrote briefly, exceedingly respectfully, and quite decently. He was quite grateful to Her Excellency Klavdia Petrovna for her virtuous concern with the orphan, for which God alone could reward her. He vaguely mentioned that, being extremely unwell, he was prevented from coming in person to bury his tenderly beloved and unfortunate daughter, and for that he placed all his hopes in Her Excellency's angelic goodness of soul. The three hundred roubles, as he further explained in the letter, were intended for the funeral and generally for the expenses incurred by the illness. If anything should be left of this sum, he most humbly and respectfully begged that it be employed for eternal commemoration for the repose of the soul of the departed Liza. The official who delivered the letter was unable to explain more; it even followed from certain of his words that it was only Pavel Pavlovich's insistent request that had made him take it upon himself personally to deliver the packet to Her Excellency. Pogoreltsev almost took offense at the phrase "expenses incurred by the illness," and resolved, having set aside fifty roubles for the burial—since it was impossible to forbid a father to bury his own child—to return the remaining two hundred and fifty roubles to Mr. Trusotsky immediately. Klavdia Petrovna decided in the end to return, not the two hundred and fifty roubles, but the receipt from the cemetery church stating that this money had been received for the eternal commemoration of the soul of the departed maiden Elizaveta. The receipt was afterward given to Velchaninov, to be handed on immediately; he sent it by mail to the rooming house.

After the funeral, he disappeared from the country house.

For two whole weeks he hung around the city without any purpose, alone, bumping into people in his pensiveness. At times he spent whole days lying stretched on his sofa, forgetful of the most ordinary things. The Pogoreltsevs sent many times asking him to come; he would promise and at once forget. Klavdia Petrovna even called on him personally, but did not find him at home. The same happened with his lawyer; and yet the lawyer had something to tell him: he had settled the lawsuit quite adroitly, and the adversaries had come to a peaceful agreement, with a very insignificant part of the disputed inheritance as compensation. It remained only to obtain the consent of Velchaninov himself. Finding him home at last, the lawyer was surprised at the extreme listlessness and indifference with which he, still recently so troublesome a client, heard him out.

The hottest days of July came, but Velchaninov was forgetful of time itself. The pain of his grief accumulated in his soul like a ripe abscess, and became clearer to him every moment in his tormentingly conscious thought. His chief suffering consisted in Liza's not having had time to know him and dying without knowing how tormentingly he loved her! The whole purpose of his life, which had flashed before him in such a joyful light, suddenly faded in eternal darkness. This purpose would precisely have consisted—he thought about it all the time now—in Liza's feeling his love upon her constantly, every day, every hour, and all her life. "No one has had or ever could have a higher purpose!" he pondered at times in gloomy rapture. "If there are other purposes, none can be holier than this one!" "By Liza's love," he dreamed, "my whole stinking and useless life would have been purified and redeemed; instead of myself, idle, depraved, and obsolete—I would have cherished for life a pure and beautiful being, and for this being everything would have been forgiven me, and I would have forgiven myself everything."

All these *conscious* thoughts came to him always inseparably from the vivid memory of the dead child, always close, and always striking his soul. He re-created for himself her pale little face, recalled its every expression; he remembered her in the coffin amid the flowers, and earlier, unconscious in fever, with open, fixed eyes. He remembered suddenly that, when she was already laid out on the table, he had noticed one of her fingers which, God knows why, had turned black during her illness; he had been so struck by it then, and had felt such pity for this poor little finger, that it had entered his mind right there and then, for the first time, to find Pavel Pavlovich at once and kill him—until that time he "had been as if insensible." Was it insulted pride that had tormented this child's little heart, or three months of suffering from a father who had suddenly exchanged love for hatred and insulted her with a shameful word, who had laughed at her fear, and had thrown her away, finally, to strangers? All this he pictured ceaselessly to himself, varying it in a thousand ways. "Do you know what Liza was for me?"—he suddenly recalled the drunken Trusotsky's exclamation, and he felt that this exclamation had no longer been clowning, but the truth, and there had been love in it. "How, then, could this monster be so cruel to a child he loved so, and is it probable?" But he hastened to drop this question each time, as if waving it away; there was something terrible in this question, something unbearable for him and— unresolved.

One day, and almost not remembering how himself, he wandered into the cemetery where Liza was buried and found her little grave. He had not been to the cemetery once since the funeral; he kept imagining that it would be too painful and had not dared to go. But, strangely, when he bent down to her little grave and kissed it, he suddenly felt better. It was a clear evening, the sun was setting; round about, near the graves, lush green grass was growing; not far away amid the eglantines, a bee buzzed; the flowers and wreaths left on Liza's little grave by the children and Klavdia Petrovna after the burial still lay there, half their leaves blown off. Even some sort of hope, for the first time in a long while, refreshed his heart. "What lightness!" he thought, feeling the silence of the cemetery and gazing at the clear, serene sky. A flood of some pure, untroubled faith in something filled his soul. "Liza has sent it to me, it's she talking to me," came the thought.

It was already getting quite dark as he went back home from the cemetery. Not too far from the cemetery gates, on the road, in a low wooden building, there was something like a chophouse or pub; through the open window clients could be seen sitting at tables. It suddenly seemed to him that one of them, placed just by the window, was—Pavel Pavlovich, and that he had also seen him and was peeking curiously at him through the window. He went on and soon heard someone coming after him; it was in fact Pavel Pavlovich running to catch up with him; it must have been the conciliatory expression on Velchaninov's face that had attracted and encouraged him as he looked out the window. Having overtaken him, he smiled timorously, but now it was not his former drunken smile; he was even not drunk at all.

"Good evening," he said.

"Good evening," Velchaninov replied.

XI

Pavel Pavlovich Gets Married

Having replied with this "good evening," he became surprised at himself. It seemed terribly strange to him that he should meet this man now with no anger at all, and that there was something quite different in his feelings for him at that moment and even a sort of urge for something new.

"Such a pleasant evening," Pavel Pavlovich said, peeking into his eyes.

"You haven't left yet?" Velchaninov said, as if he were not asking but merely pondering, and continued to walk.

"I had a slow time of it, but—I got the post, sir, with a promotion. I'll be leaving for certain the day after tomorrow."

"You got the post?" he did ask this time.

"And why not, sir?" Pavel Pavlovich's face suddenly twisted.

"I said it just . . ." Velchaninov dodged and, frowning,

looked at Pavel Pavlovich out of the corner of his eye. To his surprise, the clothing, the hat with crape, and the whole appearance of Mr. Trusotsky were incomparably more decent than two weeks before. "Why was he sitting in that pub?" he kept thinking.

"I was meaning to tell you, Alexei Ivanovich, about another joy of mine," Pavel Pavlovich began again.

"Joy?"

"I'm getting married, sir."

"What?"

"Joy follows grief, sir, it's always so in life. Alexei Ivanovich, sir, I'd like very much . . . but—I don't know, maybe you're in a hurry now, because you look as if . . ."

"Yes, I'm in a hurry and . . . yes, I'm not well."

He suddenly wanted terribly to get away; the readiness for some new feeling instantly vanished.

"And I would have liked, sir . . ."

Pavel Pavlovich did not finish saying what he would have liked; Velchaninov kept silent.

"Afterward, then, sir, if only we meet . . ."

"Yes, yes, afterward, afterward," Velchaninov muttered rapidly, not looking at him or stopping. They were silent for another minute; Pavel Pavlovich went on walking beside him.

"In that case, good-bye, sir," he spoke finally.

"Good-bye. I wish you . . ."

Velchaninov returned home thoroughly upset again. The encounter with "this man" was too much for him. Going to bed, he thought again: "Why was he near the cemetery?"

The next morning he made up his mind, finally, to go and visit the Pogoreltsevs, reluctantly made up his mind; sympathy from anyone, even the Pogoreltsevs, was much too heavy for him now. But they were so worried about him that he absolutely had to go. He suddenly imagined that he would be very embarrassed for some reason on first meeting them. "To go or not to go?" he thought, hurrying to finish his breakfast, when suddenly, to his extreme amazement, Pavel Pavlovich walked in.

Despite yesterday's encounter, Velchaninov could never have imagined that this man might someday call on him again, and he was so taken aback that he stared at him without knowing what to say. But Pavel Pavlovich took things in hand, greeted him, and sat down in the same chair he had sat in three weeks earlier during his last visit. Velchaninov suddenly remembered that visit especially vividly. Uneasily and with disgust, he looked at his visitor.

"Surprised, sir?" Pavel Pavlovich began, divining Velchaninov's gaze.

Generally he seemed much more casual than the day before, and at the same time it could be seen that his timidity was greater. His external appearance was especially curious. Mr. Trusotsky was dressed not only decently but stylishly—in a light summer jacket, tight-fitting, light-colored trousers, a light-colored waistcoat; gloves, a gold lorgnette, which for some reason suddenly appeared, linen—all impeccable; he even smelled of perfume. There was in his whole figure something at once ridiculous and suggestive of some strange and unpleasant thought.

"Of course, Alexei Ivanovich," he went on, cringing, "I surprised you by coming, sir, and—I can feel it, sir. But between people, so I think, sir, there always remains—and, in my opinion, must remain—something higher, don't you think, sir? That is, higher with regard to all conventions and even the very unpleasantnesses that may come of it . . . don't you think, sir?"

"Pavel Pavlovich, say it all quickly and without ceremony," Velchaninov frowned.

"In two words, sir," Pavel Pavlovich hurried, "I'm getting married and am presently going to my fiancée, right now. They're also in the country, sir. I wished to be granted the profound honor, so as to dare acquaint you with this family, sir, and I've come with an exceptional request" (Pavel Pavlovich humbly bowed his head), "to ask you to accompany me, sir . . ."

"Accompany you where?" Velchaninov goggled his eyes.

"To them, sir, that is, to their country house, sir. Forgive me, I'm speaking as if in a fever and may have become confused; but I'm so afraid you'll say no, sir . . ."

And he looked lamentably at Velchaninov.

"You want me to go with you now to your fiancée?" Velchaninov repeated, casting a quick glance over him and believing neither his ears nor his eyes.

"Yes, sir," Pavel Pavlovich suddenly grew terribly timid. "Don't be angry, Alexei Ivanovich, this isn't boldness, sir; I only beg you most humbly and exceptionally. I dreamed that you might perhaps not want to say no to me in this . . ."

"First of all, it's utterly impossible," Velchaninov squirmed uneasily.

"It's just my exceeding wish and nothing more, sir," the man went on imploring. "I also won't conceal that there is a reason as well, sir. But about this reason I would like to reveal only later, sir, and now I only beg exceptionally . . ."

And he even got up from his chair out of deference.

"But in any case it's impossible, you must agree . . ." Velchaninov also got up from his place.

"It's very possible, Alexei Ivanovich, sir—I planned to get you acquainted at the same time, as a friend, sir; and secondly, you're acquainted there without that, sir; it's to Zakhlebinin's country house. State councillor Zakhlebinin, sir."

"What's that?" Velchaninov cried out. It was the same state councillor he had been looking for, about a month ago, and had been unable to catch at home, who had acted, as it turned out, in favor of the adverse party in his lawsuit.

"Why, yes, of course," Pavel Pavlovich smiled, as if encouraged by Velchaninov's extreme astonishment, "the same one, you remember, you were walking along and talking with, while I watched you and stood on the other side; I was waiting then to approach him after you. Some twenty years back we even served together, sir, but at the time when I wanted to approach after you, sir, I still didn't have this thought. It's only now that it came suddenly, about a week ago, sir."

"But, listen, it seems this is quite a respectable family?" Velchaninov was naively surprised.

"So what, sir, if they're respectable?" Pavel Pavlovich's face twisted.

"No, naturally, I don't mean that . . . but as far as I could tell, having been there . . ."

"They remember, they remember, sir, that you were," Pavel Pavlovich picked up joyfully, "only you couldn't see the family then, sir; and he remembers and respects you. I spoke about you deferentially with them."

"But how can it be, if you've been a widower for only three months?"[10]

"Oh, the wedding's not right now, sir; the wedding's in nine or ten months, so that exactly a year of mourning will have gone by, sir. Believe me, it's all just fine, sir. First of all, Fedosei Petrovich has known me even since my youngest years, he knew my late spouse, how I lived, and what my reputation is, sir, and, finally, I have a fortune, and here also I've now obtained a post and a promotion—so all this carries weight, sir."

"It's his daughter, then?"

"I'll tell you all about it in detail, sir," Pavel Pavlovich hunched himself up pleasantly, "allow me to light a cigarette. Besides, you'll see for yourself today. First of all, such men of affairs as Fedosei Petrovich are sometimes highly valued in the service here in Petersburg, if they manage to attract attention, sir. But apart from the salary and the rest—supplements, premiums, emoluments, dinner allowances, or else one-time bonuses, sir—there's nothing, that is, nothing substantial, sir, that would constitute a capital. They live well, but it's impossible to save, what with the family, sir. Consider for yourself: Fedosei Petrovich has eight girls, and only one little son. If he were to die now—all that's left is a skimpy pension, sir. And there are eight girls—no, consider, just consider, sir: if it's a pair of shoes for each of them, that already comes to something! Of the eight girls, five are already marriageable, sir,[11] the eldest is twenty-four—(the loveliest girl, you'll see for yourself, sir!), and the sixth one is fifteen, she's still in school. For the five older girls suitors must be found, which ought if possible to be done well ahead of time, so the father has to take them out, sir—and what is the cost of that, may I ask, sir? And suddenly I appear, the first suitor in their home, sir, and known to them beforehand, that is, in the sense that I do actually have a fortune. Well, there you have it, sir."

Pavel Pavlovich explained with rapture.

"You proposed to the oldest one?"

"N-no, I . . . not to the oldest one; I proposed to the sixth one, the one that's still studying in school."

"What?" Velchaninov grinned inadvertently. "But you say she's fifteen years old!"

"Fifteen now, sir; but in nine months she'll be sixteen, sixteen years and three months, sir, so why not? And since for the moment it's all inappropriate, nothing's been made public yet, only with the parents . . . Believe me, it's all just fine, sir!"

"So it hasn't been decided yet?"

"No, it's decided, everything's decided. Believe me, it's all just fine, sir."

"And she knows?"

"That is, it's only for appearance, for propriety's sake, that it hasn't been talked about, as it were; but how could she not know, sir?" Pavel Pavlovich narrowed his eyes pleasantly. "So, then, will you make me a happy man, Alexei Ivanovich?" he concluded, terribly timidly.

"But what should I go there for? However," he added hastily, "since I'm not going in any case, don't offer me any reasons."

"Alexei Ivanovich . . ."

"But do you think I can really sit down beside you and go!"

A disgusted and hostile feeling came back to him again after the momentary diversion of Pavel Pavlovich's babble about his fiancée. Another minute, it seemed, and he would chase him out altogether. He was even angry with himself for something.

"Sit down, Alexei Ivanovich, sit down beside me and you won't regret it!" Pavel Pavlovich entreated in a soulful voice.

"No, no, no!" he waved his hands, catching Velchaninov's impatient and resolute gesture, "Alexei Ivanovich, Alexei Ivanovich, don't decide yet, sir! I see that you have perhaps misunderstood me: I realize only too well that I am not friends with you, nor you with me, sir; I'm not so absurd as not to realize that, sir. And that this present favor I am begging of you doesn't count for anything in the future. And I myself will leave completely the day after tomorrow, sir—altogether, sir, so it's as if there was nothing. Let this day be only one occasion, sir. I came to you basing my hopes on the nobility of certain special feelings of your heart, Alexei Ivanovich—precisely on those very feelings that may have been stirred in your heart recently, sir . . . I believe I'm speaking clearly, sir—or not quite?"

Pavel Pavlovich's agitation had grown in the extreme. Velchaninov looked at him strangely.

"You're begging for some favor on my part," he asked, pondering, "and being terribly insistent—I find that suspicious; I want to know more."

"The whole favor consists only in your coming with me. And afterward, when we've come back, I'll lay out everything before you as if at confession. Trust me, Alexei Ivanovich!"

But Velchaninov still kept refusing, and the more stubbornly as he felt in himself a certain heavy, spiteful thought. This wicked thought had already long been stirring in him, from the very beginning, when Pavel Pavlovich had only just announced about his fiancée: whether from simple curiosity, or some still entirely vague inclination, he felt drawn—to agree. And the more drawn he was, the more he defended himself. He was sitting, leaning on his hand, and reflecting. Pavel Pavlovich fussed about and implored him.

"All right, I'll go," he suddenly agreed uneasily and almost anxiously, getting up from his place. Pavel Pavlovich was boundlessly overjoyed.

"No, Alexei Ivanovich, you get yourself dressed up now," he fussed joyfully around Velchaninov, who was getting dressed, "nicely, the way you know how."

"Strange man," Velchaninov thought to himself, "why is he letting himself in for it?"

"And this is not the only favor I expect from you, Alexei Ivanovich, sir. Since you've given your consent, also be my guide, sir."

"Meaning what?"

"Meaning that there's a big question, sir: about the crape, sir? What's more appropriate: to take it off, or to keep the crape?"

"As you like."

"No, I want your decision—that is, if you were wearing crape, sir? My own thought was that if I keep it, it will point to a constancy of feelings, sir, and so will be a flattering recommendation."

"Take it off, naturally."

"Naturally, you say?" Pavel Pavlovich pondered. "No, I'd rather keep it, sir . . ."

"As you like."—"Anyhow he doesn't trust me, that's good," thought Velchaninov.

They went out; Pavel Pavlovich contemplated the dressed-up Velchaninov with satisfaction; it even seemed as if more respect and importance showed in his face. Velchaninov marveled at him and still more at himself. By the gate an excellent carriage stood waiting for them.

"And you've got a carriage all ready? So you were sure I'd go?"

"I hired the carriage for myself, sir, but I was almost certain you'd agree to go," Pavel Pavlovich responded with the look of a perfectly happy man.

"Eh, Pavel Pavlovich," Velchaninov laughed somehow vexedly when they were already settled and starting out, "aren't you a bit too sure of me?"

"But it's not for you, Alexei Ivanovich, it's not for you to tell me I'm a fool on account of that?" Pavel Pavlovich replied in a firm and soulful voice.

"And Liza?" thought Velchaninov, and at once dropped the thought, as if fearing some blasphemy. And suddenly he seemed so paltry to himself, so insignificant at that moment; the thought that was tempting him seemed such a small, such a nasty little thought . . . and he wanted at all costs to drop everything again and get out of the carriage right then, even if he had to beat Pavel Pavlovich because of it. But the man started to speak and the temptation again gripped his heart.

"Alexei Ivanovich, do you know how to judge precious stones, sir?"

"What precious stones?"

"Diamonds, sir."

"I do."

"I'd like to bring a little present. Guide me: should I do it, or not?"

"In my opinion, you shouldn't."

"But I'd very much like to, sir," Pavel Pavlovich squirmed, "only what should I buy, sir? A whole set—that is, brooch, earrings, and bracelet—or just one thing?"

"How much do you want to spend?"

"Oh, some four or five hundred roubles, sir."

"Oof!"

"Is it too much?" Pavel Pavlovich roused himself.

"Buy just a bracelet, for a hundred roubles."

Pavel Pavlovich was even upset. He wanted terribly to spend more and buy the "whole" set. He insisted. They stopped at a store. It ended, however, with their buying only a bracelet, and not the one Pavel Pavlovich wanted, but one pointed out by Velchaninov. Pavel Pavlovich wanted to take both. When the shopkeeper, after asking a hundred and seventy-five roubles for the bracelet, went down to a hundred and fifty—he was even vexed; it would have been a pleasure for him to spend two hundred, had he been asked to, so much did he want to spend more.

"Never mind my being in such a hurry with presents," he poured himself out in rapture as they drove on, "it's not high society, it's simple there, sir. Innocence likes little presents," he smiled slyly and merrily. "You grinned just now, Alexei Ivanovich, at the mention of fifteen years; but that was just what hit me on the head—precisely that she still goes to school, with a little book bag in her hand, with notebooks and little pens, heh, heh! It was the little book bag that captivated my thoughts! In fact, it's for that innocence, Alexei Ivanovich. For me it's not so much a matter of the beauty of her face, but that innocence, sir. She giggles there in a corner with a girl-friend, and how they laugh, and my God! And over what, sir: all that laughter is because the kitty jumped from the chest onto the bed and curled up . . . It really smells of fresh apples there, sir! Shouldn't I take the crape off?"

"As you like."

"I will!" He took off his hat, tore the crape from it, and threw it out on the road. Velchaninov saw the brightest hope shining in his face as he put his hat back on his bald head.

"But can he in fact be like this?" he thought, now genu-inely angry. "Can it be that there's no *trick* in his inviting me? Can he in fact be counting on my nobility?" he went on, almost offended by the last supposition. "What is he, a buf-foon, a fool, or an 'eternal husband'? But this is impossible, finally! . . ."

XII

At the Zakhlebinins'

The Zakhlebinins were actually a "very respectable family," as Velchaninov had put it earlier, and Zakhlebinin himself was quite a solid official and a visible one. Everything that Pavel Pavlovich had said about their income was also true: "They live well, it seems, but if the man were to die, there would be nothing left."

Old Zakhlebinin met Velchaninov splendidly and amicably, and from a former "enemy" turned entirely into a friend.

"My congratulations, it's better this way," he began speak-ing with a pleasant and dignified air. "I myself insisted on a

peaceful settlement, and Pyotr Karlovich" (Velchaninov's lawyer) "is pure gold in that regard. So then? You'll get about
sixty thousand and without any fuss, without temporizing,
without quarrels. Otherwise the case might have dragged on
for three years!"

Velchaninov was introduced at once to Mme. Zakhlebinin,
a rather spread-out old lady, with a simplish and tired face.
The girls also began sailing out, singly or in pairs. But far too
many girls appeared; gradually some ten or twelve of them
assembled—Velchaninov even lost count; some came in, others left. But among them were many friends from neighboring
houses. The Zakhlebinins' country place—a big wooden
house, in some unknown but fanciful taste, added on to at
various times—enjoyed the use of a big garden. But three or
four other houses gave onto this garden from different sides,
so that this big garden served as a common one, which naturally contributed to the closeness between the girls and their
summer neighbors. From the first words of the conversation,
Velchaninov noticed that he had been expected there and that
his arrival in the quality of Pavel Pavlovich's friend, wishing to
become acquainted, had been all but solemnly announced. His
keen, experienced eye in such matters soon discerned something even peculiar here: from the much too amiable reception
of the parents, from a certain peculiar look about the girls and
their dress (though, incidentally, it was a feast day), the suspicion flashed in him that Pavel Pavlovich had tricked him, and
might very well have suggested here, naturally without putting
it directly into words, something like the notion of him as a
bored bachelor, of "good society," with a fortune, who might
very, very well suddenly decide, at last, to "put an end to it"
and settle down—"the more so as he has also received an
inheritance." It seemed that the oldest Mlle. Zakhlebinin,
Katerina Fedoseevna, the one who was twenty-four and of
whom Pavel Pavlovich had spoken as a lovely person, had been
more or less tuned to this note. She stood out among her
sisters especially by her attire and some sort of original arrangement of her fluffy hair. The sisters and all the other girls

looked as if they, too, already knew firmly that Velchaninov was becoming acquainted "on account of Katya" and had come to "have a look" at her. Their glances and even certain phrases that flashed by inadvertently in the course of the day, later confirmed him in this surmise. Katerina Fedoseevna was a tall blonde, plump to the point of luxuriousness, with an extremely sweet face, of an apparently quiet and unenterprising, even drowsy, character. "Strange that such a girl has stayed like this so long," Velchaninov thought involuntarily, studying her with pleasure. "Granted she has no dowry and will soon spread out altogether, but meanwhile there are so many who love that . . ." The rest of the sisters were none too bad either, and among the girlfriends there flashed several amusing and even pretty little faces. This began to amuse him; and anyhow he had come with special thoughts.

Nadezhda Fedoseevna, the sixth one, the schoolgirl and supposed fiancée of Pavel Pavlovich, made them wait. Velchaninov waited for her with impatience, marveling at himself and chuckling inwardly. Finally she appeared, and not without effect, accompanied by a pert and sharp girlfriend, Marya Nikitishna, a brunette with a laughing face, of whom, as it turned out at once, Pavel Pavlovich was extremely afraid. This Marya Nikitishna, already a girl of twenty-three, a banterer and even a wit, was governess of the little children in the family of some neighbors and acquaintances, and had long been considered like one of their own at the Zakhlebinins', where the girls valued her terribly. It was evident that she was also especially necessary now for Nadya. From the first glance, Velchaninov could see that the girls, and even the girlfriends, were all against Pavel Pavlovich, while from the second moment after Nadya's appearance, he decided that she *hated* him. He also noticed that Pavel Pavlovich did not perceive it at all, or else did not wish to perceive it. Indisputably, Nadya was better than all her sisters—a small brunette with the air of a wild thing and the boldness of a nihilist; a thievish little demon with fiery eyes, a lovely, though often wicked, smile, amazing lips and teeth, slim, slender, with a nascent thought in the ardent expression of her face, at the same time still quite childish. Her fifteen years spoke in her every step, her every word. It turned out later that Pavel Pavlovich had actually seen her for the first time with an oilcloth book bag in her hand, but now she no longer carried it.

The giving of the bracelet was a complete failure and even produced a disagreeable impression. Pavel Pavlovich, as soon as he saw his fiancée come in, approached her at once with a grin. He offered his gift under the pretext of "the agreeable pleasure felt by him the previous time on the occasion of the agreeable romance sung by Nadezhda Fedoseevna at the piano . . ." He became flustered, did not finish, and stood like a lost man, reaching out and thrusting into Nadezhda Fedoseevna's hand the case with the bracelet, while she, not wanting to take it, and blushing with shame and wrath, kept putting her hands behind her back. She boldly turned to her mother, whose face expressed embarrassment, and said loudly:

"I don't want to take it, *Maman!*"

"Take it and say thank you," the father said with calm sternness, but he, too, was displeased. "Unnecessary, unnecessary!" he muttered didactically to Pavel Pavlovich. Nadya, since there was nothing to be done, took the case and, lowering her eyes, curtsied as little girls do, that is, she suddenly plopped down and suddenly bounced up at once, as if on a spring. One of the sisters came over to look, and Nadya gave her the case, still unopened, thereby showing that she herself did not even want to look. The bracelet was taken out and handed around; but they all looked at it silently, and some even mockingly. Only the mother murmured that it was a very nice bracelet. Pavel Pavlovich was ready to fall through the earth.

Velchaninov came to the rescue.

He suddenly started talking, loudly and eagerly, seizing the first thought that came to him, and before five minutes had passed, he already held the attention of everyone in the drawing room. He had learned magnificently the art of babbling in society, that is, the art of appearing perfectly simple-hearted and at the same time making it seem that he took his listeners for people as simple-hearted as himself. With extreme naturalness he could pretend, when necessary, to be the merriest and happiest of men. He knew how to place very deftly a witty and provocative phrase, a merry hint, a funny quip, and to do it as if quite inadvertently, as if without noticing—whereas the witticism, the quip, and the conversation itself had been prepared long ago, learned, and put to use more than once. But at the present moment his art was seconded by nature itself: he felt that he was in the spirit, that something was drawing him; he felt in himself a complete and triumphant assurance that in a few moments all these eyes would be turned on him, that all these people would be listening only to him, talking only to him, laughing only at what he said. And indeed laughter was soon heard, others gradually mixed in the conversation—he had perfect command of the skill of drawing others into a conversation—and three or four voices could already be heard talking at once. The dull and tired face of Mrs. Zakhlebinin lit up almost with joy; the same with Katerina Fedoseevna, who listened and looked as if mesmerized. Scowling, Nadya studied him keenly; one could note that she had been prejudiced against him. This fired Velchaninov up still more. The "wicked" Marya Nikitishna did manage to slip into the conversation a rather pointed barb on his account; she invented and insisted that Pavel Pavlovich had recommended him there the day before as a childhood friend of his, thus adding—and hinting at it clearly—a whole seven extra years to his age. Yet the wicked Marya Nikitishna liked him, too. Pavel Pavlovich was decidedly taken aback. He had, of course, some notion of the resources his friend possessed, and in the beginning was even glad of his success, giggling along and mixing in the conversation himself; but for some reason he gradually began to lapse as if into reflection, even, finally, into despondency, which showed clearly on his alarmed physiognomy.

"Well, you're the sort of guest who doesn't need to be entertained," old Zakhlebinin cheerily decided at last, getting up from his chair to go to his room upstairs, where, despite the feast day, he had a few business papers ready for going over, "and, imagine, I considered you the gloomiest hypochondriac of all our young people. How wrong one can be!"

In the drawing room stood a grand piano; Velchaninov asked who studied music, and suddenly turned to Nadya.

"You sing, it seems?"

"Who told you so?" Nadya snapped.

"Pavel Pavlovich said so earlier."

"Not so; I only sing for a joke; I have no voice."

"I have no voice either, but I do sing."

"So you'll sing for us? Well, then I'll sing for you, too," Nadya flashed her eyes, "only not now, but after dinner. I can't stand music," she added, "I'm sick of this piano; all this playing and singing here from morning till night—Katya's more than enough herself."

Velchaninov seized on the phrase at once, and it turned out that Katerina Fedoseevna was the only one of them all who seriously studied piano. He immediately turned to her with a request to play. Everyone was evidently pleased that he had turned to Katya, and *Maman* even blushed with satisfaction. Katerina Fedoseevna rose, smiling, and went to the grand piano, but suddenly, unexpectedly for herself, blushed all over, and suddenly felt terribly ashamed that, big as she was, already twenty-four years old, and so plump, here she was blushing like a little girl—and all this was written on her face as she sat down to play. She played something by Haydn, and played it very accurately, though without expression; but she turned shy. When she finished, Velchaninov started praising terribly, not her but Haydn, and especially the little piece she had played—and she was obviously so pleased, she listened so gratefully and happily to this praise not of herself but of Haydn, that Velchaninov involuntarily looked at her more gently and attentively. "Eh, aren't you a nice one?" shone in his eyes—and everyone understood this glance as if at once, especially Katerina Fedoseevna herself.

"A nice garden you've got," he suddenly addressed them all, looking through the glass door to the balcony. "You know, let's all go out to the garden!"

"Let's go, let's go!" came joyful squeals—just as if he had guessed the main general wish.

They were in the garden until dinner. Mrs. Zakhlebinin, who had long been wanting to sleep, also could not help herself and went out with everyone else, but sensibly stayed to sit and rest on the balcony, where she dozed off at once. In the garden, the mutual relations between Velchaninov and all the girls became friendlier still. He noticed that two or three very young men joined them from neighboring houses; one was a university student, another merely a high school boy. These two sprang over at once each to *his own* girl, and it was evident that they had come for their sake; the third "young man," a very gloomy and ruffled twenty-year-old boy in enormous blue spectacles, began hurriedly and frowningly exchanging whispers with Marya Nikitishna and Nadya. He sternly looked Velchaninov over and seemed to consider it his duty to treat him with extraordinary disdain. Some girls suggested that they go ahead and start playing. To Velchaninov's question about what games they played, they replied that they played all games, including fox and hounds, but that in the evening they would play proverbs, that is, where everybody sits down and one person stands apart for a while; all those sitting down choose a proverb, for instance: "Slow and steady wins the race," and when the person is called back, each one in turn has to prepare and tell him a sentence. The first one has to give a sentence containing the word "slow," the second a sentence containing the word "steady," and so on. And the person has to pick out all these words and from them guess the proverb.

"It must be great fun," observed Velchaninov.

"Oh, no, it's quite boring," two or three voices answered at once.

"Or else we play theater," Nadya observed, addressing him. "See that big tree with the bench around it? There, behind the tree, is like backstage, the actors sit there—say, a king, a queen, a princess, a young man—whatever anyone likes; each one comes out whenever he has a mind to and says whatever occurs to him, and something or other comes out."

"But how nice!" Velchaninov praised once more.

"Oh, no, it's quite boring! Each time it comes out as fun in the beginning, but by the end it turns senseless each time, because nobody knows how to finish; though maybe with you it would be more amusing. And we thought you were Pavel Pavlovich's friend, but it turns out he was simply boasting. I'm very glad you came . . . owing to a certain circumstance," she looked very seriously and meaningly at Velchaninov and at once stepped over beside Marya Nikitishna.

"There'll be a game of proverbs this evening," one girl-friend, whom he had scarcely noticed till then and had not yet exchanged a word with, whispered confidentially to Velchani-nov, "and this evening everybody will laugh at Pavel Pavlo-vich, so you must, too."

"Ah, how nice of you to come, we're so bored here other-wise," another girlfriend said to him amiably, one he had not yet noticed at all, and who appeared from God knows where, a little redhead with freckles, her face flushed in a terribly funny way from walking and the heat.

Pavel Pavlovich's uneasiness grew greater and greater. In the garden, toward the end, Velchaninov succeeded completely in becoming close with Nadya; she no longer peered at him scowlingly as earlier and seemed to have set aside the idea of studying him more closely, but laughed, jumped, squealed, and even seized him by the hand once or twice; she was terri-bly happy, and went on paying not the slightest attention to Pavel Pavlovich, as if not noticing him. Velchaninov was con-vinced that there existed a positive conspiracy against Pavel Pavlovich; Nadya and a crowd of girls would draw Velchani-nov to one side, while other girlfriends under various pretexts lured Pavel Pavlovich to the other; but he would tear away and at once run headlong straight to them—that is, to Velchani-nov and Nadya—and suddenly thrust his bald and anxiously eavesdropping head between them. Toward the end, he was not even embarrassed; the naivety of his gestures and move-ments was at times astonishing. Velchaninov could not help paying special attention once again to Katerina Fedoseevna; by then it had, of course, become clear to her that he had come not at all for her sake and was already much too interested in Nadya; but her face was as sweet and good-natured as before. She seemed to be happy in the fact alone that she, too, was near them and could listen to what the new visitor was saying; she herself, poor dear, had never known how to mix adroitly in conversation.

"And how nice your sister Katerina Fedoseevna is!" Velchaninov suddenly said to Nadya on the quiet.

"Katya? Why, there couldn't be a kinder soul than hers! She's an angel for us all, I'm in love with her," the girl replied rapturously.

Finally, at five o'clock, dinner was served, and it was also very noticeable that the dinner had been prepared not in the usual way, but especially for the visitor. There were two or three dishes obviously in addition to what was usually served, rather sophisticated ones, and one of them something altogether unfamiliar, so that no one could even put a name to it. Besides the usual table wines, a bottle of Tokay also appeared, obviously thought up for the visitor; toward the end of dinner champagne was served for some reason. Old Zakhlebinin, having drunk one glass too many, was in the most sunny-minded mood and was ready to laugh at everything Velchaninov said. The end was that Pavel Pavlovich finally could not help himself: carried away by the competition, he also suddenly decided to utter some pun, and so he did: from the end of the table where he sat by Mme. Zakhlebinin, the loud laughter of overjoyed girls suddenly came.

"Papa, Papa! Pavel Pavlovich has also made a pun," two of the middle Zakhlebinin girls cried with one voice, "he says we're 'young misses one always misses . . .' "

"Ah, so he's punning, too? Well, what pun has he made?" the old man responded in a solemn voice, turning patronizingly to Pavel Pavlovich and smiling beforehand at the anticipated pun.

"But that's what he said, that we're 'young misses one always misses.' "

"Y-yes! Well, so what?" the old man still did not understand and smiled still more good-naturedly in anticipation.

"Oh, Papa, what's the matter with you, you don't understand! It's misses and then misses; misses is the same as misses,
misses one always misses . . ."

"Ahhh!" the perplexed old man drew out. "Hm! Well, he'll
do better next time!" and the old man laughed gaily.

"Pavel Pavlovich, one can't have all perfections at once!"
Marya Nikitishna taunted him loudly. "Ah, my God, he's
choking on a bone!" she exclaimed, jumping up from her
chair.

Turmoil even ensued, but that was just what Marya Nikitishna wanted. Pavel Pavlovich had only swallowed his wine
the wrong way, after grabbing it to conceal his embarrassment,
but Marya Nikitishna insisted and swore up and down that it
was "a fishbone, that she'd seen it herself, and one can die
from that."

"Thump him on the back!" someone shouted.

"In fact, that's the best thing!" Zakhlebinin loudly approved, but volunteers had already turned up: Marya Nikitishna, the redheaded girlfriend (also invited for dinner), and,
finally, the terribly frightened mother of the family in person—they all wanted to thump Pavel Pavlovich on the back.
Pavel Pavlovich jumped up from the table to evade them and
spent a whole minute insisting that it was merely wine that
had gone down the wrong way, and that the coughing would
soon pass—before they finally figured out that it was all Marya
Nikitishna's pranks.

"Well, aren't you the little mischief, though! . . ." Mme.
Zakhlebinin observed sternly to Marya Nikitishna—but was at
once unable to help herself and burst into such laughter as
rarely happened with her, which also produced an effect of a
sort. After dinner they all went out to the balcony to have
coffee.

"Such fine days we're having!" the old man benevolently
praised nature, looking out at the garden with pleasure. "Only
we could use a little rain . . . Well, I'll go and rest. Have

fun, have fun, God bless you! And you have fun, too!" he slapped Pavel Pavlovich on the shoulder as he went out.

When everyone had gone down to the garden again, Pavel Pavlovich suddenly rushed over to Velchaninov and tugged him by the sleeve.

"For one moment, sir," he whispered impatiently.

They walked to a solitary side path in the garden.

"No, excuse me this time, sir, no, this time I won't let you . . ." he whispered, spluttering fiercely and grabbing Velchaninov's sleeve.

"What? How's that?" Velchaninov asked, making big eyes. Pavel Pavlovich stood silently gazing at him, moving his lips, and smiled fiercely.

"Where have you gone? Where are you? Everything's ready!" the girls' calls and impatient voices were heard. Velchaninov shrugged and went back to the company. Pavel Pavlovich went running after him.

"I bet he asked you for a handkerchief," Marya Nikitishna said, "last time he also forgot it."

"He eternally forgets!" a middle Zakhlebinin girl picked up.

"Forgot his handkerchief! Pavel Pavlovich forgot his handkerchief! *Maman*, Pavel Pavlovich forgot his handkerchief again, *Maman*, Pavel Pavlovich has caught cold again!" voices came.

"Why doesn't he say so? Pavel Pavlovich, you are so fastidious!" Mme. Zakhlebinin drawled in a singsong voice. "It's dangerous to joke with a cold; I'll send you a handkerchief right away. And why is it he's always catching cold!" she added as she left, glad of an occasion to go back to the house.

"I have two handkerchiefs, and no cold, ma'am," Pavel Pavlovich called after her, but she must not have understood, and a minute later, as Pavel Pavlovich was trotting after everyone, trying to keep closer to Velchaninov and Nadya, a maid came puffing up to him and indeed brought him a handkerchief.

"Let's play, let's play, let's play proverbs!" shouts came from all sides, as if they expected God knows what from their "proverbs."

They chose a place and sat down on benches; it fell to Marya Nikitishna to guess; they demanded that she go as far away as possible and not eavesdrop; in her absence a proverb was chosen and the words were distributed. Marya Nikitishna came back and guessed it at once. The proverb was: "Dreadful the dream, but God is merciful."

Marya Nikitishna was followed by the ruffled young man in blue spectacles. Of him still greater precautions were demanded—that he stand by the gazebo and turn his face fully toward the fence. The gloomy young man did his duty with disdain and even seemed to feel a certain moral humiliation. When he was called back, he could not guess anything, went around to each person, listening twice to what they told him, spent a long time gloomily reflecting, but nothing came of it. He was put to shame. The proverb was: "Prayer to God and service to the tsar are never in vain."

"Besides, it's a disgusting proverb!" the wounded youth grumbled indignantly, retreating to his place.

"Ah, how boring!" voices were heard.

Velchaninov went; he was hidden farther away than the others; he also failed to guess.

"Ah, how boring!" still more voices were heard.

"Well, now I'll go," said Nadya.

"No, no, now Pavel Pavlovich will go, it's Pavel Pavlovich's turn," they all shouted and livened up a bit.

Pavel Pavlovich was taken right to the fence, to the corner, and placed facing it, and to keep him from turning around, the little redhead was set to watch him. Pavel Pavlovich, already cheered up and almost merry again, piously intended to do his duty and stood like a stump staring at the fence, not daring to turn around. The little redhead kept watch some twenty paces behind him, closer to the company, by the gazebo, exchanging excited winks with the other girls; one could see that they were all expecting something, even with a certain anxiousness; something was being prepared. Suddenly the little redhead waved her arms from behind the gazebo. That instant they all jumped up and rushed off somewhere at breakneck speed.

"You run, too!" ten voices whispered to Velchaninov, all but horrified that he was not running.

"What is it? What's happened?" he kept asking, hurrying after them all.

"Quiet, don't shout! Let him stand there and stare at the fence while we all run away. Here's Nastya running, too!"

The little redhead (Nastya) was running headlong as if God knows what had happened, and waving her arms. They all came finally, beyond the pond, to a completely different end of the garden. When Velchaninov got there, he saw that Katerina Fedoseevna was having a big argument with all the girls and especially with Nadya and Marya Nikitishna.

"Katya, darling, don't be angry!" Nadya was kissing her.

"All right, I won't tell Mama, but I shall leave myself, because this is not nice at all. What must the poor man be feeling there by the fence?"

She left out of pity, but all the rest remained as implacable and pitiless as before. It was sternly demanded of Velchaninov that, when Pavel Pavlovich came back, he also pay no attention to him, as if nothing had happened. "And let's all play fox and hounds!" the little redhead cried out rapturously.

Pavel Pavlovich rejoined the company only after at least a quarter of an hour. He must have spent two thirds of that time standing at the fence. Fox and hounds was in full swing and succeeded excellently—everyone shouted and had fun. Mad with rage, Pavel Pavlovich sprang straight up to Velchaninov and again grabbed him by the sleeve.

"For one little moment, sir!"

"Oh, Lord, what's with him and his little moments!"

"Asking for a handkerchief again," the cry came after them.

"Well, this time it's you, sir; here it's you now, sir, you are the cause of it!" Pavel Pavlovich's teeth even chattered as he articulated this.

Velchaninov interrupted him and peaceably advised him to

be more cheerful, or else he would be teased to death: "They tease you because you're angry while everyone else is having fun." To his amazement, Pavel Pavlovich was terribly struck by his words and advice; he at once became quiet, even to the point of returning to the company like a guilty man and obediently taking part in the general games; for some time afterward they did not bother him and played with him like anyone else—and before half an hour had gone by, he was almost cheerful again. In all the games, he engaged himself as a partner, when need be, predominantly with the treacherous little redhead or one of the Zakhlebinin sisters. But Velchaninov noticed, to his still greater amazement, that Pavel Pavlovich hardly dared even once to address Nadya, though he ceaselessly fussed around her or near her; at least he accepted the position of one unnoticed and scorned by her as if it were proper, natural. But in the end a prank was again played on him even so.

The game was hide-and-seek. The person hiding, incidentally, had the right to change his place within the whole area in which he was allowed to hide. Pavel Pavlovich, who had managed to hide by getting himself into a thick bush, suddenly decided to change his place and run into the house. There was shouting, he was seen; he hastily sneaked upstairs, having in mind a little place behind a chest of drawers where he wanted to hide. But the little redhead flew up after him, tiptoed stealthily to the door, and snapped the lock. As before, everyone at once stopped playing and again ran beyond the pond to the other end of the garden. About ten minutes later, Pavel Pavlovich, sensing that no one was looking for him, peeked out the window. No one was there. He did not dare shout lest he awaken the parents; the maid and the serving girl had been given strict orders not to come or respond to Pavel Pavlovich's call. Katerina Fedoseevna could have opened the door for him, but she, having returned to her room, sat down in reverie and unexpectedly fell asleep herself. He sat like that for about an hour. At last, girls began to appear in twos and threes, passing by as if inadvertently.

"Pavel Pavlovich, why don't you join us? Ah, it's such fun there! We're playing theater. Alexei Ivanovich had the role of the 'young man.' "

"Pavel Pavlovich, why don't you join us, it's you one always misses!" other young misses observed, passing by.

"Who is it, again, that one always misses?" suddenly came the voice of Mme. Zakhlebinin, who had just woken up and decided finally to take a stroll in the garden and watch the "children's" games while waiting for tea.

"It's Pavel Pavlovich there." She was shown the window through which peeked, with a distorted smile, pale with anger, the face of Pavel Pavlovich.

"The man would just rather sit there alone, while others are having such fun!" the mother of the family shook her head.

Meanwhile Velchaninov had the honor, finally, of receiving from Nadya an explanation of her words earlier about being "glad he had come owing to a certain circumstance." The explanation took place in a solitary alley. Marya Nikitishna purposely summoned Velchaninov, who had participated in some of the games and was already beginning to languish greatly, and brought him to this alley, where she left him alone with Nadya.

"I'm perfectly convinced," she rattled out in a bold and quick patter, "that you are not at all such a friend of Pavel Pavlovich's as he boasted you were. I calculate that you alone can render me an extremely important service; here is today's nasty bracelet," she took the case from her pocket, "I humbly beg you to return it to him immediately, because I myself will not speak to him ever or for anything for the rest of my life. Anyhow, you may tell him so on my behalf and add that henceforth he dare not thrust his presents at me. The rest I'll let him know through others. Will you kindly give me the pleasure of fulfilling my wish?"

"Ah, no, spare me, for God's sake!" Velchaninov all but cried out, waving his hands.

"What! Spare me?" Nadya was unbelievably astonished by his refusal and stared wide-eyed at him. All her prepared tone broke down in an instant, and she was nearly in tears. Velchaninov laughed.

"It's not that I . . . I'd be very glad . . . but I've got my own accounts with him . . ."

"I knew you weren't his friend and that he was lying!" Nadya interrupted him fervently and quickly. "I'll never marry him, you should know that! Never! I don't even understand how he dared . . . Only you must return his vile bracelet to him even so, otherwise what am I to do? I absolutely, absolutely want him to get it back today, the same day—and lump it. And if he peaches to Papa, he'll be in real trouble."

Suddenly and quite unexpectedly the ruffled young man in blue spectacles popped from behind a bush.

"You must give him back the bracelet," he fell upon Velchaninov furiously, "if only in the name of women's rights, assuming you yourself stand on the level of the question . . ."

But he had no time to finish; Nadya pulled him by the sleeve with all her might and tore him away from Velchaninov.

"Lord, how stupid you are, Predposylov!"[12] she cried. "Go away! Go away, go away, and don't you dare eavesdrop, I told you to stand far off! . . ." She stamped her little feet at him, and when he had slipped back into his bushes, she still went on pacing back and forth across the path, as if beside herself, flashing her eyes and clasping her hands in front of her.

"You wouldn't believe how stupid they are!" she suddenly stopped in front of Velchaninov. "To you it's funny, but how is it for me!"

"But it's not *him,* not *him*?" Velchaninov was laughing.

"Naturally it's not *him,* how could you think such a thing!" Nadya smiled and turned red. "He's only his friend. But what friends he chooses, I don't understand it, they all say he's a 'future mover,' but I don't understand a thing . . . Alexei Ivanovich, I have no one to turn to; your final word, will you give it back or not?"

"Well, all right, I'll give it back, let me have it."

"Ah, you're a dear, ah, you're so kind!" she suddenly rejoiced, handing him the case. "For that I'll sing for you the whole evening, because I sing wonderfully, you should know that, and I lied earlier about not liking music. Ah, if only you'd come again, just once, how glad I'd be, I'd tell you everything, everything, everything, and a lot more besides, because you're so kind, so kind, like—like Katya!"

And indeed, when they went back home for tea, she sang two romances for him in a voice not yet trained at all and only just beginning, but rather pleasant and strong. When they all came back from the garden, Pavel Pavlovich was sitting sedately with the parents at the tea table, on which a big family samovar was already boiling and heirloom Sèvres porcelain teacups were set out. Most likely he and the old folks were discussing very serious things—because in two days he would be leaving for a whole nine months. He did not even glance at those who came in from the garden, least of all at Velchaninov; it was also obvious that he had not "peached" and that so far everything was quiet.

But when Nadya started singing, he, too, appeared at once. Nadya purposely did not answer his one direct question, but Pavel Pavlovich was not embarrassed or shaken by that; he stood at the back of her chair and his whole bearing showed that this was his place and he would yield it to no one.

"Alexei Ivanovich will sing, *Maman,* Alexei Ivanovich wants to sing!" nearly all the girls cried, crowding around the piano, at which Velchaninov was confidently sitting down, intending to accompany himself. The old folks came out along with Katerina Fedoseevna, who had been sitting with them and pouring tea.

Velchaninov chose a certain romance by Glinka,[13] which almost no one knows anymore:

> When you do ope your merry lips, my love
> And coo to me more sweetly than a dove . . .

He sang it addressing Nadya alone, who stood right at his elbow and closest to him of all. He had long ago lost his voice, but from what remained, one could see that it had once been

not bad. Velchaninov had managed to hear this romance for
the first time some twenty years before, when he was still a
student, from Glinka himself, in the house of one of the late
composer's friends, at a literary-artistic bachelor party. Glinka,
carried away, had played and sung all his favorite things from
his own works, including this romance. He also had no voice
left by then, but Velchaninov remembered the extraordinary
impression produced then precisely by this romance. No artistic salon singer could ever have achieved such an effect. In this
romance, the intensity of the passion rises and grows with
every line, every word; precisely because of this extraordinary
intensity, the slightest falseness, the slightest exaggeration or
untruth—which one gets away with so easily in opera—would
here ruin and distort the whole meaning. To sing this small
but remarkable thing, one had absolutely—yes, absolutely—to
have a full, genuine inspiration, a genuine passion or its full
poetic assimilation. Otherwise the romance would not only
fail altogether, but might even appear outrageous and all but
something shameless: it would be impossible to show such
intensity of passionate feeling without provoking disgust, yet
truth and *simple-heartedness* saved everything. Velchaninov remembered that he himself once used to succeed with this romance. He had almost assimilated Glinka's manner of singing;
but now, from the very first sound, from the first line, a genuine inspiration blazed up in his soul and trembled in his voice.
With every word of the romance, the feeling broke through
and bared itself more strongly and boldly, in the last lines cries
of passion were heard, and when, turning his flashing eyes to
Nadya, he finished singing the last words of the romance:

> Now I do gaze more boldly in your eyes
> My lips approach, to list I no more rise,
> I want to kiss, I want to kiss and kiss,
> I want to kiss, to kiss and kiss and kiss!

—Nadya almost started in fright, and even recoiled a little; a
blush poured over her cheeks, and at the same moment

Velchaninov saw something as if responsive flash in her embarrassed and almost abashed little face. Fascination, and at the same time perplexity, showed on the faces of all the listening girls as well; to everyone it seemed as if impossible and shameful to sing like that, and at the same time all these little faces and eyes burned and shone as if waiting for something more. Among these faces there especially flashed before Velchaninov the face of Katerina Fedoseevna, which had become almost beautiful.

"Some romance!" muttered old Zakhlebinin, slightly taken aback. "But . . . isn't it too strong? Pleasant, but strong . . ."

"Strong . . ." Mme. Zakhlebinin echoed, but Pavel Pavlovich did not let her finish: he suddenly popped forward and, as if mad, forgetting himself so much that with his own hand he seized Nadya by the hand and drew her away from Velchaninov, he then leaped up to him and stared at him like a lost man, moving his trembling lips.

"For one moment, sir," he finally managed to utter.

Velchaninov saw clearly that in another moment this gentleman might venture on something ten times more absurd; he quickly took him by the arm and, ignoring the general perplexity, led him out to the balcony and even took several steps with him down to the garden, where it was already almost completely dark.

"Do you understand that you must leave with me right now, this very minute!" Pavel Pavlovich said.

"No, I don't . . ."

"Do you remember," Pavel Pavlovich went on in his frenetic whisper, "do you remember how you demanded once that I tell you everything, *everything,* openly, sir, 'the very last word . . .'—do you remember, sir? Well, the time has come for saying that word . . . let's go, sir!"

Velchaninov reflected, glanced once more at Pavel Pavlovich, and agreed to leave.

Their suddenly announced departure upset the parents and made all the girls terribly indignant.

"At least another cup of tea," Mme. Zakhlebinin moaned plaintively.

"Why did you get so upset?" the old man, in a stern and displeased tone, addressed the grinning and stubbornly silent Pavel Pavlovich.

"Pavel Pavlovich, why are you taking Alexei Ivanovich away?" the girls cooed plaintively, at the same time glancing at him with bitterness. And Nadya looked at him so angrily that he cringed all over, yet—he did not yield.

"But in fact, Pavel Pavlovich—and I thank him for it—has reminded me of an extremely important matter, which I might have let slip," Velchaninov laughed, shaking hands with the host, bowing to the hostess and to the girls, and, as if especially among them, to Katerina Fedoseevna, which again was noticed by everyone.

"We thank you for coming and will always be glad to see you, all of us," Zakhlebinin concluded weightily.

"Ah, we're so glad . . ." the mother of the family picked up with feeling.

"Come again, Alexei Ivanovich, come again!" many voices were heard from the balcony when he was already sitting in the carriage with Pavel Pavlovich; barely heard was one little voice, softer than all the others, that said: "Come again, dear, dear Alexei Ivanovich!"

"It's the little redhead!" thought Velchaninov.

XIII

Whose Side Has More on It

He was able to think about the little redhead, and yet vexation and repentance had long been wearying his soul. And during this whole day—spent so amusingly, one would have thought—sorrow had almost never left him. Before singing the romance, he had already not known where to escape from it; maybe that was why he had sung with such feeling.

"And I could stoop so low . . . break away from everything!" he began to reproach himself, but hastened to interrupt his thoughts. And it seemed so low to lament; it would have been much more pleasant to quickly get angry with someone.

"Mor-ron!" he whispered spitefully, glancing sideways at Pavel Pavlovich, who was silently sitting next to him in the carriage.

Pavel Pavlovich remained obstinately silent, perhaps concentrating and preparing himself. With an impatient gesture he occasionally took off his hat and wiped his forehead with his handkerchief.

"He's sweating!" Velchaninov kept up his spite.

Only once did Pavel Pavlovich advert to the coachman with a question: "Will there be a thunderstorm, or not?"

"Aye, and a good one! There's bound to be, it was such a sultry day." Indeed, the sky was darkening, and distant lightning flashed. They entered the city at half past ten.

"I'm going to your place, sir," Pavel Pavlovich obligingly addressed Velchaninov, not far from his house.

"I understand; but I must warn you that I feel seriously unwell . . ."

"I won't stay long, I won't stay long!"

As they came through the gateway, Pavel Pavlovich ran over for a moment to Mavra at the caretaker's.

"Why did you go there?" Velchaninov asked sternly when the man caught up with him and they went into his rooms.

"Never mind, sir, just so . . . the coachman, sir . . ."

"I won't let you drink!"

No answer came. Velchaninov lit the candles, and Pavel Pavlovich settled at once into an armchair. Velchaninov frowningly stopped before him.

"I also promised to tell you my 'last' word," he began with an inward, still suppressed, irritation. "Here it is, this word: I consider in good conscience that all matters between us have been mutually ended, so that we even have nothing to talk about; do you hear—nothing; and therefore it might be better if you left now and I locked the door behind you."

"Let's square accounts, Alexei Ivanovich!" Pavel Pavlovich said, but with a somehow especially meek look in his eyes.

"Square ac-counts?" Velchaninov was terribly surprised. "That's a strange phrase to utter! What 'accounts' have we got to 'square'? Hah! Is it that 'last word' of yours, which you promised earlier to . . . reveal to me?"

"The very same, sir."

"We have no more accounts to square, they were squared long ago!" Velchaninov said proudly.

"Do you really think so, sir?" Pavel Pavlovich said in a soulful voice, somehow strangely joining his hands in front of him, finger to finger, and holding them in front of his chest. Velchaninov did not answer him and started pacing the room. "Liza? Liza?" moaned in his heart.

"But, anyhow, what is it you wanted to square?" he addressed him frowningly, after a rather prolonged silence. The man had followed him around the room with his eyes all the while, holding his joined hands in front of him in the same way.

"Don't go there anymore, sir," he almost whispered in a pleading voice, and suddenly got up from the chair.

"What? So it's only about that?" Velchaninov laughed spitefully. "Though you've made me marvel all day today!" he began venomously, but suddenly his whole face changed: "Listen to me," he said sadly and with profoundly sincere feeling, "I consider that I've never stooped so low in anything as I did today—first by agreeing to go with you, and then—by what happened there . . . It was so petty, so pathetic . . . I befouled and demeaned myself by getting involved . . . and forgetting . . . Well, never mind!" he suddenly recollected himself. "Listen: you happened to fall on me today when I was irritated and sick . . . well, no point in justifying myself! I won't go there anymore, and I assure you that I have absolutely no interest there," he concluded resolutely.

"Really? Really?" Pavel Pavlovich cried out, not concealing his joyful excitement. Velchaninov glanced at him with scorn and again started pacing the room.

"It seems you've decided to be happy at all costs?" he finally could not refrain from observing.

"Yes, sir," Pavel Pavlovich softly and naively confirmed.

"What is it to me," thought Velchaninov, "that he's a buffoon and his malice comes only from stupidity? All the same I can't help hating him—though he may not deserve it!"

"I'm an 'eternal husband,' sir!" Pavel Pavlovich said with a humbly submissive smile at himself. "I've long known this little phrase of yours, Alexei Ivanovich, ever since you lived there with us, sir. I memorized many of your words from that year. When you said 'eternal husband' here the last time, I realized it, sir."

Mavra came in with a bottle of champagne and two glasses.

"Forgive me, Alexei Ivanovich, you know I can't do without it, sir. Don't regard it as boldness; consider me a stranger and not worthy of you, sir."

"Yes . . ." Velchaninov allowed with disgust, "but I assure you that I'm feeling unwell . . ."

"Quickly, quickly, just one moment now!" Pavel Pavlovich hurried, "only one little glass, because my throat . . ."

He greedily drank the glass in one gulp and sat down—casting an all but tender glance at Velchaninov. Mavra went out.

"How loathsome!" Velchaninov whispered.

"It's only the girlfriends, sir," Pavel Pavlovich suddenly said cheerfully, thoroughly revived.

"How? What? Ah, yes, you're still at it . . ."

"Only the girlfriends, sir! And still so young; we're showing off out of gracefulness, that's what, sir! It's even charming. And then—then, you know, I'll become her slave; she'll know esteem, society . . . she'll get completely reeducated, sir."

"By the way, I must give him the bracelet!" Velchaninov thought, frowning and feeling for the case in his coat pocket.

"Now you say, sir, that I've decided to be happy? I must get married, Alexei Ivanovich," Pavel Pavlovich went on confidentially and almost touchingly, "otherwise what will become of me? You can see for yourself, sir!" he pointed to the bottle.

"And this is only a hundredth part—of my qualities, sir. I'm quite unable to do without being married and—without new faith, sir. I'll believe and resurrect."

"But why are you telling all this to me?" Velchaninov almost snorted with laughter. Anyhow, it all seemed wild to him.

"But tell me, finally," he cried out, "why did you drag me there? What did you need me there for?"

"As a test, sir . . ." Pavel Pavlovich somehow suddenly became embarrassed.

"A test of what?"

"Of the effect, sir . . . You see, Alexei Ivanovich, it's only a week that I . . . that I've been seeking there, sir" (he was growing more and more abashed). "Yesterday I met you and thought: 'I've never seen her in, so to speak, a stranger's, that is, a man's company, sir, apart from my own . . .' A foolish thought, sir, I feel it myself now, an unnecessary one, sir. I just wanted it so much, sir, on account of my nasty character . . ." He suddenly raised his head and blushed.

"Can he be telling the whole truth?" Velchaninov thought, amazed to the point of stupefaction.

"Well, and what then?"

Pavel Pavlovich smiled sweetly and somehow slyly.

"Nothing but lovely childishness, sir! It's all the girlfriends, sir! Only forgive me for my stupid behavior toward you today, Alexei Ivanovich; I'll never do it again, sir; and this thing won't ever happen again."

"And I won't be there anyway," Velchaninov smirked.

"That's partly what I'm referring to, sir."

Velchaninov winced slightly.

"However, I'm not the only one in the world," he observed vexedly.

Pavel Pavlovich blushed again.

"It makes me sad to hear that, Alexei Ivanovich, and, believe me, I respect Nadezhda Fedoseevna so much . . ."

"Excuse me, excuse me, I didn't mean anything—it's only a

bit strange to me that you overestimated my means so much . . . and . . . were relying on me so sincerely . . ."

"I relied on you, sir, precisely because it was after everything . . . that had already been, sir."

"Meaning that you still regard me, in that case, as a most noble man?" Velchaninov suddenly stopped. At another moment he himself would have been horrified at the naivety of his sudden question.

"And I always did, sir," Pavel Pavlovich lowered his eyes.

"Well, yes, naturally . . . I don't mean that—that is, not in that sense—I only wanted to say that despite any . . . prejudice . . ."

"Yes, sir, and despite any prejudice."

"And when you were coming to Petersburg?" Velchaninov could no longer restrain himself, feeling all the monstrousness of his curiosity.

"And when I was coming to Petersburg, I considered you the most noble of men, sir. I've always respected you, Alexei Ivanovich," Pavel Pavlovich raised his eyes and clearly, now without any embarrassment, looked at his adversary. Velchaninov suddenly turned coward: he decidedly did not want anything to happen or anything to go over the line, the more so as he himself had provoked it.

"I loved you, Alexei Ivanovich," Pavel Pavlovich said as if suddenly making up his mind, "And I loved you, sir, all that year in T———. You didn't notice it, sir," he went on in a slightly quavering voice, to Velchaninov's decided horror, "I stood too small compared with you in order for you to notice. And perhaps it wasn't necessary, sir. And for all these nine years I've remembered you, sir, because never in my life have I known such a year as that." (Pavel Pavlovich's eyes glistened somehow peculiarly.) "I remembered many of your words and utterances, sir, of your thoughts, sir. I always remembered you as an educated man, sir, ardent for good feelings, highly educated, and with thoughts. 'Great thoughts come not so much from great intelligence as from great feeling, sir'—you yourself said that, and perhaps forgot it, but I remembered it, sir. I

always counted on you, that is, as on a man of great feeling
. . . that is, I believed, sir—despite all, sir . . ." His chin
suddenly trembled. Velchaninov was completely frightened;
this unexpected tone had to be stopped at all costs.

"Enough, please, Pavel Pavlovich," he muttered, blushing
and in irritated impatience. "And why, why," he suddenly
cried out, "why do you fasten yourself on to a sick, irritated,
all but delirious man, and drag him into this darkness . . .
when—it's all a phantom and a mirage, and a lie, and shame,
and unnaturalness, and—excessive—and that's the main, the
most shameful thing, that it's excessive! And it's all rubbish:
we're two depraved, underground, vile people . . . And if
you like, if you like, I'll prove to you right now that you not
only do not love me, but that you hate me with all your
strength and are lying without knowing it yourself: you took
me and drove me there not at all for the ridiculous purpose of
testing your fiancée (what a thing to come up with!)—you
simply saw me yesterday and *got angry* and took me there to
show her to me and say: 'See her! She's going to be mine; go
on and try something now!' You challenged me! Maybe you
didn't know it yourself, but it was so, because you did feel all
that . . . And without hatred one can't make such a challenge; and that means you hated me!" He was rushing up and
down the room as he shouted this out, and most of all he was
tormented and offended by the humiliating awareness that he
was condescending so much to Pavel Pavlovich.

"I wished to make peace with you, Alexei Ivanovich!" the
other suddenly pronounced resolutely, in a quick whisper, and
his chin began to twitch again. Fierce rage took possession of
Velchaninov, as if no one had ever given him such offense
before!

"I tell you once again," he screamed, "that you are . . .
clinging to a sick and irritated man in order to tear from him,
in his delirium, some phantasmal word! We . . . but we're
people from different worlds, understand that, and . . . and
. . . a grave lies between us!" he whispered frenziedly—and
suddenly recovered himself.

"And how do you know," Pavel Pavlovich's face suddenly became distorted and pale, "how do you know what that little grave means here . . . inside me, sir!" he cried out, stepping up to Velchaninov and, with a ridiculous but terrible gesture, striking himself on the heart with his fist. "I know that little grave here, sir, and we two stand on the sides of that grave, only my side has more on it than yours, more, sir . . ." he was whispering as if in delirium, while continuing to hit himself on the heart, "more, sir, more, sir—more, sir . . ." Suddenly an extraordinary stroke of the doorbell brought them both to their senses. The ring was so strong that it seemed as if someone had vowed to tear the bell off with the first stroke.

"No one rings like that for me," Velchaninov said in bewilderment.

"But it's not for me either, sir," Pavel Pavlovich whispered timidly, having also come to his senses and instantly turned back into the former Pavel Pavlovich. Velchaninov frowned and went to open the door.

"Mr. Velchaninov, if I am not mistaken?" a young, ringing, remarkably self-confident voice was heard in the hall.

"What is it?"

"I have precise information," the ringing voice went on, "that a certain Trusotsky is presently with you. I absolutely must see him at once." It would, of course, have been very agreeable to Velchaninov to send this self-confident gentleman down the stairs at once with a good kick. But he reflected, stepped aside, and let him pass.

"Here is Mr. Trusotsky. Come in . . ."

XIV

Sashenka and Nadenka

Into the room came a very young man, of about nineteen, perhaps even somewhat less—so youthful seemed his handsome, confidently upturned face. He was not badly dressed, at least everything sat well on him; he was above medium height; thick black hair broken into locks, and big, bold dark eyes especially marked his physiognomy. Only his nose was a little too broad and upturned; had it not been for that, he would have been an altogether handsome fellow. He entered imposingly.

"I believe I have the—occasion—of speaking with Mr. Trusotsky?" he said measuredly, emphasizing the word "occasion" with particular pleasure, thereby letting it be known that there could be neither honor nor pleasure for him in talking with Mr. Trusotsky.

Velchaninov was beginning to understand; it seemed that Pavel Pavlovich, too, was already seeing some light. His face expressed uneasiness; however, he stood up for himself.

"Not having the honor of knowing you," he answered with a dignified air, "I suppose that I cannot have any business with you, sir."

"First you will hear me out, and then express your opinion," the young man said confidently and didactically, and, taking out a tortoiseshell lorgnette which he had hanging on a string, he began scrutinizing through it the bottle of champagne standing on the table. Having calmly finished his examination of the bottle, he folded the lorgnette and, again addressing Pavel Pavlovich, said:

"Alexander Lobov."

"And what is this Alexander Lobov, sir?"

"I am he. Haven't you heard?"

"No, sir."

"Anyway, how could you know. I've come with an important matter, which in fact concerns you; allow me to sit down, however, I'm tired . . ."

"Sit down," Velchaninov invited—but the young man had managed to sit down before he was invited. Despite a growing pain in his chest, Velchaninov was intrigued by this impudent boy. In his pretty, childish, and ruddy face he glimpsed some distant resemblance to Nadya.

"You sit down, too," the youth offered to Pavel Pavlovich, indicating the place opposite him with a casual nod.

"Never mind, sir, I'll stand."

"You'll get tired. I suppose, Mr. Velchaninov, that you may not have to go."

"I have nowhere to go. I live here."

"As you will. I confess, I even wish you to be present at my talk with this gentleman. Nadezhda Fedoseevna has recommended you to me quite flatteringly."

"Hah! When did she have time?"

"Just after you left. I'm coming from there, too. The thing is this, Mr. Trusotsky," he turned to the standing Pavel Pavlovich, "we, that is, Nadezhda Fedoseevna and I," he spoke through his teeth, sprawling casually in the armchair, "have long been in love and have pledged ourselves to each other. You are now a hindrance between us; I've come to suggest that you vacate that place. Will you be pleased to accept my suggestion?"

Pavel Pavlovich even swayed; he turned pale, but a sarcastic smile at once forced itself to his lips.

"No, sir, not at all pleased," he snapped laconically.

"Well, now!" the youth turned in the armchair and crossed one leg over the other.

"I don't even know with whom I am speaking, sir," Pavel Pavlovich added, "I even think there is no reason for us to continue."

Having spoken that out, he, too, found it necessary to sit down.

"I told you you'd get tired," the youth observed casually. "I just had occasion to inform you that my name is Lobov and that Nadezhda Fedoseevna and I have pledged ourselves to each other—consequently, you can't say, as you just did, that you don't know whom you are dealing with; nor can you think that we have nothing to continue talking about; not to mention me—the matter concerns Nadezhda Fedoseevna, whom you are so insolently pestering. And that alone already constitutes a sufficient reason for explanations."

All this he said through his teeth, like a fop, even barely deigning to articulate the words; he even took out the lorgnette again and, while speaking, directed it at something for a moment.

"Excuse me, young man . . ." Pavel Pavlovich exclaimed vexedly, but the "young man" at once checked him.

"At any other time I would, of course, forbid you to call me 'young man,' but now, you must agree, my youth is my chief advantage over you, and you might have wished very much—today, for instance, as you were presenting the bracelet—that you were at least a little bit younger."

"Ah, you sprat!" Velchaninov whispered.

"In any case, my dear sir," Pavel Pavlovich corrected himself with dignity, "I still do not find the reasons you have presented—improper and quite dubious reasons—sufficient for the dispute over them to be continued, sir. I see this is all a childish and empty matter; tomorrow I will make inquiries of the most esteemed Fedosei Semyonovich, but now I beg you to spare me, sir."

"See how the man is!" the youth cried out at once, unable to sustain the tone, hotly addressing Velchaninov. "It's not enough that he's chased away from there and they stick their tongues out at him—he also wants to denounce us tomorrow to the old man! Don't you prove by that, you obstinate man, that you want to take the girl by force, buying her from people who have lost their minds, but, owing to social barbarism, have kept their power over her? She has shown well enough, it seems, that she despises you; wasn't today's indecent gift—your bracelet—returned to you? What more do you want?"

"No one returned any bracelet to me, and that cannot be," Pavel Pavlovich gave a start.

"Cannot be? Didn't Mr. Velchaninov give it to you?"

"Ah, devil take you!" thought Velchaninov.

"Indeed," he said, frowning, "Nadezhda Fedoseevna entrusted me earlier with giving this case to you, Pavel Pavlovich. I didn't want to take it, but she—insisted . . . here it is . . . quite annoying . . ."

He took out the case and, in embarrassment, placed it in front of the petrified Pavel Pavlovich.

"Why hadn't you given it to him?" the young man sternly addressed Velchaninov.

"I hadn't found time, one might think," the latter frowned.

"That's odd."

"Wha-a-at?"

"It's odd, to say the least, you must agree. However, I agree to allow that it was a misunderstanding."

Velchaninov would have liked terribly to get up right then and box the boy's ears, but he could not contain himself and suddenly snorted with laughter; the boy at once laughed himself. Not so Pavel Pavlovich; if Velchaninov could have noticed the terrible look he gave him when he burst out laughing at Lobov—he would have understood that at that moment the man was crossing a certain fatal line . . . But, though he did not see his look, Velchaninov understood that he had to support Pavel Pavlovich.

"Listen, Mr. Lobov," he began in a friendly tone, "without going into a consideration of other reasons, which I do not wish to touch upon, I would merely like to point out to you that Pavel Pavlovich, after all, in proposing to Nadezhda Fedoseevna, is bringing to this respectable family—first, full information about himself; second, his excellent and respectable position; and finally, his fortune; and, consequently, he is of course surprised to see a rival such as you—a man of great merits, perhaps, but one still so young that he simply cannot take you as a serious rival . . . and is therefore right in asking you to finish."

"What do you mean 'so young'? I turned nineteen a month ago. Legally, I've been able to marry for a long time. There you have it."

"But what father would venture to give his daughter to you now—though you may be a big future millionaire or some sort of future benefactor of mankind? At the age of nineteen a man can't even answer for his own self, and you venture to take upon your conscience someone else's future—that is, the future of a child like yourself! That's also not entirely noble, do you think? I've allowed myself to speak out, because you addressed me earlier as a mediator between yourself and Pavel Pavlovich."

"Ah, yes, incidentally, his name is Pavel Pavlovich!" the youth remarked. "Why did I keep imagining it was Vassily Petrovich? The thing is this, sir," he turned to Velchaninov, "you haven't surprised me in the least; I knew you were all the same! Strange, however, that I was told you were even something of a new man. Anyway, it's all trifles, and the point is that there is nothing here that is not noble on my part, as you allowed yourself to put it, but even quite the contrary, which I hope to explain to you: we have, first of all, pledged ourselves to each other, and, besides that, I promised her directly, in front of two witnesses, that if she ever falls in love with another, or simply thinks better of having married me, and wants to divorce me, I will immediately give her a certificate of my own adultery—thus supporting, therewith, where necessary, her application for divorce. Moreover, in the event I should go back on my word later and refuse to give her this certificate, then, for her security, on the very day of our wedding I will give her a promissory note for a hundred thousand roubles in my name, so that, in the event I persist in refusing the certificate, she can immediately turn in my promissory note and have me double-trumped! In this way everything is provided for, and I'm not putting anyone's future at risk. Well, sir, that's the first thing."

"I bet it was that one—what's his name—Predposylov who thought it up for you?" cried Velchaninov.

"Hee, hee, hee!" Pavel Pavlovich tittered venomously.

"Why is this gentleman tittering? You've guessed right—it's Predposylov's thought; and you must agree it's clever. The absurd law is completely paralyzed. Naturally, I intend to love her always, and she laughs terribly—but even so it's adroit, and you must agree that it's noble, that not everyone would venture on such a thing?"

"In my opinion, it is not only not noble, but even vile."

The young man heaved his shoulders.

"Once again you don't surprise me," he observed after some silence, "all this stopped surprising me long ago. Predposylov would snap out directly that this failure of yours to understand the most natural things comes from the perversion of your most ordinary feelings and notions, first, by a long life of absurdity, and second, by long idleness. However, maybe we still don't understand each other; after all, you were well spoken of to me . . . You're already about fifty, though?"

"Get on with your business, please."

"Excuse the indiscretion and don't be annoyed; I didn't mean anything. To continue: I'm not at all a future big millionaire, as you were pleased to put it (and what an idea to come up with!), I'm all here, as you see me, but of my future I'm absolutely certain. I won't be a hero or anybody's benefactor, but I'll provide for myself and my wife. Of course, right now I have nothing, I was even brought up in their house, ever since childhood . . ."

"How's that?"

"It's because I'm the son of a distant relative of this Zakhlebinin's wife, and when all my people died and left me at the age of eight, the old man took me into his house and then sent me to school. He's even a kind man, if you wish to know . . ."

"I know that, sir . . ."

"Yes, but much too antiquated a head. Kind, though. Now, of course, I've long since left his custody, wishing to earn my own living and be owing only to myself."

"And when did you leave it?" Velchaninov was curious.

"That would be about four months ago."

"Ah, well, it's all clear now: friends from childhood! Do you have a job or something?"

"Yes, a private one, in a notary's office, twenty-five roubles a month. Of course, that's only for the time being, but when I made my proposal I didn't even have that. I was working for the railroad then, for ten roubles, but this is all only for the time being."

"So you even made a proposal?"

"A formal proposal, long ago, three weeks or more."

"Well, and what then?"

"The old man laughed a lot, but then got very angry, and she was locked upstairs in the attic. But Nadya endured it heroically. Anyway, it was all a failure, because the old man had his back up against me before then for leaving the office job he'd gotten me four months earlier, before the railroad. He's a nice old man, I repeat again, simple and merry at home, but the moment he's in the office, you can't even imagine! It's some sort of Jupiter sitting there! I naturally let him know that his manners were no longer to my liking, but the main thing here came out because of the assistant section chief: this gentleman decided to peach on me for supposedly 'being rude' to him, though I only told him he was undeveloped. I dropped them all and am now with the notary."

"And were you paid much at the office?"

"Eh, I was a supernumerary! The old man supported me himself—I told you he's kind; but even so we won't yield. Of course, twenty-five roubles is no great prosperity, but I soon hope to take part in managing the disordered estates of Count Zavileisky, and then I'll go straight up to three thousand; or else I'll become a lawyer. They're looking for people now . . . Hah! what thunder, there'll be a storm, it's a good thing I managed before the storm; I came from there on foot, running most of the way."

"But, excuse me, in that case when did you manage to talk with Nadezhda Fedoseevna—if, on top of that, you're not received there?"

"Ah, but that can be done over the fence! You did notice the little redhead today?" he laughed. "Well, she took care of it, and so did Marya Nikitishna; only this Marya Nikitishna is a serpent! . . . why did you wince? You're not afraid of thunder?"

"No, I'm unwell, very unwell . . ." Velchaninov was indeed suffering from his unexpected pain in the chest, got up from his chair, and tried to pace the room.

"Ah, then naturally I'm bothering you—don't worry, I'll leave at once!" and the youth jumped up from his place.

"You're not bothering me, it's nothing," said the delicate Velchaninov.

"How is it nothing, when 'Kobylnikov has a stomach-ache'—remember in Shchedrin?[14] Do you like Shchedrin?"

"Yes . . ."

"So do I. Well, Vassily . . . no, what's your name, Pavel Pavlovich, let's finish, sir!" he addressed Pavel Pavlovich, al-most laughing. "I'll formulate the question once more for your understanding: do you agree to renounce tomorrow, officially, in front of the old folks and in my presence, all your claims regarding Nadezhda Fedoseevna?"

"I don't agree at all, sir," Pavel Pavlovich also rose with an impatient and embittered look, "and with that I ask you once more to spare me, sir . . . because all this is childish and silly, sir."

"Watch out!" the youth shook his finger at him with a haughty smile, "don't make a mistake in your calculations! Do you know what such a mistake may lead to? And I warn you that in nine months, when you've spent everything there, worn yourself out, and come back—you'll be forced to re-nounce Nadezhda Fedoseevna here, and if you don't renounce her—so much the worse for you; that's what you'll bring things to! I must warn you that you are now like the dog in the manger—excuse me, it's just a comparison—none for yourself, none for anyone else. I repeat out of humaneness: reflect, force yourself to reflect well for at least once in your life."

"I beg you to spare me your morals," Pavel Pavlovich shouted fiercely, "and as for your nasty hints, I'll take my measures tomorrow—severe measures, sir!"

"Nasty hints? What are you referring to? You're nasty your-self, if that's what's in your head. However, I agree to wait until tomorrow, but if . . . Ah, again this thunder! Good-bye, very glad to have met you," he nodded to Velchaninov and ran, evidently hurrying to keep ahead of the thunderstorm and not get caught in the rain.

XV

Accounts Are Squared

"Did you see? Did you see, sir?" Pavel Pavlovich sprang over to Velchaninov as soon as the youth went out.

"Yes, you have no luck!" Velchaninov let slip inadvertently. He would not have said these words if he were not so tormented and angered by this increasing pain in his chest. Pavel Pavlovich gave a start, as if burnt.

"Well, and you, sir—it must have been from pity for me that you didn't return the bracelet—ha?"

"I had no chance . . ."

"From heartfelt pity, as a true friend pities a true friend?"

"Well, yes, I pitied you," Velchaninov became angry.

He did, nevertheless, tell him briefly how he had gotten the bracelet back earlier and how Nadezhda Fedoseevna had nearly forced him to take part . . .

"You understand, I wouldn't have taken it for anything; I have enough troubles without that!"

"You got carried away and took it!" Pavel Pavlovich tittered.

"That's stupid on your part; however, you must be forgiven. You saw yourself just now that the main one in the matter is not I but others!"

"Even so you got carried away, sir."

Pavel Pavlovich sat down and filled his glass.

"Do you suppose I'm going to yield to this youngster, sir? I'll tie him in a knot, that's what, sir! Tomorrow I'll go and tie everything up! We'll smoke this spirit out of the nursery, sir . . ."

He drank his glass almost in one gulp and poured more; in general he began to behave with a hitherto unusual casualness.

"See, Nadenka and Sashenka, dear little children—hee, hee, hee!"

He was beside himself with spite. There came another loud clap of thunder; lightning flashed blindingly, and the rain poured down in buckets. Pavel Pavlovich got up and closed the open window.

"And him asking you: 'You're not afraid of thunder?'—hee, hee! Velchaninov afraid of thunder! Kobylnikov has a—how is it—Kobylnikov has . . . And about being fifty years old— eh? Remember, sir?" Pavel Pavlovich went on sarcastically.

"You, incidentally, have settled in nicely here," Velchaninov observed, barely able to utter the words from pain. "I'll lie down . . . you do as you like."

"One wouldn't put a dog out in such weather!" Pavel Pavlovich picked up touchily, though almost glad that he had the right to be touchy.

"Well, so sit, drink . . . spend the night even!" Velchaninov mumbled, stretched out on the sofa, and groaned slightly.

"Spend the night, sir? Aren't you . . . afraid, sir?"

"Of what?" Velchaninov suddenly raised his head.

"Never mind, sir, just so. Last time you were as if afraid, or else I only imagined it . . ."

"You're stupid!" Velchaninov burst out and turned angrily to the wall.

"Never mind, sir," Pavel Pavlovich responded.

The sick man somehow suddenly fell asleep, a moment after lying down. All the unnatural tension of this day, not to mention the great disorder of his health recently, somehow suddenly snapped, and he became as strengthless as a child. But the pain got its own back and overcame weariness and sleep; an hour later he awoke and with suffering got up from the sofa. The thunderstorm had abated; the room was filled with smoke, the bottle stood empty, and Pavel Pavlovich was sleeping on the other sofa. He was lying on his back, his head on a sofa pillow, fully dressed, with his boots on. His lorgnette, having slipped from his pocket, hung on its string almost to the floor. His hat lay near him, also on the floor. Velchaninov looked at him sullenly and decided not to wake him up. Bending over and pacing the room, because he was no longer able to lie down, he moaned and reflected on his pain.

He feared this pain in his chest not without reason. He had begun having these attacks long ago, but they visited him very rarely—once in a year or two. He knew it was from his liver. It began as if with a still dull, not strong, but bothersome pressure gathering at some point in his chest, in the pit of his stomach or higher up. Growing constantly, sometimes over the course of ten hours, the pain would finally reach such intensity, the pressure would become so unbearable, that the sick man would begin imagining death. During the last attack, which had come a year before, when the pain finally subsided after the tenth hour, he suddenly felt so strengthless that he could barely move his hand as he lay in bed, and for the whole day the doctor allowed him only a few teaspoons of weak tea and a little pinch of bread soaked in bouillon, like a nursing infant. This pain appeared on different occasions, but always with upset nerves to begin with. It would also pass strangely: sometimes, when caught at the very beginning, in the first half hour, everything would go away at once with simple poultices; but sometimes, as during the last attack, nothing would help, and the pain would subside only after a repeated and progressive taking of emetics. The doctor confessed afterward that he had been convinced it was poisoning. Now it was still a long time till morning, he did not want to send for a doctor during the night, and besides he did not like doctors. Finally, he could not help himself and started moaning loudly. The moans awakened Pavel Pavlovich: he sat up on the sofa and listened with fear for some time, his perplexed eyes following Velchaninov, who was nearly running all around the two rooms. The bottle he had drunk also affected him strongly, not in the usual way, and for a long time he could not collect himself; finally he understood and rushed to Velchaninov; the latter mumbled something in response.

"It's from your liver, sir, I know this!" Pavel Pavlovich suddenly became terribly animated. "Pyotr Kuzmich had it, Polosukhin, he had it in exactly the same way, from the liver, sir. It's a case for poultices, sir. Pyotr Kuzmich always used poultices . . . You can die of it, sir! I'll run and fetch Mavra—eh?"

"No need, no need," Velchaninov waved him away vexedly, "no need for anything."

But Pavel Pavlovich, God knows why, was almost beside

himself, as if it were a matter of saving his own son. He would not listen, he insisted as hard as he could on the necessity for poultices and, on top of that, two or three cups of weak tea, drunk all at once—"not simply hot, sir, but boiling hot!" He did run to Mavra, without waiting for permission, made a fire with her in the kitchen, which had always stood empty, started the samovar; meanwhile he managed to put the sick man to bed, took his street clothes off, wrapped him in a blanket, and in no more than twenty minutes had cooked up some tea and the first poultice.

"It's heated plates, sir, burning hot!" he said almost in ecstasy, placing the heated plate wrapped in a towel on Velchaninov's pained chest. "There aren't any other poultices, sir, and it would take too long to get them, and plates, I swear on my honor, sir, will even be best of all; it's been tested on Pyotr Kuzmich, sir, with my own eyes and hands. You can die of it, sir. Drink the tea, swallow it—never mind if it burns you; life's dearer . . . than foppery, sir . . ."

He got the half-asleep Mavra to bustle about; the plates were changed every three or four minutes. After the third plate and the second cup of boiling hot tea drunk at one gulp, Velchaninov suddenly felt relief.

"Once you've dislodged the pain, thank God for that, sir, it's a good sign!" Pavel Pavlovich cried out and ran to fetch a fresh plate and fresh tea.

"Only to break the pain! If we can only turn the pain back!" he kept saying every moment.

After half an hour, the pain was quite weakened, but the patient was so worn out that, however Pavel Pavlovich begged, he would not agree to endure "one more little plate, sir." His eyes were closing from weakness.

"Sleep, sleep," he repeated in a weak voice.

"Right you are!" Pavel Pavlovich agreed.

"You spend the night . . . what time is it?"

"A quarter to two, sir."

"Spend the night."

"I will, I will."

A minute later the sick man called Pavel Pavlovich again.

"You, you," he murmured when the man came running and bent over him, "you—are better than I! I understand everything, everything . . . thank you."

"Sleep, sleep," Pavel Pavlovich whispered, and hastened on tiptoe back to his sofa.

As he was falling asleep, the sick man could still hear Pavel Pavlovich quietly and hurriedly making his bed, taking off his clothes, and, finally, putting out the candle and, barely breathing, so as not to make any noise, stretching himself out on the sofa.

Undoubtedly Velchaninov did sleep and fell asleep very soon after the candles were put out; he clearly recalled it afterward. But all the while he slept, till the very moment he woke up, he dreamed that he was not asleep and that it was as if he was quite unable to fall asleep, despite his weakness. Finally, he dreamed he was having a sort of waking delirium and was quite unable to scatter the visions crowding around him, despite the full awareness that it was only delirium and not reality. The visions were all familiar ones; his room was as if filled with people, and the door to the front hall stood open; crowds of people poured in and thronged the stairs. At the table, moved out into the middle of the room, sat a man—exactly as the other time, in the identical dream he had had a month earlier. Just as then, this man sat with his elbow on the table and refused to speak; but now he was wearing a round hat with crape. "What? could it have been Pavel Pavlovich then, too?" Velchaninov thought—but, peeking into the silent man's face, he convinced himself that it was someone else entirely. "Why the crape, then?" Velchaninov puzzled. The noise, talk, and clamor of people crowding around the table were terrible. It seemed these people had still greater malice toward Velchaninov than in the other dream; they threatened him with their fists and shouted at him about something with all their might, but precisely what—he was quite unable to make out. "But this is a delirium, I know it!" the thought came to him. "I know that I couldn't fall asleep and have now

gotten up, because I couldn't stay in bed from anguish! . . ."
However, the shouting and the people, and their gestures, and
all—were so vivid, so real, that he sometimes had doubts:
"Can it really be a delirium? What do these people want from
me, my God! But if it's not a delirium, then is it possible that
such a clamor has not awakened Pavel Pavlovich yet? that he's
here asleep, right here on the sofa?" Finally, something suddenly happened, again as in that other dream; everyone rushed
to the stairs and got terribly jammed in the doorway, because
a new crowd was pouring into the room from the stairs. These
people were carrying something with them, something big and
heavy; one could hear the heavy steps of the carriers resounding on the treads of the stairs and their puffing voices hurriedly calling to each other. Everyone in the room cried out:
"They're bringing it, they're bringing it!" All eyes flashed and
turned to Velchaninov; threatening and triumphant, everyone
pointed to the stairs. No longer doubting in the least that it
was all not delirium but the truth, he stood on tiptoe to see
quickly, over people's heads, what it was that they were bringing. His heart was pounding, pounding, pounding, and suddenly—exactly as then, in that other dream—there came three
loud strokes of the doorbell. And once again this was so clear,
so tangibly real a ringing, that, of course, such ringing could
not have been merely dreamed in a dream! . . . He cried out
and woke up.

But he did not, as then, go racing for the door. What
thought guided his first movement and did he even have any
sort of thought at that moment?—no, it was as if someone
prompted him to what had to be done: he snatched himself
from bed and rushed with outstretched arms, as if defending
himself and warding off an attack, straight toward where Pavel
Pavlovich lay sleeping. His arms at once met other arms already stretched out over him, and he seized them fast; someone therefore already stood bending over him. The curtains
were drawn, but it was not totally dark, because a weak light
was coming from the other room, where there were no such
curtains. Suddenly something cut the palm and fingers of his

left hand terribly painfully, and he instantly understood that he had seized the blade of a knife or razor and gripped it tightly in his hand . . . At the same moment something fell with a single weighty thump to the floor.

Velchaninov was perhaps three times stronger than Pavel Pavlovich, but their struggle continued for a long time, some three full minutes. He soon bent him down to the floor and twisted his arms behind his back, but for some reason he absolutely wanted to bind those twisted arms. With his right hand—his wounded left hand holding the murderer—he began to grope for the curtain cord, could not find it for a long time, but got hold of it at last and tore it from the window. He himself marveled later at the unnatural strength required for that. In all these three minutes neither of them said a word; one could hear only their heavy breathing and the muffled sounds of the struggle. Finally, having twisted and bound Pavel Pavlovich's arms behind his back, Velchaninov left him on the floor, stood up, opened the window curtain, and raised the blind. It was already light in the solitary street. Opening the window, he stood for a few moments taking deep breaths of air. It was just past four. Closing the window, he walked unhurriedly to the cupboard, took out a clean towel, and wound it very tightly around his left hand to stop the blood flowing from it. Under his feet he found the open razor lying on the rug; he picked it up, closed it, put it in the razor case, forgotten that morning on the little table just next to the sofa on which Pavel Pavlovich had slept, and locked this case in his bureau with a key. Only after doing all that did he go over to Pavel Pavlovich and begin studying him.

The man had meanwhile managed with effort to get up from the rug and sit in an armchair. He was not dressed, only in his underwear, even without boots. The back and sleeves of his shirt were wet with blood; the blood was not his, but from Velchaninov's cut hand. Of course, this was Pavel Pavlovich, but it would almost have been possible not to recognize him in the first moment, if one had met him like that by chance—so much had his physiognomy changed. He sat awkwardly straight in the armchair because of his bound arms, his distorted and worn-out face gone green, and shivered from time to time. Intently, but with some dark look, as if not yet distinguishing everything, he gazed at Velchaninov. Suddenly he smiled dully and, nodding at the carafe of water that stood on the table, said in a short half whisper:

"Some water, sir."

Velchaninov poured some and held the glass for him to drink. Pavel Pavlovich greedily fell upon the water; having taken three gulps, he raised his head, looked very intently into the face of Velchaninov, who was standing before him with the glass in his hand, but said nothing and went on drinking. After finishing the water, he gave a deep sigh. Velchaninov took his pillow, picked up his clothes, and went to the other room, locking Pavel Pavlovich in the first room.

His earlier pain had gone away completely, but he felt a new and extreme weakness after the momentary strain just now of that strength which had come to him from God knows where. He tried to sort the incident out, but his thoughts still connected poorly; the shock had been too strong. His eyes would now close, sometimes even for ten minutes, now he would suddenly give a start, wake up, remember everything, raise his aching hand wrapped in the blood-soaked towel, and start thinking greedily and feverishly. He decided only one thing clearly: that Pavel Pavlovich had really wanted to kill him, but that maybe a quarter of an hour before then he had not known he would kill him. The razor case had maybe only flitted past his eyes during the evening without provoking any thought, and had merely stayed in his memory. (As for the razors, they were always kept in his bureau under lock and key, and it was only the previous morning that Velchaninov had taken them out to shave off some superfluous hairs around his mustache and side-whiskers—something he used to do occasionally.)

"If he had long been planning to kill me, he would have made sure to prepare a knife or a pistol beforehand, and not have counted on my razors, which he had never seen until yesterday evening"—came to his head, among other things.

It finally struck six. Velchaninov collected himself, got

dressed, and went to Pavel Pavlovich. Unlocking the door, he could not understand what he had locked Pavel Pavlovich in for and why he had not let him out of the house then and there. To his surprise, the arrested man was already fully dressed; he must have found some opportunity for disentangling himself. He was sitting in the armchair, but got up at once, as soon as Velchaninov entered. The hat was already in his hand. His anxious eyes said, as if hurrying:

"Don't start talking; there's no point in starting; there's no reason to talk . . ."

"Go!" said Velchaninov. "Take your case," he added behind him.

Pavel Pavlovich came back from the door, took the case with the bracelet from the table, put it in his pocket, and walked out to the stairs. Velchaninov stood in the doorway to lock up after him. Their eyes met for the last time. Pavel Pavlovich suddenly stopped, the two gazed into each other's eyes for some five seconds—as if hesitating; finally, Velchaninov waved his arm weakly at him.

"Well, go!" he said in a half voice, closed the door, and locked it.

XVI

Analysis

A feeling of extraordinary, immense joy came over him; something was finished, unbound; some terrible anguish loosened and dispersed altogether. So it seemed to him. It had lasted five weeks. He kept raising his hand, looking at the blood-soaked towel, and muttering to himself: "No, now it's all completely finished!" And all that morning, for the first time in those three weeks, he almost did not think of Liza—as if this blood from his cut fingers could "square accounts" even with that anguish.

He was clearly conscious that he had escaped terrible danger. "These people," went through his mind, "it's these very people who, even a minute before, don't know if they're going to stab you, but once they take the knife in their trembling hands and feel the first spurt of hot blood on their fingers, they won't just stab you—they'll cut your head 'clean off,' as convicts say. It's quite so."

He could not stay home and went out convinced that it was necessary to do something right away, or else right away something was sure to be done to him of itself; he walked the streets and waited. He wanted terribly to meet someone, to talk with someone, even a stranger, and only that, finally, suggested to him the thought of a doctor and that his hand probably ought to be properly bandaged. The doctor, an old acquaintance, after examining the wound, asked curiously: "How could this have happened?" Velchaninov laughed him off, joked, and almost told all, but restrained himself. The doctor was obliged to take his pulse and, on learning of the previous night's attack, talked him there and then into taking a calmative he had on hand. He also calmed him down regarding the cut: "There can be no especially bad consequences." Velchaninov laughed loudly and started assuring him that there had already been excellent consequences. The irrepressible desire to tell *all* repeated itself with him two more times that day—once even with a total stranger with whom he himself started a conversation in a pastry shop. Up to then he had hated starting conversations with strangers in public places.

He stopped at shops, bought a newspaper, called at his tailor's and ordered some clothes. The thought of visiting the Pogoreltsevs continued to be disagreeable to him, and he did not think about them; besides, he could not go to the country: it was as if he kept expecting something here in town. He dined with pleasure, talked with the waiter and with a neighboring diner, and drank half a bottle of wine. He did not even think of the possibility of yesterday's attack coming back; he was convinced that his illness had gone completely the very moment yesterday when, having fallen asleep so strengthless, he had jumped from his bed an hour and a half later and with such strength hurled his murderer to the floor. Toward evening, however, he felt dizzy and it was as if something like last night's delirium in sleep began to come over him again at moments. He returned home at dusk and was almost scared of his room when he entered it. Dreadful and eerie his apartment seemed to him. He walked around it several times and even went into his kitchen, where he hardly ever went. "They heated the plates here yesterday," came to his mind. He locked the door well and lit the candles earlier than usual. As he was locking the door, he remembered that half an hour before, passing by the caretaker's room, he had called Mavra out and asked her: "Hadn't Pavel Pavlovich come by while he was out?"—as if he might really have come by.

Having locked himself in carefully, he unlocked his bureau, took out the case of razors, and opened "yesterday's" razor to have a look at it. On the white bone handle slight traces of blood remained. He put the razor back into the case and locked it up in the bureau again. He wanted to sleep; he felt that it was necessary to lie down right away—otherwise "tomorrow he won't be good for anything." For some reason he imagined the next day as fatal and "definitive." But the same thoughts that had never left him for a moment all day, even outside, also crowded and throbbed in his sick head now, tirelessly and irresistibly, and he kept thinking, thinking, thinking, and it would be a long time before he fell asleep . . .

"If we decide that he got up to kill me *inadvertently*," he kept thinking and thinking, "then had the thought come to him at least once before, at least as a dream in some wicked moment?"

He decided the question strangely—that "Pavel Pavlovich had wanted to kill him, but the thought of the killing had never once occurred to the future killer." In short: "Pavel Pavlovich had wanted to kill, but hadn't known that he wanted to kill. It's senseless, but it's so," thought Velchaninov. "He came here not to solicit a post and not for Bagautov—though he did solicit a post and call on Bagautov, and was furious when the man died; he despised Bagautov like a chip of wood. He came here for me and came with Liza . . .

"And did I myself expect that he . . . would put a knife in me?" He decided that, yes, he had expected it precisely from the very moment he had seen him in the coach following Bagautov's coffin. "I began as if to expect something . . . but, naturally, not this, naturally, not that he would put a knife in me! . . .

"And can it be, can it be that it was all true," he exclaimed again, suddenly raising his head from the pillow and opening his eyes, "all that this . . . madman told me yesterday about his love for me, when his chin trembled and he beat his breast with his fist?

"Perfectly true!" he decided, tirelessly delving deeper and analyzing. "This Quasimodo[15] from T——— is only too sufficiently stupid and noble to fall in love with the lover of his wife, in whom, for twenty years, he noticed *nothing*! He respected me for nine years, he honored my memory and remembered my 'utterances'—Lord, and I had no idea of anything! He couldn't have been lying yesterday! But did he love me yesterday when he talked about his love and said: 'Let's square accounts'? Yes, loved me *from spite;* that's the strongest love . . .

"And it could have been, and certainly was so, that I produced a colossal impression on him in T———, precisely a colossal and a 'delightful' one, and it's precisely with such a Schiller in the shape of Quasimodo that that could happen! He exaggerated me a hundredfold, because I struck him too much in his philosophical solitude . . . It would be curious to know, precisely what about me struck him? Really, it might have been fresh gloves and knowing how to put them on. Quasimodos love aesthetics, oh, how they do! Gloves are all too sufficient for some most noble soul, the more so for one of the 'eternal husbands.' The rest they'll fill out a thousandfold and they'll even fight for you if you want. And how highly he rates my means of seduction! Maybe it's precisely the means of seduction that struck him most of all. And that cry of his then: 'If even this one as well, then who can one believe in after that?' After such a cry, one could turn into a beast! . . .

"Hm! He came here so that we could 'embrace each other and weep,' as he himself put it in the meanest way—that is, he was coming in order to put a knife in me, but thought he was coming 'to embrace and weep' . . . And he brought Liza. What, then: if I had wept with him, maybe he would in fact have forgiven me, because he wanted terribly to forgive! . . . All this turned, at the first encounter, into drunken clowning and caricature, and into a vile, womanish howling about being offended. (The horns, he made horns over his forehead!) That's why he came drunk, so as to speak it out, even while clowning; he couldn't do it not drunk . . . And he did like clowning, oh, how he did! Oh, how glad he was when he made me kiss him! Only he didn't know then what he would end with: embracing or killing. It came out, of course, that the best would be both together. The most natural solution!—Yes, sir, nature doesn't like monsters and finishes them off with 'natural solutions.' The most monstrous monster is the monster with noble feelings: I know it from my own experience, Pavel Pavlovich! For a monster, nature is not a tender mother, she's a stepmother. Nature gives birth to a monster, and, instead of pitying him, executes him—and right she is. Even decent folk in our time don't get off easily with embraces and tears of all-forgiveness, to say nothing of such as you and I, Pavel Pavlovich!

"Yes, he was stupid enough to take me to his fiancée as well—Lord! His fiancée! Only such a Quasimodo could conceive the thought of 'resurrection into a new life'—by means of Mademoiselle Zakhlebinin's innocence! But it's not your fault, Pavel Pavlovich, it's not your fault: you're a monster, and therefore everything in you must be monstrous—both your dreams and your hopes. But, though you're a monster, you still doubted your dream, and that's why you required the high sanction of Velchaninov, the reverently respected. He needed Velchaninov's approval, his confirmation that the dream was not a dream but the real thing. Out of reverent respect for me, he took me there, believing in the nobility of my feelings—believing, perhaps, that there, under a bush, we'd embrace each other and weep, in the proximity of innocence. Yes! and this 'eternal husband' was bound, he was obliged, finally, to punish himself definitively for everything sometime or other, and in order to punish himself, he seized the razor—inadvertently, it's true, but even so he did it! 'Even so he did stab him with a knife, even so he ended by stabbing him, in the governor's presence!' And, by the way, did he have at least some thought of that sort when he was telling me his anecdote about the best man? And was there in fact something that night when he got out of bed and stood in the middle of the room? Hm. No, he stood there *as a joke* then. He got up for his own business, and when he saw that I was afraid of him, he refused to answer me for ten minutes, because he found it very pleasant that I was afraid of him . . . Maybe it was then that he really imagined something for the first time, as he was standing there in the dark . . .

"But all the same, if I hadn't forgotten those razors on the table yesterday—maybe nothing would have happened. Is that so? Is it so? After all, he did avoid me earlier, he didn't come for two weeks; he hid from me, *pitying* me! He did choose Bagautov to begin with, and not me! He did jump out of bed at night to warm the plates, thinking of creating a diversion—from the knife to loving-kindness! . . . He wanted to save himself and me—with warmed-up plates! . . ."

And for a long time yet the sick head of this former "man of the world" worked in this way, pouring from empty into void, before he calmed down. He woke up the next day with the same sick head, but with a totally *new* and totally unexpected horror.

This new horror came from the absolute conviction, which unexpectedly consolidated in him, that he, Velchaninov (and man of the world), today, himself, of his own free will, would end it all by going to Pavel Pavlovich—why? what for?—Of that he knew nothing and in his disgust he wanted to know nothing; he knew only that for some reason he would drag himself.

This madness—he could call it nothing else—developed, all the same, to the point of acquiring a possibly reasonable shape and a quite legitimate pretext: he still kept as if envisioning that Pavel Pavlovich would go back to his room, lock the door tightly, and—hang himself, like that cashier Marya Sysoevna told about. This yesterday's reverie gradually turned into a senseless but irrefutable conviction in him. "Why would the fool hang himself?" he interrupted himself every moment. He remembered Liza's words long ago . . . "And besides, in his place I, too, might hang myself . . ." it once occurred to him.

The end of it was that, instead of going to dinner, he did after all set out for Pavel Pavlovich's. "I'll just inquire of Marya Sysoevna," he decided. But, before coming out to the street, he stopped suddenly under the gateway.

"Can it be, can it be," he cried, turning crimson with shame. "Can it be that I'm trudging there in order to 'embrace and weep'? Can it be that the whole disgrace lacks only this last senseless abomination!"

But the providence of all respectable and decent people saved him from "senseless abomination." As soon as he reached the street, he suddenly ran into Alexander Lobov. The youth was puffing and excited.

"I was coming to see you! This friend of yours, Pavel Pavlovich, just imagine!"

"Hanged himself?" Velchaninov muttered wildly.

"Who hanged himself? Why?" Lobov goggled his eyes.

"Never mind . . . just so, go on!"

"Pah, the devil, what a funny turn of thought you've got, though! He by no means hanged himself (why hang himself?). On the contrary—he left. I put him on the train just now and sent him off. Pah, how he drinks, let me tell you! We drank three bottles, Predposylov, too—but how he drinks, how he drinks! He sang songs on the train, remembered you, waved his hand, asked to send you his greetings. A scoundrel, don't you think—eh?"

The young man was indeed tipsy; his flushed face, shining eyes, and poorly obedient tongue bore strong witness to that. Velchaninov guffawed at the top of his lungs:

"So they did finally end by pledging brotherhood!—ha, ha! Embraced and wept! Ah, you Schiller-poets!"

"No abuse, please. You know, he gave it up altogether *there*. He was there yesterday and today as well. He peached on us terribly. Nadya's locked up—sitting in the attic. Shouts, tears, but we won't yield! But how he drinks, let me tell you, how he drinks! And you know, he's such *mauvais ton*[16]—that is, not *mauvais ton,* but what's the word? . . . And he kept remembering you, but there's no comparison with you! After all, you are a decent man and in fact once belonged to high society, and only now have been forced to shun—on account of poverty or whatever . . . Devil knows, I didn't quite understand him."

"Ah, so he told you about me in such terms?"

"He . . . he—don't be angry. Being a citizen is better than high society. I mean, in our time in Russia one doesn't know whom to respect. You must agree that it's a bad disease of the time, when one doesn't know whom to respect—isn't it true?"

"True, true, but about him?"

"Him? Whom!—ah, yes! Why did he keep saying: the fifty-year-old *but* ruined Velchaninov? Why: *but* ruined and not *and* ruined! He laughs, he repeated it a thousand times. He got on the train, started a song, and wept—it's simply disgusting; it's even pathetic—the man's drunk. Ah, I don't like fools! He started throwing money to the beggars, for the repose of the soul of Lizaveta—his wife, or what?"

"Daughter."

"What's with your hand?"

"I cut it."

"Never mind, it'll go away. You know, devil take him, it's good that he left, but I'll bet that there, where he's gone, he'll get married again at once—isn't it true?"

"But don't you want to get married, too?"

"Me? I'm a different matter—what a one you are, really! If

you're fifty years old, then he's certainly sixty; we must be logical here, my dear sir! And you know, formerly, long ago now, I was a pure Slavophile in my convictions, but now we're expecting dawn from the West . . . Well, good-bye; it's lucky I ran into you without going in; I won't go in, don't ask, I have no time! . . ."

And he started to dash off.

"Ah, yes, what's the matter with me," he suddenly came back, "he sent me to you with a letter! Here it is. Why didn't you come to see him off?"

Velchaninov returned home and opened the envelope which was addressed to him.

There was not a single line from Pavel Pavlovich in the envelope, but it contained some other letter. Velchaninov recognized the hand. The letter was an old one, on time-yellowed paper, with faded ink, written to him some ten years earlier in Petersburg, two months after he left T————. But this letter had not gone to him; instead of it, he had received another one then; that was clear from the content of the yellowed letter. In this letter Natalia Vassilievna, bidding him farewell forever—just as in the letter he had received then—and confessing to him her love for another man, did not, however, conceal her pregnancy. On the contrary, to console him she promised to find an occasion for conveying the future child to him, assured him that from then on they would have other responsibilities, that their friendship was now sealed forever—in short, there was not much logic, but the goal was the same: that he should deliver her from his love. She even allowed him to visit T———— in a year—to see the baby. God knows why she had changed her mind and sent the other letter instead of this one.

Velchaninov, as he read it, turned pale, but he also imagined Pavel Pavlovich finding this letter and reading it for the first time before the opened heirloom box of ebony inlaid with mother-of-pearl.

"He also must have gone pale as death," he thought, chancing to notice his face in the mirror. "He must have been reading it and closing his eyes, and then suddenly opening them

again, hoping the letter would turn to simple blank paper
. . . He probably repeated the experiment three or four
times! . . ."

XVII

The Eternal Husband

Almost exactly two years went by after the adventure we have
described. We meet Mr. Velchaninov one beautiful summer
day in a car of one of our newly opened railways. He was on
his way to Odessa to join a friend, for the pleasure of it, and,
along with that, on account of another, also quite agreeable,
circumstance; through his friend he hoped to arrange for himself a meeting with one extremely interesting woman, with
whom he had long wished to become acquainted. Without
going into details, we shall limit ourselves to pointing out that
he had regenerated, or, better to say, improved greatly over the
last two years. Of the former hypochondria almost no traces
remained. All that remained to him of various "memories"
and anxieties—the consequences of illness—which had begun
to beset him two years ago in Petersburg during the time of
his then unsuccessful lawsuit—was some hidden shame from
the awareness of his former faintheartedness. He was partially
recompensed by the certainty that there would be no more of
it and that no one would ever know about it. True, he had
abandoned society then, had even begun to dress poorly, had
hidden somewhere from everyone—and this, of course, everyone had noticed. But he had so quickly come forth to plead
guilty, and with such a newly revived and self-confident air,
that "everyone" forgave at once his momentary falling away;
even those of them whom he had stopped greeting, these were
the first to acknowledge him and offer him their hand, and
what's more without any importunate questions—as if he had
been absent all the while somewhere far away on family business, which was no one's affair, and had only just come back.

The reason for all these beneficial and sensible changes for the better was, naturally, the winning of the lawsuit. Velchaninov got only sixty thousand roubles—no great thing, granted, but a very important one for him: first of all, he felt himself at once on firm ground again—meaning morally appeased; he knew for certain now that he would not squander this last of his money "like a fool," as he had squandered his first two fortunes, and that he would have enough for the rest of his life. "However tottering their social edifice may be, and whatever they may be trumpeting there," he thought occasionally, lending an ear and eye to all the marvelous and incredible that was being accomplished around him and all over Russia, "whatever people and thought may be regenerating into there, still I will always at least have this fine and tasty dinner which I'm now sitting down to, and thus I'm prepared for anything." This thought, tender to the point of voluptuousness, was gradually taking full possession of him and produced in him even a physical turnabout, not to mention a moral one: he now looked like a totally different man compared with that "marmot" we described two years ago, with whom such indecent stories were beginning to happen—he looked cheerful, bright, imposing. Even the malignant wrinkles that had begun to form around his eyes and on his forehead were almost smoothed out; his complexion even changed—it became whiter, rosier. At the present moment he was sitting in a comfortable seat in a first-class car, and a sweet thought was hatching in his mind: at the next station there would be a fork and a new line going to the right. "If I were to leave the direct line for a moment and bear to the right, then in no more than two stops I could visit yet another lady of my acquaintance, who has just returned from abroad and is now living in—agreeable for me, but rather boring for her—provincial seclusion; and thus the possibility arises of spending my time no less interestingly than in Odessa, the more so as Odessa won't slip away either . . ." But he was still hesitant and had not made a final decision; he was "waiting for a push." Meanwhile the station was approaching; the push was also not long in coming.

At this station the train stopped for forty minutes and the passengers were offered dinner. Just at the entrance to the waiting room for first- and second-class passengers there crowded, as usual, an impatient and hurrying multitude of people, and—perhaps also as usual—a scandal took place. One lady, who got out of a second-class car and was remarkably pretty, but somehow too magnificently dressed for a traveler, almost dragged with her, in both hands, an uhlan, a very young and handsome little officer, who was trying to tear free of her grip. The young officer was very tipsy, and the lady, in all probability an older relative, would not let him go, surely for fear he would rush straight to the buffet for a drink. Meanwhile, the uhlan was jostled in the crush by a little merchant, also on a spree, and even outrageously so. This merchant had been stuck at the station for two days already, drinking and squandering money, surrounded by all sorts of comradery, and kept being late for the train to continue his journey. There was a quarrel, the officer shouted, the merchant cursed, the lady was in despair and, drawing the uhlan away from the quarrel, exclaimed to him in a pleading voice: "Mitenka! Mitenka!" The little merchant found this much too scandalous; true, everyone was laughing, but the merchant was the more upset on account of what seemed to him, for some reason, an offense to morality.

"See that—'Mitenka'! . . ." he said reproachfully, imitating the lady's piping little voice. "They're no longer ashamed even in public!"

And, staggering over to the lady, who had thrown herself down on the first chair she could find and managed to sit the uhlan down beside her, he looked them both over with contempt and drew out in a singsong voice:

"Slut, slut that you are, your skirt tail's all tattered!"

The lady shrieked and looked around pitifully, waiting for deliverance. She was ashamed, she was afraid, and to crown it all, the officer tore from his chair and, with a yell, rushed for the merchant, but slipped and flopped back into the chair. The guffawing increased around them, while no one even thought of helping; but Velchaninov did help; he suddenly seized the little merchant by the scruff of the neck and, turning him around, shoved him some five steps away from the frightened woman. With that the scandal ended; the little merchant was greatly taken aback both by the shove and by Velchaninov's imposing figure; he was led away at once by his comrades. The dignified physiognomy of the elegantly dressed gentleman produced an imposing impression on the jeerers as well: the laughter ceased. The lady, blushing and almost in tears, began pouring out assurances of her gratitude. The uhlan muttered: "Thanksh, thanksh!"—and made as if to offer Velchaninov his hand, but instead suddenly decided to lie down across the chairs and stretch his legs out on them.

"Mitenka!" the lady moaned reproachfully, clasping her hands.

Velchaninov was pleased both with the adventure and with its setting. The lady interested him; she was, as could be seen, a rich provincial, dressed magnificently but tastelessly, and with somewhat ridiculous manners—she precisely united in herself everything that guaranteed success to a big-city fop with certain goals regarding women. A conversation started; the lady hotly told and complained about her husband, who "suddenly disappeared somewhere from the car, and that was why it all happened, because it was eternally so, when needed, he'd disappear somewhere . . ."

"For a necessity . . ." the uhlan muttered.

"Ah, Mitenka!" she again clasped her hands.

"The husband's going to catch it!" thought Velchaninov.

"What's his name? I'll go and find him," he offered.

"Pal Palych," the uhlan responded.

"Your husband's name is Pavel Pavlovich?" Velchaninov asked with curiosity, and suddenly the familiar bald head thrust itself between him and the lady. Instantly he pictured the Zakhlebinins' garden, innocent games, and the importunate bald head constantly thrusting itself between him and Nadezhda Fedoseevna.

"Here you are at last!" the wife cried out hysterically.

It was Pavel Pavlovich himself; in surprise and fear he gazed at Velchaninov, struck dumb before him as before a phantom. His stupefaction was so great that for some time he apparently understood nothing of what his insulted spouse was telling him in an irritable and quick patter. Finally he gave a start and grasped all his horror at once: his own guilt, and about Mitenka, and about this "m'sieur"—for some reason the lady referred this way to Velchaninov—"being our guardian angel and a savior, and you—you are eternally elsewhere when you should be here . . ."

Velchaninov suddenly burst out laughing.

"But he and I are friends, friends from childhood!" he exclaimed to the astonished lady, familiarly and patronizingly putting his right arm around the shoulders of Pavel Pavlovich, who was smiling a pale smile. "Didn't he ever tell you about Velchaninov?"

"No, never," the wife was slightly dumbstruck.

"But do introduce me to your wife, you perfidious friend!"

"This, Lipochka, is indeed Mr. Velchaninov, this is . . ." Pavel Pavlovich tried to begin and shamefully broke off. The wife turned red and flashed her eyes at him in spite, obviously for the "Lipochka."

"And imagine not telling me you were getting married, and not inviting me to the wedding, but you, Olympiada . . ."

"Semyonovna," Pavel Pavlovich prompted.

"Semyonovna," suddenly echoed the falling-asleep uhlan.

"You must forgive him, Olympiada Semyonovna, for me, for the sake of friends meeting . . . He's a good husband!"

And Velchaninov amicably slapped Pavel Pavlovich on the shoulder.

"But, darling, I only stayed behind . . . for a moment . . ." Pavel Pavlovich began to justify himself.

"And abandoned your wife to disgrace!" Lipochka picked up at once. "You're never where you ought to be, and where you oughn't to be, there you are . . ."

"Where you oughtn't to be—there where you oughtn't to be . . . where you oughtn't to be . . ." the uhlan kept agreeing.

Lipochka was nearly breathless with agitation; she knew it

was not nice in front of Velchaninov, and she blushed, but she could not help herself.

"Where you oughtn't to be, you're all too cautious, all too cautious!" escaped from her.

"Under the bed . . . looks for lovers . . . under the bed—where he oughtn't to be . . . oughtn't to be . . ." Mitenka, too, suddenly became terribly agitated.

But there was nothing to be done with Mitenka. Everything ended pleasantly, however; full acquaintance ensued; Pavel Pavlovich was sent for coffee and bouillon. Olympiada Semyonovna explained to Velchaninov that they were now going from O., where her husband worked, to spend two months on their estate, that it was not far away, only twenty-five miles from this station, that they had a wonderful house and garden there, that they would have guests, that they also had neighbors, and that if Alexei Ivanovich was so good as to wish to visit them "in their seclusion," she would receive him as a guardian angel, because she could not recall without horror what would have happened if . . . and so on and so forth—in short, "as a guardian angel . . ."

"And a savior, and a savior," the uhlan ardently insisted.

Velchaninov politely thanked her and replied that he was always ready, that he was a perfectly idle and unoccupied man, and that Olympiada Semyonovna's invitation was only too flattering for him. After which he at once began a merry little conversation, into which he successfully inserted two or three compliments. Lipochka blushed with pleasure and, as soon as Pavel Pavlovich returned, announced to him rapturously that Alexei Ivanovich had been so good as to accept her invitation to be their guest in the country for a whole month and promised to come in a week. Pavel Pavlovich gave a lost smile and said nothing. Olympiada Semyonovna shrugged at him and raised her eyes to heaven. Finally they parted: once more gratitude, again "guardian angel," again "Mitenka," and Pavel Pavlovich finally took his spouse and the uhlan to put them on the train. Velchaninov lit a cigar and began to stroll along the gallery in front of the station; he knew that Pavel Pavlovich would presently come running back again to talk with him before the bell rang. And so it happened. Pavel Pavlovich immediately appeared before him with an anxious question in his eyes and on his whole physiognomy. Velchaninov laughed: he took him "amicably" by the elbow and, drawing him to the nearest bench, sat down and sat him down beside him. He kept silent himself; he wanted Pavel Pavlovich to be the first to speak.

"So you're coming to visit us, sir?" the man babbled, approaching the matter with complete frankness.

"I just knew it! Hasn't changed a bit!" Velchaninov burst out laughing. "But could you really," he again slapped him on the shoulder, "could you really think seriously even for a moment that I would in fact come to visit, and for a whole month at that—ha, ha!"

Pavel Pavlovich became all aroused.

"So you—won't come, sir!" he cried out, not concealing his joy in the least.

"I won't, I won't!" Velchaninov laughed smugly. However, he himself did not understand why he found it so especially funny, but the further it went, the funnier it became to him.

"Can it be . . . can it really be as you say, sir?" And, having said that, Pavel Pavlovich even jumped up from his seat in trembling expectation.

"But I already said I won't come—what a queer fellow you are!"

"How then . . . if so, sir, how shall I tell Olympiada Semyonovna, when you don't come in a week, after she's been waiting, sir?"

"That's a hard one! Tell her I broke a leg or something like that."

"She won't believe it, sir," Pavel Pavlovich drew out in a plaintive little voice.

"And you'll catch hell?" Velchaninov went on laughing. "But I notice, my poor friend, that you do tremble before your beautiful spouse—eh?"

Pavel Pavlovich tried to smile, but it did not come off. That Velchaninov had renounced his visit—that, of course, was

good; but that he spoke familiarly about his wife—now, that
was bad. Pavel Pavlovich cringed. Velchaninov noticed it.
Meanwhile the second bell had already rung; from the faraway
car came a piping little voice, anxiously summoning Pavel
Pavlovich. He fidgeted on the spot, but did not run at the
summons, apparently expecting something more from
Velchaninov—of course, a further assurance that he would not
visit them.

"What is your wife's former name?" Velchaninov said, as if
not noticing Pavel Pavlovich's anxiety at all.

"I took her from our local vicar, sir," the man replied,
glancing at the train in bewilderment and cocking an ear.

"Ah, I understand, for her beauty."

Pavel Pavlovich cringed again.

"And who is this Mitenka to you?"

"He's just so, sir; our distant relative—that is, mine, sir, my
late cousin's son, Golubchikov, demoted for disorderly con-
duct, and now restored again; so we've equipped him . . .
An unfortunate young man, sir . . ."

"Well, well," thought Velchaninov, "everything's in order—
the full setup!"

"Pavel Pavlovich!" again a distant summons was heard from
the car, now with quite an irritated note in the voice.

"Pal Palych!" came another, hoarse voice.

Pavel Pavlovich again started figeting and fussing about,
but Velchaninov seized him firmly by the elbow and stopped
him.

"And do you want me to go right now and tell your wife
how you wanted to put a knife in me—eh?"

"How can you, how can you, sir!" Pavel Pavlovich was terribly frightened, "God keep you from it, sir!"

"Pavel Pavlovich! Pavel Pavlovich!" the voices were heard
again.

"Well, go, then!" Velchaninov released him at last, continuing to laugh good-naturedly.

"So you won't come, sir!" Pavel Pavlovich, all but in dis-
pair, whispered a last time, and even clasped his hands before
him, palms together, as in old times.

"No, I swear to you, I won't come! Run, or there'll be trouble!"

And he sweepingly offered him his hand—offered it and gave a start: Pavel Pavlovich did not take his hand, he even drew his own back.

The third bell rang.

In an instant something strange happened with the two men; they both as if transformed. Something wavered as it were and suddenly snapped in Velchaninov, who had been laughing so much only a moment before. He firmly and furiously seized Pavel Pavlovich by the shoulder.

"If I, if *I* offer you this hand here," he showed him the palm of his left hand, on which there clearly remained a big scar from the cut, "then you might well take it!" he whispered with trembling and paled lips.

Pavel Pavlovich also paled and his lips also trembled. Some sort of spasms suddenly passed over his face.

"And Liza, sir?" he murmured in a quick whisper—and suddenly his lips, cheeks, and chin quivered, and tears poured from his eyes. Velchaninov stood before him like a post.

"Pavel Pavlovich! Pavel Pavlovich!" screams came from the car, as if someone were being slaughtered there—and suddenly the whistle blew.

Pavel Pavlovich came to his senses, clasped his hands, and dashed off at top speed; the train had already started, but he somehow managed to hold on and climb into his car in flight. Velchaninov remained at the station and continued his journey only toward evening, having waited for the next train in the same direction. He did not go to the right, to his provincial lady acquaintance—he was much too out of sorts. And how sorry he was later!

BOBOK
NOTES OF A CERTAIN PERSON

This time I am including the "Notes of a Certain Person."[1] It is not I; it is an entirely different person. I think there is no need for any further preface.

Semyon Ardalyonovich hands me this the other day:

"But, pray tell me, Ivan Ivanych, will you ever be sober?"

A strange demand. I'm not offended, I'm a timid man; but, anyhow, now they've made a madman out of me. An artist had occasion to paint my portrait. "After all," he says, "you're a writer." I yielded; he exhibited it. I read: "Go look at this morbid, nearly crazy person."

Maybe it's so, but still, why come right out with it in print? In print we need everything noble; we need ideals, but this . . .

At least say it indirectly, that's what you have style for. No, he no longer wants it indirect. Nowadays humor and good style are disappearing, and abuse is taken for wit. I'm not offended: God knows I'm not such a writer as to lose my mind over it. I wrote a story—it wasn't published. I wrote a feuilleton—it was rejected. I took a lot of these feuilletons to various editorial offices, they were rejected everywhere: you lack salt, they said.

"What kind of salt do you want," I ask mockingly, "Attic salt?"[2]

He doesn't even understand. I mainly translate from the French for booksellers. I also write advertisements for merchants: "A rarity!" I say. "Red tea from our own plantations . . ." I made a pile on a panegyric for His Excellency the late Pyotr Matveevich. I put together *The Art of Pleasing the Ladies* on commission from a bookseller. I've turned out about six such books in my life. I want to make a collection of Voltaire's *bons mots*,[3] but I'm afraid it might seem insipid to the likes of us. What's Voltaire now! These days it's the cudgel, not Voltaire! They've knocked the last teeth out of each other! So that's the whole of my literary activity. Except that I also send letters to editors gratis, over my full signature. I keep giving admonishments and advice, I criticize and show the way. Last week I sent my fortieth letter to an editor in two years; four roubles on postage alone. I have a nasty character, that's what.

I think the artist painted me not for the sake of literature, but for the sake of the two symmetrical warts on my forehead: a phenomenon, they say. They have no ideas, so now they trade on phenomena. And how well my warts came out in this portrait—to the life! This they call realism.

Regarding craziness, last year they set down a lot of people as madmen. And in what style! "With such a singular talent . . ." they say, "and look what came of it in the end . . . however, it should have been foreseen long ago . . ." Still, this is rather clever; so that from the point of pure art it can even be praised. Well, but they've suddenly come back smarter still. Now, to drive someone mad is possible with us, but they've never yet made anyone smarter.

The smartest one, in my opinion, is the one who calls himself a fool at least once a month—an unheard-of ability nowadays! Formerly, in any case, a fool knew at least once a year that he was a fool, but now unh-unh! And they've confused things so much that you can't tell a fool from a smart man. They've done it on purpose.

I'm reminded of a Spanish joke, how the French built themselves the first madhouse two and a half centuries ago: "They locked up all their fools in a special house, to show what smart people they were themselves." That's just it: by locking someone else up in a madhouse, you don't prove how smart you are. "K. has lost his wits, that means we're the smart ones now." No, it doesn't quite mean that.

Anyhow, the devil . . . and what am I doing pothering over my own wits: grumble, grumble. Even the maid is sick of me. A friend stopped by yesterday: "Your style is changing," he says, "it's getting choppy. You chop and chop—then an inserted phrase, then a phrase inserted in the inserted phrase, then you stick in something in parentheses, and then you go back to chopping, chopping . . ."

My friend is right. Something strange is happening to me. My character is changing, and my head is aching. I've begun seeing and hearing some strange things. Not really voices, but as if there were someone just nearby: "Bobok, bobok, bobok!"

What is this bobok? I need some diversion.

I went out for diversion and wound up in a funeral. A distant relative. A collegiate councillor, however. A widow, five daughters, all young girls. The shoes alone, just think what that will add up to! The deceased used to provide, but now—a wretched little pension. They'll have their tails between their legs. They always gave me a cool reception. I wouldn't have gone now, either, if it hadn't been for this urgent occasion. I went to the cemetery along with the others; they snubbed me and put on airs. My uniform is indeed a bit shabby.[4] It's a good twenty-five years, I think, since I've been to the cemetery; a nice little place!

First of all, the odor. About fifteen dead people arrived. Palls of various prices; there were even two catafalques: for a general, and for some lady. A lot of mournful faces, a lot of sham mourning, a lot of outright merriment. The clergy can't complain: it's a living. But the odor, the odor. I wouldn't wish it on myself even for the odor of sanctity.

I peeked cautiously into the dead men's faces, not trusting my impressionability. Some of the expressions are soft, some unpleasant. Generally, the smiles are not nice, and in some even very much so. I don't like them; they visit my dreams.

During the liturgy I stepped out of church for some air; the day was grayish but dry. Cold, too; but then, it's October. I strolled among the little graves. Various classes. The third class costs thirty roubles: decent and not so expensive. The first two are inside the church and under the porch; now, that's a bit stiff. This time some six people were buried third class, the general and the lady among them.

I peeked into the graves—terrible: water, and such water! Absolutely green and . . . well, never mind! The grave digger was constantly bailing it out with a scoop. While the service was going on, I went for a walk outside the gates. There was an almshouse just there, and a little farther on a restaurant. A so-so restaurant, not bad: you can have a bite and all. A lot of mourners were packed in there. I noticed a lot of merriment and genuine animation. I had a bite and a drink.

After that I took part with my own hands in carrying the coffin from the church to the grave. Why is it that the dead become so heavy in their coffins? They say it's from some sort of inertia, that the body supposedly is no longer controlled by its own . . . or some such rubbish; it contradicts mechanics and common sense. I don't like it when people with only a general education among us set about resolving special questions; and it's rife among us. Civilians love discussing military subjects, even a field marshal's, and people with an engineer's education reason mainly about philosophy and political economy.

I didn't go to the wake. I'm proud, and if they receive me only out of urgent necessity, why drag myself to their dinners, even funeral ones? Only I don't understand why I stayed at the cemetery; I sat on a tombstone and lapsed appropriately into thought.

I began with the Moscow exhibition,[5] and ended with astonishment, generally speaking, as a theme. About "astonishment," here is what I came up with:

"To be astonished at everything is, of course, stupid, while to be astonished at nothing is much more beautiful and for some reason is recognized as good tone. But it is hardly so in essence. In my opinion, to be astonished at nothing is much stupider than to be astonished at everything. And besides: to be astonished at nothing is almost the same as to respect nothing. And a stupid man even cannot respect."

"But I wish first of all to respect. I *yearn* to respect," an acquaintance of mine said to me once, the other day.

He yearns to respect! And God, I thought, what would happen to you if you dared to publish that now!

It was here that I became oblivious. I don't like reading the inscriptions on tombstones; it's eternally the same. Next to me on the slab lay a half-eaten sandwich: stupid and out of place. I threw it on the ground, since it wasn't bread but merely a sandwich. Anyhow, dropping bread on the ground, it seems, is not sinful; on the floor is sinful. Look it up in Suvorin's calendar.[6]

It must be supposed that I sat there for a long time, even much too long; that is, I even lay down on the oblong stone shaped like a marble coffin. And how did it happen that I suddenly started hearing various things? I didn't pay any attention at first and treated it with contempt. But, nevertheless, the conversation continued. I listened—the sounds were muffled, as if the mouths were covered with pillows; but distinct for all that, and very close. I came to, sat up, and started listening attentively.

"Your Excellency, this is simply quite impossible, sir. You named hearts, I'm whisting, and suddenly you've got the seven of diamonds. We ought to have arranged beforehand about the diamonds, sir."

"What, you mean play by memory? Where's the attraction in that?"

"It's impossible, Your Excellency, without a guarantee it's quite impossible. It absolutely has to be with a dummy, and so that there's only blind dealing."

"Well, you'll get no dummy here."

What presumptuous words, though! Both strange and unexpected. One voice is so weighty and solid, the other as if softly sweetened; I wouldn't have believed it if I hadn't heard it myself. It seems I was not at the wake. And yet what was this card game doing here, and who was this general? That it was coming from under the gravestone, there was no doubt. I bent down and read the inscription on the memorial.

"Here lies the body of Major General Pervoedov . . . knight of such-and-such orders." Hm. "Died in August of the year . . . aged fifty-seven . . . Rest, dear dust, till the gladsome morning!"[7]

Hm, the devil, an actual general! The other grave, from which the fawning voice was coming, had no memorial as yet, just a slab; must have been a newcomer. A court councillor, by his voice.

"Oh, woe, woe, woe!" quite a new voice came, some thirty-five feet from the general's place, this time from under a perfectly fresh little grave—a male and low-class voice, but gone lax in a reverentially tender manner.

"Oh, woe, woe, woe!"

"Ah, he's hiccuping again!" suddenly came the squeamish and haughty voice of an irritated lady, seemingly of high society. "What a punishment to be next to this shopkeeper!"

"I didn't hiccup, I didn't even take any food, it's just my nature, that's all. And you, lady, with all these caprices of yours, you simply never can calm down."

"Why did you lie here, then?"

"I got laid here, I got laid by my spouse and little children, I didn't lay myself. The mystery of death! And I'd never lay next to you for anything, not even gold; but I'm laying by my own capital, according to the price, ma'am. For we're always able to pay up for our little third-class grave."

"Saved up? Cheated people?"

"Much I could cheat you, when there's been no payment from you, I reckon, since January. You've run up quite a little account in our shop."

"Well, this is stupid; I think looking for debts here is very stupid! Take yourself up there. Ask my niece; she's my heir."

"Where am I going to ask now, and where am I going to go? We've both reached the limit, and before God's judgment we're equal in our trespasses."

"In our trespasses!" the dead lady contemptuously mimicked. "Don't you dare even speak to me at all!"

"Oh, woe, woe, woe!"

"Nevertheless, the shopkeeper obeys the lady, Your Excellency."

"Why shouldn't he?"

"Well, you know, Your Excellency, considering there's a new order here."

"What sort of new order?"

"But we've died, so to speak, Your Excellency."

"Ah, yes! Well, there's still order . . ."

Well, thank you very much! Some comfort, really! If it's come to that here, what can we expect on the upper floor? But, anyhow, what antics! I went on listening, however, though with boundless indignation.

"No, I could live a little! No . . . you know, I . . . could live a little!" suddenly came someone's new voice, from somewhere in between the general and the irritable lady.

"Listen, Your Excellency, our man's at it again. For three days he's silent as can be, then suddenly: 'I could live a little, no, I could live a little!' And with, you know, such appetite, hee, hee!"

"And such light-mindedness."

"It's getting to him, Your Excellency, and, you know, he

falls asleep, he's fast asleep already, he's been here since April, and suddenly: 'I could live a little!' "

"A bit boring, though," His Excellency observed.

"A bit boring, Your Excellency, maybe we'll tease Avdotya Ignatievna again, hee, hee?"

"Ah, no, I beg you, spare me that. I can't stand that insolent loudmouth."

"And I, on the other hand, can stand neither of you," the loudmouth squeamishly retorted. "You're both utterly boring and cannot talk about anything ideal. And as for you, Your Excellency—you needn't swagger so—I know a little story of how a lackey swept you from under some marital bed one morning with a broom."

"Nasty woman!" the general growled through his teeth.

"Avdotya Ignatievna, dearie," the shopkeeper suddenly cried out again, "my dear lady, meaning no harm, tell me what it is, am I visiting the torments,[8] or is something else happening? . . ."

"Ah, he's at it again, I just knew it, because I get this smell from him, this smell, it's from him tossing around there."

"I don't toss around, dearie, and there's no special smell from me, because I preserved myself in the wholeness of my body, and it's you, dear lady, who's a bit gone off—because the smell really is unbearable, even considering the place. I don't say anything only out of politeness."

"Ah, nasty offender! Such a stink coming from him, and he shifts it onto me."

"Oh, woe, woe, woe! If only the fortieth day[9] would come sooner: to hear the tearful voices above me, the wailing of my spouse and the quiet weeping of my children! . . ."

"Well, look what he's weeping about: they'll stuff their faces with *kutya*[10] and leave. Ah, if only someone would wake up!"

"Avdotya Ignatievna," the fawning official spoke. "Wait a bit, the new ones will speak."

"And are any of them young?"

"There are young ones, Avdotya Ignatievna. Adolescents, even."

"Ah, that would be most welcome!"

"And what, they haven't started yet?" His Excellency inquired.

"Even the ones from two days ago haven't come to yet, Your Excellency, you know yourself they're sometimes silent for a whole week. It's a good thing so many suddenly got brought all at once yesterday, and the day before, and today. Otherwise, for a hundred feet around, they're all from last year."

"Yes, interesting."

"Look, Your Excellency, today they buried the actual privy councillor Tarasevich. I could tell from the voices. His nephew is an acquaintance of mine, he was lowering the coffin just now."

"Hm, is he here somewhere?"

"About five steps away from you, Your Excellency, to the left. Almost at your feet, sir . . . You ought to get acquainted, Your Excellency."

"Hm, no . . . I can't be the first."

"But he'll start it himself, Your Excellency. He'll even be flattered, leave it to me, Your Excellency, and I . . ."

"Ah, ah . . . ah, what's happened to me?" someone's frightened, new little voice suddenly groaned.

"A new one, Your Excellency, a new one, thank God, and so soon! Other times they're silent for a whole week."

"Ah, I think it's a young man!" squealed Avdotya Ignatievna.

"I . . . I . . . from complications, and so suddenly!" the young man prattled again. "Just the day before, Schulz says to me: you have complications, he says, and in the morning all at once I up and died. Ah! Ah!"

"Well, no help for it, young man," the general observed benignly, obviously glad of the newcomer, "you must take comfort! Welcome to our, so to speak, valley of Jehoshaphat.[11] We're kindly folk, you'll come to know and appreciate us. Major General Vassily Vassiliev Pervoedov, at your service."

"Ah, no! No, no, not to me! I went to Schulz; I had complications, you know, it got my chest first and I coughed, and then I caught cold: chest and grippe . . . and then suddenly, quite unexpectedly . . . above all, quite unexpectedly."

"You say it was the chest first," the official softly intervened, as if wishing to encourage the newcomer.

"Yes, the chest and phlegm, and suddenly no phlegm, and the chest, and I couldn't breathe . . . and you know . . ."

"I know, I know. But if it was your chest, you should have gone to Ecke, not to Schulz."

"And, you know, I kept thinking of Botkin[12] . . . and suddenly . . ."

"Well, Botkin's a bit stiff," the general observed.

"Ah, no, he's not stiff at all; I hear he's so attentive and tells you everything beforehand."

"His Excellency was referring to the cost," the official corrected.

"Ah, come now, just three roubles, and he examines so well, and his prescriptions . . . and I absolutely wanted to, because I was told . . . What about it, gentlemen, shall I go to Ecke or to Botkin?"

"What? Where?" the general's corpse heaved, guffawing pleasantly. The official seconded him in falsetto.

"Dear boy, dear, delightful boy, how I love you!" Avdotya Ignatievna squealed rapturously. "I wish they'd laid one like him next to me!"

No, this I simply cannot allow! And this is a contemporary dead person! However, I must listen further and not jump to conclusions. This milksop newcomer—I remember him in his coffin just now—the expression of a frightened chick, the most disgusting in the world! What next, though.

But next such a hullabaloo broke out that my memory has not retained it all, for a great many woke up at once: an official woke up, one of our state councillors, and started in with the general right there and then about a projected subcommission in the ministry of ——— affairs and about a probable reshuffling of official posts attendant upon the subcommission, which the general found quite, quite amusing. I confess, I myself learned many new things, so that I marveled at the ways in which administrative news can sometimes be learned in this capital. Then some engineer half awoke, but for a long time he went on muttering complete nonsense, so that our people didn't even bother with him, but left him to lie it out for a while. Finally, the noble lady buried in the morning under a catafalque displayed signs of sepulchral inspiration. Lebezyatnikov (for the fawning court councillor I hated, the one placed next to General Pervoedov, turned out to be named Lebezyatnikov) fussed a lot, surprised at them all waking up so quickly this time. I confess that I, too, was surprised; however, some of the ones that woke up had been buried two days before, for instance, one very young girl, about sixteen years old, who kept giggling—vilely and carnivorously giggling.

"Your Excellency, the privy councillor Tarasevich is waking up!" Lebezyatnikov announced suddenly in great haste.

"Ah, what's this?" the suddenly awakened privy councillor maundered squeamishly and in a lisping voice. The sound of his voice had something capriciously peremptory about it. I listened with curiosity, for in recent days I had heard something about this Tarasevich—tempting and alarming in the highest degree.

"It's me, Your Excellency, so far it's just me, sir."

"What is your request and what is it you want?"

"Only to inquire after Your Excellency's health; being unaccustomed, everybody feels sort of cramped here at first, sir . . . General Pervoedov wishes to have the honor of making Your Excellency's acquaintance and hopes . . ."

"Never heard of him."

"Good gracious, Your Excellency, General Pervoedov, Vassily Vassilievich . . ."

"You are General Pervoedov?"

"No, Your Excellency, I'm merely Court Councillor Lebezyatnikov, at your service, sir, but General Pervoedov . . ."

"Nonsense! And I beg you to leave me in peace."

"Leave off," General Pervoedov himself finally put a dignified stop to the vile haste of his sepulchral client.

"He's not awake yet, Your Excellency, you must keep that in view, sir; it's from not being accustomed: he'll wake up and then take it differently, sir . . ."

"Leave off," the general repeated.

"Vassily Vassilievich! Hey there, Your Excellency!" an entirely new voice suddenly shouted loudly and eagerly right next to Avdotya Ignatievna—a gentlemanly and brash voice with a fashionably weary articulation and an impudent scansion. "I've been observing the lot of you for two hours already; I've been lying here for three days; remember me, Vassily Vassilievich? Klinevich—we used to meet at the Volokonskys', where I don't know why but you, too, were admitted."

"Well, Count Pyotr Petrovich . . . but can it be that you, too . . . and so young . . . I *am* sorry!"

"I'm sorry myself, only it's all the same to me, and I want to get the most I can from everywhere. And it's not count, it's baron, just plain baron. We're some mangy little barons, from lackey ancestry, and I don't even know why—spit on it. I'm just a blackguard from pseudo-high-society and considered a 'sweet *polisson*.'[13] My father was some sort of little general, and my mother was once received *en haut lieu*.[14] Ziefel the Yid and I passed fifty thousand in false banknotes last year, but I denounced him, and Yulka Charpentier de Lusignan[15] took all the money with her to Bordeaux. And, imagine, I was already quite engaged—the Shchevalevsky girl, three months shy of sixteen, still in boarding school, comes with ninety thousand in dowry. Avdotya Ignatievna, remember how you corrupted me fifteen years ago, when I was just a fourteen-year-old page? . . ."

"Ah, it's you, you blackguard! Well, at least God sent you, otherwise here it's . . ."

"You shouldn't have suspected your negotiant neighbor of smelling bad . . . I just kept quiet and laughed. It's from me; they even buried me in a nailed coffin."

"Ah, nasty man! Only I'm glad even so; you wouldn't believe, Klinevich, you wouldn't believe what a dearth of life and wit there is here."

"Yes, yes, but I intend to start something original here. Your Excellency—not you, Pervoedov—Your Excellency, the other one, Mr. Tarasevich, the privy councillor! Answer me! It's Klinevich, the one who took you to Mademoiselle Furie last lent, do you hear me?"

"I hear you, Klinevich, and I'm very glad, and be-lieve me . . ."

"I don't believe a groat's worth, and spit on it. I'd simply like to kiss you, dear old boy, but I can't, thank God. Do you know, gentlemen, what this *grand-père* pulled off? He died two or three days ago and, can you imagine, left a whole four hundred thousand missing from the treasury? The fund was intended for widows and orphans, and for some reason he alone was in charge of it, so that in the end he wasn't audited for about eight years. I can picture what long faces they've all got there now and how they'll remember him! A delectable thought, isn't it? All last year I kept being surprised at how such a seventy-year-old codger, podagric and chiragric, could have preserved so much strength for depravity, and—and now here's the answer! Those widows and orphans—oh, the mere thought of them must have inflamed him! . . . I knew about it for a long time, I was the only one, Charpentier told me, and the moment I found out, right then, during Holy Week, I pressed him in a friendly way: 'Hand me over twenty-five thousand or else you'll be audited tomorrow.' And, imagine, he came up with only thirteen thousand then, so it seems very opportune that he died now. *Grand-père, grand-père,* do you hear me?"

"*Cher* Klinevich, I quite agree with you, and you needn't

. . . go into such detail. There's so much suffering and torment in life, and so little reward . . . I wished finally to have some peace, and, as far as I can see, I hope even here to extract all . . ."

"I'll bet he's already sniffed out about Katie Berestov!"

"What? . . . What Katie?" the old man's voice trembled carnivorously.

"Aha, what Katie? Here, to the left, five steps from me, ten from you. It's the fifth day she's been here, and if you knew, *grand-père,* what a little hellcat she is . . . from a good family, educated, and—a monster, a monster to the last degree! I never showed her to anybody there, I alone knew . . . Katie, answer me!"

"Hee, hee, hee!" answered the cracked sound of a girl's voice, but one could hear something like the prick of a needle in it. "Hee, hee, hee!"

"Is . . . she . . . blond?" the *grand-père* babbled, faltering, in three gasps.

"Hee, hee, hee!"

"I . . . I've long dreamed," the old man babbled breathlessly, "a lovely dream about a little blonde . . . fifteen or so . . . and precisely in such a situation . . ."

"Ah, abominable!" Avdotya Ignatievna exclaimed.

"Enough!" Klinevich decided. "I see the material is excellent. We'll immediately set things up here in the best possible way. Above all so as to spend the rest of our time merrily; but what sort of time? Hey, you, the official or whatever, Lebezyatnikov, I've heard they call you that!"

"Lebezyatnikov, court councillor, Semyon Evseych, at your service, and very, very, very gladly."

"Spit on your gladly, only you seem to know everything here. Tell me, first of all (I've been wondering since yesterday), how is it that we can speak here? We're dead and yet we can speak; we also move, as it were, and yet we don't speak or move? What's the trick?"

"If you wish, Baron, this can better be explained to you by Platon Nikolaevich."

"What Platon Nikolaevich? Don't mumble, get to the point."

"Platon Nikolaevich, our local homegrown philosopher, natural scientist, and magister. He put out several books on philosophy, but it's three months now and he's falling quite asleep, so it's no longer possible to shake him out of it. Once a week he mutters a few words that are quite beside the point."

"To the point, to the point! . . ."

"He explains it all with the most simple fact—namely, that up there, while we were still alive, we mistakenly regarded death there as death. Here the body revives again, as it were, the remnants of life concentrate, but only in the consciousness. It's—I don't know how to put it—life continuing as if by inertia. Everything is concentrated, in his opinion, somewhere in the consciousness, and goes on for another two or three months . . . sometimes even half a year . . . There's one here, for instance, who is almost entirely decomposed, but once in six weeks, say, he suddenly mutters some little word, a meaningless one, of course, about some bobok: 'Bobok, bobok'—which means that in him, too, an imperceptible spark of life is still glimmering . . ."

"Rather stupid. Well, and how is it that I have no sense of smell, but can feel the stench?"

"That's . . . heh, heh . . . Well, here our philosopher got himself into a fog. He observed precisely about smelling that here the stench one can feel is, so to speak, a moral one— heh, heh! A stench as if of the soul, so that one has time in these two or three months to reconsider . . . and that it is, so to speak, the last mercy . . . Only it seems to me, Baron, that this is all mystical raving, quite excusable in his position . . ."

"Enough, and the rest, I'm sure, is all nonsense. The main thing is two or three months of life, and in the final end— bobok. I suggest that we all spend these two months as pleasurably as possible, and for that we should all set things up on a different basis. Gentlemen! I propose that we not be ashamed of anything!"

"Ah, let's not be, let's not be ashamed of anything!" many voices were heard, and, strangely, even quite new voices, meaning that in the interim new ones had awakened. With especial readiness, the now completely recovered engineer thundered his consent in a bass voice. The girl Katie giggled joyfully.

"Ah, how I want not to be ashamed of anything!" Avdotya Ignatievna exclaimed with rapture.

"Do you hear, if even Avdotya Ignatievna wants not to be ashamed of anything . . ."

"No, no, no, Klinevich, I was ashamed, I was ashamed there even so, but here I want terribly, terribly not to be ashamed of anything!"

"I gather, Klinevich," the engineer bassed, "that you suggest setting up the—so to speak—life here on new and now reasonable principles."

"Well, that I spit on! Regarding that, let's wait for Kudeyarov, who was brought yesterday. He'll wake up and explain everything to you. He's such a person, such a gigantic person! Tomorrow I expect they'll drag yet another natural scientist here, another officer probably, and, in three or four days, if I'm not mistaken, some feuilletonist and, I think, his editor along with him. Anyhow, to hell with them, it's just that we'll have our little crew assembled here and it will all get set up by itself. But meanwhile I want there to be no lying. That's the only thing I want, because it's the main thing. It's impossible to live on earth and not lie, for life and lie are synonymous; but here, just for the fun of it, we won't lie. Devil take it, the grave does mean something after all! We'll all tell our stories aloud and not be ashamed of anything now. I'll tell about myself first of all. I'm one of the carnivorous ones, you know. Up there it was all tied with rotten ropes. Away with the ropes, and let's live for these two months in the most shameless truth! Let's strip and get naked!"

"Get naked, get naked!" voices shouted all around.

"I want terribly, terribly to get naked!" Avdotya Ignatievna squealed.

"Ah . . . ah . . . ah, I see it's going to be fun here; I don't want to go to Ecke!"

"No, I could live a little, no, you know, I could live a little!"

"Hee, hee, hee!" Katie giggled.

"The main thing is that no one can forbid us, and though I can see that Pervoedov is angry, he still can't reach me with his hand. *Grand-père,* do you agree?"

"I fully, fully agree, and with the greatest pleasure, provided Katie is the first to start her bi-og-raphy."

"I protest! I protest with all my strength," General Pervoedov stated firmly.

"Your Excellency!" the blackguard Lebezyatnikov, in hasty agitation and with lowered voice, babbled and persuaded, "Your Excellency, it's even more profitable for us if we agree. There's this girl here, you know . . . and, finally, all these different antics . . ."

"Granted there's the girl, but . . ."

"It's more profitable, Your Excellency, by God it's more profitable for you! Well, at least as a little sample, at least for a try . . ."

"Even in the grave they won't let me rest!"

"First of all, General, you play cards in the grave, and, second of all, we spit on you," Klinevich scanned out.

"My dear sir, I beg you all the same not to forget yourself."

"What? You can't reach me, and I can tease you from here like Yulka's lapdog. And first of all, gentlemen, what sort of general is he here? It's there that he was a general, but here—pfft!"

"No, not pfft . . . here, too, I'm . . ."

"Here you'll rot in your coffin and there'll be only six brass buttons left!"

"Bravo, Klinevich, ha, ha, ha!" voices bellowed.

"I served my sovereign . . . I wear a sword . . ."

"Your sword's good for skewering mice, and besides you never drew it."

"It's all the same, sir; I constituted part of the whole."

"We know these parts of the whole."

"Bravo, Klinevich, bravo, ha, ha, ha!"

"I don't understand what a sword is," the engineer declared.

"We'll run like mice from the Prussians,[16] they'll make mincemeat of us!" a voice farther away and unknown to me cried out, literally spluttering with rapture.

"A sword, sir, is honor," came the general's cry, but that was the last I heard of him. A long and furious bellowing, uproar, and racket arose, and only Avdotya Ignatievna's squeals, impatient to the point of hysterics, could be made out.

"Quicker, be quicker! Ah, when are we going to start not being ashamed of anything!"

"Oh, woe, woe! Truly my soul is visiting the torments!" came the voice of the simple man, and . . .

And here I suddenly sneezed. It happened unexpectedly and unintentionally, but the effect was striking: all became still, just like a cemetery, vanished like a dream. A true graveyard silence fell. I don't think they were ashamed before me: they had decided not to be ashamed of anything! I waited for about five minutes but—not a word, not a sound. It was also impossible to suppose that they feared a denunciation to the police; for what could the police do here? I'm forced to conclude that they must after all have some secret unknown to mortals, and which they carefully conceal from every mortal.

"Well, my dears," I thought, "I'll be visiting you again," and with those words I left the cemetery.

No, this I cannot allow; no, I truly cannot! It's not bobok that bothers me (so here's that bobok!).

Depravity in such a place, the depravity of last hopes, the depravity of flabby and rotting corpses and—not even sparing the last moments of consciousness! They're given, they're made a gift of these moments and . . . And, above all, above all in such a place! No, this I cannot allow . . .

I'll visit other classes, I'll listen everywhere. The point is that I must listen everywhere, and not just at one end, to form an idea. Perhaps I'll bump into something comforting.

And I'll certainly go back to those ones. They promised their biographies and various little anecdotes. Pah! But I'll go, I'll certainly go; it's a matter of conscience!

I'll take it to *The Citizen;*[17] they also exhibited the portrait of some editor. Maybe they'll print it.

THE MEEK ONE

A FANTASTIC STORY

From the Author

I beg my readers' pardon for giving them this time, instead of the *Diary* in its usual form, simply a long story. But I have in fact been occupied with this story for the better part of the month. In any case, I beg the readers' indulgence.

Now about the story itself. I have termed it "fantastic," though I myself consider it realistic in the highest degree. But there is indeed a fantastic side to it, and namely in the very form of the story, which I find it necessary to clarify beforehand.

The thing is that this is not a story and not notes. Imagine to yourself a husband whose wife is lying on the table,[1] a suicide, who a few hours earlier threw herself out the window. He is in bewilderment and has not yet had time to collect his thoughts. He paces his rooms and tries to make sense of what has happened, "to collect his thoughts to a point." Besides, he is an inveterate hypochondriac, of the sort that talks to himself. Here he is, then, talking to himself, telling the matter over, *figuring it out* for himself. Despite the seeming consistency of his speech, he contradicts himself several times, both in logic and in feelings. He justifies himself, and accuses her, and launches into extraneous explanations: there is coarseness of thought and heart here; there is also deep feeling. Little by little he actually *figures out* the matter and collects his "thoughts to a point." A series of memories he calls up brings him irresistibly to the *truth;* the truth irresistibly elevates his mind and heart. Toward the end even the tone of the story changes, as compared with its disorderly beginning. The truth is disclosed to the unfortunate man quite clearly and definitely, at least for himself.

That is the theme. Of course, the process of telling goes on for several hours, in bits and snatches, and in incoherent form: now he talks to himself, now it is as if he addresses an invisible listener, some judge. But so it always happens in reality. If a stenographer could eavesdrop and write it all down after him, it would come out a bit rougher, less polished than I have presented it, but, for all I can see, the psychological order would perhaps remain the same. Now, this supposition of a stenographer who could write it all down (after which I would polish what was written) is what I call fantastic in this story. But a somewhat similar thing has been allowed in art more than once: Victor Hugo, for instance, in his masterpiece *The Last Day of a Man Condemned to Death,* employed almost the same method, and though he introduced no stenographer, he allowed for still greater implausibility, supposing that a man condemned to death is able (and has time) to write notes not only on his last day, but even in his last hour and literally his last minute. But had he not allowed this fantasy, the work itself would not exist—the most realistic and truthful of all he wrote.

CHAPTER ONE

I

Who I Was and Who She Was

. . . So long as she's here—everything is still all right: I go
over and look every moment; but tomorrow she'll be taken
away and—how am I to stay alone? She's in the big room
now, on a table, we put two card tables together, and the
coffin will come tomorrow, a white one, white gros de Naples,
but, anyhow, it's not that . . . I keep pacing and want to
figure it out for myself. It's already six hours now that I've
been wanting to figure it out and I simply can't collect my
thoughts to a point. The thing is that I keep pacing, pacing,
pacing . . . Here is how it was. I'll simply tell it in order
(order!). Gentlemen, I'm far from being a writer, and you can
see that, and let it be so, but I'll tell it as I understand it.
There's my whole horror—that I understand everything!

This, if you want to know, that is, if we take it from the
very beginning, quite simply that she used to come to me then
to pawn things in order to pay for an advertisement in *The
Voice,*[2] saying here, thus and so, a governess, agrees to relocate,
and give lessons at home, and so on and so forth. This was at
the very beginning, and I, of course, didn't distinguish her
from the others: she comes like everybody else, well, and so
forth. But later I began to distinguish. She was so slender, fair-
haired, medium tall; with me she was always awkward, as if
abashed (I think she was the same with all strangers, and,
naturally, I was the same for her as any other, that is, taken
not as a pawnbroker but as a human being). As soon as she got
the money, she would turn and leave at once. And all silently.
Others, they argue, beg, bargain in order to get more; this one
no, just what's given . . . It seems to me I keep getting confused . . . Yes; first of all I was struck by her things: gilt
silver earrings, a trashy little locket—things worth two bits.
She knew herself they were only a bit's worth, yet I saw by her

face that they were treasures for her—and in fact it was all she had left from her papa and mama, I found out later. Once only did I allow myself to smile at her things. That is, you see, I never allow myself that, I keep a gentlemanly tone with the public: a few words, polite and stern. "Stern, stern, stern." But she suddenly allowed herself to bring the remnants (I mean, literally) of an old rabbitskin jacket—and I couldn't help myself and suddenly said something to her, as if a witticism. Goodness, how she flushed! Her eyes are light blue, big, pensive, but—how they lit up! But she didn't let out a word, she took her "remnants" and—left. It was then that I took *particular* notice of her for the first time and thought something of that sort about her, that is, precisely of that particular sort. Yes: I also remember the impression, that is, if you like, the main impression, the synthesis of everything: namely, that she was terribly young, so young, as if she were just fourteen years old. And yet she was three months short of sixteen then. But anyway that's not what I wanted to say, the synthesis wasn't in that at all. Next day she came again. I found out later that she had gone with the jacket to Dobronravov and to Moser, but they take nothing but gold and wouldn't even speak to her. But I once took a cameo from her (a trashy one)—and, on reflection, was surprised afterward: I, too, take nothing but gold and silver, yet I accepted a cameo from her. That was my second thought about her then, I remember it.

This time, that is, after Moser, she brought an amber cigar holder—a so-so little thing, for an amateur, but once again worth nothing with us, because we take only gold. Since she came after the previous day's *rebellion,* I met her sternly. Sternness with me is dryness. However, as I handed her the two roubles, I couldn't help myself and said as if with a certain irritation: "I'm doing it only *for you,* Moser wouldn't take such a thing from you." I especially emphasized the words *for you,* and precisely in *a certain sense.* I was angry. She flushed again on hearing this *for you,* but held her peace, didn't drop the money, took it—that's poverty! But how she flushed! I realized that I'd stung her. And after she left, I suddenly asked myself: can it really be that this triumph over her cost two roubles? Heh, heh, heh! I remember twice asking precisely this question: "Is it worth it? Is it worth it?" And, laughing, I resolved it for myself in the affirmative. I got quite merry then. But this wasn't a bad feeling: I had a design, an intention; I wanted to test her, because I suddenly had some thoughts fermenting in me concerning her. This was my third *particular* thought about her.

. . . Well, so from then on it all got started. Naturally, I at once made indirect efforts to find out all the circumstances and waited with particular impatience for her to come. I did have a feeling that she would come soon. When she came, I entered into friendly conversation with unusual politeness. I'm not badly brought up and have manners. Hm. It was then I guessed that she was kind and meek. The kind and meek ones don't resist for long, and though they don't really open up completely, still they can't quite avoid conversing: they reply charily, but they do reply, and the more the further, only don't get tired yourself if it's something you need. Naturally, she didn't explain anything to me herself that time. It was later that I found out about *The Voice* and everything. She was then spending her last strength to advertise, at first, naturally, with pride, something like: "Governess, willing to relocate, send letter stating conditions," but then: "Willing to do anything, teach, be a companion, keep house, tend the sick, can sew," etc., etc., the same old stuff! Naturally, all this was added to the advertisement gradually, and toward the end, when things got desperate, there was even "without salary, in exchange for board." No, she didn't find a situation! I ventured then to test her for a last time: I suddenly take today's *Voice* and show her an advertisement: "Young person, orphan, seeks position as governess of small children, preferably with an older widower. Can help with housework."

"There, you see, this woman placed an advertisement this morning, and by evening she'll certainly have found work. That's how one should advertise!"

Again she flushed, again her eyes lit up, she turned and left

at once. I liked that very much. However, I was already sure of
everything by then and had no fear: no one was going to take
cigar holders from her. And she had already run out of cigar
holders. So it was, on the third day she came, so pale,
alarmed—I understood that something had happened with
her at home, and in fact it had. I'll explain presently what had
happened, but now I just want to recall how I suddenly displayed my chic before her then and grew taller in her eyes.
The intention suddenly appeared in me. The thing was that
she brought this icon (got herself to bring it) . . . Ah, listen!
listen! Here's where it begins, and before I kept getting confused . . . The thing is that I want to recall it all now, each
trifle, each little feature. I keep wanting to collect my thoughts
to a point and—I can't, and now these little features, these
little features . . .

An icon of the Mother of God. The Mother of God with
the Child, from home, from her family, an old one, in a gilt
silver casing—worth—well, worth about six roubles. I can see
the icon is dear to her, she wants to pawn the whole icon,
without removing the casing. I tell her it's better to remove the
casing and keep the icon; because it's still an icon after all.

"Is it forbidden for you?"

"No, not really forbidden, but just so, maybe, you yourself . . ."

"Well, remove it, then."

"You know what, I won't remove it, I'll put it on the stand
over there," I said on reflection, "with the other icons, under
the lamp" (ever since I opened my shop, I've always kept an
icon lamp burning), "and you can quite simply take ten
roubles."

"I don't want ten, give me five, I'll certainly buy it back."

"You don't want ten? The icon's worth it," I added, noticing that her eyes flashed again. She held her peace. I brought
her five roubles.

"Don't despise anyone, I've felt the same pinch myself, and
even worse, and if you now see me in this occupation, miss
. . . after all I've endured it's . . ."

"You're taking revenge on society, is that it?" she interrupted me suddenly with rather caustic mockery, in which, however, there was a good deal of innocence (that is, of generality, because she decidedly did not distinguish me from others then, so that she said it almost inoffensively). "Aha!" thought I, "that's how you are, the character's coming out, of the new tendency."

"You see," I observed at once, half jokingly, half mysteriously, "I—I'm part of that part of the whole that wishes to do evil, but does good . . ."

She glanced at me quickly and with great curiosity, in which, however, there was a good deal of childishness:

"Wait . . . What is that thought? Where is it from? I've heard it somewhere . . ."

"Don't rack your brain, Mephistopheles recommends himself to Faust in those terms. Have you read *Faust*?"[3]

"Not . . . not attentively."

"That is, you haven't read it at all. You ought to read it. However, I see a mocking twist on your lips again. Please don't suppose me to be of so little taste as to wish to paint over my role as a pawnbroker by recommending myself as a Mephistopheles. Once a pawnbroker, always a pawnbroker. We know that, miss."

"You're somehow strange . . . I didn't want to say anything like that at all . . ."

She wanted to say: I didn't expect you to be an educated man, but she didn't say it, though I knew she was thinking it; I pleased her terribly.

"You see," I observed, "one can do good in any occupation. I don't mean myself, of course, I, let's say, do nothing but bad, but . . ."

"Of course one can do good in any situation," she said, glancing at me with a quick and meaning look. "Precisely in any situation," she suddenly added. Oh, I remember, I remember all those moments! And I also want to add that these young people, these dear young people, when they want to say something intelligent and meaningful, suddenly show, with all too much sincerity and naivety on their faces, that "here I am saying something intelligent and meaningful to you"—and not out of vanity, like our sort, but you can see that she herself values all this terribly, and believes it, and respects it, and thinks that you, too, respect it the same way she does. Oh sincerity! This is how they win one over. And it was so lovely in her!

I remember, I haven't forgotten anything! When she left, I made up my mind all at once. That same day I went to make my final search and found out all the rest of her then current innermost secrets; all the former innermost secrets I already knew from Lukerya, who was then their servant and whom I had bribed several days earlier. These innermost secrets were so horrible that I don't even understand how she could have laughed as she did that day and been curious about Mephistopheles' saying, being under such horror herself. But—youth! I thought precisely that about her then, with pride and with joy, because there was magnanimity in it: on the verge of ruin, yet Goethe's great words still shine. Youth is always magnanimous, be it ever so slightly, even lopsidedly. That is, I mean her, her alone. And, above all, I already looked at her then as *mine* and had no doubt of my power. You know, it is a most voluptuous thought, when one no longer has any doubts.

But what's the matter with me. If I do it this way, when will I collect it all into a point? Quickly, quickly . . . this is not it at all, oh, God!

II

A Marriage Proposal

The "innermost secrets" I found out about her can be explained in a word: her father and mother had died, already long ago, three years before, and she was left with some disorderly aunts. That is, it's not enough to call them disorderly.

One was a widow with a big family, six children, each smaller than the next; the other was a spinster, old and nasty. They were both nasty. Her father had been in the civil service, but as a scrivener, and of merely nonhereditary nobility—in short, it all played into my hands. I came as if from a higher world: a retired staff captain, after all, of a brilliant regiment, a hereditary nobleman, independent, and so on, and as for the pawnshop, the aunts could only look upon it with respect. She had slaved for the aunts for three years, but passed an examination somewhere all the same—struggled to pass it, managed to pass it, from under her merciless daily work—and that did mean something about her yearning toward the lofty and noble! After all, why did I want to get married? Spit on me, though, that's for later . . . As if that was the point! She taught her aunt's children, did sewing, and toward the end not just sewing but, with her bad chest, also scrubbed the floors. Quite simply, they even beat her, reproached her for every crumb. In the end they were intending to sell her. Pah! I omit the filth of the details. Later she told me everything in detail. For a whole year a fat neighboring shopkeeper had been observing it all, not a simple shopkeeper, but with two grocery stores. He had already given a sweet time to two wives and was looking for a third, and so he cast an eye on her: "Quiet," he thought, "grew up in poverty, and I'm marrying for my orphans." In fact, he did have orphans. He sent a matchmaker, began making arrangements with the aunts, what's more—he was fifty years old; she was horrified. It was then that she began coming to me often, so as to place advertisements in *The Voice*. Finally, she started asking her aunts to give her a bit of time to think it over. They gave her this bit, but just one, no more, because, they carped: "We don't know what we'll grub up ourselves, even without an extra mouth." I already knew it all, and after that morning I made my decision. In the evening the merchant came, bringing a pound of candy from his shop worth fifty kopecks; she was sitting with him, and I called Lukerya out from the kitchen and told her to go and whisper to her that I was at the gate and wished to tell her something most urgently. I remained pleased with myself. And generally all that day I had been awfully pleased.

There at the gate, in Lukerya's presence, I explained to her, amazed as she already was by the fact of my calling her outside, that I would consider it a happiness and an honor . . . Second: not to be surprised at my manner and that it was at the gate: "I'm a direct man," I said, "and I've looked into the circumstances of the matter." And I wasn't lying that I'm direct. Well, spit on it. I spoke not only decently, that is, showing a man of breeding, but also originally, and that's the main thing. So what, is it a sin to confess it? I want to judge myself and so I do. I must speak pro and contra, and so I do. Later I also remembered it with delight, though that is stupid: I declared directly, without any embarrassment, first, that I was not especially talented, not especially intelligent, maybe not even especially kind, a rather cheap egoist (I remember that expression, I thought it up then, on my way there, and remained pleased), and that it was very, very possible that I contained in myself much that was also unpleasant in many other respects. All this was spoken with a special sort of pride—we all know how such things are said. Of course, I had taste enough, after nobly declaring my shortcomings, not to start declaring my merits, saying: "But, on the other hand, I have this, this, and that." I could see that so far she was terribly afraid, but I didn't soften anything, what's more, seeing that she was afraid, I intensified it on purpose: I said directly that she would have enough to eat, but as for outfits, theaters, balls—there would be none of that, or not till later, when I'd reached my goal. This stern tone decidedly carried me away. I added, also as casually as possible, that if I'd taken such an occupation, that is, keeping this shop, it was that I had a certain goal, there was a certain circumstance . . . But I had the right to speak that way: I actually had such a goal and such a circumstance. Wait, gentlemen, all my life I've been the first to hate this pawnshop, but, as a matter of fact, though it's ridiculous to speak in mysterious phrases to oneself, I was in fact "taking revenge on society," really, really, really! So that her morning witticism about my "taking revenge" was unjust. That is, you see, if I had told her directly in so many words: "Yes, I'm taking revenge on society," and she had burst out laughing, as she did that morning, it would in fact have come out ridiculous. Well, but by an indirect hint, by letting in a mysterious phrase, it turned out that one could bribe the imagination. Besides, I no longer feared anything then: I knew that the fat shopkeeper was in any case more disgusting to her and that I, standing there at the gate, was a deliverer. That I understood. Oh, man understands meanness especially well! But was it meanness? How can one judge a man here? Didn't I already love her even then?

Wait: naturally, I didn't say half a word to her then about being a benefactor; on the contrary, oh, on the contrary: "It's you," I might have said, "who are *my* benefactor, not I *yours*." So that I even put it into words, I couldn't help myself, and it came out stupid, perhaps, because I noticed a fleeting wrinkle on her face. But on the whole I was decidedly the winner. Wait, if I'm to recall all this filth, I'll also recall the ultimate swinishness: I was standing there, and it was stirring in my head: you're tall, well built, well bred, and—and, finally, speaking without braggadocio, you're not bad looking. That's what was playing through my mind. Naturally, she said *yes* to me right there at the gate. But . . . but I must add: right there at the gate she thought for a long time before she said *yes*. She got so thoughtful, so thoughtful, that I already started asking: "Well, what is it?"—and even couldn't help myself, asking with a certain chic: "Well, what is it, miss?"—adding a polite touch.

"Wait, I'm thinking."

And her little face was so serious, so serious—that even then I might have read! And there I was feeling offended: "Can it be," I thought, "that she's choosing between me and the merchant?" Oh, I didn't understand then! I didn't understand anything, not anything! Until today I didn't understand! I remember Lukerya ran out after me, as I was leaving, stopped me in the street, and said breathlessly: "God will reward you, sir, for taking our dear young lady, only don't tell it to her, she's proud."

Proud, eh! I say I like the proud ones myself. The proud ones are especially good when . . . well, when one no longer doubts one's power over them, eh? Oh, mean, clumsy man! Oh, how pleased I was! Do you know, she might, when she was standing at the gate then, thinking whether to say yes to me, and I got surprised, do you know, she might even have been thinking: "If it's disaster either way, isn't it better to choose the worst straight off, that is, the fat shopkeeper, let him get drunk and quickly beat me to death!" Eh? What do you think, could she have had such a thought?

And now, too, I don't understand, now, too, I don't understand anything! I only just said that she might have had this thought: to choose the worst of two disasters, that is, the merchant? But who was worse for her then—I or the merchant? The merchant or the pawnbroker quoting Goethe? That's still a question! Why a question? And you don't understand this: the answer's lying on the table, and you say question! No, but spit on me! I'm not the point . . . And by the way, what is it to me now—whether I'm the point or not? That's something I'm quite unable to decide. I'd better go to bed. I have a headache . . .

III

The Noblest of Men, but I Don't Believe It Myself

Didn't fall asleep. How could I, some pulse was throbbing in my head. I want to take it all in, all this filth. Oh, filth! Oh, what filth I dragged her out of then! She really ought to have understood it, to have appreciated my action! I also liked various thoughts, for instance, that I was forty-one and she had just turned sixteen. This captivated me, this feeling of inequality, very sweet it was, very sweet.

I, for instance, wanted to do the wedding *à l'anglaise,*[4] that is, decidedly the two of us, with perhaps two witnesses, one of them Lukerya, and then straight to the train, say, for instance, to Moscow (I happened incidentally to have business there), to a hotel, for a couple of weeks. She protested, she wouldn't allow it, and I was forced to go visiting her aunts, honoring them as relatives from whom I was taking her. I yielded, and the aunts were rendered their due. I even gave the creatures a hundred roubles each and promised more, naturally without telling her anything about it, so as not to upset her by the meanness of the situation. The aunts at once became like silk. There was also an argument about the dowry: she had nothing, almost literally, but she also wanted nothing. I, however, succeeded in proving to her that nothing at all was not possible, and I took care of the dowry, because who else would do anything for her? Well, but spit on talking about me. My various ideas, however, I did manage to tell her then, so that she'd at least know. Even too hastily, perhaps. The main thing is that from the very first, though she tried to hold back, she threw herself to me with love, she would meet me with rapture when I came home in the evening, told me in her prattle (the charming prattle of innocence!) all about her childhood, her infancy, her parental home, her father and mother. But I immediately doused all this ecstasy at once with cold water. It was in this that my idea lay. To her raptures I responded with silence, benevolent, of course . . . but all the same she quickly saw that we were different, and that I was—a riddle. And I was, above all, aiming at a riddle! It was for the sake of posing a riddle, perhaps, that I did all this stupidity! First of all, sternness—so it was under sternness that I brought her into my house. In short, though I was very pleased, I set about creating a whole system then. Oh, it poured out by itself quite effortlessly. And it couldn't have been otherwise, I had to create this system, owing to an irresistible circumstance—what am I doing, in fact, slandering myself! The system was a true one. No, listen, if you're going to judge a man, you must know the case . . . Listen!

How shall I begin, because it's very difficult. Once you start justifying yourself—it gets difficult. You see: young people, for instance, despise money—I right away emphasized money; I stressed money. And I emphasized it so much that she began to grow more and more silent. She'd open her big eyes, listen, look, and keep silent. You see: young people are magnanimous, that is, the good ones are, magnanimous and impulsive, but they have little tolerance, the moment something's not right—there's scorn. And I wanted breadth, I wanted to implant breadth right in her heart, implant it in her own heart's view, isn't that so? I'll take a banal example: how, for instance, should I explain my pawnshop to such a character? Naturally, I didn't speak of it directly, otherwise it would have come out that I was asking forgiveness for the pawnshop, but I acted, so to speak, through pride, I spoke almost silently. And I'm a master of speaking silently, I've spent my whole life speaking silently and have silently lived through whole tragedies with myself. Oh, but I was also unhappy! I had been discarded by everyone, discarded and forgotten, and no one, no one knows it! And suddenly this sixteen-year-old girl snatched all sorts of details from mean people afterward and thought she knew everything, but the secret meanwhile remained only in this man's breast! I kept silent, and especially, especially kept silent with her, right up till yesterday—why did I keep silent? As a proud man. I wanted her to find out herself, without me, not from mean people's talk now, but that she should *guess herself* about this man and comprehend him! Receiving her into my house, I wanted full respect. I wanted her to stand before me entreatingly for the sake of my suffering—and I was worth it. Oh, I was always proud, I always wanted all or nothing! That's precisely why, because I'm no halfway man in happiness, but wanted all, that's precisely why I was forced to act as I did then, as if to say: "Guess yourself, and appreciate it!" Because, you must agree, if I myself had begun explaining and prompting, shuffling and begging for respect—it would have been as if I were begging alms . . . But anyhow . . . but anyhow, why am I talking about that?

Stupid, stupid, stupid, stupid! Directly and mercilessly (and I emphasize that it was mercilessly), I explained to her then, in a few words, that the magnanimity of youth is lovely, but— not worth a groat. Why not? Because it comes cheap, it's acquired without living, it's all, so to speak, "the first impressions of being,"[5] but let's see you do any work! Cheap magnanimity is always easy, and even to give your life—that, too, is cheap, because here it's just hot blood and surplus strength,[6] one passionately desires beauty! No, take a deed of magnanimity that's difficult, quiet, inaudible, unglamorous, with calumny, where there's much sacrifice and not a drop of glory—where you, a shining man, are presented as a scoundrel before everyone, whereas you're more honest than anyone else on earth—go and try that deed, no, you'd give it up! And I— all I've done all my life is bear that deed. At first she argued, and how she argued, but then she began to grow silent, even completely, only widening her eyes terribly as she listened, such big, big eyes, so attentive. And . . . and besides that, I suddenly saw a smile, mistrustful, silent, not nice. It was with this smile that I brought her into my house. It's also true that she had nowhere else to go . . .

IV

Plans and More Plans

Which of us was the first to begin it then?

Neither. It began by itself from the first step. I said I brought her into my house under sternness, yet from the first step I softened it. It was explained to her, while still a fiancée, that she would be occupied with taking the pledges and handing out the money, and she said nothing then (note that). What's more—she took to the business even with zeal. Well, of course, the apartment, the furniture—it all remained the same. The apartment has two rooms: one, a big room with a

partition, beyond which is the shop; and the other, also a big
one, our living room, as well as bedroom. My furniture is
scanty; even her aunts had better. My icon stand with the icon
lamp is in the other room, where the shop is; in my room
there is my bookcase with a few books in it, and a trunk, to
which I kept the keys; also a bed, tables, chairs. While she was
still my fiancée I told her that one rouble a day, no more, was
allotted for our keep, that is, food for me, her, and Lukerya,
whom I had lured to us: "I need thirty thousand in three
years," I said, "otherwise one can't make money." She didn't
object, but I raised it thirty kopecks myself. The same with the
theater. I had told my fiancée there would be no theater, and
yet I decided there should be theater once a month, and that
decently, in the orchestra. We went together, three times it
was, to see *Pursuit of Happiness* and *Songbirds*,[7] I think. (Oh,
spit on it, who cares!) We went silently, and came home silently. Why, why did we start being silent from the very beginning? In the beginning there were no quarrels, but there
was silence. She kept looking at me then, I remember, somehow on the sly; when I noticed it, I intensified my silence.
True, it was I who stressed silence, not she. Once or twice
there were impulses on her part, she would rush to embrace
me; but since these were morbid, hysterical impulses, and I
needed firm happiness, along with respect from her, I took it
coldly. And I was right: each time after such an impulse, there
was a quarrel the next day.

That is, again, there were no quarrels, but there was silence
and—and a more and more bold look on her part. "Rebellion
and independence"—that's what it was, only she didn't know
how. Yes, that meek face was becoming bolder and bolder.
Would you believe, I was becoming repugnant to her, I studied it thoroughly. And there was no doubting the fact that she
had fits of temper. So, for example, after getting out of such
filth and beggarliness, after having scrubbed floors, she would
suddenly start sniffing at our poverty! You see, sirs: it wasn't
poverty, it was economy, and, where necessary, even luxury—
with linens, for instance, with cleanliness. I had always

dreamed, before, that cleanliness in a husband is attractive to a wife. However, it wasn't at poverty, it was at my supposed stinginess in economy: "He has goals, he shows a firm character." She suddenly gave up the theater herself. And more and more of this mocking wrinkle . . . and I was intensifying my silence, intensifying my silence.

I couldn't go justifying myself, could I? It was mainly this pawnshop. Excuse me, sirs: I knew that a woman, and a sixteen-year-old one at that, can't help submitting wholly to a man. There's no originality in women, that—that is an axiom, even now it's an axiom for me! What is it that's lying there in the other room: truth is truth, and even Mill[8] himself can do nothing about it! And a woman who loves, oh, a woman who loves—will deify even the vices, even the villainies of the beloved being. He himself wouldn't seek out such justifications for his villainies as she will find for him. This is magnanimous, but unoriginal. Woman has been ruined by unoriginality alone. And what, I repeat, what are you pointing to there on the table? Is that original, what's there on the table? Ohh!

Listen: I was sure of her love then. And she did throw herself on my neck then. So she loved me, or rather—wished to love. Yes, that's how it was: she wished to love, she sought to love. And the main thing is that there were no such villainies for which she would have to seek justifications. You say: a pawnbroker, and everybody says it. But what if I am a pawnbroker? It means there are reasons, if the most magnanimous of men became a pawnbroker. You see, gentlemen, there are ideas . . . that is, you see, certain ideas, once they're uttered, expressed in words, come out terribly stupid. They come out shameful for oneself. And why? Nowhy. Because we're all trash and can't bear the truth, or else I don't know why. I said "the most magnanimous of men" just now. It's ridiculous, and yet that's how it was. That was the truth, that is, the most, the very most truthful truth! Yes, I *had the right* then to want to provide for myself and to open this pawnshop: "You rejected me, you people, that is, you drove me away with scornful silence. To my passionate impulse toward you, you responded by offending me for the rest of my life. Now, therefore, I had the right to protect myself from you with a wall, to raise these thirty thousand roubles and end my life somewhere in the Crimea, on the southern coast, amid mountains and vineyards, on my own estate, bought with this thirty thousand, and, above all, far away from all of you, but without spite toward you, with an ideal in my soul, with a beloved woman by my heart, with a family, should God send it, and—helping out the neighboring settlers." Naturally, it's good that I'm now saying this to myself, but what could have been stupider than if I had then painted it aloud for her? Hence the proud silence, hence the silent sitting. Because what could she have understood? Sixteen years, early youth—what could she understand of my justifications, my sufferings? Here was straightforwardness, ignorance of life, cheap youthful convictions, the chicken's blindness of "beautiful hearts," and, above all, here was the pawnshop, and—*basta*! (But was I a villain in the pawnshop, didn't she see how I acted and whether I took too much?) Oh, how terrible is the truth on earth! This lovely one, this meek one, this heaven—she was a tyrant, an unbearable tyrant and tormentor of my soul! I'll slander myself if I don't say it! You think I didn't love her? Who can say I didn't love her? You see: there was irony here, a wicked irony of fate and nature came out here! We're cursed, the life of men generally is cursed! (Mine in particular!) I understand now that I did make some mistake here! Something here didn't come out right. Everything was clear, my plan was clear as the sky: "Stern, proud, and needs nobody's moral consolation, suffers silently." That's how it was, I wasn't lying, I wasn't lying! "She herself will see afterward that there was magnanimity here, only she failed to notice it—and once she realizes it someday, she'll appreciate it ten times more, and will fall down in the dust with her hands clasped in entreaty." That was the plan. But I forgot something here, or lost sight of it. There was something here I failed to do. But enough, enough. And of whom shall I now ask forgiveness? What's finished is finished. Take heart, man, and be proud! It's not your fault! . . .

So, then, I'll tell the truth, I won't be afraid to stand face-to-face with the truth: it was *her* fault, *her* fault! . . .

V

The Meek One Rebels

The quarrels began with her suddenly deciding to lend money in her own way, to appraise things above their value, and she even deigned a couple of times to enter into a dispute with me on the subject. I didn't agree. But here the captain's widow turned up.

An old woman, a captain's widow, came with a locket—a present from her late husband, well, the usual thing, a keepsake. I gave her thirty roubles. She started whining pathetically, begging me not to let the thing go—naturally, I won't let it go. Well, in short, suddenly, five days later, she comes to exchange it for a bracelet that isn't worth even eight roubles. Naturally, I rejected it. She must have guessed something right then from my wife's eyes, but anyway she came when I wasn't there and my wife exchanged the locket for her.

Finding out that same day, I began speaking meekly, but firmly and reasonably. She was sitting on the bed looking down, tapping the rug with her right toe (her gesture); there was a bad smile on her lips. Then, without raising my voice at all, I declared calmly that the money was *mine,* that I had the right to look at life with *my own* eyes, and—that when I invited her into my home, I had not concealed anything from her.

She suddenly jumped up, suddenly trembled all over, and—what do you think?—suddenly stamped her feet at me; this was a beast, this was a fit, this was a beast in a fit. I froze in astonishment; I never expected such an escapade. But I was not put out, I didn't even stir, and again in the same calm voice declared to her directly that from then on I was depriving her of her participation in my concerns. She burst out laughing in my face and left the apartment.

The thing was that she had no right to leave the apartment. Nowhere without me, that was the agreement while she was still my fiancée. Toward evening she came back. Not a word from me.

The next day she was gone again from morning on, and the day after. I locked my shop and went to the aunts. I had broken with them right after the wedding—they never visited me, nor I them. It now turned out that she hadn't been there. They listened to me with curiosity and laughed in my face: "Serves you right," they said. But I had anticipated their laughter. I straightaway bribed the maiden aunt, the younger one, with a hundred roubles, and gave her twenty-five up front. Two days later she comes to me: "An officer," she says, "Yefimovich, a sub-lieutenant, your former regimental comrade, is mixed up in it." I was very amazed. This Yefimovich had caused me the most evil in the regiment, and a month ago had come to my shop once and then again, shameless as he was, on the pretext of pawning something, and, I remember, had begun laughing with my wife. I went up to him right then and told him that he dared not come to me, remembering our relations; but no such notion ever entered my head, I simply thought he was a brazen fellow. And now suddenly the aunt informs me that she has already set up a meeting with him and that the whole thing is being handled by a former acquaintance of the aunts, Yulia Samsonovna, a widow, and a colonel's widow at that—"It's to her that your spouse now goes," she says.

I'll cut this picture short. The business cost me all of three hundred roubles, but in two days it was arranged so that I would be standing in the next room, behind a closed door, listening to the first rendezvous of my wife alone with Yefimovich. In anticipation, on the eve, a brief but, for me, all too portentous scene took place between us.

She came back toward evening, sat on the bed, looking at me mockingly and tapping the rug with her little foot. As I looked at her, the idea flew into my head that for the whole past month, or, better, the past two weeks, she had not been quite in her own character, one might even say it was the opposite character: what showed was a violent, aggressive being, I wouldn't say shameless, but disorderly and seeking confusion herself. Inviting confusion. Her meekness, however, got in the way. When such a one gets violent, even if she leaps beyond all measure, you can still see that she's only breaking herself, is egging herself on, and that she herself will be the first to be unable to manage her own sense of integrity and shame. That's why her sort sometimes leap much too far beyond measure, so that you don't believe your own observing mind. The soul accustomed to depravity, on the other hand, will always soften things, making them more vile, but in the guise of an order and decency that claim superiority over you.

"And is it true that you were thrown out of your regiment because you were scared to fight a duel?" she asked suddenly, out of the blue, and her eyes flashed.

"It's true. On the decision of the officers, I was asked to withdraw from the regiment, though, anyhow, I myself had already sent in my resignation before then."

"Thrown out as a coward?"

"Yes, they judged me a coward. But I refused the duel not because I was a coward, but because I did not wish to submit to their tyrannical decision and challenge a man when I myself did not feel any offense. You know," I couldn't help myself here, "that to rise up actively against such tyranny and accept all the consequences was to show much greater courage than in any duel you like."

I couldn't help it, with this phrase I began as if justifying myself; that was just what she needed, this new humiliation of me. She laughed maliciously:

"And is it true that after that you wandered the streets of Petersburg for three years, as a vagabond, begging for kopecks and sleeping under billiard tables?"

"I also happened to spend nights in the Haymarket and in Vyazemsky's house.[9] Yes, it's true; after the regiment, there was much disgrace and degradation in my life, but not moral degradation, because I was the first to hate my actions even then. It was only the degradation of my will and mind, and was caused only by the desperateness of my situation. But that has passed . . ."

"Oh, now you're somebody—a financier!"

That is, a hint at the pawnshop. But I had already managed to control myself. I saw that she desired explanations humiliating to me and—I didn't give them. A client opportunely rang the bell, and I went out to him in the big room. Afterward, an hour later, when she suddenly got dressed to go out, she stopped in front of me and said:

"You told me nothing about it before the wedding, however."

I did not reply, and she left.

And so, the next day I stood in that room behind the door and listened to how my fate was being decided, and in my pocket there was a revolver. She was dressed up and sitting at the table, and Yefimovich was clowning in front of her. And what then: the outcome was (I say it to my credit), the outcome was just exactly what I anticipated and expected— though without being aware that I was anticipating and expecting it. I don't know whether I've expressed myself clearly.

The outcome was this. I listened for a whole hour, and for a whole hour I was witness to a combat between a most noble and lofty woman and a depraved, dull-witted society creature with a reptilian soul. And where, I thought, amazed, where did she, this naive, this meek, this taciturn woman, get to know all that? The wittiest author of high-society comedies would have been unable to create this scene of mockery, the most naive laughter, and the holy disdain of virtue for vice. And so much brilliance in her words and little phrases; such sharpness in her quick responses, such truth in her condemnation! And at the same time so much of an almost girlish simple-heartedness.

She laughed in his face at his declarations of love, at his gestures, at his offers. Having come with crude assault in mind and anticipating no resistance, he suddenly wilted. At first I might have thought it was simply her coquetry here—"the coquetry of a depraved but witty being, to put on a more costly show." But no, the truth shone like the sun, and it was impossible to doubt it. Only out of hatred toward me, affected and impulsive, could she, so inexperienced, have ventured upon this meeting, but as soon as it came to business—her eyes were opened at once. Here was simply a creature thrashing about, so as to insult me in any way possible, but, having decided upon such filth, she could not bear the disorder. And how could she, so pure and sinless, she, with her ideal, be tempted by Yefimovich or anyone else you like among these high-society creatures? On the contrary, he could only make her laugh. The whole truth rose from her soul, and indignation called up sarcasm from her heart. I repeat, toward the end this buffoon was quite withered and sat scowling and barely responding, so that I began to be afraid he might risk insulting her out of base vengeance. And I repeat again: to my credit, I heard the scene out almost without astonishment. As if I had encountered only what I knew. As if I had gone so as to encounter it. I had gone believing nothing, no accusation, though I did put a revolver in my pocket—that is the truth! And how could I have imagined her different? Why, then, did I love her, why did I esteem her, why had I married her? Oh, of course, I satisfied myself only too well as to how much she hated me then, but I also satisfied myself as to how chaste she was. I stopped the scene suddenly by opening the door. Yefimovich jumped up, I took her by the hand and invited her to leave with me. Yefimovich quickly recovered and suddenly burst into a ringing and rolling guffaw.

"Oh, I won't oppose the sacred rights of matrimony, take her, take her! And you know," he shouted after me, "though it's not possible for a decent man to fight a duel with you, still, out of respect for your lady, I'm at your service . . . If you'll risk it, that is . . ."

"Do you hear!" I stopped her on the threshold for a moment.

After that not a word all the way home. I led her by the hand, and she didn't resist. On the contrary, she was terribly struck, but only till home. Having come home, she sat down on a chair and fixed her eyes on me. She was extremely pale; though mockery formed on her lips at once, her look was solemnly and severely challenging, and it seemed she was seriously convinced in the first moments that I was going to kill her with the revolver. But I silently took the revolver out of my pocket and put it on the table. She looked at me and at the revolver. (Note this: the revolver was familiar to her. I had had it and kept it loaded ever since I opened the pawnshop. On opening the pawnshop, I had decided not to keep any huge dogs, or a muscular lackey, as Moser, for instance, does. My clients are let in by the cook. But it's impossible for someone occupied with this trade to go without self-protection, just in case, and so I kept a loaded revolver. In the first days after she entered my house, she got very interested in this revolver, asked questions, and I even explained the mechanism and system to her, and besides that, persuaded her once to shoot at a target. Note all that.) Paying no attention to her frightened look, I lay down half undressed on the bed. I was completely worn out; it was already nearly eleven o'clock. She went on sitting in the same place, without stirring, for about an hour longer, then put out the candle and lay down, also dressed, by the wall, on the sofa. The first time she didn't lie down with me—note that as well . . .

VI

A Terrible Memory

Now, this terrible memory . . .

I woke up in the morning, between seven and eight, I think, and it was already almost completely light in the room. I woke up all at once with full consciousness and suddenly opened my eyes. She was standing by the table holding the revolver in her hand. She didn't see that I was awake and watching. And suddenly I see her start moving toward me with the revolver in her hand. I quickly closed my eyes and pretended to be fast asleep.

She came to the bed and stood over me. I heard everything; and though a dead silence fell, I heard that silence. Here a convulsive movement occurred—and suddenly, irresistibly, against my will, I opened my eyes. She was looking at me, right into my eyes, and the revolver was already at my temple. Our eyes met. But we looked at each other for no more than a moment. I forcibly closed my eyes again, and at the same moment decided with all my strength of soul that I would not stir or open my eyes again, no matter what lay ahead of me.

In fact, it does happen that a deeply sleeping man suddenly opens his eyes, even raises his head for a second and looks around the room, and then, after a moment, unconsciously lays his head back on the pillow and falls asleep, remembering nothing.

When I, having met her gaze and felt the revolver at my temple, suddenly closed my eyes again and did not stir, like a man fast asleep—she decidedly could have supposed that I was in fact sleeping and had seen nothing, the more so as it was quite incredible for someone, after seeing what I had seen, to close his eyes again at *such* a moment.

Yes, incredible. But even so she might have guessed the truth—it was this that suddenly flashed through my mind, still in that same moment. Oh, what a whirlwind of thoughts and feelings swept through my mind in less than a moment, and long live the electricity of human thought! In that case (so I felt), if she had guessed the truth and knew I was not asleep, then I had already crushed her by my readiness to accept death, and her hand might now falter. The former resolution might be dashed against the new extraordinary impression. They say that people standing on a high place are as if drawn down of themselves into the abyss. I think many suicides and murders have been committed only because the revolver has already been taken in hand. Here, too, is an abyss; here, too, is a forty-five-degree slope, down which you cannot help sliding, and something invincibly challenges you to pull the trigger. But the awareness that I had seen everything, knew everything, and was silently awaiting death from her—might keep her from the slope.

The silence continued, and suddenly at my temple, through my hair, I felt the cold touch of steel. You may ask: did I have any firm hope of salvation? I'll answer you as before God: I had no hope, except perhaps for one chance in a hundred. Why, then, did I accept death? But I will ask: what did I need life for after that revolver, raised against me by the being I adored? Besides, I knew with all the strength of my being that at that very moment a fight was going on between us, a terrible life-and-death combat, the combat of that same coward of yesterday, driven out by his comrades for cowardice. I knew it, and she knew it, if only she had guessed the truth that I was not asleep.

Maybe this isn't so, maybe I didn't think that then, but it had to be so even without thinking, because all I did afterward, in every hour of my life, was think of it.

But again you will ask a question: why did I not save her from evildoing? Oh, I asked myself this question a thousand times afterward—every time that, with a chill in my spine, I recalled that second. But my soul was in dark despair then: I was perishing, I was perishing myself, could I have saved anyone else? And how do you know whether I wanted to save anyone then? Who knows what I might have felt then?

My consciousness, however, was seething; seconds passed,

there was dead silence; she was still standing over me—and suddenly I shivered with hope! I quickly opened my eyes. She was no longer in the room. I got up: I was victorious—and she was forever defeated!

I came out to have tea. The samovar was always served in the front room, and she always poured tea. I sat down at the table silently and accepted the glass of tea from her. After about five minutes I glanced at her. She was terribly pale, still paler than yesterday, and was looking at me. And suddenly— and suddenly, seeing that I was looking at her, she smiled palely with her pale lips, a timid question in her eyes. "That means she's still in doubt and is asking herself: does he know or doesn't he, did he see or didn't he?" I looked away indifferently. After tea I locked the shop, went to the market, and bought an iron bed and a screen. Coming home, I ordered the bed put in the big room and partitioned off with the screen. It was a bed for her, but I didn't say a word to her. Even without words she understood from this bed that I "had seen and knew everything" and that there was no longer any doubt. I left the revolver on the table for the night, as usual. At night she silently lay down on this new bed: the marriage was dissolved, she was "defeated, but not forgiven." During the night she became delirious, and by morning was in a fever. She lay ill for six weeks.

CHAPTER TWO

I

The Dream of Pride

Lukerya has just announced that she's not going to live with me, and once the lady is buried, she's quitting. I prayed on my knees for five minutes, and wanted to pray for an hour, but I kept thinking, thinking, and my thoughts are all sick, and my head is sick—what's the point of praying—nothing but sin!

It's also strange that I don't want to sleep: in great, in all too great grief, after the first very strong outbursts, one always wants to sleep. They say those condemned to death sleep extremely soundly on their last night. That's how it should be, it's according to nature, otherwise one's strength would fail . . . I lay down on the sofa, but didn't fall asleep . . .

. . . For the six weeks of her illness then, we looked after her day and night—I, Lukerya, and a trained nurse from the hospital, whom I had hired. I didn't spare the money, and I even wanted to spend on her. I invited Dr. Schroeder and paid him ten roubles per visit. When she regained consciousness, I tried to keep out of her sight. But, anyhow, what am I describing. When she was on her feet completely, she quietly and silently sat in my room at a special table, which I also bought for her at that time . . . Yes, it's true, we were perfectly silent; that is, we started talking later, but—all ordinary things. I, of course, purposely did not become expansive, but I noticed very well that she, too, was as if glad not to say an extra word. I thought this perfectly natural on her part: "She's too shaken and defeated," I thought, "and, of course, she must be allowed to forget and get used to it." In this fashion we kept silent, but every minute I was preparing myself for the future. I thought she was doing the same, and it was terribly entertaining for me to keep guessing: precisely what is she thinking about now?

I'll say more: oh, of course, no one knows how much I endured, lamenting over her during her illness. But I lamented to myself, and suppressed the groans in my breast even from Lukerya. I couldn't imagine, couldn't even suppose, that she might die without having learned everything. But when she was out of danger and her health began to return—this I remember—I quickly and very much calmed down. What's more, I decided to *postpone our future* for as long as possible, and meanwhile leave everything in its present way. Yes, something strange and particular—I don't know what else to call it—happened to me then: I was triumphant and the consciousness of it in itself proved perfectly sufficient for me. So the whole winter passed. Oh, I was pleased as I had never been before, and that for the whole winter.

You see: in my life there was one terrible external circumstance, which until then, that is, until that very catastrophe with my wife, had weighed on me every day and every hour—namely, the loss of my reputation and this retirement from the regiment. In two words: there had been a tyrannical injustice against me. True, my comrades disliked me for my difficult character—my ridiculous character, perhaps—though it often happens that what is most sublime for you, what is cherished and revered by you, at the same time for some reason makes the crowd of your comrades laugh. Oh, I was never liked, even at school. Never and nowhere was I liked. Lukerya is also unable to like me. The incident with the regiment, though a consequence of the dislike for me, was undoubtedly of an accidental character. I say that because there is nothing more offensive and insufferable than to perish from an accident that might or might not have happened, from an unfortunate conglomeration of circumstances that might have passed over like a cloud. For an intellectual being it is humiliating. The accident was as follows.

During intermission at the theater, I stepped out to the buffet. The hussar A———v, suddenly coming in, began loudly telling two fellow hussars, in the presence of other officers and the public, that Captain Bezumtsev of our regiment had just caused a scandal in the corridor, "and appears to be drunk." The conversation did not catch on, and the whole thing was a mistake, because Captain Bezumtsev was not drunk, and the scandal was in fact no scandal. The hussars started talking about other things, and that was the end of it, but next day the story penetrated our regiment, and right away they started talking about me being the only one from our regiment who was in the buffet, and when the hussar A———v made an impudent reference to Captain Bezumtsev, I did not go up to A———v and stop him with a rebuke. But why on earth should I? If he had a bone to pick with Bezumtsev, that was their personal affair, and why should I get involved in it? Meanwhile the officers began to say that the affair was not personal, but also concerned the regiment, and since of the officers of our regiment I was the only one there, I had thus proved to all the other officers and the public in the buffet that there could be officers of our regiment who were not so ticklish about honor—their own or that of their regiment. I could not agree with such a finding. I was given to know that I could still mend everything, if even now, late though it was, I should wish to have a formal talk with A———v. I did not wish to do that and, being annoyed, proudly refused. Right after that I handed in my resignation— that's the whole story. I came out proud, but crushed in spirit. My will and reason collapsed. Just then it also happened that my sister's husband in Moscow squandered our small fortune, including my share of it—a tiny share, but I was left penniless in the street. I could have taken a private position, but I didn't: after a splendid uniform, I couldn't work somewhere in railways. And so—if it's shame, let it be shame, if it's disgrace, let it be disgrace, if it's degradation, let it be degradation, and the worse the better—that's what I chose. Here follow three years of dark memories and even Vyazemsky's house. A year and a half ago a rich old woman, my godmother, died in Moscow, unexpectedly leaving me, among others, three thousand in her will. I thought a little and thereupon decided my fate. I decided on a pawnshop, without begging people's pardon: money, then a corner, and—a new life far away from old memories—that was the plan. Nevertheless the dark past and the forever ruined reputation of my honor oppressed me every hour, every minute. But here I got married. Accidentally or not—I don't know. But in bringing her into my house, I thought I was bringing a friend, and I needed a friend so very much. But I saw clearly that the friend had to be prepared, completed, and even won over. And how could I explain anything just like that to a sixteen-year-old and prejudiced girl? For instance, how could I, without the accidental help of this terrible catastrophe with the revolver, convince her that I was not a coward, and that I had been unjustly accused of cowardice in the regiment? But the catastrophe came just pat. Having withstood the revolver, I had revenged myself on my whole gloomy past. And though no one knew of it, *she* did, and that was everything for me, because she herself was everything for me, all my hope for the future in my dreams! She was the only person I was preparing for myself, and there was no need for any other—and now she knew everything; at least she knew that she had hastened unjustly to join my enemies. This thought delighted me. I could no longer be a scoundrel in her eyes, perhaps only an odd person, but after what had happened, I did not dislike this thought all that much: oddity is no vice, on the contrary, it sometimes attracts the feminine character. In short, I deliberately put off the denouement: what had happened was, for the moment, quite sufficient for my peace and contained quite enough pictures and material for my dreams. The nasty part of it is that I'm a dreamer: the material was enough for me, and as for her, I thought she could *wait*.

So the whole winter went by in some expectation of something. I liked to steal a look at her when she was sitting, as usual, at her table. She was busy with handwork, with linens, and in the evening she sometimes read books that she took from my bookcase. The selection of books in it also should have testified in my favor. She hardly ever went anywhere. Toward evening, after dinner, I took her for a walk each day, and we got our exercise; but not in perfect silence as before. I precisely tried to pretend that we were not being silent and talked agreeably, but, as I've already said, we both did it in such a way as not to be too expansive. I did it on purpose, and she, I thought, had to be "given time." Of course, it's strange that it never once occurred to me, almost till the end of winter, that while I liked looking at her in secret, I never once caught her glancing at me that whole winter! I thought it was her timidity. Besides, she had a look of such timid meekness, such strengthlessness after her illness. No, better to wait it out and—"and she herself will suddenly come to you . . ."

This thought delighted me irresistibly. I will add only that at times I excited myself as if on purpose and actually brought my mind and spirit to a point where I felt offended by her. And so it continued for some time. Yet my hatred could never ripen and settle in my soul. And I felt myself that it was as if only a game. And even when I dissolved the marriage and bought the bed and screen, I still could never, never see her as a criminal. And not because I took a light-minded view of her crime, but because I had had the intention of forgiving her completely from the very first day, even before I bought the bed. In short, it was an oddity on my part, for I am morally strict. On the contrary, in my eyes she was so defeated, so humiliated, so crushed, that I sometimes pitied her painfully, though for all that I sometimes decidedly liked the idea of her humiliation. It was the idea of our inequality that I liked . . .

That winter I happened deliberately to do several good deeds. I forgave two debts, I gave one poor woman money without any pledge. And I did not tell my wife about it, and I did it not at all so that my wife would find out; but the woman herself came to thank me, all but on her knees. So it became known; it seemed to me that she was actually pleased to learn about the woman.

But spring was coming, it was already the middle of April, the storm windows had been taken down, and bright sheaves of sunlight began to light up our silent rooms. Yet a veil hung before me and blinded my reason. A fatal, terrible veil! How did it happen that it all suddenly fell from my eyes, and I suddenly recovered my sight and understood everything! Was it an accident, or had the appointed day come, or did a ray of sun light up the thought and the answer in my stupefied mind? No, there was no thought or answer here, but here suddenly some nerve began to play, some nerve, grown numb, began to tremble and came alive and lit up my whole stupefied soul and my demonic pride. Just as if I'd suddenly jumped up from my seat then. And it did happen suddenly and unexpectedly. It happened toward evening, at five o'clock after dinner.

II

The Veil Suddenly Fell

A couple of words first. Already a month ago I noticed a strange pensiveness in her, not silence now, but real pensiveness. This, too, I noticed suddenly. She was sitting over her work then, her head bent to her sewing, and didn't see that I was looking at her. And right then it suddenly struck me that she had become so thin, so slender, her little face pale, her lips white—all that, as a whole, together with the pensiveness, struck me extremely and all at once. Even before then I had heard a dry little cough, especially at night. I got up at once and went to invite Schroeder to come, telling her nothing.

Schroeder came the next day. She was very surprised and kept looking first at Schroeder and then at me.

"But I'm well," she said, with a vague smile.

Schroeder did not examine her much (these medical men are haughtily careless at times), and only told me in the other room that it was a leftover from her illness and that come spring it wouldn't be a bad idea to go somewhere to the sea, or if that was impossible, simply to take a country house. In short, he said nothing except that there was weakness or some such thing. When Schroeder left, she suddenly said to me again, looking at me terribly seriously:

"I'm quite, quite well."

But having said this, she straightaway blushed all at once, apparently with shame. Apparently, it was shame. Oh, now I understand: she was ashamed that I was still *her husband,* looking after her, still as if I were a real husband. But I didn't understand it then and ascribed her color to humility (the veil!).

And then, a month after that, between four and five o'clock, in April, on a bright sunny day, I was sitting in my shop making calculations. Suddenly I heard her, in our room, at her table, at her work, softly, softly . . . singing. This novelty produced a tremendous impression on me, and to this day

I haven't understood it. Up to then I'd hardly ever heard her sing, except in the very first days, when I brought her into my house and we could still frolic, shooting at a target with the revolver. Then her voice was still rather strong, ringing, though unsteady, but terribly pleasant and healthy. Now, however, her little song was so feeble—oh, not that it was plaintive (it was some romance), but in her voice there was something as if cracked, broken, as if her little voice couldn't manage it, as if the song itself were sick. She was singing in a half voice, and suddenly, after rising, the voice broke off— such a poor little voice, and it broke off so pitifully; she coughed and again softly, softly, barely, barely began to sing . . .

My alarm will be laughed at, but no one will ever understand why I was so alarmed! No, I wasn't sorry for her yet, it was something quite different as yet. To begin with, at least in the first minutes, there suddenly came perplexity and terrible astonishment, terrible and strange, painful and almost vengeful. "She's singing, and with me here! *Has she forgotten about me, or what?*"

All shaken, I sat where I was, then suddenly got up, took my hat, and walked out, as if uncomprehending. At least I don't know why or where. Lukerya started helping me with my coat.

"She sings?" I said to Lukerya involuntarily. She didn't understand and stared at me, continuing not to understand; however, it was actually impossible to understand me.

"Is it the first time she's singing?"

"No, she sometimes sings when you're out," Lukerya replied.

I remember everything. I went down the stairs, walked out, and let my feet take me wherever they wanted to go. I walked as far as the corner and began staring somewhere. People were passing by, pushing me, I didn't feel it. I hailed a cab and told the driver to go to the Police Bridge, I don't know why. But then I suddenly dropped him and gave him twenty kopecks:

"It's for having bothered you," I said, laughing to him

senselessly, but in my heart some sort of rapture suddenly began.

I turned toward home, quickening my pace. The cracked, poor, broken little note suddenly began to ring again in my soul. I was breathless. The veil was falling, falling from my eyes! If she'd begun singing with me there, it meant she'd forgotten about me—that's what was clear and terrible. This my heart felt. Yet rapture shone in my soul and overcame fear.

Oh, the irony of fate! There was and could have been nothing else in my soul all winter except this very rapture, but where had I myself been all winter? had I been there with my soul? I ran up the stairs in great haste, I don't know whether I walked in timidly. I remember only that the whole floor was as if undulating and I was as if floating on a river. I walked into the room, she was sitting in the same place, sewing, her head bent, but no longer singing. She gave me a passing, uncurious glance—not a glance, but merely the gesture, ordinary and indifferent, when someone comes into a room.

I went straight over to her and sat down on a chair right beside her, like a crazy man. She gave me a quick look, as if frightened: I took her hand, and I don't remember what I said to her, that is, wanted to say, because I couldn't even speak properly. My voice faltered and wouldn't obey me. And I didn't know what to say, only I was suffocating.

"Let's talk . . . you know . . . say something!" I suddenly babbled some stupid thing—oh, as if intelligence was the point! She gave another start and drew back in great fright, looking me in the face, but suddenly—*stern astonishment* showed in her eyes. Yes, astonishment, and it was *stern*. She was looking at me with big eyes. This sternness, this stern astonishment, all at once demolished me: "So you also want love? love?"—this astonishment as if suddenly asked, though she was silent. But I could read everything, everything. Everything in me shook, and I simply collapsed at her feet. Yes, I fell at her feet. She quickly jumped up, but with extraordinary strength I held her back by both hands.

And I fully understood my despair, oh, I understood it!

But, would you believe, rapture was seething in my heart so irrepressibly that I thought I would die. I was kissing her feet in ecstasy and happiness. Yes, in happiness, boundless and endless, and that while understanding all my hopeless despair! I was weeping, I was saying something, yet I couldn't speak. Fright and astonishment were suddenly replaced in her by some worried thought, an extraordinary question, and she looked at me strangely, wildly even, she wanted to understand something very quickly, and she smiled. She was terribly ashamed that I was kissing her feet, and she kept pulling them away, but I at once kissed the place on the floor where her foot had been. She saw that and suddenly started laughing from shame (you know how one can laugh from shame). Hysterics were coming, I could see that, her hands twitched—I wasn't thinking about that and kept mumbling to her that I loved her, that I wouldn't get up, "let me kiss your dress . . . let me worship you like this all my life . . ." I don't know, I don't remember—and suddenly she began sobbing and shaking; a terrible fit of hysterics came. I had frightened her.

I carried her over to the bed. When the fit passed, she sat up on the bed, seized my hands with a terribly crushed look, and begged me to calm down: "Enough, don't torment yourself, calm down!"—and again she started weeping. All that evening I never left her side. I kept telling her I'd take her to Boulogne[10] to swim in the sea, now, at once, in two weeks, that she had such a cracked little voice, I'd heard it that day; that I'd close the shop, sell it to Dobronravov, that everything would begin anew, and, above all, to Boulogne, to Boulogne! She listened and kept being afraid. Kept being more and more afraid. But for me the main thing was not that, but that the desire kept growing greater and more irrepressible in me to lie at her feet again, and again to kiss, to kiss the ground on which her feet stood, and to worship her and—"nothing more, I'll ask nothing more of you," I kept repeating every moment, "don't answer me anything, don't notice me at all, just let me look at you from the corner, turn me into a thing of yours, into a little dog . . ." She was weeping.

"And I thought you'd just let me stay like that," suddenly escaped her involuntarily, so involuntarily that she perhaps didn't notice at all how she had said it, and yet—oh, this was her most important, her most fatal phrase, the clearest for me that evening, and it was as if my heart was slashed by this phrase as by a knife! It explained everything to me, everything, but as long as she was near, before my eyes, I hoped irresistibly and was terribly happy. Oh, I made her terribly weary that evening, and I understood that, but I was constantly thinking I was going to remake it all right then! Finally, toward night-time, she became totally strengthless, I convinced her to go to sleep, and she fell asleep at once, soundly. I expected delirium, there was delirium, but very little. During the night I got up almost every minute and went quietly in my slippers to look at her. I wrung my hands over her, looking at this sick being on this poor little cot, the iron bed I had bought for her then for three roubles. I knelt down, but didn't dare to kiss the sleeper's feet (without her will!). I'd start praying to God, but would jump up again. Lukerya watched me closely and kept coming in from the kitchen. I went to her and told her to go to bed and that the next day "something quite different" would begin.

And I believed it blindly, insanely, terribly. Oh, rapture, rapture flooded me! I was only waiting for the next day. Above all, I did not believe in any calamity, despite the symptoms. Sense had not fully returned, despite the fallen veil, and it took a long, long time to return—oh, till today, till this very day!! And how, how could it return then: why, she was still alive then, she was right there before me, and I before her: "She'll wake up tomorrow, and I'll tell her all this, and she'll see it all." That was my reasoning then, simple and clear— hence the rapture! Above all, there was this trip to Boulogne. I kept thinking for some reason that Boulogne was—everything, that Boulogne contained something definitive. "To Boulogne, to Boulogne! . . ." I waited insanely for morning.

III

I Understand All Too Well

And this was only a few days ago, five days, only five days, last Tuesday! No, no, if she'd only waited a little longer, only a little bit longer, I—I would have dispelled the darkness! And, anyway, didn't she calm down? The very next day she listened to me with a smile now, despite her bewilderment . . . Above all, throughout this time, all five days, there was bewilderment or shame in her. She was also afraid, very afraid. I won't argue, I'm not going to contradict like some insane person: there was fear, but how could she not be afraid? We'd been strangers to each other for so long, had grown so unused to each other, and suddenly all this . . . But I didn't consider her fear, the new thing was shining! . . . True, unquestionably true, I had made a mistake. And maybe even many mistakes. And when we woke up the next day, still that morning (it was Wednesday), I right away suddenly made a mistake: I suddenly made her my friend. I hurried too much, too much, but a confession was needed, was necessary—yes, and much more than a confession! I didn't conceal from her even what I'd been concealing from myself all my life. I said straight out that all I'd done that whole winter was feel certain of her love. I explained to her that the pawnshop was nothing but the degradation of my will and intelligence, a personal idea of self-castigation and self-exaltation. I explained to her that I had actually turned coward in the buffet that time, owing to my character, to insecurity: I was struck by the surroundings, by the buffet; struck by how I was going to come out in this, and wouldn't it come out stupid? I turned coward not at the duel, but that it would come out stupid . . . And afterward I didn't want to admit it and tormented everyone, and tormented her for it, and that was why I had married her, so as to torment her for it. Generally, I spoke for the most part as if in a fever. She herself took me by the hands and begged me to stop: "You're exaggerating . . . you're tormenting yourself"—and again the tears would start, again all but fits! She kept begging me not to say any of it, not to remember.

I paid little or no regard to her begging: spring, Boulogne! The sun was there, our new sun was there, that was all I kept saying! I locked the shop, handed the business over to Dobronravov. I suddenly suggested to her that we give everything away to the poor, except for the capital of three thousand inherited from my godmother, which we'd spend on going to Boulogne, then come back and start a new life of labor. So it was decided, because she didn't say anything . . . she only smiled. And, it seems, she smiled more out of delicacy, so as not to upset me. I did see that I was burdening her, don't think I was so stupid or such an egoist that I didn't see it. I saw everything, everything to the last little feature, I saw and knew it better than anyone else; all my despair stood in full view!

I told her all about me and about her. And about Lukerya. I told her I had wept . . . Oh, yes, I also changed the subject, I also tried by all means not to remind her of certain things. And she even became animated a couple of times, I remember, I remember! Why do you say that I looked and saw nothing? And if only *this* hadn't happened, everything would have been resurrected. She even told me just two days ago, when the conversation turned to reading and what she'd read that winter—she even told me, laughing as she recalled it, about the scene between Gil Blas and the archbishop of Granada.[11] And what childlike laughter, so dear, just as before, when she was my fiancée (one instant! one instant!); how glad I was! I was terribly struck, however, about this archbishop: so she had after all found peace of mind and happiness enough to laugh over the masterpiece as she sat there this winter. So she had already begun to be fully at peace, to believe fully that I would just let her stay *like that*. "I thought you'd just let me stay *like that*"—that's what she had said then on Tuesday! Oh, a ten-year-old girl's thought! And she believed, she did believe that everything would in fact stay *like that*: she at her table, I at mine, and both of us like that till we're sixty years old. And suddenly—here I come, a husband, and a husband in need of love! Oh, incomprehension, oh, my blindness!

It was also a mistake that I looked at her with rapture; I should have restrained myself, because rapture is frightening. But, after all, I did restrain myself, I didn't kiss her feet anymore. I never once showed that . . . well, that I was a husband—oh, it never even entered my mind, I only worshipped! But it was impossible to be quite silent, it was impossible not to speak at all! I suddenly said to her that I delighted in her conversation and that I considered her incomparably, incomparably better educated and developed than myself. She turned bright red and said abashedly that I was exaggerating. Here, like a fool, unable to help myself, I told her how enraptured I had been when, standing behind the door, I had listened to her combat, the combat of innocence with that creature, and how I had delighted in her intelligence, her sparkling wit, together with such childlike simple-heartedness. She shuddered all over, as it were, tried to murmur again that I was exaggerating, but suddenly her whole face darkened, she covered it with her hands and began to sob . . . Here I, too, couldn't stand it: I fell down before her again, again started kissing her feet, and again it ended with a fit, the same as on Tuesday. That was last evening, but in the morning . . .

In the morning?! Madman, that morning was today, just now, only just now!

Listen and try to fathom: when we came together over the samovar just now (this after yesterday's fit), I was even struck by her calm, that's how it was! And I'd spent the whole night shaking with fear over yesterday. But suddenly she comes up to me, stands in front of me, and, clasping her hands (just now, just now!), began saying to me that she was a criminal, that she knew it, that her crime had tormented her all winter, torments her still . . . that she values my magnanimity only too highly . . . "I'll be your faithful wife, I'll respect you . . ." Here I jumped up like a crazy man and embraced her! I was kissing her, kissing her face, her lips, like a husband, for the first time after a long separation. And why did I ever leave just now, for only two hours . . . our passports . . . Oh, God! Five minutes, if only I'd come back five minutes earlier? . . . And here this crowd in our gateway, those looks at me . . . oh, Lord!

Lukerya says (oh, now I'll never let Lukerya go, she knows everything, she was here all winter, she'll tell me everything), she says that when I left the house, and only something like twenty minutes before I came back—she suddenly went into our room to ask the lady something or other, I don't remember, and saw that her icon (that same icon of the Mother of God) had been taken down and was standing in front of her on the table, as if the lady had just been praying before it. "What's the matter, ma'am?" "Nothing, Lukerya, go now . . . Wait, Lukerya," she went up to her and kissed her. "Are you happy, ma'am?" "Yes, Lukerya." "You should have come to the master long ago, ma'am, to ask forgiveness . . . Thank God you've made things up." "All right, Lukerya," she says, "you may go, Lukerya," and she smiled, and so strangely. So strangely that Lukerya suddenly went back ten minutes later to look at her: "She was standing by the wall, right by the window, her hand leaning on the wall and her head pressed to it, she was standing like that, thinking. And she was so deep in thought that she didn't hear how I stood and looked at her from the other room. I saw that she was as if smiling—standing, thinking, and smiling. I looked at her, turned quietly, walked out, also thinking to myself, only suddenly I heard the window being opened. I went at once to tell her, 'It's chilly, ma'am, you might catch cold,' and suddenly I see her standing on the windowsill, already standing up straight in the open window, her back to me, holding the icon in her hands. My heart just sank, I shouted: 'My lady, my lady!' She heard me, made as if to turn toward me, then didn't, but took a step, pressed the icon to her breast, and threw herself out the window!"

I only remember that when I came in the gate, she was still warm. Above all, they were all staring at me. First they shouted, but then they suddenly fell silent and everyone makes way for me and . . . and she's lying there with the icon. I remember, as if through darkness, that I went up silently and looked for a long time, and everyone surrounded me, saying something to me. Lukerya was there, but I didn't see her. She says she spoke to me. I remember only that tradesman: he kept shouting to me that "a handful of blood came out of her mouth, a handful, a handful!" and showing me the blood right there on the stone. It seems I touched the blood with my finger, got it on my finger, looked at it (I remember that), while he kept telling me: "A handful, a handful!"

"And what of this handful?" I screamed, so they say, at the top of my lungs, raised my arms, and hurled myself at him . . .

Oh, wild, wild! Incomprehension! Implausibility! Impossibility!

IV

I Was Only Five Minutes Late

Or not so? Is it plausible? Can you say it's possible? Why, for what reason, did this woman die?

Oh, believe me, I understand; but what she died for—is still a question. She got frightened of my love, asked herself seriously: to accept or not to accept, and couldn't bear the question, and preferred to die. I know, I know, there's no point racking one's brain: she made too many promises, got frightened that she couldn't keep them—it's clear. Here there are several quite terrible circumstances.

Because what did she die for? the question still stands. The question throbs, it's throbbing in my brain. I would even have let her stay *like that,* if she'd wanted it to stay *like that.* She didn't believe it, that's what! No—no, I'm lying, that's not it at all. Simply because with me it had to be honest; if it's love, it must be total love, and not like the love of some merchant. And since she was too chaste, too pure to consent to the kind of love a merchant needs, she didn't want to deceive me. Didn't want to deceive me with half love, under the guise of love, or with quarter love. Too honest she was, that's what, sirs! I wanted to implant breadth of heart in her, remember? A strange thought.

I'm terribly curious: did she respect me? I don't know, did she despise me or not? I don't think she did. It's terribly strange: why did it never occur to me, during the whole winter, that she despised me? I was in the highest degree certain of the opposite, until that very moment when she looked at me with *stern astonishment. Stern,* precisely. Then I understood at once that she despised me. Understood irrevocably, for all eternity! Ah, let her, let her despise me, even all her life, but— let her live, live! Just now she still walked, talked. I don't understand at all how she could throw herself out the window! And how could I have supposed it even five minutes before? I've called Lukerya. I won't let Lukerya go now for anything, not for anything!

Oh, we could still have come to some agreement. We only got terribly unused to each other over the winter, but couldn't we have got accustomed again? Why, why couldn't we have come together and begun a new life again? I'm magnanimous, so is she—there's the point of connection! A few words more, two days, no longer, and she'd have understood everything.

Above all, the pity is that it was all chance—simple, barbaric, insensate chance. That's the pity of it! Five minutes is all, I was only five minutes late! If I'd come five minutes earlier—the moment would have flown over like a cloud, and would never have entered her head afterward. And it would have ended with her understanding everything. And now again empty rooms, again I'm alone. There's the pendulum ticking, it doesn't care, it's not sorry for anything. No one's here—that's the trouble!

I pace, I keep pacing. I know, I know, don't prompt me: you find it ridiculous that I complain about chance and about five minutes? But it's obvious here. Consider one thing: she didn't even leave a note saying something like "blame no one for my death," as they all do. Couldn't she have considered that they might even give Lukerya trouble: "You were the only one with her, so it was you who pushed her." At the least, they'd be pestering her for no reason, if four people in the courtyard hadn't seen from windows in the wing and from the courtyard how she stood with the icon in her hands and threw herself down. But this, too, is chance, that people were standing there and saw it. No, all this is a moment, just one unaccountable moment. Suddenness and fantasy! So what if she prayed before the icon? That doesn't mean it was before death. The whole moment lasted maybe only some ten minutes, the whole decision—precisely as she was standing by the wall, her head leaning on her hand, and smiling. The thought flew into her head, whirled around, and—and she couldn't resist it.

There's an obvious misunderstanding here, like it or not. She still could have lived with me. And what if it was anemia? Simply from anemia, from an exhaustion of vital energy? She got tired over the winter, that's what . . .

I was late!!!

How thin she is in the coffin, how sharp her little nose is! Her eyelashes lie like little points. And how she fell—didn't crush, didn't break anything! Only this "handful of blood." A teaspoon, that is. Internal concussion. A strange thought: if only it were possible not to bury her? Because if she's taken away, then . . . oh, no, it's almost impossible that she'll be taken away! Oh, I know they must take her away, I'm not crazy and not raving at all, on the contrary, never before has my mind shone so—but how can it be that again there's no one in the house, again two rooms, and again myself alone with the pledges. Raving, raving, there's where the raving is! I wore her out—that's what!

What are your laws to me now? What do I need your customs, your morals, your life, your state, your faith for? Let your judge judge me, let them take me to court, to your public court, and I'll say I recognize nothing. The judge will shout: "Silence, officer!" But I'll shout back at him: "Where did you get such power now that I should obey you? Why did dark insensateness smash what is dearest of all? Why do I need your laws now? I separate myself." Oh, it makes no difference to me!

Blind, blind! Dead, she doesn't hear! You don't know what paradise I'd have surrounded you with. Paradise was in my soul, I'd have planted it all around you! Well, so you wouldn't love me—let it be, what of it? Everything would be *like that*, everything would stay *like that*. You'd tell me things as you would a friend—and we'd be joyful, and we'd laugh joyfully looking into each other's eyes. And so we'd live. And even if you came to love someone else—well, let it be, let it be! You'd walk with him and laugh, and I'd watch from the other side of the street . . . Oh, let it all be, only let her open her eyes at least once! For one moment, only one! she'd look at me as she did just now, when she stood in front of me and swore to be my faithful wife! Oh, in one look she'd understand everything.

Insensateness! Oh, nature! People are alone on the earth—that's the trouble! "Is there a living man on the field?" the Russian warrior cries. I, too, though not a warrior, cry out, and no one answers. They say the sun gives life to the universe. Let the sun rise and—look at it, isn't it dead? Everything is dead, and the dead are everywhere. Only people, and around them silence—that's the earth! "People, love one another"—who said that? whose testament is it? The pendulum ticks insensibly, disgustingly. It's two o'clock in the morning. Her little boots are standing by her bed, just as if they were waiting for her . . . No, seriously, when she's taken away tomorrow, what about me then?

THE DREAM OF A RIDICULOUS MAN

A FANTASTIC STORY

I

I am a ridiculous man. They call me mad now. That would be a step up in rank, if I did not still remain as ridiculous to them as before. But now I'm no longer angry, now they are all dear to me, and even when they laugh at me—then, too, they are even somehow especially dear to me. I would laugh with them—not really at myself, but for love of them—if it weren't so sad for me to look at them. Sad because they don't know the truth, and I do know the truth. Ah, how hard it is to be the only one who knows the truth! But they won't understand that. No, they won't understand it.

Before, it caused me great anguish that I seemed ridiculous. Not seemed, but was. I was always ridiculous, and I know it, maybe right from birth. Maybe from the age of seven I already knew I was ridiculous. Then I went to school, then to the university, and what—the more I studied, the more I learned that I was ridiculous. So that for me, all my university education existed ultimately as if only to prove and explain to me, the deeper I went into it, that I was ridiculous. And as with learning, so with life. Every passing year the same consciousness grew and strengthened in me that my appearance was in all respects ridiculous. I was ridiculed by everyone and always. But none of them knew or suspected that if there was one man on earth who was more aware than anyone else of my ridiculousness, it was I myself, and this was the most vexing thing for me, that they didn't know it, but here I myself was to blame: I was always so proud that I would never confess it to anyone for anything. This pride grew in me over the years, and if it had so happened that I allowed myself to confess to anyone at all that I was ridiculous, I think that same evening I'd have blown my head off with a revolver. Oh, how I suffered in my youth over being unable to help myself and suddenly somehow confessing it to my comrades. But once I reached early manhood, I became a bit calmer for some reason, though with every passing year I learned more and more about my terrible quality. Precisely for some reason, because to this day I cannot determine why. Maybe because a dreadful anguish was growing in my soul over one circumstance which was infinitely higher than the whole of me: namely—the conviction was overtaking me that everywhere in the world it *made no difference.* I had had a presentiment of this for a very long time, but the full conviction came during the last year somehow suddenly. I suddenly felt that it would *make no difference* to me whether the world existed or there was nothing anywhere. I began to feel and know with my whole being that *with me there was nothing.* At first I kept thinking that instead there had been a lot before, but then I realized that there had been nothing before either, it only seemed so for some reason. Little by little I became convinced that there would never be anything. Then I suddenly stopped being angry with people and began almost not to notice them. Indeed, this was manifest even in the smallest trifles: it would happen, for instance, that I'd walk down the street and bump into people. It wasn't really because I was lost in thought: what could I have been thinking about, I had completely ceased to think then: it made no difference to me. And it would have been fine if I had resolved questions—oh, I never resolved a single one, and there were so many! But it began to *make no difference* to me, and the questions all went away.

And then, after that, I learned the truth. I learned the truth last November, precisely on the third of November, and since that time I remember my every moment. It was a gloomy evening, as gloomy as could be. I was returning home then, between ten and eleven o'clock, and I remember I precisely thought that there could not be a gloomier time. Even in the physical respect. Rain had poured down all day, and it was the coldest and gloomiest rain, even some sort of menacing rain, I remember that, with an obvious hostility to people, and now, between ten and eleven, it suddenly stopped, and a terrible dampness set in, damper and colder than when it was raining, and a sort of steam rose from everything, from every stone in the street and from every alleyway, if you looked far into its depths from the street. I suddenly imagined that if the gaslights went out everywhere, it would be more cheerful, and that with the gaslights it was sadder for the heart, because they threw light on it all. I'd had almost no dinner that day, and had spent since early evening sitting at some engineer's, with two more friends sitting there as well. I kept silent, and they seemed to be sick of me. They talked about something provocative and suddenly even grew excited. But it made no difference to them, I could see that, and they got excited just so. I suddenly told them that: "Gentlemen," I said, "it makes no difference to you." They weren't offended, but they all started laughing at me. It was because I said it without any reproach and simply because it made no difference to me. And they could see that it made no difference to me, and found that amusing.

When I thought in the street about the gaslights, I looked up at the sky. The sky was terribly dark, but one could clearly make out the torn clouds and the bottomless black spots between them. Suddenly in one of these spots I noticed a little star and began gazing at it intently. Because this little star gave me an idea: I resolved to kill myself that night. I had firmly resolved on it two months earlier, and, poor as I was, had bought an excellent revolver and loaded it that same day. But two months had passed and it was still lying in the drawer; but it made so little difference to me that I wished finally to seize a moment when it was less so—why, I didn't know. And thus, during those two months, returning home each night, I thought I was going to shoot myself. I kept waiting for the moment. And so now this little star gave me the idea, and I resolved that it would be that night *without fail*. And why the star gave me the idea—I don't know.

And so, as I was looking at the sky, this girl suddenly seized me by the elbow. The street was empty, and almost no one was about. Far off a coachman was sleeping in his droshky. The girl was about eight years old, in a kerchief and just a little dress, all wet, but I especially remembered her wet, torn shoes, and remember them now. They especially flashed before my eyes. She suddenly started pulling me by the elbow and calling out. She didn't cry, but somehow abruptly shouted some words, which she was unable to pronounce properly because she was chilled and shivering all over. She was terrified by something and shouted desperately: "Mama! Mama!" I turned my face to her, but did not say a word and went on walking, but she was running and pulling at me, and in her voice there was the sound which in very frightened children indicates despair. I know that sound. Though she did not speak all the words out, I understood that her mother was dying somewhere, or something had happened with them there, and she had run out to call someone, to find something so as to help her mother. But I did not go with her, and, on the contrary, suddenly had the idea of chasing her away. First I told her to go and find a policeman. But she suddenly pressed her hands together and, sobbing, choking, kept running beside me and wouldn't leave me. It was then that I stamped my feet at her and shouted. She only cried out: "Mister! Mister! . . ." but suddenly she dropped me and ran headlong across the street: some other passerby appeared there, and she apparently rushed from me to him.

I went up to my fifth floor. I live in a rented room, a

furnished one. It's a poor and small room, with a half-round garret window. I have an oilcloth sofa, a table with books on it, two chairs, and an armchair, as old as can be, but a Voltaire one. I sat down, lighted a candle, and began to think. Next door, in another room, behind a partition, there was bedlam. It had been going on for two days. A retired captain lived there, and he had guests—some six scurvy fellows, drinking vodka and playing blackjack with used cards. The previous night they'd had a fight, and I know that two of them had pulled each other's hair for a long time. The landlady wanted to lodge a complaint, but she's terribly afraid of the captain. The only other tenants in our furnished rooms are a small, thin lady, an army wife and out-of-towner, with three small children who had already fallen ill in our rooms. She and her children are afraid of the captain to the point of fainting, and spend whole nights trembling and crossing themselves, and the smallest child had some sort of fit from fear. This captain, I know for certain, sometimes stops passersby on Nevsky Prospect and begs money from them. They won't take him into any kind of service, yet, strangely (this is what I've been driving at), in the whole month that he had been living with us, the captain had never aroused any vexation in me. Of course, I avoided making his acquaintance from the very start, and he himself got bored with me from the first, yet no matter how they shouted behind their partition, and however many they were—it never made any difference to me. I sit the whole night and don't really hear them—so far do I forget about them. I don't sleep at night until dawn, and that for a year now. I sit all night at the table in the armchair and do nothing. I read books only during the day. I sit and don't even think, just so, some thoughts wander about and I let them go. A whole candle burns down overnight. I quietly sat down at the table, took out the revolver, and placed it in front of me. As I placed it there, I remember asking myself: "Is it so?" and answering myself quite affirmatively: "It is." Meaning I would shoot myself. I knew that I would shoot myself that night for certain, but how long I would stay sitting at the table before then—that I did not know. And of course I would have shot myself if it hadn't been for that girl.

II

You see: though it made no difference to me, I did still feel pain, for instance. If someone hit me, I would feel pain. The same in the moral respect: if something very pitiful happened, I would feel pity, just as when it still made a difference to me in life. And I felt pity that night: I certainly would have helped a child. Why, then, had I not helped the little girl? From an idea that had come along then: as she was pulling and calling to me, a question suddenly arose before me, and I couldn't resolve it. The question was an idle one, but I got angry. I got angry owing to the conclusion that, if I had already resolved to kill myself that night, it followed that now more than ever everything in the world should make no difference to me. Why, then, did I suddenly feel that it did make a difference, and that I pitied the girl? I remember that I pitied her very much; even to the point of some strange pain, even quite incredible in my situation. Really, I'm unable to express the fleeting feeling I had then any better, but the feeling continued at home as well, when I had already settled at my table, and I was extremely vexed, as I hadn't been for a long time. Reasoning flowed from reasoning. It seemed clear that, if I was a man and not yet a zero, then, as long as I did not turn into a zero, I was alive, and consequently could suffer, be angry, and feel shame for my actions. Good. But if I was going to kill myself in two hours, for instance, then what was the girl to me and what did I care then about shame or anything in the world? I turned into a zero, an absolute zero. And could it be that the awareness that I would presently cease to exist *altogether,* and that therefore nothing would exist, could not have

the slightest influence either on my feeling of pity for the girl,
or upon the feeling of shame after the meanness I had committed? And I had stamped and shouted at the unfortunate
child in a savage voice precisely because, "you see, not only do
I feel no pity, but even if I commit some inhuman meanness,
I can do so now, because in two hours everything will be
extinguished." Do you believe this was why I shouted? I'm
now almost convinced of it. It seemed clear that life and the
world were now as if dependent on me. One might even say
that the world was now as if made for me alone: I'd shoot
myself and there would be no more world, at least for me. Not
to mention that maybe there would indeed be nothing for
anyone after me, and that as soon as my consciousness was
extinguished, the whole world would be extinguished at once,
like a phantom, like a mere accessory of my consciousness, it
would be done away with, for maybe all this world and all
these people were—just myself alone. I remember that, sitting
and reasoning, I turned all these new questions, which came
crowding one after another, even in quite a different direction
and invented something quite new. For instance, there suddenly came to me a strange consideration, that if I had once
lived on the moon or on Mars, and had committed some most
shameful and dishonorable act there, such as can only be
imagined, and had been abused and dishonored for it as one
can only perhaps feel and imagine in a dream, a nightmare,
and if, ending up later on earth, I continued to preserve an
awareness of what I had done on the other planet, and knew
at the same time that I would never ever return there, then,
looking from the earth to the moon—would it *make any difference* to me, or not? Would I feel shame for that act, or not?
The questions were idle and superfluous, since the revolver
was already lying in front of me, and I knew with my whole
being that *this* was certain to be, but they excited me, and I
was getting furious. It was as if I couldn't die now without
first resolving something. In short, this girl saved me, because
with the questions I postponed the shot. Meanwhile, everything was also quieting down at the captain's: they had ended

their card game and were settling down to sleep, grumbling and lazily finishing their squabbles. It was then that I suddenly fell asleep, something that had never happened to me before, at the table, in the armchair. I fell asleep quite imperceptibly to myself. Dreams, as is known, are extremely strange: one thing is pictured with the most terrible clarity, with a jeweler's thoroughness in the finish of its details, and over other things you skip as if without noticing them at all—for instance, over space and time. Dreams apparently proceed not from reason but from desire, not from the head but from the heart, and yet what clever things my reason has sometimes performed in sleep! And yet quite inconceivable things happen with it in sleep. My brother, for instance, died five years ago. Sometimes I see him in my dreams: he takes part in my doings, we are both very interested, and yet I remember and am fully aware, throughout the whole dream, that my brother is dead and buried. Why, then, am I not surprised that, though he is dead, he is still here by me and busy with me? Why does my reason fully admit all this? But enough. I'll get down to my dream. Yes, I had this dream then, my dream of the third of November! They tease me now that it was just a dream. But does it make any difference whether it was a dream or not, if this dream proclaimed the Truth to me? For if you once knew the truth and saw it, then you know that it is the truth and there is and can be no other, whether you're asleep or alive. So let it be a dream, let it be, but this life, which you extol so much, I wanted to extinguish by suicide, while my dream, my dream—oh, it proclaimed to me a new, great, renewed, strong life!

Listen.

III

I said that I fell asleep imperceptibly and even as if while continuing to reason about the same matters. Suddenly I dreamed that I took the revolver and, sitting there, aimed it straight at my heart—my heart, not my head; though I had resolved earlier to shoot myself in the head, and precisely in the right temple. Having aimed it at my chest, I waited for a second or two, and my candle, the table, and the wall facing me suddenly started moving and heaving. I hastily fired.

In dreams you sometimes fall from a height, or are stabbed, or beaten, but you never feel pain except when you are somehow really hurt in bed, then you do feel pain and it almost always wakes you up. So it was in my dream: I felt no pain, but I imagined that, as I fired, everything shook inside me and everything suddenly went out, and it became terribly black around me. I became as if blind and dumb, and now I'm lying on something hard, stretched out on my back, I don't see anything and can't make the slightest movement. Around me there is walking and shouting, there is the captain's bass and the landlady's shrieking—and suddenly another break, and now I'm being carried in a closed coffin. And I feel the coffin heave and I start reasoning about that, when suddenly for the first time I'm struck by the idea that I'm dead, quite dead, I know this and do not doubt it, I can't see, I can't move, yet I feel and reason. But I quickly come to terms with it and, as is usual in dreams, accept the reality without arguing.

And now they bury me in the ground. Everyone leaves, I'm alone, completely alone. I can't move. Always before, whenever I actually imagined to myself how I would be buried in the grave, my only association with the grave proper was the feeling of dampness and cold. So now, too, I felt that I was very cold, especially the tips of my toes, but I didn't feel anything else.

I lay there and, strangely—didn't expect anything, accepting without argument that a dead man has nothing to expect. But it was damp. I don't know how much time passed—an hour, or a few days, or many days. But then suddenly a drop of water that had seeped through the lid of the coffin fell on my closed left eye, another followed it in a minute, then a third a minute later, and so on and so on, with a minute's interval. A deep indignation suddenly blazed up in my heart, and suddenly I felt physical pain in it. "It's my wound," I thought, "it's my shot, there's a bullet there . . ." The drop kept dripping, each minute and straight onto my closed eye. And I suddenly called out, not in a voice, for I was motionless, but with my whole being, to the master of all that was coming to pass with me.

"Whoever you are, if you're there, and if there exists anything more reasonable than what is coming to pass now, allow it to be here, too. And if you are taking revenge on me for my unreasonable suicide by the ugliness and absurdity of my subsequent existence, know, then, that no matter what torment befalls me, it will never equal the contempt I am silently going to feel, even if the torment were to last millions of years! . . ."

I called out and fell silent. For almost a whole minute the deep silence lasted, and one more drop even fell, but I knew, boundlessly and inviolably, I knew and believed that everything was certain to change presently. And then suddenly my grave gaped wide. That is, I don't know whether it was opened and dug up, but I was taken by some dark being unknown to me, and we found ourselves in space. I suddenly could see again: it was deep night, and never, never has there been such darkness! We were rushing through space far from earth. I did not ask the one carrying me about anything, I waited and was proud. I assured myself that I was not afraid and swooned with delight at the thought that I was not afraid. I don't remember how long we rushed like that, and cannot imagine it: everything was happening as it always does in dreams, when you leap over space and time and over the laws of being and reason, and pause only on the points of the heart's reverie. I remember that I suddenly saw a little star in the darkness. "Is that Sirius?" I asked, suddenly unable to restrain myself, for I did not want to ask about anything. "No, it is the very star you saw between the clouds, as you were returning home," the being who was carrying me replied. I knew that it had as if a human countenance. Strangely, I did not like this being, I even felt a deep revulsion. I had expected complete nonexistence and with that had shot myself in the heart. And here I am in the hands of a being—not a human one, of course—but who *is,* who exists: "Ah, so there is life beyond the grave!" I thought with the strange light-mindedness of dreams, but the essence of my heart remained with me in all its depth: "And if I must *be* again," I thought, "and live again according to someone's ineluctable will, I don't want to be defeated and humiliated!" "You know I'm afraid of you, and you despise me for it," I said suddenly to my companion, unable to hold back the humiliating question, which contained a confession, and feeling my humiliation like the prick of a needle in my heart. He did not answer my question, but I suddenly felt that I was not despised or laughed at, and not even pitied, and that our journey had an unknown and mysterious purpose which concerned me alone. Fear was growing in my heart. Something was being communicated to me, mutely but tormentingly, from my silent companion, and was as if penetrating me. We were rushing through dark and unknown spaces. I had long ceased to see constellations familiar to the eye. I knew that in the heavenly spaces there were stars whose light reached the earth only after thousands or millions of years. Maybe we were already flying through those spaces. I awaited something in a terrible anguish that wrung my heart. And suddenly the call of some highly familiar feeling shook me: I suddenly saw our sun! I knew it could not be *our* sun, which had generated *our* earth, and that we were at an infinite distance from our sun, but for some reason I recognized, with my whole being, that it was absolutely the same as our sun, its replica and double. The call of a sweet feeling sounded delightfully in my soul: the native power of light, the same light that gave birth to me, echoed in my heart and resurrected it, and I felt life, the former life, for the first time after my grave.

"But if this is the sun, if this is absolutely the same as our sun," I cried out, "then where is the earth?" And my companion pointed to the little star that shone in the darkness with an emerald brilliance. We were rushing straight toward her.

"And are such replicas really possible in the universe, is that really the law of nature? . . . And if that is the earth there, is it really the same as our earth . . . absolutely the same, unfortunate, poor, but dear and eternally beloved, giving birth to the same tormenting love for herself even in her most ungrateful children? . . ." I cried out, shaking with irrepressible, rapturous love for that former native earth I had abandoned. The image of the poor little girl whom I had offended flashed before me.

"You will see all," my companion replied, and some sadness sounded in his words. But we were quickly approaching the planet. It was growing before my eyes, I could already make out the ocean, the outlines of Europe, and suddenly a strange feeling of some great, holy jealousy blazed up in my heart: "How can there be such a replica, and what for? I love, I can love, only the earth I left, where the stains of my blood were left, when I, the ungrateful one, extinguished my life with a shot in the heart. But never, never did I cease to love that earth, and even on that night, as I was parting from her, I perhaps loved her more tormentingly than ever before. Is there suffering on this new earth? On our earth we can love truly only with suffering and through suffering! We're unable to love otherwise and we know no other love. I want suffering, in order to love. I want, I thirst, to kiss, this very minute, pouring out tears, that one earth alone which I left, and I do not want, I do not accept life on any other! . . ."

But my companion had already left me. Suddenly, as if quite imperceptibly, I came to stand on this other earth, in the bright light of a sunny day, lovely as paradise. I was standing, it seems, on one of those islands which on our earth make up the Greek archipelago, or somewhere on the coast of the mainland adjacent to that archipelago. Oh, everything was exactly as with us, but seemed everywhere to radiate some festivity and a great, holy, and finally attained triumph. The gentle emerald sea splashed softly against the shores and kissed them with love—plain, visible, almost conscious. Tall, beautiful trees stood in all the luxury of their flowering, and their numberless leaves, I was convinced, greeted me with their soft, gentle sound, as if uttering words of love. The grass glittered with bright, fragrant flowers. Flocks of birds flew about in the air and, fearless of me, landed on my shoulders and arms, joyfully beating me with their dear, fluttering wings. And finally I got to see and know the people of that happy earth. They came to me themselves, they surrounded me, kissed me. Children of the sun, children of their sun—oh, how beautiful they were! Never on our earth have I seen such beauty in man. Maybe only in our children, in their first years, can one find a remote, though faint, glimmer of that beauty. The eyes of these happy people shone with clear brightness. Their faces radiated reason and a sort of consciousness fulfilled to the point of serenity, yet they were mirthful faces; a childlike joy sounded in the words and voices of these people. Oh, at once, with the first glance at their faces, I understood everything, everything! This was the earth undefiled by the fall, the people who lived on it had not sinned, they lived in the same paradise in which, according to the legends of all mankind, our fallen forefathers lived, with the only difference that the whole earth here was everywhere one and the same paradise. These people, laughing joyfully, crowded around me and caressed me; they took me with them and each of them wished to set me at ease. Oh, they didn't ask me about anything, but it seemed to me as if they already knew everything, and wished quickly to drive the torment from my face.

IV

You see, once again: well, let it be only a dream! But the feeling of love from these innocent and beautiful people remained in me ever after, and I feel that their love pours upon me from there even now. I saw them myself, I knew them and was convinced, I loved them, I suffered for them afterward. Oh, I at once understood, even then, that in many ways I would never understand them; to me, a modern Russian progressive and vile Petersburger, it seemed insoluble, for instance, that they, while knowing so much, did not have our science. But I soon realized that their knowledge was fulfilled and nourished by different insights than on our earth, and that their aspirations were also quite different. They did not wish for anything and were at peace, they did not aspire to a knowlege of life, as we do, because their life was fulfilled. But their knowledge was deeper and loftier than our science; for our science seeks to explain what life is, it aspires to comprehend it, in order to teach others to live; but they knew how to live even without science, and I understood that, but I could not understand their knowledge. They pointed out their trees to me, and I could not understand the extent of the love with which they looked at them: as if they were talking with creatures of their own kind. And you know, perhaps I wouldn't be mistaken if I said that they did talk to them! Yes, they had found their language, and I'm convinced that the trees understood them. They looked at the whole of nature in the same way—at the animals, who lived in peace with them, did not attack them, and loved them, won over by their love. They pointed out the stars to me and talked of them with me about something I couldn't understand, but I'm convinced that they had some contact, as it were, with the heavenly stars, not just in thought, but in some living way. Oh, these people did not even try to make me understand them, they loved me even without that, but on the other hand I knew that they would also never understand me, and therefore I hardly ever spoke to them about our earth. I only kissed before them that earth on which they lived and wordlessly adored them, and they saw it and allowed me to adore them without being ashamed of my adoring them, because they loved much themselves. They did not suffer for me when sometimes, in tears, I kissed their feet, joyfully knowing at heart with what force of love they would respond to me. At times I asked myself in astonishment: how could they manage, all this while, not to insult a man such as I, and never once provoke in a man such as I any feeling of jealousy or envy? Many times I asked myself how I, a braggart and a liar, could manage not to speak to them about my knowledge—of which they, of course, had no notion—not to wish to astonish them with it, if only out of love for them? They were frisky and gay as children. They wandered through their beautiful groves and forests, they sang their beautiful songs, they ate their light food—fruit from their trees, honey from their forests, and milk from the animals who loved them. For their food and clothing they labored little and but lightly. There was love among them, and children were born, but I never observed in them any impulses of that *cruel* sensuality that overtakes almost everyone on our earth, each and every one, and is the only source of almost all the sins of our mankind. They rejoiced in the children they had as new partakers of their bliss. Among them there was no quarreling or jealousy, they did not even understand what it meant. Their children were everyone's children, because they all constituted one family. They had almost no illnesses, though there was death; but their old people died quietly, as if falling asleep, surrounded by those bidding them farewell, blessing them, smiling at them, and receiving bright parting smiles themselves. I saw no sorrow or tears at that, there was only love increased as if to the point of rapture, but a rapture that was calm, fulfilled, contemplative. One might think they were in touch with their dead even after their death and that the earthly union between them was not interrupted by death. They barely understood me when I asked them about eternal life, but they were apparently so convinced of it unconsciously that it did not constitute a question for them. They had no temples, but they had some essential, living, and constant union with the Entirety of the universe; they had no faith, but instead had a firm knowledge that when their earthly joy was fulfilled to the limits of earthly nature, there would then come for them, both for the living and for the dead, a still greater expansion of their contact with the Entirety of the universe. They waited for this moment with joy, but without haste, without suffering over it, but as if already having it in the presages of their hearts, which they conveyed to one another. In the evenings, before going to sleep, they liked to sing in balanced, harmonious choruses. In these songs they expressed all the feelings that the departing day had given them, praised it, and bade it farewell. They praised nature, the earth, the sea, the forest. They liked to compose songs about each other and praised each other like children; these were the most simple songs, but they flowed from the heart and penetrated hearts. And not in songs only, but it seemed they spent their whole life only in admiring each other. It was a sort of mutual being-in-love, total, universal. And some of their songs, solemn and rapturous, I hardly understood at all. While I understood the words, I was never able to penetrate their full meaning. It remained as if inaccessible to my mind, yet my heart was as if unconsciously pervaded by it more and more. I often told them that I had long ago had a presentiment of all this, that all this joy and glory had already spoken to me on our earth in an anguished call, sometimes reaching the point of unbearable sorrow; that I had had a presentiment of them all and of their glory in the dreams of my heart and the reveries of my mind, that I had often been unable, on our earth, to watch the setting sun without tears . . . That my hatred of the people of our earth always contained anguish: why am I unable to hate them without loving them, why am I unable not to forgive them, and why is there anguish in my love for them: why am I unable to love them without hating them? They listened to me, and I saw that they could not imagine what I was talking about, but I did not regret talking to them about it: I knew they understood all the intensity of my anguish for those whom I had abandoned. Yes, when they looked at me with their dear eyes pervaded by love, when I felt that in their presence my heart, too, became as innocent and truthful as theirs, I did not regret not understanding them. The feeling of the fullness of life took my breath away, and I silently worshipped them.

Oh, everyone laughs in my face now and assures me that even in dreams one cannot see such details as I'm now telling, that in my dream I saw or felt only a certain sensation generated by my own heart in delirium, and that I invented the details when I woke up. And when I disclosed to them that perhaps it was actually so—God, what laughter they threw in my face, what fun they had at my expense! Oh, yes, of course, I was overcome just by the sensation of that dream, and it alone survived in the bloody wound of my heart: yet the real images and forms of my dream, that is, those that I actually saw at the time of my dreaming, were fulfilled so harmoniously, they were so enchanting and beautiful, and so true, that having awakened, I was, of course, unable to embody them in our weak words, so that they must have been as if effaced in my mind, and therefore, indeed, perhaps I myself unconsciously was forced to invent the details afterward; and of course distorted them, especially with my so passionate desire to hurry and tell them at least somehow. And yet how can I not believe that it all really was? And was, perhaps, a thousand times better, brighter, and more joyful than I'm telling? Let it be a dream, still it all could not but be. You know, I'll tell you a secret: perhaps it wasn't a dream at all! For here a certain thing happened, something so terribly true that it couldn't have been imagined in a dream. Let my dream have been generated by my heart, but was my heart alone capable of generating the terrible truth that happened to me afterward? How could I myself invent or imagine it in my heart? Can it be that my paltry heart and capricious, insignificant mind were able to rise to such a revelation of the truth! Oh, judge for yourselves: I've concealed it so far, but now I'll finish telling this truth as well. The thing was that I . . . corrupted them all!

V

Yes, yes, it ended with me corrupting them all! How it could have happened I don't know, but I remember it clearly. The dream flew through thousands of years and left in me just a sense of the whole. I know only that the cause of the fall was I. Like a foul trichina, like an atom of plague infecting whole countries, so I infected that whole happy and previously sinless earth with myself. They learned to lie and began to love the lie and knew the beauty of the lie. Oh, maybe it started *innocently,* with a joke, with coquetry, with amorous play, maybe, indeed, with an atom, but this atom of lie penetrated their hearts, and they liked it. Then sensuality was quickly born, sensuality generated jealousy, and jealousy—cruelty . . . Oh, I don't know, I don't remember, but soon, very soon, the first blood was shed; they were astonished and horrified, and began to part, to separate. Alliances appeared, but against each other now. Rebukes, reproaches began. They knew shame, and shame was made into a virtue. The notion of honor was born, and each alliance raised its own banner. They began tormenting animals, and the animals withdrew from them into the forests and became their enemies. There began the struggle for separation, for isolation, for the personal, for mine and yours. They started speaking different languages. They knew sorrow and came to love sorrow, they thirsted for suffering and said that truth is attained only through suffering. Then science appeared among them. When they became wicked, they began to talk of brotherhood and humaneness and understood these ideas. When they became criminal, they invented justice and prescribed whole codices for themselves in order to maintain it, and to ensure the codices they set up the guillotine. They just barely remembered what they had lost, and did not even want to believe that they had once been innocent and happy. They even laughed at the possibility of the former happiness and called it a dream. They couldn't even imagine it in forms and images, but—strange and wonderful thing—having lost all belief in their former happiness, having called it a fairy tale, they wished so much to be innocent and happy again, once more, that they fell down before their hearts' desires like children, they deified their desire, they built temples and started praying to their own idea, their own "desire," all the while fully believing in its unrealizability and unfeasibility, but adoring it in tears and worshipping it. And yet, if it had so happened that they could have returned to that innocent and happy condition which they had lost, or if someone had suddenly shown it to them again and asked them: did they want to go back to it?—they would certainly have refused. They used to answer me: "Granted we're deceitful, wicked, and unjust, we *know* that and weep for it, and we torment ourselves over it, and torture and punish ourselves perhaps even more than that merciful judge who will judge us and whose name we do not know. But we have science, and through it we shall again find the truth, but we shall now accept it consciously, knowledge is higher than feelings, the consciousness of life is higher than life. Science will give us wisdom, wisdom will discover laws, and knowledge of the laws of happiness is higher than happiness." That's what they used to say, and after such words each of them loved himself more than anyone else, and they couldn't have done otherwise. Each of them became so jealous of his own person that he tried as hard as he could to humiliate and belittle it in others, and gave his life to that. Slavery appeared, even voluntary slavery: the weak willingly submitted to the strong, only so as to help them crush those still weaker than themselves. Righteous men appeared, who came to these people in tears and spoke to them of their pride, their lack of measure and harmony, their loss of shame.

They were derided or stoned. Holy blood was spilled on the thresholds of temples. On the other hand, people began to appear who started inventing ways for everyone to unite again, so that each of them, without ceasing to love himself more than anyone else, would at the same time not hinder others, and thus live all together in a harmonious society, as it were. Whole wars arose because of this idea. At the same time, the warring sides all firmly believed that science, wisdom, and the sense of self-preservation would finally force men to unite in a harmonious and reasonable society, and therefore, to speed things up meanwhile, the "wise" tried quickly to exterminate all the "unwise," who did not understand their idea, so that they would not hinder its triumph. But the sense of self-preservation quickly began to weaken, proud men and sensualists appeared who directly demanded everything or nothing. To acquire everything, they resorted to evildoing, and if that did not succeed—to suicide. Religions appeared with a cult of nonbeing and self-destruction for the sake of eternal peace in nothingness. Finally, these people grew weary in meaningless toil, and suffering appeared on their faces, and these people proclaimed that suffering is beauty, for only in suffering is there thought. They sang suffering in their songs. I walked among them, wringing my hands, and wept over them, but I loved them perhaps still more than before, when there was as yet no suffering on their faces and they were innocent and so beautiful. I loved their defiled earth still more than when it had been a paradise, only because grief had appeared on it. Alas, I had always loved grief and sorrow, but only for myself, for myself, while over them I wept, pitying them. I stretched out my arms to them, in despair accusing, cursing, and despising myself. I told them that I, I alone, had done it all; that it was I who had brought them depravity, infection, and the lie! I beseeched them to crucify me on a cross, I taught them how to make a cross. I couldn't, I hadn't the strength to kill myself, but I wanted to take the suffering from them, I longed for suffering, I longed to shed my blood to the last drop in this suffering. But they just laughed at me and in the end began to consider me some sort of holy fool. They vindicated me, they said they had received only what they themselves had wanted, and that everything could not but be as it was. Finally, they announced to me that I was becoming dangerous for them and that they would put me in a madhouse if I didn't keep quiet. Here sorrow entered my soul with such force that my heart was wrung, and I felt I was going to die, and here . . . well, here I woke up.

It was already morning, that is, not light yet, but it was about six o'clock. I came to my senses in the same armchair, my candle had burned all the way down, everyone was asleep at the captain's, and around me was a silence rare in our apartment. First of all, I jumped up extremely surprised; nothing like that had ever happened to me, even down to trifling little details: for instance, never before had I fallen asleep in my armchair like that. Here suddenly, while I was standing and coming to my senses—suddenly my revolver flashed before me, ready, loaded—but I instantly pushed it away from me! Oh, life, life now! I lifted up my arms and called out to the eternal truth; did not call out, but wept; rapture, boundless rapture, elevated my whole being. Yes, life and—preaching! I decided on preaching that same moment, and, of course, for the rest of my life! I'm going out to preach, I want to preach—what? The truth, for I saw it, saw it with my own eyes, saw all its glory!

And so, since then I've been preaching! What's more—I love those who laugh at me more than all the rest. Why that's so I don't know and can't explain, but let it be so. They say I'm already getting confused now, that is, if I'm already so confused now, how will it be later? The veritable truth: I'm getting confused now, and maybe it will be worse later. And of course I'm going to get confused a few times before I discover how to preach, that is, in what words and in what deeds, because it's very hard to do. I see it clear as day even now, but listen: is there anyone who doesn't get confused? And yet ev-

eryone goes toward one and the same thing, at least everyone
strives for one and the same thing, from the sage to the last
robber, only by different paths. This is an old truth, but what
is new here is this: I cannot get very confused. Because I saw
the truth, I saw and I know that people can be beautiful and
happy without losing the ability to live on earth. I will not and
cannot believe that evil is the normal condition of people. And
they all laugh merely at this belief of mine. But how can I not
believe: I saw the truth—it's not that my mind invented it,
but I saw it, I saw it, and its *living image* filled my soul for all
time. I saw it in such fulfilled wholeness that I cannot believe
it is impossible for people to have it. And so, how could I get
confused? I'll wander off, of course, even several times, and
will maybe even speak in other people's words, but not for
long: the living image of what I saw will always be with me
and will always correct and direct me. Oh, I'm hale, I'm fresh,
I'm going, going, even if it's for a thousand years. You know, I
even wanted to conceal, at first, that I corrupted them all, but
that was a mistake—already the first mistake! But truth whispered to me that I was *lying*, and guarded and directed me.
But how to set up paradise—I don't know, because I'm unable
to put it into words. After my dream, I lost words. At least all
the main words, the most necessary ones. But so be it: I'll go
and I'll keep talking, tirelessly, because after all I saw it with
my own eyes, though I can't recount what I saw. But that is
what the scoffers don't understand: "He had a dream," they
say, "a delirium, a hallucination." Eh! As if that's so clever?
And how proud they are! A dream? what is a dream? And is
our life not a dream? I'll say more: let it never, let it never
come true, and let there be no paradise (that I can understand!)—well, but I will preach all the same. And yet it's so
simple: in one day, *in one hour*—it could all be set up at once!
The main thing is—love others as yourself, that's the main
thing, and it's everything, there's no need for anything else at
all: it will immediately be discovered how to set things up.
And yet this is merely an old truth, repeated and read a billion
times, but still it has never taken root! "The consciousness of

life is higher than life, the knowledge of the laws of happiness is higher than happiness"—that is what must be fought! And I will. If only everyone wants it, everything can be set up at once.

And I found that little girl . . . And I'll go! I'll go!

A NASTY ANECDOTE (1862)

1. The Neva River divides into three main branches as it flows into the Gulf of Finland, marking out the three main areas of the city of St. Petersburg. On the left bank of the Neva is the city center, between the Neva and the Little Neva is Vasilievsky Island, and between the Little Neva and the Nevka is the so-called "Petersburg side," which is thus some distance from the center.

2. These three gentlemen are all in the civil service, not the military. But civil service ranks had military equivalents, which were sometimes used in social address. The following is a list of the fourteen civil service ranks from highest to lowest, with their approximate military equivalents:

1. Chancellor   Field Marshal
2. Actual Privy Councillor   General
3. Privy Councillor   Lieutenant General
4. Actual State Councillor   Major General

5. State Councillor — Colonel
6. Collegiate Councillor — Lieutenant Colonel
7. Court Councillor — Major
8. Collegiate Assessor — Captain
9. Titular Councillor — Staff Captain
10. Collegiate Secretary — Lieutenant
11. Secretary of Naval Constructions
12. Government Secretary — Sub-lieutenant
13. Provincial Secretary
14. Collegiate Registrar

The rank of titular councillor conferred personal nobility; the rank of actual state councillor made it hereditary. Wives of officials shared their husbands' rank and were entitled to the same mode of address—"Your Honor," "Your Excellency," "Your Supreme Excellency." Mention of an official's rank automatically indicates the amount of deference he must be shown, and by whom.

3. The star was the decoration of a number of orders, among them the Polish-Russian Order of St. Stanislas (or Stanislav) and the Swedish Order of the North Star.

4. Certain Russian decorations had two degrees, being worn either on the breast or on a ribbon around the neck.

5. "Botched existence" or "failed life" (French).

6. "Talker" and "phrase-maker" (French).

7. A tax-farmer was a private person authorized by the government to collect taxes in exchange for a fixed fee. The practice was open to abuse, and tax-farmers could become extremely rich, though never quite respectable. Tax-farming was eventually abolished by the economic reforms of the emperor Alexander II in the 1860s, to which reference is made here.

8. A reference to Christ's teaching: "Neither do men put new wine into old bottles: else the bottles break, and the wine runneth out, and the bottles perish: but they put new wine into new bottles, and both are preserved" (Matthew 9:17).

9. "That's the word" (French).

10. "Good sense" (French).

11. Pralinsky is mulling over the "problem" of the abolition of corporal punishment with birch rods, then still allowed in the army and in the schools as well as with serfs.

12. The clerk's name is absurdly close to the Russian *psevdonym* ("pseudonym"), a fact Pralinsky later mentions himself. Pseldonymov is a collegiate registrar.

13. "Mlekopitaev" is also an absurd, though just plausible, name derived from the Russian word for "mammal."

14. Clerks in the civil service had to have their superiors' permission to change departments, to move elsewhere, and even to marry.

15. The leader of the romantic movement in Russian art, K. P. Briullov (1799–1852), was most famous for his enormous historical painting *The Last Day of Pompeii,* evidently the epitome of turmoil and confusion for Pralinsky.

16. "Ladies join hands; swing!" (French).

17. Harun-al-Rashid, or Harun the Just (?766–809), Abbasid caliph of Baghdad (786–809), is known in legend for walking about the city anonymously at night, familiarizing himself with the life of his subjects. He became a hero of songs and figures in some of the tales in *The Thousand and One Nights.*

18. A parodical *Dream Book of Contemporary Russian Literature,* written by N. F. Shcherbina, was circulated in manuscript at the end of the 1850s.

19. Ivan Ivanovich Panaev (1812–62), a now-forgotten writer and journalist, published some important memoirs in *The Contemporary,* a liberal magazine he co-edited for a time with the poet Nikolai Nekrasov.

20. The "new lexicon" in question was the government-subsidized *Encyclopedic Dictionary Composed by Russian Scholars and Writers,* which began to appear in 1861. When A. A. Kraevsky (1810–89), then editor of the magazine *Fatherland Notes,* was named editor in chief of this project, there was general indignation, since he was neither a scholar nor a writer. N. D. Alferaki (d. 1860), a merchant from Taganrog in the south of Russia, was a notorious entrepreneur of the time. The exposé (which Dostoevsky jocularly refers to here, as he would later in *Notes from Underground,* with the mispronunci-

ation "esposé"), was the favorite journalistic form of the young radicals of the 1860s.

21. It was possible at that time (and long after) to rent not a room but only part of a room. This living "in corners" signified the direst poverty (or, in Soviet Russia, the direst shortage of housing).

22. That is, not from Jerez in Spain, home of true sherry.

23. The folk dance called "the fish" was described by Ivan Turgenev in his *Old Portraits* (1881) as one in which a male soloist imitates the movements of a fish taken out of the water.

24. The slow and mournful "Luchinushka" is perhaps the most well known of all Russian songs.

25. The *Petersburg Bulletin* was published by the Academy of Science in Petersburg; hence the telltale nickname.

26. *Frühstück* is "breakfast" in German.

27. Fokine, "hero of the can-can," was popular in Petersburg during the 1860s. His dancing was considered the ultimate in shamelessness.

28. The "Little Cossack" is a folk dance imitative of military steps.

29. The drink Christ was offered just before the crucifixion (Matthew 27:34).

30. Peski ("The Sands") was a neighborhood at the opposite end of the city from the Petersburg side.

31. Refers to the old custom among anchorites and monks of sleeping in their own coffins.

32. "One fine morning" (French).

THE ETERNAL HUSBAND (1870)

1. The Black River, a small stream now well within the limits of Petersburg, was then a country spot outside the city suitable for summer houses.

2. "Worthless person" or "good-for-nothing" (French).

3. Turgenev's play *The Provincial Lady* (1851) portrays the young wife of the elderly provincial official Stupendiev, who makes a visiting count fall in love with her.

4. The sect of the flagellants emerged among Russian peas-

ants in the seventeenth century. Its adherents practiced self-flagellation as a means of purification from sin. Both sect and practice were condemned by the Church.

5. God destroyed the city of Sodom on the Dead Sea because its inhabitants practiced "sodomy" (Genesis 19:1–28), but in Russian use "Sodom" means a more general sort of disorderly life. For that reason, we sometimes translate it as "bedlam."

6. A quotation from the ballad *Der Siegesfest* ("The Victory Banquet") by the German poet and playwright Friedrich von Schiller (1759–1805). Pavel Pavlovich quotes the Russian translation by Vassily Zhukovsky, published in 1828. Interestingly, the great Russian prose writer Nikolai Gogol quoted these same lines in reference to himself and the poet Alexander Pushkin in a letter written on the occasion of the latter's death.

7. The terms appeared in an article by the critic N. N. Strakhov on Tolstoy's *War and Peace,* in which he supported the opinion of the poet Apollon Grigoriev that ". . . our literature represents an incessant struggle between these two types . . . the predatory and the placid" (*Zarya,* Feb. 1869).

8. In the Orthodox marriage service, crowns are held above the heads of the bride and groom.

9. It was customary in Russia to lay out the body of a dead person on a table until the coffin arrived.

10. The customary period of mourning was one year at least; to remarry before then was considered scandalous.

11. Sixteen was marriageable age for a girl.

12. Another of Dostoevsky's plausible but wonderfully absurd names, derived from *predposylka,* Russian for "premise" or "presupposition."

13. Mikhail Glinka (1804–57), founder of the modern Russian school of music, composed this romance to words by the great Polish poet Adam Mickiewicz (1798–1855), translated into Russian by S. Golitsyn in 1834.

14. "Shchedrin" was the pseudonym of the Russian writer Mikhail Saltykov (1826–89), author of *The Golovlovs, The*

History of a Certain Town, and much else. He was a liberal publicist and often Dostoevsky's ideological opponent. The quotation is from his story *For Children.*

15. Quasimodo is the hunchbacked bell ringer in Victor Hugo's *Notre-Dame de Paris* (1831), who is unhappily in love with the beautiful Esmeralda.

16. "Bad tone" in the social sense (French).

BOBOK (1873)

1. This and the following two stories were first published in Dostoevsky's *Diary of a Writer,* which appeared periodically between 1873 and 1881. Here and in *The Meek One,* he offers brief introductory remarks for the readers of the *Diary.*

2. "Attic salt" refers to the subtle witticisms for which the Athenians, inhabitants of the region of Attica, were famous in ancient times.

3. The French writer and philosopher François-Marie Arouet, called Voltaire (1694–1778), was one of the most famous figures of his age and a great producer of salty witticisms *(bons mots).* Dostoevsky admired his philosophical tale *Candide,* of which he long planned to write a Russian variant. Several of Dostoevsky's characters, including the narrator of *The Dream of a Ridiculous Man* at the end of this collection, sit in a variety of chair known as a "Voltaire armchair."

4. Civil servants also wore uniforms in Russia, which varied according to rank.

5. This would be an exhibition of the painters known as *Peredvizhniki* ("Wanderers"), a group opposed to the Academy of Art in Petersburg and therefore controversial.

6. The publisher Suvorin, an enlightener of the people, produced extremely cheap editions, including tear-off calendars giving a bit of art or literature, a saying or a saint's life, along with the date.

7. This epitaph was in fact composed by the Russian writer and historian Nikolai M. Karamzin (1766–1826). Dostoevsky and his brother Mikhail had it placed on their mother's tombstone in 1837.

8. According to a popular notion, as a person's soul ascends toward heaven after death, it meets evil spirits that try to force it down into hell. Only the souls of the righteous avoid these "torments" (there are said to be twenty of them).

9. According to another popular belief, the soul is finally separated from this world forty days after death. On the fortieth day, a prayer service is customarily held and the relatives visit the grave.

10. *Kutya* (accented on the final syllable) is a special dish offered to people after a memorial service (and, in some places, on Christmas Eve), made from rice (or barley or wheat) and raisins, sweetened with honey.

11. According to tradition, the valley of Jehoshaphat, near Jerusalem, is the burial place of the Judean king Jehoshaphat. In the prophecy of Joel (3:17) it is the place where God will judge all the nations in the last days.

12. S. P. Botkin (1832–89) was a famous doctor and scientist, founder of physiological and experimental medicine.

13. "Young scamp" or "dissolute person" (French).

14. "In high places" (French).

15. A ludicrous name compounded of the Russian diminutive for Yulia (Julie), the common French name Charpentier, and Lusignan, the name of one of the most illustrious French feudal families, rulers of Angoulême and La Manche, one branch of which became the royal family of Cyprus and Jerusalem (1192–1489).

16. After defeating the French in 1871, the Prussians, under Kaiser Wilhelm I and his chancellor Bismarck, became the dominant military power in Europe, thus posing a threat to Russia much spoken of in the press.

17. In January 1873 Dostoevsky became editor of the newspaper *The Citizen*, continuing in that position until March 1874. The first installments of his *Diary of a Writer* appeared there (the later installments of 1876–77, 1880, and 1881 he published by subscription on his own). The "certain person" apparently succeeded in placing his "notes" there.

THE MEEK ONE (1876)

1. See note 9 to *The Eternal Husband*.

2. *The Voice* was a liberal weekly published in Petersburg between 1863 and 1884, edited by A. A. Kraevsky (see note 20 to *A Nasty Anecdote*).

3. *Faust* is the monumental two-part poetic drama by German poet Johann Wolfgang von Goethe (1749–1832). The narrator distorts the line slightly; Mephistopheles says he is "part of that power which eternally wills evil and eternally works good."

4. "English style" (French).

5. The quotation is a paraphrase of a line from Alexander Pushkin's poem "The Demon" (1823).

6. "Hot blood and surplus strength" is a free quotation from the poem "Do not, do not believe yourself, young dreamer" (1839) by Mikhail Lermontov.

7. *Songbirds,* or *Pericola,* is an operetta by the French composer Jacques Offenbach (1819–80). The other play has not been identified.

8. John Stuart Mill (1806–73), English economist and utilitarian philosopher, is a singularly inappropriate choice here, since he would certainly have agreed with the narrator.

9. The Haymarket was a square in a poor quarter of Petersburg (much of *Crime and Punishment* takes place there). Vyazemsky's house was a flophouse on the Haymarket.

10. In June–July 1862, on his way home from England, Dostoevsky stopped in Boulogne-sur-Mer, a French port on the English Channel famous as a seaside resort.

11. Gil Blas is the hero of the French picaresque novel *Histoire de Gil Blas de Santillane* (1715–36) by Alain-René Lesage (1668–1747). Serving as secretary to the archbishop of Granada, Gil Blas becomes his favorite by praising his sermons. The archbishop enjoins him always to criticize his sermons sincerely. When Gil Blas permits himself one small criticism, the archbishop fires him for tastelessness and ignorance.

THE DREAM OF A RIDICULOUS MAN (1877)